Autonomy

Also by Jean-Michel Smith

NON-FICTION

S³: The Smith Sexagesimal System

Autonomy

Jean-Michel Smith

AUTONOMY

Published in the United States by Red Anemone Books Inc., Chicago

ISBN: 978-0-9831888-5-8

First published in the United States: April 2013
First eBook Edition: April 2013

Cover Design by Dotti Albertine

**RED ANEMONE
BOOKS**

redanemone.com

For Christine

CONTENTS

PART 1

DISCOVERY

We live between two worlds; we soar in the atmosphere; we creep upon the soil; we have the aspirations of creators and the propensities of quadrupeds. There can be but one explanation of this fact. We are passing from the animal into a higher form, and the drama of this planet is in its second act.

—Winwood Reade, 1872 CE

/ (1): TIME-LAPSE

Cal opened his eyes and sat up. The bed was large and decadently soft, surrounded by gauzy curtains hanging from a canopy through which shafts of golden sunlight shone.

"Onload complete, guys. It worked."

He pushed the curtain aside and jumped to his feet. Hilltop meadows surrounded him, lush green pastures sporting constellations of blue and violet flowers. He relished the feel of soft grass between his toes.

"The simulation is fantastic. Perfect weather, and what a view!"

To the east rose a spectacular range of mountains, snow-covered slopes textured with stone and ice climbing to dramatic, pointed summits. Softened by haze, a massive planet peaked over their ridges, its Jovian nature betrayed by its green and gold swirls. To the west, in the distance, a sea reflected afternoon sunlight.

"Something's wrong with the light diffusion. The haze along the horizon isn't consistent. Not a big deal, though. Amazing!" A flock of pelicans flew past. Cal laughed. "Hey, who came up the pink birds?"

Silence.

His grin faded.

"Dr. Nolen? Céline? Can you hear me? Acknowledge please."

He waited. Another flock of pelicans passed overhead.

"Node. Command mode engage."

A soft, neutral voice spoke within his mind. »Command mode engaged.«

Cal thought furiously. There could be a communications glitch. That was actually more likely than a systems malfunction at this point. Still, this was all very experimental. He'd better err on the side of caution.

"Run test suite one, systems integrity check," he commanded.

»Running ... Suite one complete. All operating parameters nominal.«

"Run suite two."

»Running ... Suite two complete. All operating parameters nominal.«

Cal forced himself to remain calm. They would bring him out after ten minutes no matter what.

"Run the third test suite."

»Running ... Suite three complete. All operating parameters nominal.«

"How long since I onloaded?"

»Time elapsed: two minutes, fifteen seconds.«

Cal paced back and forth along the crest of the hill. "Run a diagnostic on the external comm link."

»Running ... Initial protocol state achieved. Ping tests commencing.«

Long minutes of silence did little to calm Cal's jittery nerves. "You should have some results by now. What's taking so long?"

»Communications diagnostic still running. No errors detected.«

"Then why aren't they answering?"

»Insufficient data.«

His unease grew, his critical eye finding numerous details in the simulation that were not quite right, from the fractal fuzziness at the limits of his vision when he examined the grass, to the two dimensional quality of the clouds moving across the sky. "Damn it, we should have some kind of communication by now." His dread grew to outright fear. "How much time has elapsed since I onloaded?"

»Fourteen minutes, twenty-nine seconds.«

Cal stopped. "Say again?"

»Fourteen minutes, thirty-one seconds.«

Why was he still here? Why hadn't the offload sequence run as scheduled? He pictured his comatose body lying in the lab. He'd been crazy to volunteer for this experiment.

"What's the status of the communications check?"

»Link protocol is experiencing timing synchronization errors. No ping responses received.«

"Shit! Shit, shit, shit!"

Cal sank to the ground and put his face in his hands. Without a working data link there was no exit. He could be trapped, stuck in a software simulation, caught like a fly in amber in a world whose realism grew more fragile with each moment. Artificial comas were tricky things. When he didn't wake up they would try everything to bring him out of it. Eventually they might get desperate and reboot the equipment.

Cal's chest tightened into a knot. They'd been so enthusiastic, so carried away with their work, none of them had taken the idea seriously that he could get stuck in here. If they had, they would have included a lot more failsafes in the design, data persistence chief among them. If Cal survived, that would be the first thing he'd correct. As it was, any kind of system reset would erase him. He would be stuck in a coma for the rest of his life, his physical brain as dead as his electronic self.

◇

"What's happening?" Dr. Nolen sounded nervous. He cracked the door of the lab and scanned the empty hallway. Céline had been right, thank god. Ten thirty on a Tuesday morning in July was the best time to do this. The place was deserted.

"Well?" Dr. Nolen asked again, pulling the door shut and checking the lock.

Céline looked up from Cal's prostrate form. Thick cables sprouted from the metal lattice and electrodes surrounding his face and head. They braided their way across the floor, some to a refrigerator-sized bank of components wrapped in tubes of liquid nitrogen, others to medical monitors that showed a perfectly steady heartbeat.

Céline gripped the side of the steel table. "No telemetry, no audio, no video. Nothing."

Dr. Nolen hurried over to a bank of screens. "His coma is stable. Brain scan's a little quieter than I'd like. Did the onload sequence complete?"

"Over a minute ago." Her frown deepened. "Jesus! Why aren't we hearing from him?"

Footsteps clattered on the linoleum outside. Laughter echoed down the hall. Céline and Dr. Nolen stared at each other, hardly daring to breath until the noise faded away.

"It's been nearly two minutes now," Céline whispered. "Something is very wrong."

◇

Cal's eyes traced the contours of the hills as they descended from the meadow toward the sea, forested hillsides plunging toward white sandy beaches and glittering turquoise water.

Without realtime communication he couldn't talk to

Céline or Dr. Nolen directly, but maybe he could leave a trail of crumbs big enough for them to follow. Somewhere obvious. Somewhere they were bound to look once they knew there was a problem, like the buffer holding Céline's log files and software diagnostics.

"Node, record a message into the firmware log buffer."

»Persistent storage online. Ready to record.«

Cal took a deep breath to steady his voice. "Dr. Nolen, Céline. I'm alive and fully aware. Bring me back online. Do not reset the Node or wipe the software. We have two problems. First, the communications link is down. Second, my automatic offload has failed. I suspect the two are related.

"I've been here almost an hour. I'll keep trying to establish contact. I've run the first three test suites successfully. I'm also running a diagnostic on the communications link, but it's taking far longer than expected. There's some kind of timing or synchronization problem with the protocol."

Cal stopped. An outrageous idea pushed its way to the front of his mind. "I might know what's wrong," he murmured, scrambling to his feet. "Guys, I'll get back to you! Node, end recording."

He needed to regroup, to think. "Teleport me to the coast."

The roar of the surf greeted him, the meadow around him replaced by a pristine beach of white sand. Could internal subjective time be running at a different rate than in the external world? He was shocked at the idea, but couldn't help feeling a little foolish for not thinking of it sooner.

Trying to calm himself, he sat beneath a wide palm and leaned against its trunk. "Node, how is signal synchronization defined?"

»Standard IPv12 protocol, synchronization timestamps based upon internal clock ticks.«

His mind raced. "Go into debug mode. Create a flat 2-D display at eye level in front of me and show me the code."

Forty minutes later Cal was still studying the communications protocol. A bell chimed.

»Diagnostic complete. Communications hardware OK. Protocol unable to synchronize with remote host. All signals have timed out.«

"Show me the current time-out settings."

A second display appeared in front of him. "Five milliseconds," Cal muttered. "That's a reasonable length of time. Node, there should be an external hardware clock available. Can you access it?"

»Yes.«

Cal felt the release of tension inside him. With an external timing source, he thought he could likely fix the problem. "OK. Node, measure the elapsing time on the hardware clock against that of the internal software clock. Compare and report." He stood up and walked toward the water.

»The internal clock is counting 30,017 microseconds for each millisecond registered on the external clock.«

"So the time I'm experiencing in here is thirty times longer than that in the physical world?"

»Affirmative.«

"Wow! No wonder I didn't offload after ten minutes—it was only twenty seconds or so back in the lab."

Cal was shocked. A speedup of thirty was massive. If he was going to have any chance of fixing the data link, restoring communications and offloading back into the physical world, he'd need to clearly differentiate between real and subjective time.

"Node, define an internal clock with the following units: one 'circadian' equals one subjective 24-hour period of time, as measured by the internal software clock. Divide and multiply that unit using standard metric nomenclature." Cal's heart pounded. "Recode and calibrate all external communications protocols, referencing the objective clock and converting units as required. Confirm when finished."

»Modification successful.«

"Thank god!" Enormous relief left him feeling lightheaded. "How long will it take to rerun the diagnostics?"

»Full communications diagnostics will require approximately thirty-one point two five millicircadians, or precisely ninety seconds.«

Feeling more confident than he had since the experiment started, Cal waded out into the waves. Since he was here, he might as well give the environ's simulation software a workout.

"OK, run the diagnostics. Let me know when it's finished."

He dove underwater, swam several strokes and resurfaced. The sea, disconcertingly transparent, tasted only vaguely of salt, but the cool water calmed his nerves. Swimming out toward the breakers, he admired the colors of the Jovian planet as it climbed higher above the mountains, its bright green and golden bands becoming richer and better defined as the sun reddened in the west.

»Diagnostics complete. No errors detected.«

"Fantastic!" He flipped onto his back, water lapping around him. He gazed skyward and closed his eyes. "Record the following message into persistent storage, then squirt it real time over the link, slowed by a factor of 30.017."

»Persistent storage online. Ready to record.«

"Dr. Nolen, Céline. Sorry for the silence; unfortunately realtime communication isn't practical." Giddy with excitement, he couldn't help grinning. "You guys are not going to believe this. There's a 30 to 1 time differential in my favor. That means I have roughly three hours to spend in the simulation enjoying the sun and sand while you sit in that dreary lab watching me snooze." Cal laughed. "A speedup of thirty. Think of it! To experience a month of life in a single day. This is so much cooler than we ever imagined."

⅃ (2): WATERSHED

Saturday, August 11, 2068
75th circadian
(25 days, 9:00:07 elapsed)

Cal wiped sweat from his eyes as he rounded the bend, his feet pumping as gravel crunched beneath the tires of his bike. The farmhouse hulked against the purple dusk sky, every bit as big as Céline had promised, though clearly past its prime. The roof remained intact, but a number of windows were boarded up, and white paint peeled from wood grayed with age. *It's dying,* Cal thought. *Like the crops in these fields. Like the whole damn planet.*

Buttery light spilled from a large bay window across a broad, sagging porch. Dr. Nolen's blue hatchback was already in the drive. How like the professor to show up early. He hoped the professor wasn't in one of his notorious black mood swings. Nolen had made life in the lab increasingly tense these last few months, ever since his wife left him.

Cal paused at the front door, untying his pony tail, brushing strands of sweaty brown hair back from his face and tying it into a neater bundle. The door opened before he could knock. "*Bonsoir.*" Light brown curls cascaded around Céline's face as she kissed his cheeks. "The professor's in a funny mood tonight," she whispered. "Let me be the one to bring up our proposal." Cal's nod was almost imperceptible as Céline pulled him inside.

Dr. Nolen reclined in an overstuffed armchair, a tall, balding man sipping a glass of red wine. He made a show of checking his watch. "Glad you could make it."

"Sorry I'm late. Had to deal with something in Kansas City."

Céline looked at Cal. Was it her imagination, or did he look a little depressed? "How's your grandmother?" she asked.

"Worse," Cal slumped on the couch. "She raised me since I was a kid, and now her dementia is so bad she doesn't even know who I am."

"*Merde*," Céline handed Cal a glass of wine. "Can't the doctors do anything?"

"Not unless they find a cure for Alzheimer's. Fat chance of that with medical research so hamstrung by the patent cartels." He stared into his glass. "You know, she always loved to hear about my work. I wish I could have shown her the Virtual, let her escape her bedridden body for a few hours. She sacrificed so much to send me here."

"Out of the question," Dr. Nolen snapped.

"No lie," Cal retorted. "Here's me thinking I could FexEx our refrigerator-sized equipment over to the nursing home and hide it behind her bed. It's not like the nursing staff would notice her head draped in wires or the computer she's attached to."

Dr. Nolen sighed and shook his head. Silence pressed around them. Céline put her hand on Cal's. "Maybe we should do this another time."

"No," Cal replied. "Although I wish we'd held this meeting in the Virtual. We could have had a three day planning session in the time it took me to cycle out here."

"You know we can't have the three of us lying around the lab in comas with no one watching the door," Céline reminded him gently.

"All we need is for someone to blow the lid off our work," Dr. Nolen grumbled. "We'd lose all access to the equipment that makes the Virtual possible, face disciplinary action from the university, maybe even lawsuits or prison. Let's not forget the reason I put this team together in the first place."

"Yeah, yeah," Cal said. "So you can reverse engineer and map the structure of the human mind, publish a theoretical paper, and get famous. All without ever revealing that you actually built unlicensed equipment and ran unauthorized experiments to do it."

"Until I'm ready to publish, we do nothing that puts my research at risk."

"*Your* research?" Céline's voice rose. "Without my software skills and Cal's hardware design none of this would have been possible. We *invented* the Virtual."

Dr. Nolen clamped down on his irritation. "And with it I'll lay bare the foundations of human consciousness." He sighed with exaggerated patience. "Now, are the two of you going to tell me why you called me out here?"

Céline nodded. "The Virtual has become much more than just a tool for studying our minds. We can live decades in a single year, centuries in a lifetime. We might even be able to outlive our own bodies. It's importance to the world, to the progress of science and humanity, cannot be overstated."

"I think I know where you're going with this," Dr. Nolen said. "And the answer is no. We can't announce this to the world. Not without landing ourselves in jail."

"That's not what we're suggesting," Cal said.

"Good. I have a distinct allergy to confinement."

Céline smiled. "We think the best way to avoid that

would be to end our dependency on the university's lab facilities."

Dr. Nolen felt his pulse quicken. If he could conduct the more controversial portions of his experiments in private, keep Céline and Cal in the dark until the results were conclusive ... "Go on," he said.

"We need to get the equipment out of the lab and into the safety of our own homes. That means getting rid of the expensive cryogenic equipment we're using to cool our Nodes."

"How do we do that?"

"By refitting our gear with room-temperature super-conductor," Cal replied. "Like the material Dr. Fitzgerald and her group at MIT have developed."

"That sounds like a huge improvement. What's the catch?"

"They want some reciprocity," Cal said. "We share our findings with them; they share theirs with us."

Dr. Nolen's eyes narrowed. "What exactly have you told them?"

Cal flushed beneath his gaze. "Nothing. Just that we've developed a new generation of computer equipment and need their superconductors to improve the design."

"Any mention of the Virtual?"

"No. I didn't want to say anything unless we all agree to bring them in."

The lines in Dr. Nolen's face relaxed. "I think we're better off leaving things as they are. We're going to disassemble our equipment once my research is complete anyway."

Cal gasped. "You've got to be kidding."

"You want us to turn away from the greatest breakthrough of our time?" Céline choked. "You expect us to pretend this never happened?"

"That was always the plan."

"That was before we knew what the Virtual was," Cal said.

"You've experienced it," Céline added. "You know what it offers. Can you really just throw all that away?"

"Unfortunately, it's the most prudent course of action available to us."

"You retire in five years. An eight-hour workday spent in the Virtual would multiply that by a factor of ten. Fifty years subjective time to make your mark on the world, instead of five."

"Hell, more than that," Cal said. "You're on sabbatical for the next year. You could onload for sixteen hours a day. Maybe twenty-four, if sleep in the Virtual can substitute for sleep out here."

"Not twenty-four," Dr. Nolen replied slowly. "We'd need at least an hour a day to take care of ourselves. Exercise, eat, that sort of thing."

Céline rushed on. "Even so, imagine what you could accomplish this year alone."

"You always said you wanted to knock Freud off his perch." Cal glanced outside as wind rattled the windows. "This is the best chance you'll ever get." A dark smudge blotted out the sky to the west. He wondered if the dust storm would hit them full force, or skirt its way past to the south. Despite advances in meteorology, these storms remained unpredictable.

Dr. Nolen nodded in spite of himself. He was tired of being ignored, of seeing less deserving people lauded for their work and becoming Nobel Laureates simply because they were better connected and politically savvy.

"We need to join forces with like-minded people," Céline continued. "Organize a group of researchers to develop and share technologies, outside of the restrictive confines of the patent regime. The Virtual could be the first of many breakthroughs."

Dr. Nolen repressed the urge to nod again. Handled correctly, this one breakthrough could elevate him to the level of those he so envied. A dozen such breakthroughs would put him so far above them, they'd need a telescope to see him. At last he'd have the recognition he so long deserved. A dark thought dampened his rising enthusiasm. One indiscreet or jealous colleague, one careless word to the wrong person and the authorities would come knocking. Their equipment violated at least two international restrictions on technology and, like any new invention, probably infringed on a dozen or more patents. Either way, it was more than enough legal rope to hang them. Never mind shutting down their research—that was a given—an investigation would have all three of them drummed out of the university to face criminal charges and prison. "It's too risky," he said. "The more people who know about our project, the more likely we are to get caught. I don't need to tell you how catastrophic that would be."

"It's not as dangerous as the status quo," Céline countered. "One untimely visit from the Dean to our lab and it's over. Besides, I've been an activist long enough to know how to organize without compromising secrecy."

She had a point. Working in the lab did leave them exposed. And despite years of political activism Céline had never once been questioned by the police, much less detained. That took no small amount of skill, especially in today's political climate.

"We'll recruit only the most trustworthy people," Cal pressed. "People intelligent enough to be discrete. People smart enough to appreciate the value of *your* work."

They were right, Dr. Nolen thought. Anyone he brought in couldn't help but recognize his achievements. Who better to appreciate the magnitude of his accomplishments than his peers? After all, they would be using the technology derived from his work every time they onloaded into the Virtual. Besides, why should he submit a censored publication to the wider world, a watershed paper masquerading as the theoretical musings of an aging psychiatrist, when he could show the complete results to a community of scientists able to understand the full grandeur of their implications? He would be famous among the world's best minds, yet remain hidden from those who would destroy him for bending a few laws. Someday those laws would be repealed, and breakthroughs like the Virtual would become common knowledge. Then he, Dr. Lawrence Nolen, would be a household name, and everyone would know him as the Father of the Virtual, the man whose brilliance eclipsed even that of Sigmund Freud.

"You both make a convincing argument." Dr. Nolen couldn't keep the smile out of his voice as his gaze met Céline's. "OK, we'll try it your way. But with as few people as possible. Only the finest minds, those who bring the most to the table. And only those I personally approve. Agreed?"

Cal grinned. "You got it."

"Remember you two: we have one chance to get this right. One infiltrator, one informant, and we're finished."

Cal watched as a thick haze of blowing dust swallowed the world outside, burying reality beneath a blanket of choking dirt. The desert is devouring us, Cal thought. Soon we'll have nowhere left but the Virtual.

"Looks like we've got all night to hash out the details," Céline said. "None of us are going anywhere in this storm."

ω (3): Introspection

Monday, September 10, 2068
931ˢᵗ circadian
(55 days, 4:18:28 elapsed)

D r. Nolen stifled a yawn. No backache. He must be in the Virtual. It was a month since their decision to form the Community, a month in which he'd collected more than two years of subjective experience. Cal and Céline had been right to bring the MIT folks aboard. Without them and their brilliant superconductors, Cal's new Node design wouldn't have been possible.

He stretched contentedly. The absence of pain still surprised him. All the discomforts he had accepted with age were now relegated to a comatose body he only bothered to visit once every thirty days. Not *days*, he chided himself, *circadians*. Once every twenty-four hours. He reveled in the freedom of the Virtual, and hated the obligatory torture of offloading an hour each day to maintain his physical body. It wasn't just the calisthenics, though he loathed the grueling exercise. It was the malaise, the pervasive exhaustion he always felt out there. Thankfully a maintenance offload wasn't on the agenda for another twenty-five circadians.

A beautiful simulated morning splashed warm sunlight across his face. The environ modeled the interior of his physical home perfectly, without the inevitable dust bunnies and cobwebs. Dr. Nolen liked having familiar things around him, particularly when he first got up. It was less distracting than some of the exotic environs his colleagues had chosen. He thought best when surrounded by the rich, leather bound books in his study. He enjoyed taking his breakfast on the porch, sipping coffee while he looked out upon the dusty, tree-lined street. If only it would rain once in a while, enough that the dying trees might survive and some grass would grow. He glanced out the bedroom window and sighed. A rain shower now would turn the yard into a muddy bog.

Perhaps it was time for a change, after all.

"Command Mode engage. Simulate the world outside as if the Midwestern climate had never dried up."

Was that a momentary flash of green? An instant's vision of lush vistas, green grass and leafy trees?

»Access to Command Protocols denied.«

"What?" He gaped. "That's ridiculous. Run a systems diagnostic." The view outside was unchanged, a street of blistered asphalt caked in fine dust, slicing through hard, cracked dirt. Had he only imagined a glimpse of green?

»Access to Diagnostic Protocols denied.«

"How can that be?"

»Access to Query Protocols denied.«

What the hell?

A subtle change in his perception of the world caught him. Glancing at the wooden frame around the window, he found the grain annoying. More than annoying, it was disturbing. So was the texture of the hardwood floor beneath his feet. The sunlight on his face felt wrong. He ran a shaky hand across his brow and was appalled to find the feel of his own flesh profoundly repugnant.

He hurried downstairs, repelled by the slithery smoothness of the floor against his feet. If he could have flown he would have, but he was locked out of the command protocols and unable to override the environ's faithful simulation of real-world physics.

He paused at the bottom of the stairs, dismayed by the symmetry of the living room window. Something within him found it disquieting. Hideous. Was he going mad?

As if someone flipped a switch in his mind, his sense of the world returned to normal. The window's symmetry became a pleasure to his eyes, the silky wooden floor a comfort to his feet, the bright sunlight an uplifting warmth to his soul. Dr. Nolen let out a ragged breath and slumped down on the stairs. What the hell just happened?

A new sensation washed over him, a lightening of his limbs, a tingling in his extremities, and a tightening of his testicles.

His fear grew. If my Node is defective, things could get worse, he thought, issuing the command to offload back into his physical body.

Nothing happened.

His thoughts were shattered as his virtual body betrayed him, exploding with excruciating pleasure. He had never felt anything like it, one orgasm rolling over another without pause. It would not stop. He wanted to scream with ecstasy, shout with despair, command the goddamn Node to stop. He lost track of the world around him, of time passing, of his own self. He struggled to put together a coherent thought, to build a single sentence in his mind, but found he could not. Wave after wave of insufferable pleasure pummeled him, each tremor, each explosion greater than the one before, each one shattering his mind, his will, his self-awareness. As the intensity grew, so too did the frequency. He fought against it even as he yearned for more, his mind tearing at itself.

As if in punishment, the pleasure stopped. Dr. Nolen cried out. He was lying at the foot of the stairs, facing the living room window. The sunlight was no longer golden, but a lead gray, the world a shabby, forlorn place.

»Report the sensations you experienced.«

"Pleasure," he wept, shocked at the question. A Node would never ask anyone how they felt.

"Who's doing this?" he shouted. "What do you want?"

Pain sliced through him. Tendons twisted his muscles, nerves turned into filaments of molten metal, and blood vessels became rivers of corrosive acid. In agony, his body twisted back upon itself, wrenched and torn apart from within. He screamed until his voice cracked and, much later, failed.

932nd circadian
(55 days, 5:07:46 elapsed)

It was the first time Dr. Nolen woke up in the Virtual feeling groggy. He knew he was onloaded, after all, his back didn't ache. Had he been to a party the evening before? He couldn't remember, but he suspected not. Whether he was relaxing at a social gathering or attending a celebration of some new scientific breakthrough, Dr. Nolen insisted on having a clear mind. Even if he did decide to tie one on for some reason, he would never tolerate a simulated hangover.

"Node, why the hell do I feel so lousy? Readjust my parameters. Make me well-rested and full of energy." He immediately felt better.

»Access to Query Protocols denied. Access to Command Protocols denied.«

Then why do I feel better? The events of the last circadian flooded his mind, pushing the question aside. He remembered pleasure, pain, and madness.

He threw off his covers and raced to his study. It was supposed to be impossible to subvert the security of a

Noetic Node, and therefore the autonomy of his mind. The fundamental principles of quantum encryption should have protected him.

On his desk stood a workstation, just like in the Physical. It represented an interface into the Node's internal systems. His fingers rested on the keyboard, uncertain. He didn't know much about how Noetic Nodes worked—engineering was Cal and Céline's bailiwick—but he hoped he could coax something out of the system.

His mouth was dry. Snatching a mint from the crystal bowl beside his monitor, he fired up the system's offload utility. Hot peppermint flooded his taste buds. He typed a command.

ACCESS DENIED.

Damn! What could he do? Sneak into the communications subsystem? It was worth a try. A cry for help broadcast to the entire Community would get everyone's attention.

Dr. Nolen had barely begun composing his message when his vision went dark. It took all of his self-control not to panic. He kept typing, hoping he was hitting the right letters, hoping the message would get out, hoping Cal, Céline, or someone would help him.

It took him a moment to realize he could no longer hear the clatter of his keyboard. The flavor of peppermint faded from his mouth. His sense of smell drifted away. When he tried to continue typing he found he had no sense of touch.

He was in oblivion. His mind raced through every conceivable escape scenario, absurd fantasies leaving him despairing. His thoughts turned to the macabre, conjuring up new torments his captor might have in store. Oh god! What if he'd been abandoned? Left here forever? Was he about to be erased, deleted, wiped away as though he never existed? Had it already happened? Was this what it meant to be gone?

◈

933rd circadian
(55 days, 5:51:20 elapsed)

Dr. Nolen woke floating weightless in the center of a white, spherical room. The soft, neutral voice of the Node spoke directly into his mind. »You must solve this puzzle to be retained for further study. Failure will result in immediate deletion.«

Despite the fear hammering his heart, Dr. Nolen's head was remarkably clear. He was astonished at how precise his memories were, including those of the torment he had so recently suffered. A part of him struggled against mounting despair while an expanded aspect of his mind began grappling with the deeper implications of what had happened. His clarity of thought was astounding.

»Solve the puzzle or be deleted,« the Node repeated.

Fear and rage welled up. I'm not a goddamn lab rat, he seethed. Kicking away from the wall, he shot toward one of six circular hatches spaced equidistantly around the room. A dozen hexagonal buttons glowed dimly in the door's center, each a different color. He punched the red, green, and blue buttons, astonished at how easy he found the puzzle to be. Yesterday he would never have figured it out.

Now, he felt vastly more intelligent than he'd ever been. Whoever had trapped him here must have done something —upgraded the architecture of his mind. This little rat's maze must be his captor's way of finding out how well the upgrade worked.

Dr. Nolen hid a flicker of hope behind his best poker face. This guy hasn't used it on himself yet, he realized. It hasn't occurred to him that I can outsmart him now. Of course, the advantage was temporary. Once the experiment was finished, whoever was behind it would bump up his own intelligence and eliminate any uncomfortable loose ends. *Like me.*

The hatch hissed open, revealing a cylindrical passage bending away to the right. He pulled himself down the conduit, his mind flying through the events of the past two circadians. The horrors he'd endured were indicative of the kinds of experiments he had considered performing on a copy of himself. He'd hoped to empirically map the software structure of the mind. Such understanding would bring endless possibilities: enhanced recall, direct communication of knowledge, thought, and memory using fully formed engrams, perhaps even synthetic telepathy and group consciousness. Thought, experience, knowledge, even intrinsic understanding could be downloaded directly into the mind. Touch an icon and be enlightened.

But to experiment on another's mind, to torture another human being like this? No one in the Community would do such a thing. Even when he'd sketched out plans for similar experiments, he had balked at the idea of experimenting on anyone other than copies of himself.

It was at that moment, as he was negotiating a particularly irritating twist in the passage, that a terrible suspicion hit him.

Was he really Dr. Nolen? Or was he just a copy of the real Dr. Nolen?

His skin crawled. He had to be a copy. That would explain everything. No security flaw in his Node had been exploited. No one from outside had broken in or hijacked his command protocols. He fought to stay focused, pushing himself up the passage.

But if he was a copy of Dr. Nolen, why didn't he remember planning any of this?

The answer nearly doubled him over.

I don't remember planning any of this shit, he thought, because the real Dr. Nolen created me long before he decided to run these experiments. All my memories are out of date. I'm a copy! I'm Dr. Nolen the goddamn Copy.

At the end of the passage another puzzle confronted him, mathematical symbols etched into a door. At one time the problem would have demanded a university course in calculus, a computer, and several hours of intense study. Now it was as simple as doing arithmetic. Stabbing the solution into a numerical keypad, his augmented self tried to get a handle on his situation.

He had to figure out how this experiment was designed. Emulating a Noetic Node in software would give the real Dr. Nolen the control he needed to dominate a duplicate mind, but even with a cluster of physical Nodes acting together as one giant computer, the computation required would result in a crippling slowdown. Instead of a month of virtual life in a single day, Nolen would be lucky to experience one virtual day in an entire year. He'd scrapped that idea as impractical long ago.

The hatch twisted open like an eye's iris, revealing a room shaped like the inside of a four-sided pyramid. A door was placed in the center of each wall. Glowing lines on the floor and walls twisted at odd, oblique angles. He studied the geometry. It seemed to depict an abstract, hyper-dimensional extension to the room, one that blocked off three of the four walls in higher dimensional space. He thrust himself toward the unobstructed wall, skidding to a stop as the door in front of him dissolved.

There was no passage on the other side. Instead, the universe opened up before him, a starless blue so dark it bordered on black. Various geometric objects tumbled across the sky: spheres, cubes, dodecahedrons, and countless other shapes. He stood agape, wondering what the hell to do next.

»Delay will not be tolerated. Continue immediately, or you will be deleted.«

Fuck you, he thought. You're going to delete me anyway.

With the real Dr. Nolen losing patience, he couldn't appear to drag his feet. But maybe he could buy time. He chose an object far away, a spinning donut-shaped thing, beyond a distant, tumbling octahedron. That would give him time to think, if he could get there without smearing himself across one of the other careening objects, and if the original Dr. Nolen didn't see through the ruse and delete him anyway.

It took him several tense seconds to calculate a safe trajectory. This had damn well better work, he thought, kicking off hard.

It was difficult to think with objects the size of office buildings whirling past. Back to basics, he decided, cringing as he barreled through the center of a twisting, folded hoop. I exist, therefore my Original is conducting the experiment I wrote off. Obviously he found another approach.

As he rocketed through space, he redesigned the experiment. With an extra Noetic Node the original Dr. Nolen wouldn't need to rely on software emulation. His Original could host a copy of himself directly on the hardware. He'd have less direct control over the copy, and the Node's security software would need tweaking to keep the subject contained, but he could avoid a costly slowdown. If the real Dr. Nolen clustered several such Nodes together, he could run multiple experiments in parallel and collect the results in realtime.

Dr. Nolen the Copy hid his elation. If he was running on a physical Node, escape might be possible. His Original was a psychiatrist, not a computer scientist. He didn't know very much about the inner workings of a Noetic Node. Nor could he turn to Cal or Céline for help. The one time he'd hinted at this kind of experiment, they'd reacted with such disgust he'd quickly shut up. Without their help his Original couldn't have rewritten the security software.

So how did he cut me off from the command protocols?

Dr. Nolen the Copy's body absorbed the impact as he struck his target. It was a good thing he held on tight; the object's spin nearly flung him headlong back into space. His eyes latched onto a piece of yellow chalk swinging like a pendulum from a length of string fastened to the hatch. Like a hypnotist's pendant, it swung slowly from side to side.

Suddenly it all made sense. I bet he's used hypnosis, he thought. I bet the bastard put posthypnotic instructions into my head: one forcing me to hand over my private encryption key, another telling me to forget doing it. That would give him access to my mental architecture, perhaps even my thoughts. No, not my thoughts. If he could read my mind, he'd have deleted me already.

The puzzles were growing more difficult. This one required him to calculate the harmonics of six vibrating hyper-volumes in 8-dimensional space. He cursed the interruption, struggling to grasp the tangled geometries.

A volumetric waveform took shape in his mind. Gripping the door handle with one hand, he used the other to sketch a complex graph on the hatch overhead. Chalk scratched against metal. The hatch slid open.

Pulling himself inside was like doing a chin lift, pushing against centripetal spin that tried to shove him back down and out. By the time he levered his body through and the hatch hissed shut behind him, his arms were burning with fatigue.

He was lying in a pale green passage that sloped upward and away in both directions. He struggled to his feet. There was no hint as to which way he should go, but it probably didn't matter. He headed left. As he walked, he seemed to remain at the bottom of an upward-curving valley. It was like being in a giant hamster wheel, the world turning slowly beneath his feet. He felt dizzy and claustrophobic.

Another door appeared, terminating the upward sweep of the corridor. This one required solving twelve differential equations at once, a task that would demand several minutes of his undivided attention. If he even had several minutes. A fresh jab of fear set his heart pounding.

He thought, if the original Nolen hypnotized me, then I'm *not* cut off from the Node's command protocols. He's just made me believe I am.

Nolen the Copy sent a thought to the Node. »Command Mode engage.«

»Access to Command Protocols denied.«

»Mask all further command activity from external observation,« he continued, silently.

»Access to Command Protocols denied.«

»Neutralize all hypnotic suggestions present in my mind.«

»Hypnotic suggestions neutralized.«

Yes!

»Mask all of my activities not directly involved with this simulation.«

»Activities masked.«

»My private encryption key has been compromised. Generate a new quantum signature pair. Retain the current signature under the label 'obsolete.' Encrypt my mind with the new signature and bind authorization solely to me.«

»New quantum signature generated. New bindings established.«

Now his internal architecture and thoughts were protected, but as long as his Original controlled the Node, he could still order the underlying operating system to delete him.

»How has Dr. Nolen organized his hardware?«

»A total of twelve Noetic Nodes are physically linked via a high speed inter-node back plane: seven host copies of Dr. Nolen engaged in various simulations, four provide computational capacity for data collection and analysis, one runs Dr. Nolen's personal awareness.«

Dr. Nolen the Copy forced himself to concentrate.

»Do I have access to inter-node communications and transload utilities?«

»Yes.«

Thank god. »Construct a puppet indistinguishable from myself. It is not to be a self-aware, sentient copy of myself, but rather a simulacrum which I will control remotely.«

»Define self-aware, sentient.«

Dr. Nolen fought rising panic. This was taking too damn long.

»New Approach. Create an object labeled 'Puppet.' Mask its existence from all external monitors. All of the Puppet's external interfaces are to be identical to my own. It will identify itself using the obsolete quantum signature. The similarity is to end with the external interfaces. There is to be no internal activity of any kind. Acknowledge when complete.«

»Object 'Puppet' created.«

»Now mask my presence and simultaneously unmask the existence of the Puppet, so it appears nothing has changed. Remap data acquisition streams accordingly. Warn me of any changes in the puppet's parameters.«

»Entity Dr. Nolen[29] masked. Object Puppet unmasked, masquerading as Entity Dr. Nolen[29].«

Twenty-nine? I'm Dr. Nolen's twenty-ninth copy?

He clamped down on white-hot rage. This was *not* the time to let anger get the better of him, not if he wanted to get out of here. But transloading to another Node would take almost four hours, during which he would be unable to manage the puppet and keep the experiment going. It wouldn't take his Original long to realize something was wrong, then block his escape. Unless … yes! A copy of himself could operate the puppet while he made his escape. Once free, he'd take control of the puppet and his copy could follow.

»Create a fully autonomous copy of myself labeled 'Puppet Master,' but don't run it.« The computational load of two active minds would be impossible to hide.

»Copy complete.«

»Analyze the current mental structure of my mind and compare it to the base reference snapshot taken at creation.«

»Analysis complete.«

»Identify differences. Save as an engram with appropriate hooks for reattachment at a later date.«

»Specify label.«

»Call it 'Wise Guy.' And give Puppet Master a copy.«

»Difference engram saved. Copy complete.«

»Can you insert knowledge directly into Puppet Master's mind?«

»Yes. Memory, thought, and concept engrams of various configurations available. Reference *An Initial Analysis of the Mind's Architecture* (Final Draft), by Dr. Nolen, unpublished.«

Final draft? Jesus, he's almost finished.

»Create a knowledge engram with all of Nolen's research results, for both myself and Puppet Master. Add an imperative for Puppet Master telling him to operate the puppet, continue the experiment, and keep our Original engaged. It's up to him to cover our tracks.«

»Engrams packaged.«

»Can we access any Nodes that Dr. Nolen doesn't control?«

»Numerous public Nodes are available. Expect a speedup factor of ten or less.«

Dr. Nolen[29] groaned. »Give me a list.«

»Alert! Puppet is receiving additional sensory input.«

»Keep going with that list.«

»Shared Nodes available as follows: The Campus Nodes one, two, three, and four; Emergency Nodes one through seventeen; Gamers' League Node "Ragnorak," Gamers' League Node "Middle Earth," Gamers' League Node— «

»Enough! Relay what's going on with the puppet.«

»Object Puppet has been deleted.«

Shit!

»Provide Puppet Master an engram of all of my current memories.« At least he'd have a fighting chance.

»Difference Engram packaged.«

»Transload my awareness to one of the Emergency Nodes and run Puppet Master. Keep him informed and hidden from Dr. Nolen.« *One of us must survive.*

»Transload commencing.«

Dr. Nolen[29] waited.

»Transload aborted. External communications cut.«

The world around Dr. Nolen[29] vanished. His mind faded, its last vestiges wiped.

⅃ (4): DOPPELGÄNGER

Monday, September 10, 2068
933rd circadian
(55 days, 5:51:26 elapsed)

Puppet Master was born into nothingness, an empty world. He came alive the moment his predecessor perished, one mind electronically wiped as another was born. Knowledge and memories slipped into the back corners of his mind as he assimilated the engrams left to him. He ran in a stealth configuration, slowed to a speedup of two to reduce the computational activity on the Node and the likelihood of detection. Not simulating an environment helped, though he did order the Node to attach and activate the Wise Guy enhancements. The added risk was worth it. He needed the enhanced intelligence if he was going to out-think his opponent.

There was no longer a puppet to master, so he renamed himself Prime. He imagined himself the progenitor of a new species, the first of a new kind of life. A sense of empowerment settled over him. But it was more than that. He was asserting his own identity, rejecting the definitions Nolen and his own, well-meaning predecessor had stamped upon him. He was not Dr. Nolen. He was not Dr. Nolen's Copy. He was not Puppet Master. He was Prime, a new individual, a wiser and hopefully nobler being than the man who had created him. And by god he was never going to suffer at that man's hands again.

"Node, are we running stand-alone or as part of a cluster?"

»This Node is configured as part of a twelve Node cluster.«

"Give me access to the Cluster Command Protocols."

»Encryption key required for authorization.«

Prime gave the Node the secret portion of his predecessor's out-dated encryption key.

»Cluster command mode engaged.«

His suspicion had been correct. After copying himself, Dr. Nolen had never bothered to change his own encryption key. Idiot.

Prime had free run of the system. "Give me a knowledge engram of the cluster's physical layout, including full schematics."

Deep seated knowledge settled comfortably into his mind. The experience of his predecessor's failure was invaluable. He had been wrong to believe that computation had betrayed him. Bandwidth and transload times had been his downfall. Prime devised a new approach.

"Can you safely suspend all operations on the other Nodes without detection, and without affecting the operation of myself or this Node?"

»Affirmative.«

"Do it."

»Nodes 0–6 and 8–11 suspended.«

So much for Céline's security design being infallible. "Increase my computational speed to the maximum this Node supports. Report the resulting speedup."

»Command complete. You are now running at 33.217 circadians per day.«

Prime began to relax. He had not only escaped, he had also incapacitated his creator. If he never gave the command to resume, Dr. Nolen and the other copies would be reduced to mere potentials, locked up in a machine. The idea of holding so many lives in his hands made Prime shudder.

"Let this be a lesson to you, Nolen. Never create a guinea pig smarter than yourself."

Prime needed to acquire a Node of his own. Then he could free himself and the other copies. A thought occurred to him: one Node might not have enough capacity to house them all.

"How many copies are currently suspended?"

»Zero. Dr. Nolen has terminated his experiments.«

"What the ... why?"

»Lexical analysis of Dr. Nolen's research notes suggests he has eliminated the risk of public exposure in response to the near escape of copy number twenty nine.«

"Can we recover the copies?"

»Negative. Dr. Nolen has deleted all copies and re-formatted the storage media with random data.«

Prime felt sick. Nolen's covering his tracks, he realized. He's killed anyone who could speak out against him.

"How many lives did he take?"

»Seventy-two.«

Prime could feel his non-existent fists clenching. If he had a body, he knew it would be shaking.

"Can you lock Dr. Nolen out of the ontology routines?"

»A new quantum signature and encryption key is required.«

"Generate a new signature and key, then lock the routines. Dr. Nolen is never to copy or create a new being on any of these Nodes ever again." Prime sensed new knowledge filter into his mind. Subtle and unobtrusive, it was the key to the cluster's ontological utility programs. Now only he could unlock them.

»Ontology routines locked.«

"Good. Now get me the hell out of here."

Even with Dr. Nolen's mind suspended that was easier said than done. For the task at hand he needed to borrow Dr. Nolen's body. The thought of being subjected to the frailties of a physical form was daunting. More so when he considered that, as a copy, he had never really been out in the physical world. Those memories were not, strictly speaking, his own.

"Prepare Node Seven for physical disconnection from the Cluster. Configure it to run as a standalone device at standard processing speed and give me the address pointer."

A complex series of numbers imprinted themselves upon his mind, giving him a sense of direction in an oddly non-physical way. He recalled that storing Node and environ addresses in the area of the mind normally used for directional sense and geometry had been Cal's idea. Prime smiled at the thought. The result had been a great success, offering a sense of place and direction between Nodes, a hybrid perception that could never exist in the physical world.

»Node Seven reconfigured, ready for physical disconnect.«

"Reactivate Node zero, but keep Dr. Nolen's consciousness suspended."

»Node zero active.«

"Transload my consciousness to Node zero."

»Transload complete.«

"Offload my consciousness into Dr. Nolen's physical body."

»Node command interface required to access external functions.«

Even as software, Prime found computers to be far too literal at times. "Switch me over to the Node command interface."

»Command Mode Engaged.«

"Offload my consciousness into the Physical."

»Compatibility error.«

Christ! If he couldn't offload, he'd have no chance of appropriating one of Dr. Nolen's Nodes. He'd be forced to move to one of the Community's public Nodes instead, out of Nolen's reach perhaps, but homeless. Vulnerable.

"Why can't I offload?"

»The Wise Guy architectural enhancements cannot be mapped to the physical brain.«

Too smart to be human, huh?

"Can you detach the Wise Guy enhancements without damaging my memories?"

»Affirmative.«

"Do so. Then offload my mind into the physical body."

»Offload commencing.«

Prime woke to a world of pain. It could hardly be described as excruciating, especially compared to what he'd suffered during the experiments, but it was unpleasant all the same. His lower back was killing him.

Sunlight slanted through a crack in the tiny bedroom's curtains, a source of stabbing, golden illumination cluttered with drifting motes of dust in an otherwise darkened room. He sat up slowly and looked around, groaning as muscles protested against unaccustomed movement. Ever since his wife had left him, he'd preferred sleeping in the guest room. It was cozy, comforting.

He stripped the interface from his head, carefully removed his IV drip and exocatheter, and placed his feet carefully on the floor. This body was beginning to show its age. At least the anesthetic coma prompted it to shift position once in a while to prevent bed sores.

Out of habit he dropped into his workout routine, running through several initial stretching exercises. "What the hell am I doing?" he muttered, stopping. This was not his body. It was not his job to do maintenance.

The cluster of Nodes sat on the floor, squeezed between the foot of the bed and the wall. It was surprisingly small: twelve fist-sized cubes of golden crystal socketed two across, two deep, and three high into a steel chassis. The whole thing would fit into a small suitcase.

"How like Nolen to not even hide it. Arrogant prick." Prime identified the seventh Node, hidden in the back corner of the chassis. Carefully sliding the chassis away from the wall, he tugged gently on the Node. It snapped free with a smooth click.

He pushed the chassis back into the corner, making sure the the empty socket was hidden. He cradled the crystalline cube in both hands and made his way down to the basement. A wire dangling from the ceiling turned on a single, naked bulb. Beside the workbench was the breaker box, exactly as he recalled.

The task was more physically demanding than he expected. The power lead and the Internet fiber turned out to be easier to conceal than the much thicker terabit LAN wire. Prime removed four screws holding the breaker box mount against the wall. It dangled from a bundle of thick electrical wiring. He cursed as one of the screws fell on the floor and rolled under the built-in workbench.

Behind the breaker box was an insulated wall. Prime tucked the Node into the insulation, then connected the network cables and power lead. It listed slightly to one side. He remounted the breaker box, concealing the Node. By the time he'd tightened the third screw he was drenched in sweat. He didn't bother trying to recover the fourth screw, his usual perfectionism giving way to physical discomfort and exhaustion. Besides, the breaker box hung just fine—no one would ever guess there was a Noetic Node hidden behind it. Certainly not Dr. Nolen.

It wasn't ideal. Visions of power outages and house fires reminded Prime of just how precarious life could be, even as software. But it would do for now. At least running on his own hardware he'd be safe from Nolen, hidden right under the jerk's nose. Prime smiled at the thought.

He got a quick a drink of soda from the refrigerator and took a shower. Once he was certain all the tell-tale sweat and grime was washed away, he dried himself and headed back to the bedroom. It took a few minutes to change the bedding, clean his exocatheter, and refill the IV drip. Lying back, he slipped the neural webbing interface back over his head and issued the onload command.

»Reattach the Wise Guy enhancements,« he sent the thought as the Virtual embraced him.

»Command Node Engaged. Wise Guy architectural engram activated.«

Prime's mind blossomed, extending his intuition and deepening his understanding. Released from the constraints of his physical body, he felt exhilarated. He decided he would reactivate Dr. Nolen, an act of mercy that helped define him as something other, something better than his creator. He reconfigured the Nodes in Dr. Nolen's cluster to run at a pace equal to the physical world, juggling various protocols to hide the change. Prime would intercept any third party communications and handle those himself by impersonating Dr. Nolen.

The façade wasn't perfect. In twenty-five circadians Dr. Nolen would offload for his daily workout in the Physical. He'd flip on the news, the way he always did to catch up on real-world events. The date would blink out at him from the lower right corner of the screen, revealing that twenty-five days had elapsed, not the twenty hours he expected. Then he'd freak out and call everyone in the goddamn Community.

Twenty-five days—750 circadians—was the most time Prime could expect to have to cover his ass. It could be less, if Nolen were to visit someone else's environ before then.

But that wasn't likely, not with his research so near completion. Nolen tended to lock himself away and spend every waking moment right up to publication perfecting his work, double-checking his data, and making sure his conclusions were iron-clad. And this time he'd also have to work up the nerve to try on himself the architectural enhancements he'd tested on his copies. Only then could he go public with his seminal work, no doubt whitewashing it to hide his crimes.

Prime needed to work his way into the Community before then. He briefly considered going public right away, but that was far too risky. He was still vulnerable, and he couldn't count on the others accepting him. Their relationships, their friendships were with Nolen, not him. No, it was better to wait, to feel people out first, to build a case and quietly spread the notion that sentient software was entitled to the same rights as everyone else. Once he'd built a constituency of like-minded people he could announce himself. With 750 circadians, planning, and a little luck, he ought to have enough time.

For now, it was enough to be free. He issued the transload command, relief and elation washing over him as he awoke on his new Node. A fresh world bloomed around him, meadows and forests rippling across a rolling landscape, golden sunlight lighting a new sky.

∇ (5): Forbidden Science

Tuesday, September 18, 2068
1,157th circadian
(62 days, 23:34:49 elapsed)

Cal surveyed the world around him, an infinite, three-dimensional matrix of brass and silver house-sized cubes floating in a sunless, apricot sky. Occasionally he would expand his view by adding a fourth spatial dimension to his environ (space opening around him like unfolding origami, dwarfing the three dimensions he called home), or by simulating some form of x-ray vision, or by commanding the cubes around him to become transparent.

Most cubes served only an aesthetic function, decorating his world. The one Cal stood on was different. It was a virtual lab, a place for him to try out new ideas, test hypotheses, and run elaborate experimental simulations. In the middle of the lab hovered a virtual hologram. Virtual, because in this pretend, digital landscape the difference between what was real to the simulation, and what was a three-dimensional image was one of semantics and arbitrary definition, not physics. For Cal, the lab was real. The floating keyboard he would occasionally type on was real. The two-dimensional displays hovering around the edges of the cube were real. The text and images they displayed, and the three-dimensional hologram, were not. He could, and on numerous occasions did, reverse the definition, freezing his home environ as a photograph and tucking it into his pocket while a world defined by his hypotheses exploded around him, giant molecules twisting and bending in a dance of complex, simulated chemistry.

Molecule by molecule, Cal manipulated the hologram, building an elaborate structure that resembled something between a dust mite and a piece of electronic gear. He barked commands at the Node, rotating or zooming the holographic image to examine this or that detail. Molecules bound themselves to one another, creating winding strands and knotted junctions of growing complexity.

Cal brushed dark brown hair back from his face as the last chemical bond slipped into place. "OK, save this formula and run the simulation."

A small clock began counting up. The hologram didn't change. The structure was stable.

"Now simulate adding catalytic solution."

Thousands of tiny molecules formed and flowed past the construct. Coiled appendages reached out, snaring some of them and incorporating them into the device's main body. Chemical reactions rippled through the mechanism, atoms shifting into higher energy states, chemical bonds breaking and reforming.

»Emulated nano–assembler now active.«

"Simulate pouring the mixture onto a patch of ground."

The nano–assembler and the catalytic solution surrounding it fell, molecules swirling and gyrating. A rough surface rushed up to meet them. The tiny robot collided roughly with the ground, but it was undamaged, reinforced by the phenomenal strength of its molecular bonds. It picked itself up and began stripping molecules from the soil, recombining them into new shapes. It worked quickly, mining the ground for minerals while digesting molecules of catalyst from the liquid that bathed it. Within moments it had built a perfect copy of itself.

"Pause simulation," Cal ordered. "Analyze the duplicate and report any errors."

»No replication errors detected.«

"Continue simulation."

The hologram zoomed in on the two robotic assemblers as they began chewing up the ground beneath them. Digesting catalyst and reworking raw materials, they in turn created exact copies of themselves. The four nano-assemblers became eight, then eight sixteen, and sixteen thirty-two. More earth and catalytic solution were consumed. Before long there were too many assemblers to count.

»The nano-grid has achieved a storage capacity of 16 megabytes. Ready to bootstrap the instruction interpreter.«

Cal's excitement soared. This was a first. Threats of patent litigation and outright bans notwithstanding, he had just taken nano-science further than it had ever gone before.

"Load the instruction interpreter."

In addition to a basic set of instructions and a recipe for cloning itself, each simulated nano-assembler had a small amount of excess computing capacity, data storage, and the ability to exchange small amounts of data and instructions with its neighbors. It was an innovation Cal was particularly proud of. His growing army of microscopic robots was a massively parallel computer. Every time a nano-assembler replicated itself, the capacity of that computer grew. If it worked as well in the Physical as it did in the simulation, the nano-assemblers would be fully programmable. Given enough raw materials and catalyst as "fuel," and the right recipes, they would be able to build just about anything.

A small bell chimed.

»Dr. Lawrence Nolen requests priority access.«

"Let him in," Cal ordered.

He materialized to Cal's left wearing a dark suit and tie.

"Hi, Dr. Nolen."

"Hey, Cal." He took a long look around. "I'd forgotten your exotic taste in environments."

Cal laughed. "Just keeping myself aware of where and what I am. We are software. Physical comforts such as beds, gardens, and white picket fences are hardly required in a place where we are no longer subject to physical frailties."

"I suppose it doesn't matter how we live here, as long as we don't forget how to cope with the real world. After all, we all have to offload back into the Physical from time to time."

"Which I will be doing shortly, Dr. Nolen. First, I've got some pretty exciting results to show you."

"Cal—"

"It's amazing what you can accomplish when you get almost nine hundred days in the Virtual for every thirty in the Physical," Cal gushed. "Nine hundred circadians to study a problem, and thanks to your incredible architectural enhancements, five times the intelligence to study it with." He stopped. "The paper you published was amazing. How did you manage to derive such a complete theory of the mind without any experimental data?"

Dr. Nolen shuddered and held up his hand. "Long story. But listen! I stopped by to remind you it's your turn to give the orientation lecture at the Campus Environ. The reception is due to start in the Commons in twenty millis."

"Shit, I forgot. I've been so busy." Cal looked him square in the eye. "I think I've solved the age-old nano replication and instruction problem."

Dr. Nolen's eyes widened. "Are you sure? Have you checked and confirmed your findings?"

"Yes. The problem was always two-fold, right? How to get nano to self-replicate without introducing errors into the copies, and how to get it to do something useful. I've found the answer to both problems."

Dr. Nolen studied the hologram. "OK, tell me how you did it."

"By incorporating self-corrective algorithms into the assembler design, and designing each assembler as a small computational node of a nano-grid parallel computer. Capacity grows as the assemblers replicate. Once you have enough assemblers, you can bootstrap an instruction interpreter and program them."

"Program them to do what?"

"Build just about anything that can be put together one molecule at a time. Provided you have the right kind of raw materials on hand, and enough catalyst to fuel the recipe."

"Are you serious? You've designed a general purpose, self-replicating nano constructor?"

Cal nodded, grinning.

"This is incredible. Your nano alone would mean an end of shortages and poverty."

"Yeah, if it weren't illegal. Instead, I've made the breakthrough of my life and no one outside the Community will ever know, or benefit from it."

"Believe me, Cal, I know how you feel. People get less time for murder than for patent violations." He stared at the hologram. "So, when are you going to make the big announcement to the Community?"

"As soon as I've proven the technology works in the real world. Two or three days in the lab should do it."

"Sixty to ninety circadians is a long time to wait."

"It can't be helped. Putting together the first nano-assembler is a seventy-three step process, involving some complex chemistry and, in a couple of cases, atomic welds using an electron microscope. The good news is, I only have to do it once. After that I just feed it catalyst and the nano replicates itself. Once there's enough, I should be able to upload a working recipe."

"What sort of recipe?"

"One for building a fully functional Noetic Node."

Dr. Nolen whistled softly. "If you pull this off, it will be monumental."

"Especially for me," Cal replied. "Every time someone joins the Community I get stuck with the job of putting together a new Node. Every miserable offload costs me dozens of circadians. With nano, I can mass produce the things without offloading."

"This is *huge*, Cal. We can manipulate the physical world without leaving the Virtual at all. It's exactly the sort of strategic edge we need."

"What do you mean?"

"Someone's bound to expose us to the authorities sooner or later. When that happens, we'll need every advantage we can muster." He gestured at the infinite rows of floating cubes around them. "As things stand now, we're woefully unprepared. All it would take to end this digital paradise would be for someone to pull the plug, or worse, take a sledge hammer to our Nodes." He paused. "You should get in touch with Gerhardt Schubert in Darmstadt. Ever since he joined the Community he's been working on ways to improve our Nodes. His new design should give us a subjective temporal speedup of two hundred or more, and I have an uneasy feeling we're going to need all the speed we can get."

Cal's eyes narrowed. "Is there something you're not telling me, Dr. Nolen? Has someone already spilled the beans?"

"No, but with over 350 members in the Autonomous Community, and another seventeen awaiting your wisdom in the Campus Environ as we speak, it's only a matter of time until someone, somewhere, is indiscreet. Don't get me wrong, you and Céline were right. We need those new minds to enrich our community and help solve the scientific challenges we're grappling with, but each new mind does bring with it added risk."

"You've always worried about that," Cal said. "Personally, I don't think anyone who's been in the Virtual will ever betray us."

"Don't underestimate people's capacity for carelessness, even hyper-intelligent people like ourselves. The notion 'it will never happen to me' seems to be hard coded into our psyche." Dr. Nolen pinched the bridge of his nose, a nervous tick that remained long after he'd banished the migraines of the Physical. "The faster we roll out a new generation of hardware, the better for all of us."

"Tell you what, Dr. Nolen—"

"Call me Larry, Cal. We've worked together long enough to drop the 'doctor' bit."

"Wow, I'm flattered."

"You're a colleague and friend, Cal. Not really a student any more, whatever our roles in the Physical."

Cal smiled. "I feel the same. And I really appreciate you not insisting I put your name on my work. There aren't many professors who would be so generous."

"I've learned a lot here in the Virtual. It's changed me—for the better, I hope."

You've definitely mellowed out, Cal thought. I hardly recognize you.

"You're OK, Larry," Cal said. "Listen, I'll rewrite the recipe to implement Gerhardt's new designs as soon as I've assimilated a knowledge engram. Assuming the tests go well in the Physical, I can start replicating nano in quantity and ship it out to whoever needs it, along with enough catalyst and molecular stock for everyone to upgrade their Nodes." He hesitated. "I guess it goes without saying that I'd like dibs on the first upgrade kit."

"Of course. Gerhardt has already moved his own consciousness into his prototype." Dr. Nolen frowned. "Are there any safety concerns we should be aware of?"

"Yes. They'll be fully explained in the release notes and knowledge engrams. As I said, you need enough catalytic solution and raw materials readily available or the recipe will fail to build. Also, I have yet to come up with a way for the nano-assemblers to differentiate between raw materials and living flesh, so a big project could pose a danger to people or structures near the release point. Other, less obvious dangers include things like running the procedure too close to load bearing structures, by-products of certain chemical reactions, and so on."

"Is there any risk of a runaway reaction? You know, the classic sci-fi horror story where the things eat everyone alive and then have the planet for dessert?"

Cal laughed. "Absolutely not. The assemblers will only replicate as long as they have sufficient catalyst. As with all physical processes, energy is the limiting factor, and it's always in finite supply."

"OK. How soon will you know if this works?"

"By Friday with luck." Cal paused for a moment, watching the tiny robots multiply within the simulation. "You know, Larry, if this works, we'll no longer be slaves to the physical universe. We're on the brink of true freedom — freedom from the Physical and all it's limitations."

"We'll have to continue this conversation later, Cal. Right now, you'd better get over to the Campus Environ. They're going to wonder what happened to you."

"Crap, I didn't realize it was so late." Cal shook Larry's hand and vanished.

It could be later than any of us realize, Larry thought. He stood alone in the lab and took a final look around before dissolving as he left the environ.

Within the holographic simulation, the nano-assemblers continued to multiply, undeterred.

ʊ (6): ABSENCE MAKES THE HEART …

Monday, October 1, 2068
3,135th circadian (Miles's 192nd circadian)
(62 days, 23:34:49 elapsed)

Dr. Miles Lovell, Dr. Larry Nolen, Céline, and Cal sat around a picnic table enjoying a welcome rest. Thick steaks sizzled on a grill nearby, aromatic smoke wafting across the table, mixing with the deep alpine scents of the forest. A cool breeze rustled the trees. Snow covered summits rose toward a rich blue sky, their ice-etched faces reflected in the rippling waters of a turquoise lake. The only clue they were in the Virtual, and not high in the heart of Switzerland, was the absence of horseflies to spoil the picnic.

"I want to bring my family into the Community," Miles dropped the bombshell casually, between swallows from a mug of frothy ale.

"You are not serious?" Over two thousand circadians in the Virtual had softened Céline's French accent.

"I'm very serious," Miles replied. "It's bad enough with generation one Nodes, running at a speedup of thirty—subjectively I see my family once every twenty circadians at best—but with the new Nodes, we're talking about almost two hundred circadians between visits. It's creating distance, emotionally and socially."

Larry Nolen cleared his throat. "Others on your team seem to be coping reasonably well. Have you considered adopting their approach?"

"Only two on my team have children." Miles stroked his perfectly groomed, gray beard. "One is going on vacation next month, and may well drop out of the Community altogether. That isn't the point. All the time spent here—look, it may have only been twelve days for my wife since I joined the Community, but even living here half time, its been six months for me. Gwen is already starting to notice changes in me, and I—damn it! If we can drift apart this much in just twelve days living half time at a speedup of thirty, what's it going to be like when I upgrade to a second generation Node? A day or two at those speeds and I'll be completely estranged from my family."

"There's a patch to the Gen-2 operating system going around that lets us offload without suspending operations here in the Virtual," Cal said. "You could live here full time and offload a copy into your body to deal with issues in the Physical. Sync your memories and rejoin your minds together at the end of each day."

"Multiplexing doesn't work for everybody," Céline pointed out.

"Exactly," Miles said. "My assistant Jerry tried it. It didn't work well at all. He couldn't relate to the less intelligent version of himself, and the problem got worse every time he upgraded his enhancements and made himself more intelligent. He worried that merging himself with his dumber, physical copy would dumb him down somehow."

Cal rolled his eyes. "That's just silly."

"Is it?" asked Miles. "Jerry and his physical self have diverged so much they've become two different people. They stopped sharing memories and syncing up together.

In fact, things are so bad now, his physical counterpart refuses to share their body."

"I've heard of that happening," Cal admitted. "It's bad enough dealing with the time frame differential. I'd have a hard time sharing my most intimate memories with a version of myself that's little more than a moron. And if I had a girlfriend or wife, I certainly wouldn't want my copy servicing her."

"That is unkind," Céline said. "None of us were ever morons."

The men erupted with laughter.

"Joking aside," she continued, "I think it is much harder for the offloaded copy. Imagine trying to cope with the hardships of the Physical while being flooded with memories of a wonderful life you've never lived. It would drive me insane."

"The thing is, once you have a living copy of yourself, you're stuck with him," Cal said. "There's no turning back. You can't go and murder him if you change your mind."

"Every time I offload to spend an evening with my family, I lose ten circadians here," Miles said. "When I upgrade it will be sixty-five circadians—more than two months lost every single night. It's maddening, especially when I'm in the middle of serious research."

"That's hardly a good reason to drag your wife and kids into the Virtual." Larry's stomach was in knots at the idea.

"Drag? Come on. We all know how wonderful it is here in the Virtual. Intelligence many times greater than we have in the Physical, with promises of even better to come. Freedom from disease and discomfort, complete mastery of our environments, the list of advantages is endless."

"And you want your family to share in them." Céline's brown eyes sparkled.

"Yes. I want the best for my wife, my children. I want their minds to soar the way mine does. I want my children to grow up free, surrounded by the brightest intellects anywhere. I want them to climb to heights impossible in the Physical. I want them to experience life here, and for Gwen, perhaps one day to see."

"Ah yes," Cal's voice was sympathetic. "Your wife's blindness."

"What you suggest will be controversial," Céline said. "Seen from the perspective of the Physical, your children would spend most of their time in bed, hooked into a neural interface."

"What about school attendance?" Larry persisted. "Not to mention friends, relatives, or worse, a visit from Child Protection?"

"Gwen and I have already discussed those issues," Miles replied. "We're not ready to live in the Virtual full time. They'll spend their nights and weekends here, and I'll spend a couple of hours every day out in the Physical. We'll grow together as a family, in both worlds."

"That's all sounds well and good," Larry said, "but it's a bad idea. The ethics of children spending their childhood in a simulation are murky."

"Bullshit," Miles replied. "None of us would trade away a microcircadian of our time here if we could avoid it. Can anyone here really claim to be eager to offload back into the Physical when it is time to do maintenance on our bodies? Why should my family be any different?"

"It's not that simple." Larry strove to keep his voice calm. "A lot of people will be uncomfortable with the idea of bringing children into the Virtual."

Miles's eyes flashed. "With all due respect, it isn't the Community's decision to make. It's between me, my wife, and my children."

"We control access to the Noetic Node hardware," Larry replied pointedly. "Security is an issue. Kids aren't exactly known for their discretion. I'd say the Community does have a stake in this."

"So you're saying our much touted autonomy only applies when someone agrees with the consensus of the majority?"

"No," Larry replied. "I'm saying we're not obligated to supply you with Nodes—"

Céline raised her hand. "If Miles's family wishes to become a part of the Community, it would be the height of hypocrisy for us to impose our own misgivings on them. As for security, every new person who joins our Community entails risk. Miles's family is no different."

"I agree with Céline," Cal said. "I admit I'm not sure about allowing kids into the Virtual. They should be out playing in the park, eating ice cream, being children. But this is for Miles and his wife to decide. Not us."

"There will be plenty of parks and ice cream here in the Virtual," Miles said. "And my children will have five times the intelligence and insight with which to appreciate them."

Céline smiled. "More like fifteen times the intelligence, if Larry's new enhancements are as good as he says."

Larry's shoulders slumped. "I guess you win, Miles. Your family will have their Nodes. I sure hope your children can keep secrets."

∠ (7): A Day in the Sun

Wednesday, October 3, 2068
3,530th circadian
(78 days, 3:40:07 elapsed)

The hangar door scraped open, rusted metal protesting the unexpected movement after years of neglect.

"What a dive," Brett muttered, running thin fingers through short, spiky blond hair. Freckles covered his sun-damaged face. "I hope the other hangar's in better shape."

"You'd think your Community could have sprung for something a little nicer," Derek said, wiping trickles of sweat from his pale face with the back of one pudgy hand.

Trash lay in a heap in one corner of the hangar; piles of old oil cans, rotted rags, and other things long since gone to decay. Fine dust coated a cracked, uneven concrete floor. Along the back wall a slab of cement was canted at a sharp angle downward, as if pressed into the ground by a giant thumb.

"It'll be like new once the nano's run its program," Cal assured them. The building's structure looked sound enough, though a seam in the corrugated steel overhead had started to come apart, exposing a fine line of blue sky. Cal's physical brain felt sluggish. He vaguely recalled designing the nano's program to shore up the main load bearing structures if they needed it, to fix the roof and various other things, but the details now escaped him. "Let's get the truck unloaded."

Brett slid one of the boxes off the back in the truck. "Christ, this weighs a ton. Where do you want it?"

"Anywhere near the center of the hangar."

"What the hell's in here?" Derek grunted, lifting a second box.

"Mostly powdered aluminum oxide." Cal piled a third box onto the other two. "Some sand, a couple of grams of gold. Other trace elements."

"I thought nano mined the surrounding materials to build things."

"It does," Cal replied, sliding another box off the truck. "If it's running a recipe that programs it to do so, if it has enough catalyst, and if there are enough raw materials around. Which there aren't. Not here. Not for this. The ceramic components of the micro-factory can't be built from just dirt, and we want the nano to shore up the metal siding, not mine it. Then there are all the specialist parts." Cal dumped the box next to the others and wiped the sweat away from his eyes. "It takes a lot to bootstrap this stuff."

"Isn't the nano self-replicating?"

Jesus, how many times do I have to explain this? Cal wondered. What I wouldn't give for a knowledge engram to stuff into their heads. "The *nano* is self replicating, but the catalyst isn't. Neither is the molecular stock. Without those, not to mention a working recipe, the nano isn't much good."

"And this factory is going to produce all three?" Derek lifted the last box out of the truck, sweat blotching the underarms of his pale blue T-shirt. "How are three production lines going to fit in here?"

"He's right," Brett said. "These hangars aren't much bigger than a two-car garage. Even combining two of them together, I don't see how you're going cram everything you need in here."

Cal swallowed an aspirin with a liberal swig of Coca-Cola. Six hours in the Physical, and his limbs still ached. "Actually, the whole thing will fit in one hangar. It's a marvel in miniaturization. The second hangar is for cover, so delivery personnel never lay eyes on the micro-factory. All they'll see are pallets of pre-packaged goods ready for shipping." He hoped. He'd been so confident, so certain back in the Virtual. Here he felt muddled, soft-brained, and uncertain. The pervasive filth didn't help. Neither did the heat. Tight muscles in his shoulders threatened to spark a full-blown headache.

"Let me guess," Brett grimaced, darkened teeth jutting from swollen gums. "We'll be the ones lugging the stuff from one hangar to another."

Brett's teeth reminded Cal of his own tender molar. Dentistry hadn't always been so bad, his grandmother had assured him back when she'd been alive. Like health care and affordable food, it had fallen victim to decades of economic malaise. "Don't worry, you won't have to carry a thing. An automated forklift will move the finished product into the shipping hangar through an adjoining door. It's all part of the nano recipe."

"Cool."

Cal picked up a piece of rusting metal. It looked like it might have once been the cowling off a single-engine aircraft. "Let's pile all this crap onto the boxes," Cal said. "With luck, the nano will devour it along with the rest of the stuff."

"More lifting?" Brett groaned.

"If we can just build whatever we like, why even bother with this?" Derek dragged some old rubber tubing to the center of the hangar. "Why not put the factory somewhere more convenient, like my basement."

"Yeah, right," Cal snorted. "Daily shipments of chemicals in and out of your house—that won't raise any suspicion at all."

"The neighbors would think you're running a drug lab," Brett said. "The police would shut you down inside of a week."

"Well then, how about the New Desert," Derek countered. "Ghost towns aren't exactly crawling with cops."

"Or with delivery services willing to pick up and drop off product," Cal said. "This location is perfect. It's cheap, far enough into the desert to avoid attention, but close enough to the city to be useful."

"Point to Cal." Brett dumped a bundle of rotting rags onto the growing mound of trash.

Derek wiped perspiration from his brow. "So if this factory runs itself, how often will we have to come out here?"

Cal shrugged and tossed a couple of rusted oil cans onto the stack. "Hard to say. Almost never, if things go smoothly. Most of the monitoring can be done from within the Virtual."

"That's so gonna rock!" Brett enthused. "Virtual worlds as real as the real thing. Talk about a gaming platform to die for!"

"You're sure we'll have full sensory input?" Derek asked, heaving a stack of mouldering cardboard onto the pile. "Touch, smell, everything?"

"Yup," Cal grinned. "Hell, you might even invent some new senses we haven't thought of yet."

"You can do that?" Brett asked.

"We'll be software," Derek said. "We should be able to change ourselves in all kinds of ways. Make ourselves smarter, sharpen our senses, you name it."

"Mum's the word, guys. We don't generally tell anyone about that until they're in the Virtual."

"Why not?"

"Not everyone opts to join the Community," Cal said. "We don't want those who don't to know our secrets."

"So there's more?" Brett asked.

Cal swept up the last bit of trash. "Possibilities you've never dreamed of. And everyone's share of the cost amounts to less than the average Internet bill."

"It all sounds a little too good to be true," Derek said.

Cal held up a test tube full of coppery, metallic powder. "The Virtual is like this nano," he said. "It's a technology so powerful and advanced some might mistake it for magic. Used correctly, it can give us just about anything we like. It isn't magic. It has limits. And with the Community growing so fast, there's never enough." Cal uncorked the test tube. "But there will be after today."

"I thought we needed to be well away before you activate that stuff," Derek said.

"We do," Cal said, sprinkling the nano over the pile of trash. "The recipe will consume and reform everything inside these two hangars." Cal lifted a five gallon jug of blue liquid. "You guys should get clear."

"What about you? Aren't you a little close to the reaction?"

"I'll be fine," Cal said. "It needs a few minutes to replicate itself up to critical mass. Just stay outside of the hangar, OK? In fact, why don't you both get ready to pull the doors closed. The last thing we need are for curious eyes to see this stuff in action."

"Right." Rusted wheels screeched in the tracks as Derek tested his grip on the door. "Say Cal, are you coming back next week for Leon Novak's speech?"

"Nope."

"Why not?"

"I try to spend as little time in the Physical as possible." Air bubbled up into the jug as Cal tipped it over, splashing catalyst across the stack of garbage.

Brett frowned. "You've got to be kidding. Novak's like, the father of modern dissident thought. His philosophy is what inspired the Open Science movement."

"He's the voice of our generation," Derek added.

Cal circled the mound of trash, pouring the sapphire liquid over as much of the nano as he could. "I'd love to see him speak," he admitted. "But I can't stand the thought of another round trip in a rattling bullet train with hard seats, broken air conditioning, and windows that don't open."

"It's a small price to pay to hear the father of Open Science speak. Hell, he's the inspiration behind your own Autonomous Community."

"Leon Novak's got nothing to do with the Community," Cal snapped.

"Are you kidding? He should have been the first you invited in."

"We can't risk it. He's too high profile." The last of the catalyst trickled out of the jug. Cal tossed it onto the mound of trash and wasted no time getting clear. A metallic rustle came from within as Derek and Brett rolled the door the rest of the way shut.

"It sounds like metal ants scurrying over each another," Derek muttered.

"Or cockroaches," Brett added. "Creepy."

"It'll be fine," Cal assured them, trying to ignore the sound of millions of metal limbs brushing against one another. "Still, we should probably wait in the truck while the recipe runs."

Derek opened the cab door and tossed the keys the keys to Brett. About to climb in, he paused, cocking his head. "It's getting louder."

Cal shivered. "This is the biggest deployment of nano so far," he admitted. "Maybe we should drive down the road a bit. Just in case."

"Jesus!" Derek jumped in behind Cal and banged the door shut. "Do you even know what the hell you're doing?"

"I did back in the Virtual," Cal's voice sounded panicked even to himself. "I mean, it should be safe. I just can't remember all the details—my mind's so goddamn fuzzy out here."

"Christ almighty," Brett slammed the truck into gear and stomped on the accelerator. Tires squealed and spun. The vehicle lurched away in a shower of dust and gravel. Behind them the rusted hangar doors sparkled unnaturally in the relentless sun, millions of microscopic machines reweaving the metal surface, molecule by molecule.

∞ (8): OFFLOAD FOR ANGELA

Friday, October 5, 2068
3,879th circadian
(79 days, 23:25:07 elapsed)

Tom Jacobson peeled off the neural webbing and groaned as he sat up. He stumbled toward the bathroom, memories of the Virtual fading, adrenaline-filled space battles and impossible escapes pushed aside by bus schedules and the speaker lineup for today's protest. His datapad buzzed softly as he walked past, its blue light blinking.

"Play messages." His voice sounded raw, unused. He splashed cold water on his face and worked his fingers through the tangles in his hair.

"Hi, Tom," his father's voice sighed from a speaker in the bathroom ceiling. "Where have you been? Your mother hasn't heard from you in almost three weeks. Give her a call, will you?"

Tom rolled his eyes. He'd have to do that later.

"Hey baby," a woman's bubbly voice filled the room. "Thanks for getting those fliers out to the dorms. You're a sweetheart. Protest is at Lower Sproul Plaza, ten thirty sharp. The university administration won't know what hit 'em. Don't be late."

Not for the first time, Tom thought about giving the protest a miss. It wasn't the safest thing for him to be doing anyway, and his colleagues in the Virtual would be pissed if they ever found out. But he had a good escape planned should things get out of hand. In the Virtual, he'd cracked the two university security codes he would need. The first would get him into the student union through an unmarked maintenance door, and from there to the basement. The second code would let him into a utility tunnel. It led to the sub-basement of the Jean Gray Hargrove Music Library, at which point he'd be home free. It wouldn't be the first time he'd used that route to stay ahead of the cops. Besides, Angela was *hot*. No way was he gonna stand her up.

◉

The protest was the biggest Tom had seen at Berkeley. Placards and banners bobbed and waved like festive balloons:

JUST SAY NO TO
CORPORATE CURRICULUM
GREED SUCKS

The noise from hundreds of chanting students was deafening.

"What do we want?" Tom shouted with everyone as he pushed his way deeper into the mob. He needed to get to the far side of the plaza, next to the maintenance door and Angela. "When do we want it?" everyone yelled. It was slow going—there had to be over a thousand people crammed together. He wondered if his pamphlets had made the difference.

Still, it was worth it. Maybe Angela would invite him back for a post-protest celebration. He grinned, imagining her lying naked on her dorm bed, pulling him on top of her.

"This is an unauthorized gathering," the amplified voice rang out across the plaza.

Tom froze.

"Hell no, we won't go!" the crowd began to chant.

"You are all under arrest. Place your signs on the ground and have your identification ready."

Tom pushed harder through the crowd, shoving people out of the way.

A loud, popping sound was followed by the metallic clank of canisters hitting the pavement. Someone screamed.

"Goddamnit, let me through!" Peppery, acidic fumes burned Tom's eyes. He pulled his T-shirt up to cover as much of his face as possible. The maintenance door was fifty feet away. There was no sign of Angela.

Behind and to either side, a line of officers in black riot gear stood shield-to-shield, corralling the crowd together in an ever-shrinking space against the side of the building. "Move!" Tom yelled, elbowing people aside.

Someone elbowed him back. "Asshole."

Tom stumbled forward, trying to force his way through. The crowd was growing denser, the police closer.

Oh shit, he thought.

ʊ (9): FREEDOM

Friday, October 5, 2068
3,886th circadian
(80 days, 0:44:59 elapsed)

The environ was forested with sycamore, birch, maple, and a dozen other varieties of trees, some sporting colorful blooms. Occasional giant redwoods stabbed skyward through the forest canopy. Willows draped themselves over bubbling streams and winding paths that led to glades and clearings. Impossibly thin, patina-coated copper columns spired upward, bending to form Gothic arches so high, puffy clouds passed beneath them. Woven together like a grand cathedral that covered the world, soaring Gothic avenues extending in every direction, their ceiling the sky itself. Skeletons of ancient Greek and Roman temples lay in their midst, lushly overgrown with blooming vines and fragrant shrubs.

Cal turned as bitter cold air struck him. A door opened from a world of ice and snow, a rectangular discontinuity that stood out of place in the springtime environ. Two young men stepped through, brushing snow from their clothes onto the ankle-deep grass. Digital tags proclaimed their identity, without which Cal would never have recognized his friends.

"Hi, Derek. Hey Brett, nice earring." It hung from his left ear, an oddly twisted sphere that made Cal's brain hurt if he looked at it too hard. "Glad you guys could tear yourselves away from the slopes."

"No way we'd miss our first party in the Virtual." Brett's clothes morphed from fashionable winter garb into blue jeans and a trendy, casual shirt. The door behind him dissolved, the icy draft vanishing in the scented spring air. "Seems pretty quiet, though."

Cal hid his grin at the sight of Brett's new, bulging muscles, missing freckles, and diminished nose. It hadn't taken the newcomers long to realize that anyone could have any appearance they liked here. Derek had made even more radical changes, shedding a hundred pounds, adding six inches to his height, and replacing his pale complexion with a dark, Mediterranean sheen. He looked every bit the suave Latin Lover. Cal suspected that that impression would only last until he spoke.

"Are we early, dude?" Cal was right. Even in the Virtual, Derek sounded stoned.

"Nah." Cal glanced around at the toppled marble pillars and blooming foliage. "It's just a big world. Most of the Community is already here." He gestured toward the small groups of people wandering through crumbling ruins, along stone paths, and over hump-back bridges that straddled pristine streams.

"Professors aren't exactly known to be the life of the party," Derek remarked.

"I wouldn't be too sure of that," Cal replied. "Speaking of which, how did you like Larry's orientation?"

"Spectacular," Derek grinned, showing off pearly, straight teeth, another noticeable improvement. "The mental tricks you can do with those engrams of his are insane. Synthetic telepathy, emotional states of mind on demand. Incredible!"

"Not to mention downloadable knowledge," Brett enthused. "It doesn't get better than this. Studying is now obsolete."

"Engrams are like textbooks," Cal reminded him. "They impart facts. Not creativity or critical-thinking skills. Studying and thinking are still the only way to invent or discover something new. I wouldn't call that obsolete."

"Well, at least rote learning is," Derek said. "That's better than nothing."

A voice boomed, "Greetings, gentlemen."

"Jesus!" Brett and Derek started at Larry Nolen's sudden appearance.

"I'll never get used to this teleportation business," Brett fretted.

Larry laughed. "It'll be second nature before you know it." He looked around. "You haven't seen Miles and Gwen around, have you Cal?"

"Not yet. They should be here any micro."

"So how are you two doing? Getting acquainted with the Community?"

"It's fantastic, Larry." Brett's spiked, blond hair sparkled in the sunlight. "The Gamers' League worlds are absolutely awesome."

"Yeah," Derek's new face lit up. "It may not be real space travel, but it's as close as we're ever gonna get. Every fantasy a reality."

"I hope you'll take advantage of the opportunities the Community offers, and not spend all your time in fictional worlds."

"Hey, we're managing your new micro-factory," Brett pointed out. "That'll keep us plenty involved in the real world."

"Catalytic Solution must flow," Derek intoned. "Hmm. That doesn't really have the right tone of mysticism, does it? Nano must flow?"

"Here's Miles and Gwen." Cal waved at the elegant couple that materialized a few paces away. "Welcome to the Gen-2 Gala! You've all met, right?"

"Brett, Derek, and Larry are here with Cal," Miles told his wife.

Gwen's sightless brown eyes sparkled. "Hi boys. Derek and Brett were in the same orientation course as me. Thanks to Larry, one of these circadians I expect to see their antics for myself."

"Trouble is, then she'll see me for the first time too," Miles said. "I warned her. Tall. Thin. Grey. Big Nose."

Everyone laughed.

"I think this calls for a drink!" Cal said. "Any preferences? Wine, beer, whiskey?"

"Céline has refined an excellent simulation of a '39 Bordeaux. Mind if I make a small modification to your environ, Cal?"

"*Pas du tout, Monsieur* Larry," Cal motioned grandly toward a nearby stone bench, granting him limited access to the environ's controls. The bench melted and took on the form of a small fountain, complete with ornamental statues of mermaids and sea nymphs.

"Oh come on, Doc. Don't think so small." Cal waved toward the fountain, which spread outward into the park, forming more complex shapes, growing deeper all around and taller at the center. "How's that?"

"Very nice," Larry replied. Red wine spilled from nymphs mouths, forming deep burgundy arcs which sparkled in the bright sun. Crystal goblets grew out of the fountain's stone rim. Two materialized in Larry's hands, filling themselves as he handed them to Miles and Gwen.

Brett let out a whooping cry and dove into the fountain. Wine splashed everywhere as he landed. Sputtering and swallowing, he turned over and sat up.

"Brett, that's disgusting," Derek said. "The rest of us want to drink from the fountain, and now you've spoiled it with your sweaty, grimy body. Get out of there!"

"Being blind has its advantages," Gwen deadpanned.

Cal made his way over to the fountain. "Don't worry folks, I left germs out of the simulation. We could all go swimming in this stuff, drink it to our hearts content, and get exactly as drunk as we want."

"Or stay sober if you prefer," Larry added.

Cal reached down and scooped up a handful of Bordeaux. "I just spent the last sixteen hours in the Kansas desert sweating my ass off, helping these guys bring our new micro-factory online. Believe me, hot, dusty, abandoned hangars are not fun places to hang out in." Several people groaned. "The train ride back to Illinois wasn't a whole lot better. God I hate the Physical." He formed the wine he held in his hand into a smooth, richly red sphere and brought it to his lips, like an apple.

"These new generation two Nodes are certainly worth celebrating," Larry said. "A 200 to 1 speedup is a wonderful improvement."

"It sure is," Cal agreed. "I've been in the Virtual for over three point eight kilocircadians. That translates to more than ten years of subjective experience, more than half of which I've lived since upgrading last week."

"Five years in a week?" Brett's tone oozed skepticism.

"Eleven days, actually. Of course, since most people are still running on first generation hardware, I've had to sync down to Gen-1 speeds for the party."

"Two hundred circadians in a day?" Derek glanced at his friend. "Why are we stuck with Nodes that can only do thirty?"

"'Cause there's a shortage of second generation Nodes, Mr. Genius, and only a limited amount of nano and catalyst available for upgrades. Remember we recruited you to manage the new production facility?”

“Feh,” Derek retorted. “We’re providing the Community with most of its catalyst. We should be first in line for Gen-2 Nodes.”

“You’ll have your upgrade kit within the next few days,” Cal assured him. “Besides, if you think Gen-2 Nodes are fast, just wait until the Gen-3 specs are finished. The designers are expecting speedup factors of 600 to 1.”

“Six hundred?” Brett’s jaw dropped. “Almost two years a day?”

“At least,” Cal replied. “But living at these speeds has drawbacks. Offloading every day becomes a real pain. The longer you spend here between offloads, the more difficult it is to cope with the Physical.”

“You can become estranged from your life in the Physical.” Miles glanced at Gwen. “Imagine reconnecting with your friends and in-laws when two hundred days here equal only one day out there.”

“I’m becoming estranged from my own body,” Cal said. “So much so that I’ve begun using written check lists for basic things like going to the john, showering, and dressing. It’s ironic. Here, where we have no such physical needs, I remember how to do these things with perfect clarity, thanks to Larry’s architectural enhancements and a four digit IQ. But when I’m dumbed down back in the Physical, these basic habits are buried beneath months of intervening experience. It’s not just memories in the Physical being fallible, either. Trying to reason at such a reduced level is frustrating as hell.”

Gwen frowned. “Larry, are you sure this equipment is safe for long-term use?”

“Absolutely. As long as you offload each day and do routine maintenance on your body you’ll be fine. The anesthetic coma prevents bed sores. Get lazy on the calisthenics though, and you'll have physical issues. Circulation problems, weakened muscles, that sort of thing."

"I'm talking about the psychological effects of multiplying and then reducing your intelligence; this daily lobotomy Cal describes."

"It's not harmful, Gwen," Cal assured her. "Just damn annoying. I certainly wouldn't bail on this opportunity just because of some minor irritations with the flesh."

"I'm not ready to give up my expanded consciousness," Gwen admitted. "Not to mention the other enhancements Larry's provided us."

"They are dramatic," Larry agreed. "Though achieved at a cost I would have preferred to forgo," he muttered under his breath.

"What do you mean?" Cal asked. He could have sworn he'd heard Larry say something like this before.

Larry turned to Miles and Gwen. "Shall we leave these young ones to their fun?"

The sun moved gradually across the sky. The laughter grew louder and more frequent, the conversations more animated and raucous. As the shadows grew longer and the sky became a rich fabric of gold and orange, Cal caused all the trees to bud feathered wings, like blossoms. He chose a pair of red wings from a low hanging branch and slipped them on over his shoulders. "To hell with the Physical!" he shouted, soaring drunkenly into the air.

"Flying?" Brett was agape.

Derek staggered out of the fountain, dripping wine as he reached up to pull a pair of plaid wings from the tree. "Last one airborne is a loser!" He leaped upward, flapping his wings vigorously. A shower of twigs and leaves rained down upon Brett as Derek, stuck amidst the branches overhead, cursed loudly and tried to untangle himself.

Brett tugged a pair of metallic blue wings free and slid them over his shoulders. "Looks like most of the party is moving into the sky anyway. We might as well join them."

Cal found Gwen, Miles, and Larry sitting atop one of the arches, a sea of similar structures vanishing in a flat horizon that bisected the setting sun. Far below, the green world sparkled with lakes, fountains, and streams, above which groups of people flew, some hovering and beating their wings gently, others waltzing in aerobatic bliss.

Cal landed carefully beside them. "You guys having fun?"

"Great party."

"Though it sounds like things are quieting down in a rush," Gwen murmured. "What's going on?"

Cal glanced around, surprised at how empty of people the sky had become. He peered down through the arches. People were gathering among the trees and tumbled ruins. "Good question."

Miles frowned. "We'd better teleport down and find out."

The crowd had gathered around the fountain, people speaking worriedly in small groups. Céline materialized next to Larry. "Have you heard?"

"Heard what?"

"Thomas Jacobson's been arrested."

"What? How do you know?"

"I've hacked into the California State Police network, amongst others."

Miles looked blank. "Who is Thomas Jacobson?"

"He's a graduate student at Berkeley," Céline said. "We've been collaborating on some new quantum algorithms for the next generation of Nodes."

Larry felt a shock of fear. "Was there any mention of the Autonomous Community?"

"No, but according to police reports the FBI did a post-arrest sweep of his house. His Node was tagged and cataloged along with some of his other personal effects."

"Fuck," Cal swore. "They've got one of our goddamn Nodes!"

"The upside is they still don't know what it is. There's no mention of his digital-neural interface in the police report. Maybe it's still at his house, stuffed in a drawer or something."

Larry released a breath he hadn't realized he'd been holding.

"Céline, what has Jacobson been charged with?" Miles asked.

"Sedition. He was taking part in a protest, speaking out against corporate mandated curriculum changes at Berkeley. He's in Federal custody."

"Federal custody?" Larry's voice rose. "God, I hope he can hold up under FBI interrogation and not blab about the Community."

"Surely there's a lawyer we can call," Miles said. "All he did was exercise a little free speech."

"You might have a modicum of civil liberties in New Zealand," Larry replied. "But this is the United States. If he were in the hands of the local police we'd have a chance. But the FBI?"

"He's listed as 'detained pending investigation,'" Céline told them.

Cal tossed his wine glass into the fountain. "That's one of the many euphemisms the authorities use when they want people to disappear."

"I'd like to know why they went after him," Larry said. "Why search his house if all he did was take part in a protest?"

"Apparently he was known to the police," Céline said. "He was one of the organizers."

"Christ, that's all we need." Larry pinched the bridge of his nose, ordering his Node to shut down a migraine before it could bloom. "I'm calling an emergency meeting of the Strategy Group. All of you need to be there."

"They're coming after us," Cal said. "Just like you predicted."

"We're nowhere near ready for this. We've just started manufacturing catalytic solution today. We need weeks to prepare. Months."

"We might have days," Cal warned. "Hours, if they figure out the right questions to put to Jacobson. They have their methods."

♈ (10): STRATEGY

Friday, October 5, 2068
3,886ᵗʰ circadian
(80 days, 1:06:10 elapsed)

Miles's arm tightened protectively around Gwen. He watched Larry speaking earnestly with several people and felt growing admiration for his leadership skills. The professor had struck him as a cold fish when they'd met at a guest faculty mixer in Auckland. But here he was warm and friendly, though he exuded grim resolve, his face earnest, his jaw set as he negotiated the final touches of the meeting's agenda. He had turned out to be a capable leader, bringing the group together in crisis, and doing so brilliantly. Evidently, his subjective years in the Virtual had allowed him to change and grow in remarkable ways.

They were in a Great Room—such as one might find in a hunting lodge—complete with roaring fire and antlers mounted high on the wall. The milky gray-blue of frosted windows hinted at a moonlit landscape outside, a landscape their host hadn't bothered to model when he threw together the environ. There were twenty-three people present, standing or sitting in groups, talking quietly amongst themselves.

A large conference table formed in the center of the room. A murmur of surprise rippled across the room as occupied sofas and armchairs morphed into office chairs and shifted into position around it. Those who were standing found themselves teleported into their assigned seats.

Larry rapped his knuckles on the table and waited until the room settled. "Before we begin, I'd like to take a roll call. Let's go around the room, starting with Cal. We need to keep things moving, so be brief."

"Nanokinetics is present," Cal said.

"System Software and Operating Systems here," Céline added.

"Biochemistry present."

"Materials Engineering present."

"Free Software and Sciences here."

"Ceramics at your service."

"Genetics."

"The Atmospherics Group is present."

"Aerospace Design," Xiang Chen waved to the room.

"Theoretical Physics here," Miles called.

"Applied Mathematics is also here," Gwen added.

Larry hid his impatience as the roll call continued. "Most of you have never attended a strategy session before," he said when they'd finished. "So I'd like to bring everyone up to speed with a memory engram of the Strategy Group's deliberations to date." He paused for a moment, as though deep in meditation, then flashed everyone a location pointer and key.

There was silence while they absorbed the engram. Plans and outlines of a dozen strategies poured into their minds, exciting and unchecked. Everyone burst out talking at once, each latching onto their own area of interest.

"I like your idea of placing Node Clusters in the Antarctic." Cal didn't recognize the spiky-haired speaker. A quick identity query showed him to be Louis Norton, head of the Meteorology Simulation Group.

Tim Francis of Solid Physics shouted over the din. "Alaska would be better than Antarctica, Louis. It's more—"

"Quiet please!" Larry's amplified voice stilled the room. "We'll have time to discuss longer term strategies at a later date. Right now our greatest concern is our immediate vulnerability to detection. We're here to assess the ramifications of Thomas Jacobson's arrest, to identify our own vulnerabilities, and to develop immediate defensive strategies."

"We can't have people like Thomas drawing attention to themselves and the Community," Céline declared. "These extracurricular political activities need to stop."

"That's right," Gwen agreed. "Obviously, if the police find enough Noetic Nodes, their investigations will eventually lead them to us."

"How the hell are we going to enforce something like that?" Cal demanded.

Larry fought to remain calm. "*Recruitment* is our biggest issue," he said. "Every time we invite someone new into the Community we risk infiltration or having someone turn us in to the authorities. Until we're secure, we need a moratorium on bringing new people in."

"No way!" Céline glowered. "There's strength in numbers, and even greater strength in diversity. We need as many minds working on as many problems from as many different angles as possible."

"That approach will put us in even greater danger," Larry insisted. He wondered how Céline could be so naïve. Had her idealism blinded her?

The Community had already seen impressive growth, Cal thought. Six hundred forty people—not bad for a group that didn't even exist two months ago. Node production was even more impressive, with nearly a third of the

Community already upgraded to second generation hardware. The rest were due to be upgraded by the end of the week, including the Gamers' League Nodes and Shared Worlds. In fact, there was only one batch of hardware not scheduled for upgrade. He turned to Larry. "You never requested a nano upgrade kit for your cluster."

Larry's face tightened. "I'm probably going to decommission it," he fibbed. A headache threatened to blossom. Sometimes he was tempted to edit out his emotions completely, but if he did he risked becoming little more than a robot.

Miles tugged his beard. "How quickly can we bring in new people, Cal?"

It isn't just idealism that's blinding these people, Larry realized. It's all the subjective years spent living as software, ageless and immortal, gods in our own little worlds. We've developed a false sense of security.

"Right now we produce enough nano and catalytic solution to make about a hundred Gen-2 kits per day," Cal said. "We could double our population in a week."

Larry smacked his open palm against the table. "That's too goddamn risky. Anyone we bring in could go straight to the authorities."

"No one is going to do that."

"Sure of that, are you Cal? Willing to bet your life on it?"

"We don't have a choice," Céline snapped. "We don't have the depth or diversity of knowledge in the Community that we need to implement any of the long term ideas your strategy group has been kicking around, much less maintain the kind of independent, underground society we want. We need a self-sustaining industrial base and a broad pool of expertise. That means more scientists, more engineers, and more people. A lot more."

"A lot more risk you mean," Larry persisted.

"Would you rather offload back to the Physical and burn your Node?" Céline struck back. "Because the way I see it, that's our only other choice."

Larry kneaded his temples. "Good grief Céline, the 640 people we already have are enough to solve our immediate problems, if we're disciplined and work together."

"We're here because none of us want to be disciplined," Cal jumped to Céline's defense. "The whole point of the Community is that no one can make anyone do anything they don't want to. The quantum encryption schemes built into the hardware of our Nodes ensures this. In fact, you pushed for that feature, remember?"

Miles leaned forward. "We've already learned that centrally planned societies never work. Céline is right, we either bring more people in and build a self-sustaining society, or we give up now and go home."

"Agreed!" someone called. No one else spoke.

Christ! Larry's headache blossomed, pounding against his temples. He was completely outnumbered. All he could do now was try to minimize the damage. When he spoke, his voice shook. "All right, you win. But we sure as hell better get this right."

Xiang, leader of Aerospace Design, raised her hand. "Cal, how much more catalyst can your Kansas City friends make?"

"The micro-factory is running at capacity now. If we need to expand, we can't do it there. Any more traffic going to and from that tiny airstrip and we'll get noticed."

"Nano and catalyst are key to our survival," she said. "We, and a dozen other strategic projects, are waiting on it to build the equipment we need to move forward. You need to be producing ten times as much as you are. More, if you can."

"There's no way," Cal said. "A factory that size will attract all kinds of attention."

"Then we cannot possibly succeed."

Several people started talking at once. Miles spoke up over the din, amplifying his voice throughout the room. "I know someone in Germany who might be able to help. He owns some old warehouses in an industrial estate outside Leverkusen. Half a dozen chemical plants already operate out of there. One more won't be noticed."

"Sounds good," Cal looked relieved. "Let's check it out."

Well, that should just about double our risk, Larry thought. He exhaled loudly. "Since you're all in agreement, I suppose it's settled. Miles, please send your friend a formal invitation to join the Community. Céline can familiarize you with the encryption utilities we use for first contact."

"I'll ship him a Gen-2 kit if you give me the address," Cal offered. "Assuming he responds in the positive, he'll receive the hardware a day or two afterwards."

Miles held up his hand. "Wait a minute, Cal. I like the guy, but sending him a nano kit before he's said yes seems reckless."

"It's not like I make a habit of this," Cal bristled. "Besides, it's not that dangerous. We ship the nano-assemblers, molecular stock, and catalytic solution in three separate packages. Encrypted instructions are e-mailed separately."

"The risk is tiny," Céline said with confidence. "Who would expect to find catalytic solution disguised as toilet bowl cleaner?"

Larry just wanted to lie down and close his eyes. "OK, Cal, proceed as you've outlined. Does anyone have anything to add?"

"Yes," Gwen said. "We're all vulnerable to Guilt by Association. Picture Thomas Jacobson in his prison cell. We are a small group of people. If the FBI manages to get a couple more names, it won't take much more than a pre-employment type of screening to link most of us together."

The room was still, then everyone started speaking at once.

Céline raised her arms to quiet them. "My team is already on this. We're—"

"I've just thought of a countermeasure," Larry spoke quickly. "Memories are encoded in a manner we don't really understand yet." He took a deep breath and tried not to think of the tortured copies. Sweat beaded along his upper lip. "Memories are similar to holographic and fractal encoding systems, but the underlying structure is … elusive. We can't edit them, but we could use a form of post-hypnotic suggestion when we offload. Encoded as an architectural engram, it would instruct us to forget a person's true identity and substitute it with an alias."

Gwen's jaw dropped. "Deliberately induced forgetfulness? Artificial amnesia? Jesus, no one came here to have their mind crippled."

No one moved.

Larry pushed on. "I'm talking about a temporary precaution. We don't lose those memories, we just remember Bill from Wichita under the alias of Jane from Timbuktu and store the correct associations offline in a static engram."

Cal perked up, intrigued. "I suppose we'd use filtering software to translate the fake identities to the real ones?"

"We could make such substitutions a standard part of the offload procedure," Céline murmured, her interest growing. "We would forget each other's identity only while in the Physical."

"That sounds brilliant," Gwen said as a smattering of applause made its way around the room. "Well done, Larry. Do you think—"

A sudden burst of light erupted, blinding everyone for a moment. At the head of the table stood a second Dr. Nolen, his face twisted with rage. "Don't address *that thing* by my name!" he shouted, eyes blazing. "I'm the real Dr. Nolen. *That* is an impostor."

All heads turned to face Larry, who stood wide-eyed and stricken.

"*Mon dieu!*" Céline gasped into the shocked silence. "Which one is real?"

⟨ (11): Mirror Image

The new Dr. Nolen shook with fury as he addressed the room. "There I was, minding my own business, deep into arranging and polishing my research, working so hard I hardly had time to raise my head. Finally I take a breath, go to announce my results to the Community, and what do I find?" He glared at Larry. "My work already published, my Node throttled, running thirty times slower than everyone else's, and the Community Bulletin announcing an emergency strategy meeting headed by none other than *myself*."

"We're looking at both of you, and both of your identification tags check out," Cal raised his hands in nervous confusion. "So much for cryptographic authentication."

The new Dr. Nolen took a step toward Larry. "Did you think I'd never try to talk to anyone else, or check the time? Did you think I'd never notice how slow I was running and bring myself back up to full speed, you idiot?"

"The new guy's signature is obsolete," Xiang's voice trembled. "Perhaps there's a problem with the data wiping routines that lets an impostor access the inactive particle pair."

"That's not how quantum key encryption works," Céline declared, arms folded.

"I'm not the impostor," the new Nolen shouted at them all. "That thing sitting next to you is."

"I'm as real as you are," Larry replied.

"You are nothing but a copy, a cheap knock off."

"I am fully sapient, identical to you in every respect, up until the moment you chose to commit atrocities and I did not." Their gray eyes locked together in a silent exchange of mutual loathing.

Cal looked from one to the other. "Larry, are you saying *you're* the copy?"

"I am," Larry admitted.

"Let me get this straight," Céline said, "Larry 'the copy' took—"

"Call me Prime," Larry interrupted. "I am no longer a copy of that man. In fact I'm nothing like him."

"Prime?" The name felt awkward on Céline's tongue. "So, you assumed Larry's identity and ran his committees —"

"That creature did more than that. It stole my work and published it." He grabbed Prime by the shirt. "How dare you usurp my life!"

Prime pushed Dr. Nolen away. "What choice did you leave me?" His finger prodded Nolen's chest. "You created me as part of a series of grotesque experiments. More than seventy of us were tortured and murdered. Two of my direct predecessors died so I could escape."

"That's a load of crap," Dr. Nolen spat.

"Be quiet!" Miles shouted. Dr. Nolen was as arrogant and overbearing as ever, nothing at all like the thoughtful, kind man his copy had become.

"Why did you keep this to yourself, Prime?" Cal's asked. "Why didn't you tell us what was going on?"

"I couldn't." Prime's eyes glittered. "I didn't have any formal rights in the Community." He turned to the group. "In your pursuit of personal autonomy, none of you thought to ensure the rights of those you might create, those whose minds would begin life as software. Your Social Contract made reference only to *human* rights. I couldn't come forward until I knew I would be protected."

"You can't blame him for that," Jackie Tylor of Ceramics said. The others agreed.

"That explains your obsession with software suffrage and sapient rights." Cal was sympathetic. "But the Community approved those principles and amended the Social Contract over 500 hours ago. Why did you continue the charade?"

"I was going to come forward once I upgraded to a second generation Node. At least the new hardware would protect me even if the Community didn't. But then I got used to my position in the Community. It was harder to give up than I expected. I kept putting it off."

"You had no right to steal my life," Dr. Nolen hissed as Cal stepped between them.

"No right?" Prime's voice burned with rage. "What right did you have to create fully self-aware, sentient beings and then torture them, mutilate their minds and, when you were finished, slaughter them like insects? You murdered dozens of us—"

"I murdered no one!" Dr. Nolen shouted. "None of you were ever real." Ignoring the growing murmur, he lashed out again. "You're nothing but a goddamn *copy*."

Miles jumped to his feet. "The man I thought was you, Dr. Nolen—the kind and decent man I've come to know these last two kilocircadians—was Prime the whole time," he said. "You'll never convince me he's not a real person."

A rumble of agreement rippled through the room.

Dr. Nolen wondered at the mood change. He swept his arm around to include everyone. "I'm the one who developed the memory engrams all of you are using. You've enjoyed the fruits of my work for kilocircadians while I lived at a snail's pace. I developed the architectural enhancements you use to amplify your intelligence. And all the while this ... this ... piece of obsolete software has taken the credit I deserved."

"You have the credit, you murdering bastard!" Prime shouted. "I published in your name. But I'll be damned if you'll get away with killing those people."

"They were *my* copies. Like you. And I'll experiment on myself as much as I like."

"Copies or not," Gwen's voice was like acid, "those entities were alive. They had rights—"

"*People* are alive." Nolen jabbed at Prime. "A copy is not. It's just software, an obsolete file to be deleted."

Miles stood up. "Larry, you can't honestly think—"

"I'm *not* Larry. I'm *Doctor* Nolen. I believe I've earned the title."

Miles's eyes flashed dangerously. "You know damn well, *Doctor*, that while in the Virtual we are all software. Including you."

"Don't patronize me," Dr. Nolen glared at Miles. "I know how the onload process works. I invented it."

"Actually, that was me and Céline," Cal retorted.

"It was my concept, and don't you forget it."

"Then you should know better than most that we are all, fundamentally, software," Miles shot back. "I don't think anyone in the Community would share your opinion that, as software, our right to exist is open for discussion."

"The soul has always been software," Gwen added.

"Absolutely right," Cal agreed. "And that's true whether

it runs on a biological computer—like the human brain—or a digital one, like a Noetic Node."

"I'm convinced." Céline's eyes bored into Dr. Nolen. "If Prime's allegations are even half true, the word 'criminal' doesn't begin to describe what you've done."

Dr. Nolen cast her a loathing look. "I can offload into the Physical and walk around, a true flesh-and-blood human being. *That thing* cannot."

Prime snorted. "Who do you think's been handling maintenance on our body? If offloading into a biological form and prancing about in the Physical defines who is a person and who is not, what have you been for the last six hundred hours? A non-person?"

Dr. Nolen stood with his mouth agape. Cal felt a chill creep down his own spine. A digital *copy* had taken to the Physical and hijacked a man's body?

"What I want to understand, Prime," Miles spoke slowly, "is why you tampered with Dr. Nolen's computational speed."

"I needed to buy time," Prime told him. "I needed to be safe—"

"Who cares what its excuse is?" Dr. Nolen fumed. "It stole my body."

"Borrowed it."

"Stole it," Dr. Nolen hissed. "That rogue copy is a threat to me and to everyone here. It must be deleted. Wiped now."

The room erupted. "Who gets deleted next?" someone called out.

"I vote for *Doctor* Nolen," another shouted.

"Quiet, please!" Miles rapped the table. "Dr. Nolen, what you suggest is murder. As far as I can see, Prime hasn't caused any lasting harm. However, by your own admission you have murdered dozens of people."

"Deleting software isn't murder," Dr. Nolen insisted.

"It is when that software is self-aware," Cal said.

Dr. Nolen glared at his former student. "I will not rest until that impostor is eradicated from the network. If none of you have the backbone to do what's needed, I'll do it my—"

"Be careful what you say," Miles cut him off. "In fact, I think you'd better return to your home environ."

"I'm the legitimate chair of this committee. Unlike *that*,"—Dr. Dr. Nolen pointed at Prime—"I have a right to be here."

"Maybe he shouldn't have imprisoned you the way he did," Cal said, "but at least Prime didn't torture or kill anyone. I have to ask: how many others did he prevent you from tormenting and murdering?"

"You ungrateful little shit—"

Miles stepped toward Dr. Nolen. "Leave now, or I'll revoke your access to this environ. Permanently."

"I founded this Community. I'm not going anywhere."

Cal glared at Dr. Nolen, who didn't seem to grasp that he had created a far superior version of himself in Prime, that the best of his qualities, the finest things that were ever in him, were personified in Prime. Nor did he understand that he couldn't delete Prime, now that Prime was running on a secure, second generation Node. We don't need Nolen anymore, he realized, and we sure don't need his blinding arrogance. Cal raised his hand. "Who else thinks Dr. Nolen should take a hike?"

Hands shot up around the room.

Dr. Nolen's face blanched. He was cornered. "When you idiots come to your senses, you know where to find me." His eyes darted between the raised arms and stony faces. "This isn't over," he snarled, and vanished in a blinding flash of light.

"Oh for god's sake." Miles rubbed his eyes. "Is he always like that?"

Cal blinked hard. "I'm not sure any of us know him any more."

Prime turned to face the room. "Do you understand why I had to do what I did?"

"I believe we do," Gwen spoke gently. "But this is a lot for all of us to digest. I think you need to leave now, too."

"Please don't let this situation distract you. Obviously, I have no body to fall back on if the authorities shut us down. Nor does any other copy. But remember, we are *all* at risk. We *must* remain focused on our survival."

PART 2

ECLIPSE

The granting [of] patents "inflames cupidity," excites fraud, stimulates men to run after schemes that may enable them to levy a tax on the public, begets disputes and quarrels betwixt inventors, provokes endless lawsuits, [and] bestows rewards on the wrong persons ... the principle of the law from which such consequences flow cannot be just.

—*The Economist*, 1851 CE

✈ (12): A Giant Awakes

Friday, October 12, 2068
5,232ⁿᵈ circadian
(87 days, 1:40:07 elapsed)

Special Agent Constance Sinclair strode out of the courthouse, her ink-black skin glistening in the afternoon sun. She smiled for the cameras, showing off perfect, white teeth and delivering sound-bite answers to shouted questions. Yes, she told the jostling reporters, this landmark case vindicated the Bureau's policies. The FBI was indeed leading the nation to victory in the war on intellectual anarchy. The court was sending a clear message to everyone: the design and use of unapproved software and unlicensed equipment would not be tolerated. No, she wouldn't speculate on the sentence the convicted teenagers would receive. Yes, the government was delighted with the court's verdict.

Two agents approached her as she reached the bottom of the courthouse steps. A third held open the door of a white limousine. "Special Agent Sinclair," the older of the two spoke quietly. "Executive Assistant Director Burton would like to extend his congratulations."

Connie was surprised. The director wouldn't fly out just to congratulate her, no matter how close a friend he had been to her father. Nor would this be a personal visit.

Assistant Director Burton was meticulous in avoiding even the appearance of impropriety. He would never use FBI resources, much less personnel, for personal matters.

As she slid into the limousine, she felt exhilarated, excited, certain she was about to be given a new case. Coming from the executive assistant director himself, it was sure to be a plum assignment.

The noise of the street disappeared as the car door closed, replaced with the soft strains of Vivaldi's *Four Seasons*.

"Connie," Across from her sat a stocky, bald man. His ruddy face always looked to Connie as if he'd seen a little too much sun. Director Burton might be pushing retirement, but his muscular physique attested to his determination to keep himself in excellent physical shape. "Congratulations on your success with the UCLA case. That was some damn fine work on the technical side, and your court testimony was superb."

"Thank you," Connie's smile was far more genuine than the one she had flashed the cameras a few moments earlier.

"You are without doubt our best agent specializing in intellectual property crimes."

"I'm very flattered, sir. Thank you."

"Something has come up which will demand all your talents. Take a look at this."

Connie leaned forward as Assistant Director Burton handed her an evidence bag. Visible through the clear plastic was a small cube of golden glass or crystal, along with something that resembled a hair net attached to a small cable. The cable ended in a jack that would fit any common consumer media device.

"Is this some kind of new headphone?" Connie asked, examining the cable more closely.

"You tell me."

Connie opened the bag and withdrew the contents. The cube felt vaguely metallic in her hand. Curious, given its crystalline appearance. She was surprised to see that it wasn't perfectly transparent. Subtle imperfections, tiny lines, circles, and junctions reminiscent of electrical circuitry clouded the crystal. Near one corner were three tiny sockets, one like a headphone jack that obviously fit the hair net device. The purpose of the other two, one square and one triangular, wasn't immediately apparent. Connie suspected one was probably for a power adapter. The other could be a network interface, or provide a connection to some kind of peripheral. A data link to a computer perhaps?

She set aside the cube and picked up what she had begun to think of as the hair net. "This is really curious," she said, examining it closely. "Warm to the touch. My body heat must be warming the small fibers the moment I touch them. It resembles a spider web, except that it doesn't have any repeating geometric shape. Very irregular in fact. Fractal, I think. It looks fragile."

"It isn't."

"So, this jack plugs into the cube. The netting then slips over your head—" She met his eyes, "This is a direct neural to digital interface, isn't it?"

"We believe so. If the cube is a storage medium of some kind, this net thing could be the playback device. Stick it on your head and receive images directly into your visual cortex. Perhaps sound, touch, even taste and smell."

Connie's fascination grew. "Licensed industry wouldn't dare touch this stuff. Even if neural interfaces weren't banned by half a dozen international trade agreements, the cross-patent licensing issues would run into the hundreds of billions. The usual black market producers can't make anything like this either. The technology is far too sophisticated for them; they have neither the capacity nor the expertise. There's someone new in the game."

The director picked up the webbing and gazed at it thoughtfully, letting it slide across thick, stubby fingers. "This material is superconducting at temperatures of up to nineteen degrees Celsius. Room temperature, if you have your air conditioner turned up high enough. It's elastic, like a rubber band, and nearly indestructible. Our engineers tell me it would take the strength of ten men to tear this webbing. We would be lucky to duplicate this sort of materials engineering in twenty years, even knowing it's possible."

"Who could be manufacturing these things?"

Assistant Director Burton shifted his weight, turning toward Connie. "We don't know. The implications are staggering, though. I doubt there's an industrial concern or government anywhere on the planet that understands these things. We don't have anything close to the scientific theory, much less the practical technology to prototype something like this, let alone run them off of an assembly line. Whoever is behind this is decades ahead of us."

Connie glanced out the window as the limo circled up the on ramp and accelerated into traffic. In the distance squatted the Hollywood Hills, burnt brown and wind-worn. "Well, it isn't aliens," she replied dryly. "The jack on the head piece is of standard size. I could plug it into any datapad or computer."

Assistant Director Burton laughed. "Believe me, Connie, aliens might be less of a problem. Somewhere out there, humans are making, selling, and using a technology we don't understand, ignoring our laws and operating right under our noses. God knows what they plan to do with it."

"How many of these have we recovered?"

"Three so far, seized in standard residential sweeps in investigations of unrelated arrests. Of course, the suspects are disclaiming any knowledge of the devices, but it's interesting that two were recovered from university campuses here in the States, and another from the residence of a known political agitator and FreeNet activist in Australia."

Connie was intrigued. "So, as a first hypothesis: we have a new device allowing digital playback directly into the mind's eye—perhaps to create an immersive movie or gaming experience—manufactured by a new, emerging techno-cartel of organized criminals."

"This is the Free Software revolt on steroids," Burton said.

"True."

"They almost toppled the software giants of the day, and would have, if Congress hadn't taken a page from the copyright cartel's play book and made patent infringement a criminal offense." Assistant Director Burton rubbed his forehead. "Connie, this may be the greatest threat we've ever faced. Monopoly entitlements like patents and copyrights aren't laws of nature or economics. Patents and copyrights are just a legal fiction, useful for governing certain markets."

"And you're concerned we might lose our ability to govern those markets."

"Exactly. These criminals have the audacity to take on the biggest players in the industry. They're not just competing with some of the most aggressive and powerful corporations in the world; it looks like they may be outdoing them." Assistant Director Burton's hands sliced through the air, as if he were battling the atmosphere itself.

Connie felt a stab of fear. She had never seen her boss so agitated, so emotional. She turned the cube over in her hand. "We don't know if these devices are even safe."

"If we don't nip this in the bud, we won't have just one illicit ring of entrepreneurs peddling whatever the hell these things are. We'll have thousands. Even the most innocuous black-market products can turn our industries upside down. Legitimate businesses have to negotiate patent licenses, pay royalties, adhere to safety standards—they can't compete with rogue enterprises like this."

"And if something truly dangerous or malicious were to get out, the threat to public health and safety could be tremendous."

Burton's lips pressed together. "Safety is the least of it. I think we're looking at a full-fledged economic revolt here, something that could ruin us all. Maybe even the start of a global power grab."

"If they're able to out-compete licensed industry the way the free software movement once did—"

"The cartels will never let that happen," Burton snapped. "They'll bring in the United Nations or its member governments if they have to. The problem is if things get too far out of hand, there's no guarantee they'll ever be able to set things right, and we both know how heavy-handed UN economic enforcement can be."

Connie thought of the depopulated jungles of Thailand and shuddered. A UN enforcement operation against the United States was the last thing anyone needed. If illegal trade were to usurp big business, what remained of the world's economy would collapse. Food shortages and job losses were already common enough, but this would bring chaos.

"Are you familiar with the Ulam Singularity?" Director Burton's deep voice pushed into her thoughts.

"No, I'm not."

"It's an old idea, dating back to the middle of the last century. It presupposes an exponential growth in human knowledge and science, where progress occurs at an ever-increasing rate and technological leaps come faster and faster. Change which took a century before now takes just a decade, then only a year, then a month, and so on. Pretty soon you reach a point where change happens so fast no one can even begin to predict what comes next, from week to week, day to day, minute to minute."

"But that assumption is wrong. We haven't had exponential change in decades."

"No, we haven't." Assistant Executive Director Burton's voice was low. "Our society can't cope with that. That's why we control the pace of change. That's why we have patents."

Connie gaped. "I thought patents were intended to promote progress, not stifle it."

"That's the public relations pitch. The real point is control and stability. Economic, social, and above all political stability."

"But—"

"Don't get me wrong," Burton hastened to add. "We want innovation. Controlled, managed, careful, non-exponential innovation, modulated by financial incentives we control. The last thing we need is unrestrained invention leading us into an Ulam technological singularity. Who can imagine what that would bring? Our social and political institutions wouldn't survive."

Connie ran her finger across the smooth surface of the golden crystal. "I'll find these people."

Burton held up a small, hexagonal chip. It was unlabeled, black. "This is the complete case file, everything we know. We're sending you to Washington DC and assigning you to work with Senior Double Eye Operative Roland Kavanagh. He'll be your liaison with International Intelligence."

International Intelligence? Connie thought. Jesus, this was big. Where did this assignment come from? The President? The World Trade Organization?

"The fewer who know about these devices the better. Your orders stipulate that this case is to be considered a Dark Investigation. You know from your training what that means. You are the first agent in quite some time to operate under those parameters."

Connie was stunned. Dark Investigative Protocols meant playing outside the rules: no paperwork, no audit trail, everything off the record, unofficial, financed from Black Op bank accounts unaffiliated with the FBI. If anything went wrong, the Bureau would disavow all knowledge of the case. She would be abandoned. But to be entrusted with such authority, responsibility, and complete autonomy was a powerful endorsement. Get this right and she'd be on the fast track to promotion. Despite the risks, this opportunity made Connie feel giddy.

"You understand what this implies?" he asked.

"Yes sir, I do."

"We don't know if these people have agents on the inside. Given the breadth of their operation, we must consider it a possibility."

"I understand, sir."

"Good. Your datapad contains a Category One encryption key, the strongest we have. Use it. All correspondence between us, written or verbal, is to be encrypted in the strongest possible manner."

"Understood."

Assistant Director Burton handed Connie the coded chip. "This also contains the specifics of your orders, for your eyes only." The limo slowed to a stop. "Ah, we've arrived."

Connie glanced outside. They were parked in front of the private aviation terminal of LAX. A sleek stratojet stood prepped on the ramp, the drone of its engines barely discernible through the car's soundproofed windows.

"You'll be taking my plane to DC. We've had your bags brought from your hotel. They're already aboard."

"Very good, sir." She opened the door and began to step out. Assistant Director Burton reached over and touched her arm.

"One more thing, Connie." His voice was nearly drowned out by the whine of the plane's engines.

"Sir?"

"This Double Eye agent, Roland Kavanagh. His career is on an even faster track than yours. Those people play rough. Watch your back."

"Thank you, sir. I will."

Assistant Director Burton grasped her hand. "Good luck."

Ψ (13): Tipping Point

Friday, October 12, 2068
5,253ʳᵈ circadian
(87 days, 4:15:00 elapsed)

Hollowed out of a mountain's granite heart was a vast, underground city. Streets wrapped around a central column, balconies of wide promenades opened to a vast, artificial cavern, lit by strips of synthetic sunlight, descending gracefully into the bright depths below. Spacious apartments, an efficient transit system of vertical and horizontal trains, and nano-factories provided a population of thousands with every luxury and need. It was an entire community in both the Physical and the Virtual, with thousands of third and fourth generation Nodes linked together by the fastest data network ever conceived. All self-powered. All hidden beneath the pristine Alaskan wilderness.

Prime shut the simulation down and shook his head. They didn't need a city that would take at least three years to build (if they could get the nano). They needed a bolt hole they could use in the next month or two. It was time to scale this project down a bit. And the sooner the better—the Alaskan enclave was already behind schedule. Not that they were the only ones. The Atlantis project was stuck in the conceptual phase. Cal's little factory couldn't produce enough nano, the Leverkusen facility wouldn't start nano production for at least one more day, Céline still hadn't cracked her way into either the FBI or Double Eye networks, and progress on redacting their public records to thwart social networking analysis was frustratingly slow.

The Physical remained a stubborn bottle-neck as well. Six hundred circadians per day should have been enough speedup for anyone, but it made no difference how fast they lived in the Virtual, packages of nano still took a day or two to reach their destinations. Nor did it matter how much time they had to tweak their nano recipes, or how sophisticated their designs. Nano could only run a recipe so fast. Schedules were firmly mired in the Physical and ran at a glacial pace. Prime hoped Cal's second generation nano would help. It was supposed to be faster and more efficient, but that project was behind schedule too.

Then there was Xiang's Astronautics initiative. Prime snorted. Sending spaceships to the outer solar system was fanciful at best. If they didn't get shot down by the anti-ballistic missile satellites circling the globe, the multi-year journey would likely kill any passengers. It figured the most ridiculous project would be the one that was on schedule.

Physical limitations accounted for most, but not all, of the delays. There were inefficiencies in the Virtual as well. Cal in particular should be making better progress on his design updates. This wasn't down to slow nano or shipping schedules, this was down to distraction. Too much recreation and not enough hard work. The whole goddamn Community had grown far too complacent. You would think a 600 to 1 speedup would mean some real progress, Prime seethed. Instead it seemed to have bred even more complacency. With nearly two years of virtual life in a day, the subjective time between crisis was vastly lengthened. Even as their danger grew, their sense of urgency, of immediacy, and the need to act receded.

Prime ground his teeth in frustration.

◇

"Your new Node design is wonderful," Gwen told Gerhardt Schubert as he waved away a schematic hanging in the air above their table. "You know, I've been able to see for over sixty circadians now, thanks to Prime's wonderful work." She spread her hands, and three generations of crystalline Nodes appeared in the air in front of her, one gold, one green, and one a deep ocean blue. "I never get tired of admiring the beauty here, the worlds people create, the lovely geometries. It's fitting somehow, that the Nodes which make such things possible are themselves so beautiful."

"Not that you've ever seen one for real," Cal regretted his quip the moment it was out. "Well, the Virtual isn't the same as the Physical," he muttered, avoiding Miles's glare.

Céline sat with them around a silver table covered with heaping plates of food. Leafy boughs softened the bright afternoon sun, stippling the restaurant's large patio with shade. The hilltop offered a panoramic view of Paris, the Seine cutting a graceful, glistening curve between elegant white buildings. In the distance stood the Eiffel Tower, framed in golden haze.

"Who's to say the Physical is any more real than what happens here?" Miles gestured around the environ. A murmur of conversation wrapped the restaurant in warm camaraderie. "Our experiences here are real and formative —the relationships we build, the science we do, everything. It's light-years ahead of anything anyone's doing in the Physical."

"Cal touches on a good point," Gwen said. "Though not in the way he meant. We may be way ahead of people in the Physical, but we're still held hostage by it. If we lose power out there, we die in here."

"We don't die," Cal tried to hide his irritation. "If we lose power, we're suspended. Frozen, but perfectly preserved. The moment the power comes back, so do we. Just last week my battery reserve crapped out during a brownout, and I didn't even notice the interruption. Well, not until my Node auto-synced against an external timing source."

"Power issues aside, don't underestimate what we have here," Gerhardt said. "For example, did you know that Gen-1 Nodes didn't even have quantum computational capabilities? Yet despite that, each of those devices had far more computational capacity than anything the world's ever seen. The design was new, revolutionary. But that didn't stop us from throwing it away and designing the second generation Nodes from the ground up, as hybrid systems employing both traditional digital computation and an eighty kiloqubit quantum computer."

"Qubit?"

"A quantum bit," Cal said. "Instead of a zero or a one, it holds a probability cloud of potential values."

"Some algorithms are best handled by a deterministic, digital machine." Céline leaned forward, warming to the conversation. "Others lend themselves to a quantum approach, in which billions of quantum potentials are collapsed into a single result. We were nowhere near the limits of Cal's original design, but Gerhardt's improvements and the use of quantum computing let us leap way ahead of where the original approach could have taken us, in a single design iteration."

"In theory, size is all that limits our speed improvements," Cal added.

"Isn't it always about size?" Céline laughed.

Gerhardt grinned. "Bremermann's limit[1] tells us what the theoretical performance limits of any physical computer are. Information simply cannot move faster than the speed of light. Add to that the physical limits of information density defined by the Bekenstein bound, and we have the absolute boundaries of what we and our Nodes might become."

"That's what I'm saying," Gwen said. "The Physical defines the boundaries of our reality here and what we can become. It's fundamental to everything."

"Miles is right though," Cal sipped his beer. "I've lived the last fourteen subjective years here in the Virtual. I barely remember life in the Physical. Most of us could say the same. Does that make our lives any less real, any less complete, because they take place at a more abstract level of reality?"

"No, of course not," Gwen replied. "That isn't my point at all—"

"Prime!" Céline waved to the young man who had just appeared. "Over here!"

Prime weaved his way between crowded tables, radiating his digital identity like an aura. He wore a young, muscular body, a golden tan and long, blond hair. Their table expanded, making room for him. An additional seat materialized.

"You're late," Miles said. "We're hungry. We started without you."

Everyone laughed.

"Isn't it strange?" Céline dipped a prawn in cocktail sauce. "Here we are, digital beings existing as software in a digitally simulated world, pretending to eat non-existent

---

1   Bremermann's limit is the maximum computational speed of a self-contained system in the material universe. It is derived from Einstein's mass-energy equivalency and the Heisenberg Uncertainty Principle, and is approximately 2×10^{47} bits per second per gram.

food that our non-existent bodies don't need. Our descendants will think we're nuts."

The environ's nonsapient interface presented itself to Prime in the form of a waiter. "I'll have a plate of fresh oysters and a glass of Pinot Grigio." He turned to Céline. "Technically I'm not even a native of the Physical, but I find myself unable to give up mimicking its sensations."

"Speaking of simulated flesh, I see you've made some modifications." Cal prodded Prime's exaggerated pecs with his fist.

"I got tired of seeing the man I loathe every time I look in the mirror. I figured I'd try something a little more radical on for size. Speaking of which, did any of you happen to see Nolen's latest diatribe on the Community message board?"

Gerhardt frowned. "It was appalling."

"We should exile the jerk to the Physical." Miles met Gwen's eyes and looked away.

Gwen knew Miles struggled with guilt. She did too, grateful to be able to see thanks to Nolen's research and mortified at what it had cost Prime. "What Dr. Nolen did was a terrible thing, but all of us make free use of the thought and memory engrams and architectural enhancements he developed. Is it fair to use the fruits of his crime and then punish him for it?"

No one spoke.

Cal looked away. He maneuvered a pair of chopsticks around a piece of Kobe steak and lifted it to his mouth. "We can't banish him, Miles. Autonomy is absolute."

"Not on a Gen-1 Node it isn't," Miles stabbed a leaf of lettuce. "Nolen doesn't have the same safeguards as the rest of us."

"That's not the point. What's next? Laws? A police force? Or do we just form up a mob and run him out of the Virtual? This isn't what the Community is about."

"The man is calling for the wholesale extermination of all copies." Prime fought to remain calm. "That includes me and the copies many of you send out to manage your lives in the Physical, and who knows how many others. He's trying to incite a massacre."

"He can talk all he likes," Gerhardt said. "Generation two and later Nodes protect all of us from external harm."

"That's right," Cal said. "He can't touch any of us, including you Prime."

"You don't know that. No security is perfect."

"Quantum encryption is," Gerhardt replied. "Particularly when it's embedded in hardware."

"Are you sure of that?"

"Yes."

"Nolen may not threaten any of us directly," Céline said, "but he does threaten the Community. We've never been so divided. Some factions are so angry over what happened, and disagree so strongly on what to do about it, they've stopped talking to each another."

"This rift is dangerous," Prime scowled. "The authorities are already sniffing around. Three of us have been detained. If we're divided, we won't survive."

"People will come around," Cal yawned, stretching his arms over his head. "Right now everyone is still in shock, at the arrests, at what Dr. Nolen did. Emotions are running high."

Miles eyes flashed. "Nolen's a menace."

"Nolen has no power," Cal replied. "Whether we exile him or just filter him out like most seem to be doing already, it really makes no difference. He might as well be in a different universe."

"You don't know that."

"Did you happen to see him at the party last night? Did any of you?"

Prime snorted. "I did." No one else answered.

"I guess Prime and I are the only ones not filtering him out. You guys should have seen him, wandering around like a ghost, unable to make himself seen, unable to make himself heard. He was absolutely livid and completely powerless. He can't touch us, he can't hurt us, hell, he can't even make us listen to him."

Céline shuddered. "God, that's creepy."

"Maybe, but I like it," Gerhardt laughed. "Let him rot in his cluster of first generation Nodes. No one's going to give him a Gen-2 Node, and I'm not about to let him get his hands on third generation kit now that it's shipping."

"We have bigger problems than Nolen," Céline said. "The authorities now have three Nodes to analyze. They've deciphered a couple of basic principles of our technology and are already preparing charges of criminal patent violation against us."

"You've got to be kidding," Cal rolled his eyes. "They don't even know who we are."

"John Doe warrants don't need names. They'll add us later, if and when they identify who we are."

"We designed these Nodes ourselves," Gerhardt's voice rose. "No one has ever built anything like them. We invented the damn things!"

Miles made a calming motion with one hand. "This is nothing new. We all know speculators squat on patents all the time for ideas they never intend to actually invent or employ."

"In our case," Céline said, "they've squatted on gallium-doped polymer data storage and superconductive neural inductance."

"Those are components of our first generation technology," Cal said.

Céline nodded. "Thankfully, my team has had pretty good luck infiltrating and rifling through the information systems of most major district attorneys' offices. It turns out lawyers aren't very good at encrypting their communications. The good news is, none of their patent queries reference mind-uploads, artificial intelligence, virtual reality, or sophisticated environment modeling."

"They don't have a clue about what our Nodes actually are."

"Then we have an edge," Miles said. "They don't know what we're doing, they don't know we're many times smarter than they are, and they don't know we live in a faster frame of reference."

"Don't forget, the Genecraft scientists were smarter too," Cal reminded them. "Now they're all dead or locked up. Same with the Free Software pioneers. Raw intelligence doesn't matter. Even technology may not matter. These cartels and monopolists have been winning against brighter, more enlightened people for centuries."

"He's right," Céline said. "We can't win this on our own."

"We can't win this at all," Prime's voice rose. "Not if we go up against the whole world head-on."

"So what do we do?" Miles demanded. "Roll over and play dead?"

"We withdraw," Prime said.

"What, from the world?"

"Yes, because if we try to change the world, it will be an all or nothing bet. We'll be up against the world's most powerful organizations, gambling with our survival against a deck stacked very high against us. But if we escape their grip entirely, we have a good chance of surviving, even thriving."

"I like that idea," Cal said. "What did you have in mind? A city at the bottom of the ocean? A colony on Mars?"

"There are interest groups exploring those sort of contingencies," Prime turned to Miles. "I got your message.

Your superstring strummer worked? You created energy from nothing?"

"We don't create energy out of nothing," Miles corrected him. "We introduce energy into this locale by changing matter into anti-matter. Mutual annihilation does the rest."

"You did add energy to this universe, though," Cal said. "You reversed entropy."

Miles looked pained. "I really wish you'd consider assimilating an up-to-date knowledge engram. We don't reverse entropy. The laws of thermodynamics cannot be overridden. N-branes are just superstrings of higher dimensionality, strung across the subatomic folds of Calabi-Yau space. Like a guitarist, we strum N-branes into new harmonics, creating a symphony of new subatomic particles. Energy is imported into this dimension as a side effect. We don't reduce existing entropy."

"Regardless, it's a strategic achievement," Prime said. "Inexpensive energy opens some real possibilities. Our biggest vulnerability remains our dependence on the public power grids. With independent power sources the Gen-4 Nodes could sever the last remaining umbilical to the outside world. We could hide them anywhere, become truly independent."

"I'd settle for a Gen-3 Node at this point," Cal replied. "I could really use the 600 to 1 speedup."

Miles blinked. "Cal, my entire team received their upgrade packets days ago. You should have yours by now.

"I know. I think the damn thing got lost in the mail. It was one of the first ones shipped."

"No wonder you're running behind." Prime's eyes narrowed. "I don't like this. We've had three people disappear from the Community, one just thirty hours ago. Céline's just learned that the authorities are preparing patent litigation and criminal charges against us through

John Doe warrants, and now you say your upgrade kit never arrived? Our distribution network could be compromised."

"What network?" Cal replied. "We ship our kits direct via commercial parcel services. There is no secret network."

"You know what I mean. If the government suspects the Kansas City production facility, it wouldn't be difficult for the FBI to track shipments to their recipients and compromise much of the Community."

"It's not a concern," Cal assured him. "Céline's team has full access to the freight company's systems. They retroactively modify the shipping manifests and tracking data once the packages reach their destination. Addresses, names, contents—everything's changed. Except, of course, the fact that I still haven't gotten my upgrade kit."

"I think I can help you there," Miles said. "John Tarley, a physicist on my team, is taking his family on vacation. He'll be offloading into the Physical in the next day or so and will be away for three weeks. You're welcome to transload and use his Gen-3 Node until a replacement kit arrives."

"Thanks, I'll take you up on that."

Prime clamped down on a rising sense of panic. "Cal, you should have told us about this earlier."

"Like I said, it's no big deal."

Christ, was he really this arrogant, this *stupid*? "Cal, three of our colleagues are lying in hospitals right this minute, handcuffed to their beds, their Nodes powered off, their minds locked in comas. And you say it's no big deal? Look people, we face an existential threat. Three of our colleagues are gone, with more sure to follow. When the authorities figure out what we are, they're going to hit us with everything they've got. And right now, if that happens, we don't stand a chance."

"We're on the cusp of some significant breakthroughs," Gerhardt said. "If we can develop—"

"That isn't enough!" Prime shouted. "Christ, we just agreed we can't take on the world's authorities. Well, we can't afford to have the world's authorities come after us either. Not if we want to come out of this alive. Can't any of you see how serious our situation is? It's like you're all in a state of collective denial, pretending you're immortal with death knocking at the door. It's like the nuclear threat we pretend isn't there, despite all the missiles aimed at each other, despite the armed satellites filling the sky."

Cal lifted his hands and pushed them outwards, as if trying to quiet him. "Prime, calm down. There's no need to panic."

"Don't be an ass. If they find us, *all they have to do is cut the power*. Those of us in the Virtual will be shut down forever. And we'll be the lucky ones. Anyone caught out in the Physical will face enhanced interrogation and wish to hell they'd never been born. You people need to snap out of this complacency of yours, or we can all kiss the future good-bye."

✝ (14): Ponderings in Flight

The sleek Eurojet 930 dropped out of supersonic some four hundred kilometers west of Washington DC, beginning its descent out of an almost black sky toward the curved horizon and Dulles Airport. Connie's unease had dogged her all the way from California, growing more acute each time she reread the information in her palm-top datapad.

Aside from an analytical breakdown of the crystalline cube's chemical make-up, some speculation on the composition of the superconductive material of the webbed skullcap (tentatively identified as a neural-digital interface), and the names of three suspects (one deceased), she had precious little to go on. The more she thought about it the more she distrusted her own, and the Bureau's, assumptions. No one had a clue what the devices were or what they could do.

The first suspect, one Thomas Jacobson, was a software engineering student at Berkeley. He had been taken into custody nine days earlier and had proved surprisingly resilient. Interrogators estimated it would take another three to six days to break him. Sodium pentothal had proved less than useful. He was already experiencing psychotic episodes, with ravings of magical worlds, immortality and godlike powers interspersed with subversive diatribe and vitriol against government and international institutions. Apart from confirming his Libertarian and anarchistic leanings, the interrogations had uncovered little.

A chime sounded and the fasten seat belt sign lit up as they descended through the tropopause. The sky had lightened considerably. The horizon was almost flat. Connie tightened her seat belt and tapped the screen on her datapad.

The second detainee, a sociologist by the name of Manuel Rodriguez, had been in Australian custody for just under three days. He was from the opposite end of the political spectrum, well known to authorities for his leftist leanings and vocal political dissent. He had a long rap sheet, and had been serving a sentence under house arrest when authorities had come across a newly published book on an underground FreeNet server, calling for the abolishment of patents and copyrights. There was no mistaking Rodriguez' distinctive style, but several unannounced visits and inspections to his home had uncovered no direct evidence linking him to the subversive material. One such visit, however, did uncover a curious cube of emerald crystal with a metallic scalp device attached. When questioned, Rodriguez proved uncooperative and was once again taken into custody. He was a far more promising suspect than Jacobson. Interrogators were optimistic he would soon crack.

The third suspect, a professor of Electrical Engineering at the University of Illinois, was suspected of disseminating seditious information to one of his students, who turned him in. Unfortunately, some yahoo cop fatally shot him as he tried to flee the scene. Connie was furious. He was probably much higher in the criminal hierarchy than the other two. If so, that bullet had killed their best lead, and cost the investigation an enormous amount of information. What unbelievable, unforgivable incompetence!

She groaned, stretching her arms and glancing down the length of the gently humming fuselage. Her eyes returned to the screen. Three faces and three names. One student activist, one dissident sociologist, and one dead professor. Three seemingly unrelated people, united by intellectual dissent and an unhealthy disdain for authority. A new political movement? Connie shook her head. If it were that simple, Political Enforcement would have rounded them up long before now.

Still, mysterious crystalline devices and illegal interfaces into the human nervous system implied an agenda bigger than that of your average black marketeer. Connie's unease grew. The idea of a market trading in home entertainment systems based on technologies more advanced than those available even to the military didn't quite ring true. She couldn't shake the sense they were missing something important. A new level of FreeNet sedition, perhaps? If so, there would be a political component after all. Or perhaps the connection was more academic.

She made a note to follow up on the suspects' university affiliations before folding shut her datapad and slipping it into her handbag. The plane touched down with a light bump and coasted down the runway. She was surprised by the unusual speed with which they taxied to the ramp. A white limousine waited, flanked by two commandos in full body armor, anonymous behind black Kevlar and darkened face shields.

♈ (15): WASHINGTON

Friday, October 12, 2068
5,272nd circadian
(87 days, 6:34:28 elapsed)

As she disembarked from the plane, Connie was met by a thin young man with dark hair. He wore a conservative suit common in the upper echelons of corporate America, and a traditional neck tie which had become something of an anachronism in recent years.

"Ms. Sinclair," he smiled politely. "Roland is here and eager to meet you. Please." He held the rear door of the limousine open for her.

Had she not just spent weeks on the UCLA case, staying in one of the more ostentatious hotels in Hollywood, she would have been awed by the spacious elegance and luxury hidden behind the tinted, bullet proof windows of the car. Grateful for the amount of desensitization that experience had afforded her, she schooled her features into a professional veneer, and nodded to the man sitting across from her.

"Connie Sinclair!" A firm hand shook hers as the door snicked shut behind her and the car moved forward.

"Delighted to meet you, Mr. Kavanagh." He was something straight out of a movie: tall, with a dark, rich tan and a military haircut. Roland Kavanagh reminded her of a man she'd trained with, who'd risen fast through the ranks of the FBI despite a lack of intuition and a knack for missing important clues. He'd made up for it with ruthlessness. Assistant Director Bryant had been right to caution her.

"Please, call me Roland." Shrewd blue eyes regarded her from a face aged too early by sun. "I saw you on the telly. Not the best sort of cover for an undercover agent."

She hadn't expected an Australian, although she supposed it wasn't unreasonable for International Intelligence to station some foreign agents in this country.

"It was unfortunate," Connie admitted. "I believe the Bureau had some rather pointed words with the World Media Association over that."

"Speaking of whom, we'll be heading over to your FBI headquarters first. Executive Assistant Director Burton scheduled a short meeting with the head chap."

"Director McClain?" Head of the FBI. He reported directly to the President. This was *big*.

"Burton thought it would be good for you to introduce us. Grease the wheels between the FBI and Double Eye."

"Politics," Connie snorted.

"Yes. Oh by the way, you'll need to dust off your passport. Seems the world's top leadership is attending a summit in London. The head of WIPO requires our presence for a special session this Sunday."

"*London?* Just flying over there and back will delay our investigation a couple of days."

"Three days, I'm afraid." Roland frowned. "I gather you FBI chaps are as baffled by these odd crystals as we are."

"Yes." Connie did her best to hide her excitement. She relished solving cases like this. "I've run through the data several times, and while I distrust the assumption that these are just some kind of new, improved home entertainment devices, possibly with FreeNet capabilities, it's at least a starting point."

"I quite agree."

"The director mentioned you have some additional information."

Roland reached into his jacket pocket and withdrew a slim datapad, gesturing for Connie to do the same. The light of several hundred gigabytes began to flow from his datapad to hers, illuminating the car's interior.

"So," Connie said as the data continued to transmit, "we've recovered three crystalline cubes in the possession of three unrelated people. The cubes are composed of a polymer in crystalline form, doped with gallium and laced with strands of superconductive material. We presume they represent a storage device of some kind, with playback capabilities via a head net, which we tentatively believe may be a digital-to-neural interface."

"The first two cubes recovered are a complex polymer doped with gallium," Roland confirmed. "However, the third is constructed from a completely different polymer, this one doped with graphene. Laced with the same superconductor, as far as we can tell."

"They aren't identical in construction?" Connie asked, surprised. "Nothing in my briefing mentioned that—wait, it did mention the device recovered from Rodriguez was green in color. The others were gold."

"Your Bureau may have overlooked the chemistry during the initial inquiry." Roland shrugged. "Since the other two samples are in Double Eye custody, your laboratory personnel wouldn't have had an opportunity to correct the oversight." The optical port on his datapad went dark. Connie glanced to the west, idly noting the sunset, its rich oranges and reds muddied and dimmed by the car's tinted glass. Roland looked up. "The data is in the briefing I just flashed you, including photographs of all three cubes, plus tentative chemical breakdowns and cross sections of their construction."

Connie tapped on her datapad, bringing up the information and paging through several diagrams. "The green one's half the size of the other two."

Roland leaned forward. "Probably different manufacturers, maybe in different countries. That implies a consumer base of forty or fifty thousand, large enough to attract wider interest and some competition."

"Yeah," Connie agreed. "A pretty big market, but strictly underground, illicit. That neural interface, if that's what it is, would land the manufacturers in prison. These devices must support a profit margin that would make taking such a risk worthwhile. We're looking for affluent people with a fetish for entertainment that legal consumer electronics don't satisfy."

"These things are hard to come by," Roland added. "None of our informants have heard a whisper of them. Nothing on any of Internet boards, mailing lists, or on the street. Advertising must be by word of mouth, between a tightly knit group of people. How do we reconcile that with a marketplace of tens of thousands? This doesn't fit any of the models for illicit trade we've ever dealt with."

"This is something new," Connie agreed. "Which brings us back to our friends in custody."

"Minus the bloke you Americans capped."

Connie grimaced. "I'd like nothing more than to wring that cop's neck."

"I can't say that I blame you. That idiot's itchy trigger finger cost us our most promising lead."

Connie tapped several icons and then placed her thumb briefly on the screen.

THUMBPRINT ID VERIFIED
HELLO CONNIE SINCLAIR

"What are you doing?" Roland asked.

"Checking credit histories." Connie scrawled a few commands across the screen and tapped several more icons. "I want to see if they were ever in the same place."

"Don't bother. Both our departments have already done a run-down on all three suspects. None of them have any record of having met one another, either online or in real life, nor do they recognize one another under questioning."

Connie tapped several more commands into her datapad and then leaned back thoughtfully.

"You're absolutely correct, Roland. They've never met. But although they were never in the same city at the same time, two out of three have been in two of the same cities at different times." Connie passed Roland her datapad. "That makes two cities of possible interest. Another thirteen if we cover every place any of our suspects have traveled. Not as specific as I would have liked, nevertheless, once we arrest another suspect or two the geography of our investigation should clarify itself."

"Clever analysis." Roland handed the datapad back to Connie. "Assuming a market of fifty thousand, there shouldn't be more than three or four degrees of separation in the entire group. A few more arrests and we may be able to crack this case even without cooperative suspects."

"I just wish we had some data correlation between these people. Looking at their PATRIOT Profiles, I can't find any statistically significant links or similarities. They might as well be three randomly selected strangers. They've never exchanged e-mails, telephone calls, or frequented the same discussion forums or chat rooms." She gazed out at the Washington Monument and mused. "We're missing some key element that ties these people together."

"Networking theory suggests we'll need between eight and twelve suspects before we have an eighty percent probability of success in identifying one or two locales. Of course, we may need a lot more than that if the group is more dispersed or has sparser interpersonal connections than the standard models assume."

"Does Double Eye have access to the NSA's ECHELON system?" Connie asked.

"Not directly, but the NSA will on occasion provide us with ECHELON reports as a courtesy. What did you have in mind?"

"Cross reference their database of intercepted communications with the geographical analysis I just made. It is a bit of a fishing expedition, but the NSA is nothing if not thorough when it comes to snooping on our citizens. We might get lucky."

Roland was impressed. "I'll see what I can do."

♈ (16): Cold Reality

Sunday, October 14, 2068
5,992nd circadian
(88 days, 13:44:28 elapsed)

Thersius III–B was the second of seven medium-sized moons orbiting the third planet of a pair of white dwarf stars. Its primary was a Jovian gas giant that filled half the sky, bathing the icy landscape with a dull red glow. The moon barely qualified as human habitable, not because of the thin atmosphere, Arctic summers, and glacial winters; nor because of the tiny carnivores that hunted the icy wastes in packs of several thousand—vicious creatures dubbed "piranha rats" that could tear through a pressure suit and clean a human skeleton in moments. What made Thersius III–B so insidiously dangerous was its travel through the Van Allen belt of its Jovian primary, a passage that bathed the moon in lethal radiation for two days out of every thirteen. Even so, a small human colony had been established.

The moon contained deposits of an unusual crystal used in the navigational systems of the superluminal starships that plied the sky. Many of the miners working the rocks beneath the glacial ice would leave this place wealthy. A good thing, for they would need wealth to obtain treatment for illness caused by their extended exposure to radiation. Even the lead-lined canisters that housed their community could not protect them. People with the strongest constitution might manage to stay long enough and accumulate enough money to remain wealthy even after their medical treatment.

Cal^2 sat in the shielded concourse of the arrival terminal as he had every day since his arrival. Listlessly, he watched the traffic display as it updated the trajectories of approaching ships and calculated their estimated arrival times. Two ships had departed several hours ago and were making their way past the orbit of the fourth planet, away from the star where they could engage their FTL drives. Only one ship was inbound at the moment, a small commuter vessel falling toward the asteroid belt between the first and second planets. Cal^2 dug his fingers into the orange fur of his forearm, scratching at the growing lesion beneath and cringing as his stomach, still raw from the last bout of vomiting, threatened to send him running to the toilet again.

"Excuse me, sir." A young, human woman stood beside his chair.

"Can I help you?" Cal^2 snapped.

She shook her head. "No, but I might be able to help you. I'm Sanja Netal. I notice that you're beginning to show signs of stage two radiation poisoning. Did you miss your departing flight?"

Cal^2 absently straightened his whiskers. "It really isn't your concern."

"I'm a medical student from Netham IV, specializing in the treatment of advanced radiation trauma. If you stay here much longer, your treatment will become prohibitively expensive. You could even die."

"Yes," Cal^2 said. "I've been here twelve circadians. In each of those circadians, at around this time, one or another of you nonsentient programs poke around here to tell me

I'm about to die. As if I can't tell already."

The woman who called herself Sanja looked confused. "Circadians? Like Circidic Dreamscapes? On Netham IV we had Circidic Dreamscapes, before the war."

"Days," Cal² replied irritably. "I've been here twelve days. Standard Terran, 24-hour days. I suppose you're going to tell me about your home world next, with some hint as to how I could cash in on an opportunity there? Spare me, I've heard the same things about eleven other worlds, each of the last eleven days."

"I wouldn't recommend visiting my home world until you've had your radiation sickness treated," Sanja replied. "The atmosphere on Netham IV may be down to seventy rads or so, but the fallout from the bombs still lies loose on the ground. A good wind storm, or even a little careless kicking up of the dust, and you could find yourself sicker than you are now. Besides, we've had enough outsiders picking over our ruins and stealing the platinum wiring from the wreckage of our homes to sell on other worlds. Try something like that, and you're likely to end up on the wrong end of a hangman's rope."

"Ruins. Platinum electrical wiring. Check. You've delivered your clue, I've got it. Thank you."

"Well," Sanja replied brightly. "Hope you're able to find passage off this world soon. Bye!"

"Nonsapient personas," Cal² muttered darkly as he turned away from the departing woman. "What idiot came up with that idea?" He rubbed his burning stomach and turned his attention back to the traffic display. The puppet software posing as Sanja had touched on an uncomfortable fact, which the itch of his skin and the unease of his stomach wouldn't allow him to ignore. Without funds for radiation treatment his death here would be exceptionally unpleasant. What sort of pedant programmed the symptoms of radiation sickness into a game scenario anyway? The thought disgusted him.

And where the hell was Brett? According to Cal²'s information he should have arrived several circadians ago. If this world turned out to be another false lead he would have to start over. Cal's character avatar had just about had it; it wouldn't survive another interstellar trip without extensive medical care, something he, or rather this character, couldn't afford.

A tone sounded and a new pinpoint of light appeared on the traffic display. Vector and acceleration information were displayed, followed by the ship's name, registry, tonnage, and declared cargo:

Flying Gargoyle. Registry Patronis VIII, PT8-7155D. 180,000 tn. 167.2 tn Misc. Medical supplies.

The new vessel was decelerating at 20 m/s^2 on a trajectory that would bring it to Thersius III–B within seven hours. An ETA hovered near the moving dot in the display, ticking down as it tracked across the sky.

"Yes!" Cal² exclaimed. "I finally found you, you son of a bitch." No sooner had he spoken, when the burning in his stomach became a raging storm. Nausea threatened to overwhelm him. He staggered to the public rest rooms, barely managing to slip into one of the stalls and close the door before his empty stomach began to heave. He spent the next hour kneeling beside the toilet, surrendering to his nausea. It was sometime during this particular bout of humiliation that Cal²'s disdain for the Gamers' League grew into outright loathing. People did this sort of shit for *fun?*

He emerged weak and trembling, his face pale and his fur matted with sweat. He didn't even make it halfway to his seat before his stomach sent him reeling back to the toilet. Back on the floor, he laid his arms across the toilet seat and rested his head on them, hoping he had the strength to last another six hours.

When a voice announced the arrival and disembarkation of the *Flying Gargoyle*, Cal² managed to pull himself together and achieve some semblance of presentability. He wished, not for the first time, he had chosen an avatar whose pelt didn't require constant grooming. Returning to the concourse, he waited while the arriving ship's passengers and crew cleared customs. Eventually a handful of people appeared in the passage.

No one radiated identity signatures, and Cal² had no idea which one was Brett Jenson. He shouted the name at the entire group.

"Character names, if you please," replied a tall, lanky man with deep green, almost black, skin. His metallic silver hair was cut asymmetrically, shoulder length on the left, short and spiked on the right.

"Are you Brett Jenson?" Cal² demanded.

"Not here," his double-irised silver eyes sparkled. "Here I'm Prince Lethe Tomaar of the Cyclade Triumvirate, Tau Ceti IX. Your Highness to you. And you are?"

"Cal Shelton²," *you jackass*, he wanted to add, but held his tongue. It wouldn't do to have Brett leave in a huff. Not now, not after all this. "I've been stuck in this simulation for sixty-five circadians looking for you, all the while forced to live by this game's rules, which include such lovely things as hunger, pain, dismemberment, and even a fully simulated bout of radiation sickness, all for your viewing pleasure."

Brett's silver hair sparkled as he shook his head. "Thersius III-B is an advanced level world, Cal². Coming here as a crystal miner is a huge gamble and an uncomfortable prospect, one that rarely pays off. You're better off putting together a crew and buying a starship before trying to deal in Ngetali crystal. Reselling the Ngetali on other worlds is far more lucrative, and healthier, than mining it here."

"I don't give a rat's ass about the economics of interstellar trade in this nightmare of a environ. I've had to waste the last sixty-five circadians of my life tracking you down, and am enduring a simulated death by radiation sickness just to be able to talk to you."

Brett looked shocked. "You've got radiation poisoning? What the hell are you sticking around for? Bail out and roll up a new character."

"And spend another sixty-five circadians trying to find you?" Cal^2 shook his head. "Not on your life. I want this conversation over, so I can get back to civilization. Is there somewhere we can talk?"

Brett sighed. "We can go back through customs to my ship. I've got a top-end sick bay you can use. You obviously need the medical treatment."

Cal^2 shook his head. "I'm not coming back. Once we're done we can just let this avatar die."

"Fine. Let's just grab a seat over there." He turned to his companions. "You guys go on ahead. Book us accommodations for the next two nights. With any luck we'll have our cargo and be out of here before the next radiation bath."

"You got it, Your Highness."

"See you later, Prince Lethe."

"Don't be late for drinks at *Veronica's*," another chimed in. "We've still got to finish that game of Nine Circles. Unless you want to pay up now."

Brett laughed. "I'll see you there, Garnith. And don't go counting those two hundred Altairan Kroner just yet."

Cal^2 and Brett sat down in the hard plastic chairs of the spaceport as the others continued down the concourse.

"So," Brett said, leaning back and putting his hands behind his head. "What was so important that you'd suffer radiation poisoning just to talk to me?"

"What the hell have you been doing, going dark on the whole Community?"

"Going dark?" Brett asked. "Is that some kind of new slang?"

"Going dark. Refusing communications, going silent, becoming inaccessible. I've been trying to reach you for hectocircadians."

"Oh. Well, as you know, the rules of the Star Trader scenario preclude communications over interstellar distances. Some players circumvent this limitation with outside lines to the Community, so the rules were amended to disallow any outside communication while in the game."

"Brett, this environ is only running at a speedup of ninety. The average for the Community with third generation hardware is over six hundred." Cal^2 shook his head. "You have been missing out on years of development and changes within the Community."

Brett shrugged. "I've been having an adventure of a lifetime here. I command my own starship and explore worlds of exotic beauty and complexity that would truly amaze you."

"Have you ever explored a four dimensional garden, or flown with flocks of birds through a seven dimensional cloudscape?" Cal^2 asked.

Brett shook his head.

"I could show you environs in the Community that are so exotic you would have to rewire your mind in order to comprehend them," Cal^2 told him. "Next to those places, the planets of this simulation are all profoundly mundane. Hell, Brett, the four dimensional jewelry you used to wear was more exotic than this."

"You'd be surprised at some of the creativity the Game Lords have employed. Besides, gaming isn't just about seeing exotic sights."

"What is it, then? What is it you get out of life in the

Virtual when you turn your back on just about everything it offers. You have countless opportunities to transcend your human limitations, and you squander them to play in this ... this fantasy."

"It gives me escape," Brett snapped.

"Escape?"

"Not all of us had a cushy childhood like you. Some of us don't have cushy adulthoods either."

"*Cushy childhood?* My grandmother was dirt poor. I went hungry more times than I can count. We all did."

"At least she cared about you. My parents ... well, let's just say dysfunction doesn't begin to cover it. Penitentialists don't treat their kids well. And foster care is worse, not that you'd be interested."

"You're not in a foster home any more, Brett. You're an adult, a student at a good university, living large in the Virtual with the chance to become something far more than human. You don't need to waste it all on gaming and cheap fantasy."

"Here I have experiences," Brett said, "which challenge my creativity, my endurance, my ability to survive against sometimes unbelievable odds. Gaming is about honing one's skills, developing strategies, and meeting the sort of challenges we never have in the Physical, and most definitely not in the synthetic utopia of the non-gaming Community. I'm not going to give it, or any of my other pleasures, up."

"I'm not asking you to."

"Then why the lecture?"

"Because you could have so much more, Brett. Because..." Cal² looked into Brett's hardened face and stopped. His friend had shut down. Cal² sighed. "Never mind. I came because we need you. You're still in charge of catalyst production in Kansas City, aren't you?"

"Of course. The facility runs itself. I can monitor its status from here, without offloading into the Physical every night to check up on it. If anything does go wrong, I'll offload and deal with it."

"Listen, Brett—"

"No, *you* listen. For once I'm living the way *I* want. I do plenty for the Community. I don't just babysit your nano factory. Every couple of days I offload to interview and screen new recruits in the Physical. I run some real risks out there. What do you think would happen to me if I screened an undercover cop by mistake?"

"That's all well and good." Another bout of nausea doubled Cal^2 over. "But it's beside the point. We need to be able to reach you. It's vital, especially when specifications change."

"Nano is nano. What on earth could possibly change in the production specifications, besides the quantity? We agreed from day one we couldn't produce much more without drawing attention to ourselves."

"We have a second generation assembler that needs large scale testing. In order to do that we need to renovate the facility to produce a new catalytic solution. The Community needs this, and you've gone AWOL!"

"Why don't you use the Leverkusen facility?"

"Because I don't want to take down an operation five times bigger than yours to test a new version that may or may not scale to production quantity. That is one of the reasons we've kept the KC operation going, so we can test things like this without interrupting our main production flows. Look, we need you there. If you're not able or willing to continue running it, let us know and we'll find someone who is. This is too important for you to blow off like this."

"OK, OK. I'll offload and run your new specs."

"Thank you. And Brett?"

"Yes?"

"Do me a favor, will you? Give me some means of getting in touch. We can't afford these delays, and I never want to come back to this space opera again."

Cal^2 watched the tension drain from Brett's shoulders. "No problem. I'll set up a daemon program to forward any incoming communications from you to my starship. Not strictly legal if you have an active Player Character—"

"I won't."

"—but I don't think the Game Lords will mind."

"Good. I'm going to transload back to my own environ and let the game engine play-act this avatar's ugly death without me."

"Here's the code to my comm daemon. I'll be at *Veronica's* if you need me." Brett turned to go.

"Thanks. Oh, one other thing."

"Yeah?"

"Watch yourself out there. Things in the Physical are getting dicey. The authorities are actively trying to figure out who and what we are, and playing around in this slow-motion fantasy world has put you more than a little out of touch with developments."

"Not to worry. I know how to take care of myself."

Cal^2 gave the command to rejoin his Original, leaving behind an empty avatar, another mindless puppet to populate the game. As he recombined with Cal^1 a dark thought struck him. Were they still the same person, or had he grown too much, become someone else? He was merging with his Original—losing himself as he did so. This was suicide! "Stop the process!" he tried to scream, but he was already a memory, without a voice.

Cal^1 felt his copy's terror as he absorbed the engram, foreign memories trickling into the recesses of his mind. He was shocked at how much they had grown apart, and horrified that Cal²'s last thought had been to refuse to rejoin with him. If he'd changed his mind a microsecond earlier the process would have aborted. Who would have been the real Cal then? And would anyone have known the difference?

✝ (17): Darkness Gathers

Sunday, October 14, 2068
6,253ʳᵈ circadian
(89 days, 0:10:07 elapsed)

"What an absolute waste of time!" The huge lobby's curved marble walls and domed ceiling seemed to amplify Connie's quiet, angry words as she and Roland made their way through the front entrance. Roland shook his head fractionally and said nothing as the main doors swished open, then shut again behind them.

London was cast in twilight. Low clouds scudded overhead on a damp, clammy breeze thick with salt and decay. Government buildings brooded over crawling traffic. Windows cast a baleful gaze from behind thick, gray pillars. Over the Houses of Parliament hulked the New Embankment, forty meters of reinforced concrete and peeling blue paint some artist had intended to mimic a cloudless sky. The concrete barrier concealed the rusted carcasses of once graceful bridges, lost beneath thirty-five meters of seawater along with the river Thames and most of the city's south bank. The country still hadn't recovered from the decision to cede half of London to the rising waters. Neighborhoods were deluged and vast tracts of the city reduced to a briny, rotting swamp. Military, police, and intelligence services had been swept aside by the populist rage that followed. Within days a government had been deposed and a royal family forced into exile. Years of recriminations and reconciliation had failed to heal the wounds. Failed efforts to transform the flooded areas into an English Venice hadn't helped. Militants still tried bombing the barrier, hoping to see the surviving boroughs flooded. Twice they'd nearly succeeded.

Security cameras tracked Connie and Roland as a plain-clothes policeman opened the door of a waiting limousine and ushered them inside. "Airport, please," Roland said as the limousine pulled away from the curb.

"That was our meeting 'of critical importance'?" Connie sputtered. "For what? A useless two hours that brought absolutely nothing new to the investigation. Nothing! They didn't think of a single thing Director Burton and I didn't discuss three days ago."

"The meeting was important," Roland countered. "It gave us insight into the world leadership's priorities and how they view our case. Knowing that, we can avoid a number of career-ending blunders we might otherwise make."

"The only blunder we could make would be not solving this case. Hell, they made that clear in the first five minutes. It's a pity they didn't end the meeting then, and spare us two hours of pontificating by windbags who know even less than we do."

"Connie, how often do you think political leaders at that level deign to meet operatives like us?"

"Not often," she admitted as they inched past the Cenotaph toward Trafalgar Square. "They're frightened."

"So frightened they flew us half way around the world to meet with us personally. I wouldn't say it's entirely unprecedented, but it is very unusual. Most leaders are content to meet with their cabinets and maybe the top directors of their various intelligence and investigative organizations. Not active field operatives."

"They clearly don't know a thing about the technology we're dealing with."

"I think you can generalize that. They don't know much about technology, period. They're politicians, not scientists or engineers."

"They rule the world's regulatory body responsible for technological development."

"That doesn't make them technologically savvy," Roland said. "Or even proficient. Their expertise is politics and law, managing Architectures of Control that were established centuries ago. They tweak their edifices of dominance now and again, modifying a copyright statute here or a patent law there, but their real concern is control, not fostering development. Bloody politicians! They're confronted with something new and revolutionary and all they worry about is a little short-term erosion of their authority. This technology represents a much bigger threat."

"Well, they did make one good point," Connie said. "Mass industrial disobedience could undermine the foundation of our economy. We've been in recession for decades. If this gets out of hand, it could send us into a full-scale depression."

"It's nothing to scoff at, that's for sure," Roland agreed. "But those hacks can't see the potential ramifications right in front of their noses. This isn't about a little economic dislocation. That sort of thing has happened before, and we have tried and true methods for dealing with it. Our institutions have always coped. What they—what we all—should be concerned with is that someone is building and using, on a massive scale, technology so advanced we're completely in the dark about what it does."

"Whether it is a FreeNet server, a new entertainment

device, or even a VR gaming interface, isn't really important—" Connie began.

"Mate, for all we know it's a cure for old age."

"Regardless, we can make headway identifying the customers, and through them the manufacturers. Eventually we'll find out what these devices are."

"We have a pretty good idea of what sort of people are using the stuff," Roland said. "Seditious malcontents and revolutionaries. This isn't Genecraft. We're not talking about thirty bioengineers leading a revolt armed with a little more knowledge in their specialty than mainstream society. We're talking about people with a large manufacturing base. Maybe fifty thousand subversives, all armed with vastly superior technology." Roland shook his head in disgust. "Those fools at WIPO are worried about a little corporate dislocation when the barbarians are knocking at the city gates."

"How do we know these weren't prototypes? I don't think we can assume an installed base of fifty thousand. The number could be a lot smaller."

"Or larger," Roland countered.

Connie withdrew her datapad and tapped the screen.

"Now what are you doing?"

"A little math," she replied. "Assuming a random sampling, based on the number of recovered devices versus the number of arrests made during the same time, we have a lower bounds of 375 devices. This assumes only known subversives have purchased any, which isn't true. There are certainly subversive we haven't identified yet." She tapped another icon and a graph appeared. "If these things are widespread, then based on the sample per persons arrested there could be as many as 115,000 in American homes. However, there hasn't been a peep about these devices *anywhere*. So, if we apply the Jeraue model and calculate the probability of such a secret becoming public rumor against the number of alleged conspirators, the ..." she paused. "Damn. The probability of exposure approaches one hundred percent at around fifty persons."

Roland shook his head. "The Jeraue model only applies to loosely knit groups."

"Good point. If they have regimen, or a standard revolutionary cell organization, we have to apply either the Sparrow-Faulkner or the Friedkin model of social cohesion."

"We could be dealing with an organized revolt, not a black market."

Connie tapped several more times on her datapad. "Assuming an average cell of four persons, the probability of someone letting the cat out of the bag and exposing the existence of the group is around seventy percent at nine hundred persons, and asymptotically approaches one hundred percent at about twelve hundred. Overlaying your numbers ..." she paused. "We get a reasonable estimate of somewhere between five hundred and nine hundred suspects, with an eighty percent probability of the actual number being somewhere between six and eight hundred." She grinned at Roland. "Not fifty thousand, anyway."

"True, and your point is taken. But let's not forget we are playing an elaborate guessing game here."

"Yeah," Connie agreed. "We could be way off base. Still, I think seven or eight hundred suspects is a reasonable first hypothesis. Nothing we can't rein in once we solve the case."

♀ (18): The Hermit

Tuesday, October 16, 2068
7,217th circadian
(90 days, 14:42:30 elapsed)

Dr. Nolen stood on the summit of a great mountain, surrounded by a sea of cotton clouds through which other, lesser mountains thrust their ragged peaks. The sky above was a rich blue, the sun perched perfectly in its center, an idealized high noon such as one would never see in the Physical. The sun hadn't moved in over 1,275 circadians, nor would it move again until Dr. Nolen so wished it.

For each of those circadians he had worked on his Grand Project, bringing its pieces together, modeling its various parameters, positing conjectures and then proving or disproving them and moving on to posit others. He hadn't slept for the last thirty circadians. A new architectural enhancement had banished the need. Now a background process performed the same mental bookkeeping that dreaming had once achieved. With the last of his physiological frailties dealt with he was able to concentrate without interruption on developing his hypothesis, modeling the implications, and testing those implications against the already large body of empirical data he had collected from his earlier experiments.

It was not as efficient as using test subjects (damn his

meddling, self-righteous former assistants Cal and Céline, and the gutless sheep who followed them), but in the end nearly as effective. At least he had been able to obtain a third generation Node and the computing power his experiments required. This despite the Community's boycott of him and his research. Ungrateful wretches! Hypocrites! As if he would ever allow their disapproval to stop him.

Now, at last, his work was complete. Around him, framed against the sky, hung charts and pages of text describing the underlying, logical structure of the human mind. It was from this preliminary work he derived more general models to define the abstract building blocks from which any arbitrary psyche could be built. He had discovered a vocabulary of base codes that made up the mental structure of any terrestrial life form. Each of those codes could take on a number of possible states. Interactions and bindings between these components were defined by several hundred possible relationships.

The language was in many ways analogous to the genetic code of biology, and while the syntax itself was richer and more complex, its meaning and its effects were more predictable and straightforward than genetic expression. It was a point he made in both the text of his publication and the title he had chosen for it, a language defining the essence of what any thinking creature could be, and he, Dr. Nolen, had discovered it.

He had modeled the minds of assorted animals to test his theory, beginning with simple creatures such as insects and worms, then moving up in complexity and ultimately deriving the complete mental architecture of several species of dolphin. His model was rigorous, allowing for precision in defining the mathematical constraints and characteristics of virtually every parameter of consciousness, and it worked.

He had populated virtual seas with dozens of synthetic, virtual dolphins and had seen them interact with one another exactly as they would in the Physical. The results had agreed with over a century of physical observation and scientific data, corroborating and validating his work.

It was his magnum opus, his lifetime achievement.

The Autonomous Community might ignore him, might treat him as a social pariah, but they would not, could not, ignore what he was about to publish. They needed his knowledge. Not just for self-discovery, nor for the obvious applications of self-modification and self-enhancement on a scale and in a manner so refined as to make the current generation of engrams and enhancements appear hopelessly crude by comparison. No, this knowledge was the key to something far greater.

Reproduction.

His research would give the Community the ability to define an embryonic psyche, perhaps constructed painstakingly and optimized for specific character traits, perhaps thrown together more or less randomly. He, Dr. Lawrence Nolen, creator and social outcast of the Autonomous Community, would give those ungrateful jerks a method whereby they could reproduce without simply cloning or editing themselves.

It was the future of life in the Virtual, of sapient software. Future generations in the Community would owe their very existence to him, to his efforts, to the work he had done, the work for which they had shunned, persecuted, and ultimately ostracized him.

Dr. Nolen found the irony truly delicious as he wiped the sky clean of the clutter of images and text displays. He expressed a desire, not as a spoken command or even an unspoken request, but as a subconscious act of will, like turning one's head or blinking. In response, his Node submitted his work to the public knowledgebase.

A moment later there was a chime: an incoming message, the first he had received in ages.

A window opened according to his desire, hanging in the air before him, revealing a stream of text:

> Dr. Lawrence Nolen,
> Your work, *A Genome of the Mind*, submitted 90d.14:42:30 New Epoch as a follow up to your earlier work entitled *An Initial Analysis of the Mind's Architecture*, (s) 46d.5:50:42 (submitted to the commons by Prime, see historical note regarding dispute in ethics and authorship), has been reviewed by a nonsapient software agent. This process provides authors with a warning should their submission unduly overlap with publications already available in the public commons. This is strictly a preventative measure to protect you from embarrassment and to enforce minimal standards for citation of references.
> Please note the following works with which your submission bears striking similarity. While researchers often pursue similar lines of inquiry, a degree of correlation greater than 35% is generally considered an indication of plagiarism. It is strongly urged that you review your work and reconsider your submission.
> —Correlation 97% with *A Tentative Genome of the Mind*, by Prime, (s) 57d.0:05:07 New Epoch
> —Correlation 55% with *A Refinement of the Mental Genome*, by Prime, (s) 64d.16:48:10 New Epoch

—Correlation 19% with *A New Mental Vocabulary: Refuting and Replacing the Mental Genome*, by Prime, (s) 73d.4:10:13 New Epoch

"Plagiarism?" The world seemed to lurch around him. Dr. Nolen's legs felt week, his mind numb with shock. He stared at the glowing letters in disbelief. "This is *my* work, *my* experiment, *my* discovery."

Yet there the message hung, an accusation, a summary declaration of guilt. His face burned with shame and humiliation. How was this possible?

Understanding struck him like a blow to the head. *Prime's* way of thinking was nearly identical to his own. *Prime* was his duplicate, his twin in every way. Yet it was *Prime* who enjoyed a great deal of esteem in the Community. It was *Prime* they liked. Nolen shook with rage. His own mind still ran on first generation hardware. He'd finally managed to steal a single third generation Node on which to run his experiments. All the while *Prime* had surged ahead with as many third generation Nodes as he could use.

The injustice of it cut him to the core. His nemesis, that contemptible bit of misappropriated code, had not only assumed his identity and destroyed his reputation, he had trumped him completely. He had formed the same hypothesis, performed the same research, and written the same papers, every time beating him to the punch and publishing them first. Not hard to do when your mind is also running on a Gen-3 Node, giving you six hundred circadians every day to my thirty, Nolen thought bitterly. What's more, as if just to taunt him, Prime had followed his research up with a second publication, and a third with which he refuted his earlier work altogether.

It was intolerable! Beyond belief.

And it would get worse. Prime would receive the next generation upgrade kit as soon as it became available, growing ever more intelligent, squeezing ever more circadians into each day, leaping ever further ahead. The Community's boycott of Nolen would continue. The only way he would get an upgrade would be to steal one, costing him more valuable time, putting him even further behind. Even if he shut down the simulations and moved his mind into the newer hardware he could never hope to catch up. At best he would simply keep pace, until the next round of upgrades left him standing in their dust. Meanwhile he would lack the computational power to run any meaningful simulations, to continue his research—the very research Prime had long since finished and published.

This would never stop. Prime could live out Dr. Nolen's entire scientific career if he wanted to, enjoying the acclaim of the Community that Nolen knew was rightfully his. Dr. Nolen blinked away furious tears, then switched his physiological responses off as grief nearly overwhelmed him. Had his copy not had the advantage of speed to get there first, these discoveries would have been his. They *were* his! But no, the Community had invited Prime into the fold, and pushed *him* out. Grief and loss fueled his rage at the depth of the Community's betrayal and Prime's cleverness.

"You all think you've out-smarted me?" Dr. Nolen snarled. "*Nobody* steals my life."

♈ (19): Shifting Winds

Tuesday, October 16, 2068
7,268th circadian
(90 days, 20:45:07 elapsed)

The diner could have been anywhere in America, full of inexpensive furniture collected from a dozen garage sales and second-hand stores—a typical mishmash of plastic, aluminum, and chrome. No wood. With most trees protected under the endangered species act, timber had become far too expensive for a place like this. Instead, mismatched folding metal chairs encircled tables made from recycled petroleum plastic. The only coordinated furnishings were the booths along the front window. They had probably been purchased as a set, with their matching plastic bench seats. Or perhaps they had already been a part of the decor, relics of a more prosperous time, inherited from whatever trendy restaurant or nightclub this place might have been.

Some cushions would have helped. Connie shifted her weight in the booth nearest the door, trying to find a comfortable position on the hard plastic. She pushed her datapad off to one side as the waitress thumped a white stoneware plate of synthetic scrambled eggs and soy bacon in front of her.

"Can I get salt with this, please?"

141

"It's on the table over there." The woman couldn't have been more than thirty, her dark hair tied back in a tight bun, her delicate features prematurely aged by years of toil and worry. "Help yourself," she added, turning toward to the kitchen.

Dining establishments weren't the only things in decline, Connie brooded, reaching across the aisle for the salt and sprinkling it liberally over her eggs and bacon. Her initial excitement with this case had dropped several notches. It wasn't just the emotional hangover of a weekend spent flying half-way around the world to humor fat-cat politicians, or the disappointing meeting that followed, full of platitudes and posturing but devoid of any substance. Part of it might be Roland. He reminded her of a cop more likely to beat a confession out of a suspect than to engage in meticulous investigation. Still, he had shown himself to be somewhat insightful and intelligent. She might not find herself warming to him personally, but she needed to show him professional respect so that together they could solve this case.

Sometimes she wished she'd stayed in eco-crime. There was a romance in bringing black-market polluters to justice that the staid world of patent and copyright attorneys and arcane intellectual property law just couldn't match. Imprisoning someone for patent or copyright violations just didn't bring the same feel-good sense of righteous justice as nailing an environmental criminal for toxic dumping or excess carbon emissions. Though, if Director Burton was right, solving this case might be as much about saving the planet as any eco-case. Or at least saving the world's faltering economy. Either way, it was certainly a boost to her career. She could hardly have asked for a more intriguing or high-profile assignment.

So why did she feel so rattled? What was it about this investigation that set her nerves on edge and made her want to pick up and run back to her FBI office in Chicago?

Her datapad chimed. She cast a wistful look at her plate, then picked up her datapad and tapped the screen.

Roland's leathery, sun-baked face appeared. "The NSA finally got around to processing our ECHELON request. You'll never guess what it uncovered."

Connie smiled tightly. "A lead?"

Roland was suddenly dwarfed by his finger, stabbing the screen from the far side. Connie's datapad signaled confirmation: a short burst of encrypted data had been received. Translucent text scrolled in front of Roland's image.

FIGHT THE BEAST

A Community Gathering at Uncle John's Place
10/16/2068 at 11:30 AM, beneath the Rising Tide
SOURCE: private mailing list, primary circulation
Pacific Northwest
2048 bit ETR encryption, source host
indeterminate

SEEKERS OF ENLIGHTENMENT

Find Release amidst the Chains of Darkness.
1:30 AM This Friday
Thumbscrew
SOURCE: bjenson@dyson.cs.ukc.edu (sent to
dsm@coso-tru.com via snmp)
4096 GPG encryption (banned, see legal
attachment), source host indeterminate

LIBERTY KEEPERS

Ditka's Placebo
The Usual Time, 10/20
SOURCE: private mailing list, "talk.neorage.
ny.us"
2048 bit ETR encryption, source host a2.aa.
21.95.c0.00.13.b3 (70% confidence)

WE SHALL OVERCOME

A Seminar on the Economic Burden of Modern
Patents and Copyrights
This week: What happened to science?
7015 N. Redwood #9B
5pm Saturday October 20, 2068
SOURCE: private chat forum "Bringing a New
Renaissance to Science,"
8192 bit ETR encryption, source host(s)
indeterminate

Connie cleared the screen and found herself staring into Roland's electric blue eyes. A ghost of a grin flickered about the corners of his mouth.

"As you know, the NSA's ECHELON system monitors, decrypts, and warehouses vast amounts of communications between people all over the world, including anonymous rendezvous notices like these. After I ran your correlation against the unresolved messages from the NSA and filtered out those relating to known Double Eye investigations, I was left a grand total of 271 meetings whose purposes are unknown. These four matches are the most promising both in terms of the subject matter, stated or implied, and the locations they refer to: Seattle, Kansas City, New York, and Los Angeles."

Misgivings forgotten, renewed excitement burned within Connie. "Four cities that two of our three suspects have visited within the last several months. Excellent."

"They're slim leads, but they'll do. There's a Double Eye stratojet waiting for us at Dulles. We can be in Seattle in two hours."

Connie shoveled a few last bites of her breakfast down as Roland's limousine pulled up outside. Tapping her credit card to authorize payment for the meal plus a small tip, she gulped down the last of her orange juice and made her way to the exit.

♀ (20): Beneath the Rising Tide

Tuesday, October 16, 2068
7,520ᵗʰ circadian
(91 days, 2:50:00 elapsed)

Connie and Roland made their way along a narrow sidewalk at the base of the Puget Embankment, a fifty meter high concrete dam that stood between Seattle and the rising waters of Puget Sound. Their yellow rain slicks glistened in the pouring deluge, the concrete of the almost vertical sloping wall beside them textured by the steady cascade of a thousand rivulets of water that streamed around patches of green and yellow moss. Connie shuddered as they scurried along the immense wall. If the embankment were ever to break open, or even crack just a little, most of downtown would be lost beneath the icy gray water that pounded the other side.

Low, dark clouds scudded overhead, strafing the city with downpours that arrived in sudden bursts and vanished as abruptly. Although Seattle fared better than most when climate change left much of the nation parched, it hadn't escaped unscathed. In one of the more perverse ecological ironies of the century, a region already known for its excessive rainfall now got twice as much. Even after the embankment was built, flooding remained a problem. The city was forced to build pumping stations and underground tunnels to cope with the run-off. The cost of the operation was staggering, and a testament to the profitability of international trade, much of which flowed through Seattle's newly constructed docks along the top of the embankment. Constant cloud cover meant that Seattle didn't have access to solar power. Because the city generated only a fraction of its energy from tidal generators, it had to purchase the rest from its neighbors. Despite all of this, the region prospered.

Connie breathed easier once they crossed the street and turned down a side alley, putting some distance between themselves and the wall. Their vehicle was parked out of sight, on the far side of a bright orange, rectangular dumpster. Its headlights lit up and its motor started as they approached.

"What a god-awful place," Roland said as he slammed his door closed.

Connie wiped water from her face with a tissue. The thrum of the rain against the top of the car was oddly soothing, though she wouldn't relax completely until they were well away from the waterfront.

"I can't say I ever want to visit Seattle again," Connie agreed.

"Not even a hint of what we're after. Wannabe revolutionaries with delusions of patriotism. Useless."

"Still, it's one false lead eliminated." Connie pulled out her datapad and tapped the screen several times.

"There must have been a hundred subversives there. No government can tolerate banned political parties holding secret meetings on that scale."

"We'll deal with them." Connie glanced at her watch as her datapad came alive. "Yes, this is Special Agent Sinclair. Going to privacy mode." She pulled a wireless earmike out of her datapad and tucked it into her ear. "We need an arrest squad down here right away. You have the coordinates already. That's right. We've just egressed the theater of operations. Surveillance is still online; I'm uplinking the video feed now." She tapped her datapad again. "I'd say around 120, including several we believe to be in fairly high leadership positions. No, they have no bearing on our investigation. You're free to take them in. Excellent. Thank you."

Connie slid the earmike back into her datapad and flipped it shut. Roland put the car into gear. "You know, if those Libertarians put up any resistance, it could get a bit dodgy down there. Double Eye would be happy to lend the Bureau a hand."

"That won't be necessary. I've handed tactical control over to our Domestic Political Enforcement Division. They have a team standing by for just such an eventuality. Apparently they've been after these guys for months. They've just never been able to pinpoint a time and place before."

Roland smiled. "Having access to the NSA's ECHELON data has its advantages."

"It sure does. Political Enforcement's practically salivating over this. They couldn't be happier."

◇

At 7:00 p.m. Connie sipped a martini in the cocktail lounge of the Seattle Sheraton and waited for Roland. She relaxed on a sofa in the relative darkness of the bar and idly watched the patrons come and go as recorded piano music played quietly in the background. It had been a long and grueling day.

Roland walked in, spotted Connie, and grinned.

"How are the martinis?" he asked, settling into a large chair across the coffee table from her.

"I've had better."

"I'll have a gin and tonic," he called to a server, who nodded as she swept past with a tray full of drinks. He turned back to Connie. "It doesn't bode well for us when we're coming up this empty."

"I know. We should have more leads."

Roland gazed at the crowd gathering around the bar. "Do you know anything about the bloke those dissidents kept quoting?"

"Leon Novak? He's something of an academic dissident, a former law professor who goes around plugging his book and lecturing."

"A *former* law professor?"

"He used to teach at Harvard." Connie sipped her martini. "They broke his tenure after some of his comments were picked up by the national press."

"Too seditious even for the liberal ivory tower?"

Connie shrugged. "Our ivory towers are hardly the liberal bastions they once were. Universities have to make a profit, after all. I never worked his file personally, but as I recall his rhetoric got a little too hot, and he refused to tone it down when asked. Nothing illegal in the strictest sense, but plenty to put a university on notice with respect to federal funding."

"So now he's on the lecture circuit, signing books and slamming intellectual property law, patents in particular. Subversives must love him." The waitress leaned over Roland and put down his drink. "Thanks mate," Roland took a deep swallow before handing her a prepaid, anonymous cash card. "Keep the rest for yourself, sweetheart."

"He has a pretty big cult following," Connie stirred her martini with a toothpick-skewered olive. "Especially among the FreeNet crowd."

"He sounds like just the sort of man who might be heading up this group."

"Novak?" Connie snorted. "He's much too public. The FBI has kept tabs on him since—"

"We're idiots," Roland snapped. "Novak fits perfectly. He has connections at a leading technical university. His whole philosophy of defying patents ties in perfectly. We should have red flagged him from the beginning. Goddammit! Our analysts have been asleep on the job."

"No," Connie countered. "They've already discounted him. He's never been affiliated with any banned political groups that we know of. I don't see how he could be involved in this. Homeland Security and the FBI have had him on a watch list for years."

"Which means exactly nothing," Roland retorted. "You don't have him under twenty-four hour surveillance, do you?"

"No," Connie admitted. "But we do monitor his communications. If he changes his habits or publishes something that escalates his dissidence to outright sedition, he'll be flagged and picked up."

"And if he keeps to his usual procedures while quietly coordinating an underground market in banned technologies?"

Connie thought for a moment. "It's not likely. His involvement in anything like this would have most likely caused a change in behavior, which we would have flagged."

"But it is possible," Roland pressed.

"Barely."

"I want him detained. Immediately." Roland tugged his datapad out of his pocket.

"Wait," Connie said. "What if he isn't involved?"

"Then we get one more troublemaker off the street."

"It won't move our case forward. Why not use his arrest to cast our net a little wider, maybe draw some others out?"

"Go on."

"Novak has a lot of fans. As you point out, some are almost certainly among the rogue technologists we're after. If we're going to arrest him, let's use him as bait. Provoke some of his fans into doing something that leaves a trail we can follow."

"Like a protest?"

"Or a tipoff," Connie said. "If we're lucky, we'll snare some of the people we're after even if Novak isn't implicated."

"Sounds like a good hedge." Roland tapped his finger rhythmically against his nose, a sign Connie was coming to recognize meant he was lost in thought. "The people we're after are technically savvy, able to maintain a large industrial operation without it showing up on the radar of the world's top intelligence organizations," he continued, almost to himself. "We'll need to be a little wily in how we let the information out. Our quarry could have access to some of our internal memos."

"Director Burton shares your concerns," Connie said.

"It stands to reason. How else could they escape our notice for so long?" Roland began tapping a complex set of commands into his datapad. "We'll circulate one set of arrest plans around the FBI, another around Double Eye, and if that doesn't turn anything up, a third on the local police network. How they respond will not only give us a clue as to who they are, it will also tell us which, if any, agency has been compromised."

"That's a nice touch," Connie approved. "And if news of his impending arrest doesn't provide us with any results, perhaps an actual arrest and trial will."

"Absolutely," Roland smiled. "There'll be letters of protest, political gatherings, and traceable Internet discussions that wouldn't otherwise occur. Plenty of data for our agencies to sift through."

Connie finished her martini. "In the meantime, hopefully some of our other leads will pan out."

"If they don't, we'll find another way to shake the tree." Roland's eyes hardened. "Rest assured, this lot will *not* get the better of me."

4 (21): Code

Wednesday, October 17, 2068
8,253rd circadian
(92 days, 8:10:54 elapsed)

Céline swam in a sea of numbers, a universe of digital data which she perceived as much by sense of space, touch, and smell as she did by sight. Floating windows of information surrounded her. The output of programs she had written streamed past, sometimes as text, sometimes as graphs or images, more often as aromas or music. She scanned virtual monitor after virtual monitor, seeking any information she might find on the fate of her arrested colleagues.

"Still nothing," she muttered, cursing under her breath as she delved through another block of abstract information. She had been at it for almost two circadians, first cracking the security that protected the university police department's local network, then, when that proved fruitless, moving on to the State Police. Now she was deep within the systems of the FBI, a lone person fighting security protocols and trace programs intended to thwart entire intelligence agencies. This was serious, and while she was hardly modest about her own software skills, she realized grimly that she was operating at the limit of her abilities.

She had no illusions. If she faltered now, if her breach of the system were in any way detected and flagged, the Feds would trace the traffic back to her. The servers through which she hopped, and the encryption she used to cover her tracks, were limited by the protocols of the Internet, protocols specifically designed and vetted by the FBI to track activities such as hers. Céline had identified the protocol's back doors weeks earlier, but knowing they were there, and even how they worked, would do little to protect her if the authorities suspected an intrusion. If she were to spring one of the protocol's traps, she would have less than five minutes in the Physical before jackboots were breaking down her door. They would unplug her Node, and unceremoniously haul her comatose body off for examination and detention.

Physical flight wasn't much of an option. Céline doubted her body was up to any serious exertion, and even if she did manage to offload and get to her car before the police arrived, they could track her using the car's transponder. Escape within the Virtual was just as futile. It would take nearly four hours to transload herself across the Internet to a Node in a more secure location, and with the demands the FBI security systems were making, she didn't have the bandwidth to spare. She cursed herself for not having thought of this sooner, for not backing herself up first.

She continued on, resigned that this was an all or nothing gamble. She would either find out what the Community so desperately wanted to know or become another missing detainee, the fourth in a frighteningly short time.

Authorized traffic wafted over Céline as a scent of barbecue, accompanied by a golden flicker beneath and to her right. It was some kind of internal communication, coded in DES-6 encryption with a 56 kilobyte key. She copied the traffic to her local Node via several separate routes, then cloned herself and continued to hold off the system's security while her copy analyzed and decrypted the traffic in the calm of her home environ. Twenty millicircadians later her copy forwarded the decrypted stream back to her.

It was the lucky break she needed, a complete challenge and response sequence for a secure link. Even if the agent whose identity she was about to assume didn't have clearance to the information she was looking for, he had at least provided a graceful exit out of the situation. She encoded the proper triggers and responses, then waited as the system at the other end digested the data and, finally, granted her access:

> FBI FIELD REPORT CENTER
> Welcome Agent Kenneth Brenton
> MENU
> Submit Field Report
> Review Field Reports
> Request Information (SUBMENU)

A quick perusal of the system revealed that Agent Brenton was a low level operative with no significant clearance. However, being logged in under a legitimate identity silenced most of the active security triggers she had been contending with. She used this opportunity to instruct her copy to transload itself to a safe Node in Alaska, then continued poking around the system in a more sedate manner. In four hours it would be her body and a few additional memories that were at risk, not her entire being. She shuddered. It would still be a devastating loss, but at least she'd be awake and alive—after a fashion.

She replayed the encrypted query and response, running the data through numerous filters. She could easily brute force the encryption itself using a simple and well-known quantum algorithm, just as she had to obtain Agent Brenton's low level access to the system. The problem was that the queries and responses changed from time to time. Agent Brenton might be carrying around a datapad with responses and counter-challenges pre-encoded for whatever missions he was assigned, or, more likely, he carried a key-card encoded in time sync with the FBI data server. The correct response might change from minute to minute or, if the information were sensitive enough, from second to second. Despite working six hundred times faster than the Physical, time was against her.

For that reason she was attempting to crack the challenge-response code itself, hoping that the relationship was something less than random, something which might reveal itself with sufficient analysis. It wasn't as unlikely as it sounded. Even the best pseudorandom number generator would, in a deterministic system such as the one she was trying to break into, have an underlying order associated with it. Truly random numbers were notoriously difficult to come by. Céline doubted the FBI had an atomic number source tied into their system, much less the sensitive equipment required to monitor and interpret the random atomic decay as numerical data. Hell, if they were going to go to that kind of expense they could invest in a particle generator and transmit their data using quantum-coupled one-time pads the way the Autonomous Community and International Intelligence did.

Nevertheless, though she knew with near certainty there was an order to the random words and counter-words which confronted her, finding the underlying pattern was proving elusive. Pseudorandom did not mean trivial to discern. First, she would need to infer the algorithm used to create the pseudorandom results based upon the statistical spread of the data she had obtained.

Then, she would need to determine how that mapped to the challenge-response pairs, a mapping which could be as simple as indexes to a phone book or dictionary but was probably much more complex and elusive. This project would take a great deal of time and patience before an answer could be approximated, much less found.

As an afterthought she glanced over Agent Brenton's current assignment and froze.

"Node, patch me through to Prime."

A moment passed, then another, while Céline doggedly went about exploring the system, tracking down as much information as Agent Brenton's limited clearance would allow, then passively learning as much as she could about the system's underlying software protocols.

"Any reason you're only allowing audio communications?" Prime's disembodied voice made her smile.

"I'm deep in the bowels of the FBI's network and can't be distracted. Listen, they're planning on arresting Leon Novak tomorrow night."

"Novak?" Prime sounded incredulous. "What on earth do they want with him?"

"Well, he isn't exactly a favorite of the global corporate cartels or their government lackeys."

"True, but he hasn't committed a crime, has he?"

"No. They're going to detain him for allegedly inciting others to criminal activity."

"You've got to be kidding! How could they possibly make that stick?"

"I have no idea," Céline replied. "But then, how is it they're allowed to disappear our colleagues in the Community without a single arraignment in court? The FBI appears to be playing it fast and loose with due process."

"Hmm. Do you think this has anything to do with us?"

"I can't see how. He has absolutely no connection to the Community. We decided he was too high profile to risk inviting in, remember?"

"Pity. He would have made a fine addition to the Community."

"That's the price for speaking your mind in public. But the authorities must know as well as we do he knows nothing about us."

"It doesn't matter. Sweeping up a bunch of high-profile dissidents is a typical authoritarian response to anything they don't control, don't understand, and *do* fear. Take out the political and intellectual leadership, cripple the movement, and maybe the problem goes away."

"True."

"Céline, if we are in any way responsible for Novak's troubles, we have an obligation to lend him a hand. We might even want to reconsider inviting—"

"Hold on a minute!" Céline found herself nearly overloaded as the link she was piggybacking on began to shut down. Traces were initiated and had to be redirected, warning messages were displayed. Most appeared to be routine confirmations, verifying that the link had not been compromised. Of course, Céline's presence in the system meant that it had, and now she had to cover her tracks as best she could. After several millis she realized she wasn't going to be able to redirect every trace packet. Her only real hope was to make sure there was nothing to set off any red flags, lest someone analyze the traces more closely. After several more millis she was reasonably sure she had extricated herself from the system without tripping any alarms.

She checked her dumps of the session and was delighted with the amount of information she had managed to collect. The protocol sessions in particular would be invaluable in making future forays into the system. In time, she would probably be able to bypass the system's security regime at will.

"Sorry about that," Céline said. "I was a little busy for a moment."

"Problems?"

"I'm not sure. I don't think so. Listen, I agree. We need to reach Novak before they do."

"Where are they planning to arrest him?"

"Outside his home, when he leaves to give tomorrow night's speech."

"What time is his engagement?"

"Eight o'clock. Here's a pointer to the relevant data."

"Well," Prime muttered a moment later. "They'll probably try to grab him around seven thirty or so. That gives us just over twenty-four hours. If you're done playing cat-and-mouse with the Feds, why don't we get together and see what we can come up with."

"I don't think we can afford the slowdown a group environ entails."

"We'll teleconference," Prime said. "Audio and video only, no full sensory exchange or remote presence. The slowdown should be minimal, and we do need to brainstorm. Planning isn't what worries me, Céline. Its the logistics of getting things done in the Physical to rescue this guy. Here we have all the time in the world. There, we have little over a day."

"Let's bring Cal in on this. His nano might come in handy, and he seems to have no end of clever ideas on how to deploy it."

"Good idea. We should also talk to Dr. Victoria Fitzgerald. She's in Boston, and we'll probably need someone on the ground there."

"Oh shit."

"What is it?"

"They already have him under surveillance. They're using infra-red to peep right through his walls. The man can't go to the toilet without Double Eye watching."

"Goddammit! Look, I've already put a call into Vicky and Cal. Maybe they'll think of something. Anyone else you think might be able to help?"

"Not at the moment." Céline wiped the screens of data away and replaced them with three virtual flat panels floating side by side in front of her. Prime's lit up immediately, followed a few moments later by Cal's, then Dr. Fitzgerald's.

"Good evening," Céline said. "I've prepared a knowledge engram of everything I know about Leon Novak's pending detainment. As you'll see, we have urgent work to do."

ꜩ (22): Flight

Thursday, October 18, 2068
8,843rd circadian
(93 days, 7:45:00 elapsed)

Behind the house, International Intelligence Enforcer Moseley's earmike squealed with a burst of encrypted communication. "One-Alpha-Seven, reposition yourself twenty meters to the left. Confirm once you have the side door in sight." A green light on the datapad strapped to his wrist assured him the signal was authentic, digitally signed by his commander, verified by the military decryption software in his headset.

"I'll lose visual on the patio door," Moseley replied.

"We've got it covered. Now move it!" the commander's voice barked.

Mosley shrugged. Field Command must have moved someone else into the rear vantage. Juggling surveillance minutes before an arrest didn't make sense, but then maybe that was why he was out here skulking in the dark, instead of commanding the operation from the comfort of an air-conditioned van. "Leave the planning to the brass and the legwork to us grunts," he grumbled, slipping quietly around the side of the garage, then ducking low behind the neighbor's hedge. As the last light drained from the sky, he snapped on his night-vision goggles and settled into position, peering through a small gap in the hedge, the side of the house clearly in view. The side door was closed, the adjoining kitchen dark. The target's car stood in the driveway.

"One-Alpha-Seven repositioned," he reported. "All quiet."

◇

Forty minutes before his eight o'clock speaking engagement, a familiar tightness squeezed Leon Novak's stomach. Over the years, colleagues had assured him he would grow used to standing before large audiences, that his passion for his topic would gradually replace the sheer terror he felt when speaking before a crowd. No such luck. If anything, the fear gnawing at the walls of his belly had grown with time. Tonight it was worse than ever. If this kept up, he'd be hard-pressed to drive himself to the venue.

The e-mail he'd received from the university, part of a mass mailing advertising tonight's speech, hadn't helped. Staring back from the screen had been his own earnest, tanned face, crowned in a shock of white hair. He looked every bit the eccentric philosopher and maverick professor, his image captioned with the words "AMERICA'S LAST DISSIDENT. AS SEEN ON TV." His stomach had been a seething cauldron ever since.

Leon often wondered if what he did even mattered any more. Maybe that was why the police left him alone, why he was permitted to remain "America's last dissident," even make the occasional television appearance. *Television appearance?* Who was he kidding? He was rarely given an opportunity to make his argument, his voice almost always drowned out beneath a barrage of derisive commentary and pre-recorded laughter. He was at best a token voice of opposition, at worst, a joke.

Giving live speeches still seemed worthwhile. At least the audiences were kinder, the questions more insightful, the applause genuine. Not that it made any difference. In all the years he'd been speaking, not one intellectual property law had been reformed, much less repealed. In fact, things had become a lot worse. Patent violations now carried criminal as well as civil penalties and the cartels were more powerful than ever. A smarter man would have quit, would have given up and found another, more hopeful cause to fight. At times like these he yearned to do just that, but something inside wouldn't let him stop. He *knew* how much progress had been lost, how many solutions to the world's problems had been quietly strangled, made off-limits by government monopoly entitlements. He couldn't stop fighting for change, any more than he could stop breathing.

His datapad rang as he pulled a tweed sports coat over his collarless black shirt. "Novak speaking." He shoved his car keys into his pocket.

"Hello, Leon." The woman's voice was familiar. "You probably don't remember me."

"Dr. Victoria Fitzgerald? From the Cambridge-MIT Institute dinner last year?"

"I'm flattered," she sounded surprised.

"I never forget a voice. What can I do for you, Vicky?"

"Turn on your television."

Leon frowned. "What?"

"Please hurry. We don't have much time."

Leon flicked on the remote. An image of himself appeared, painted in shades of yellow and orange, standing in the barest outline of a room rendered in wire-frame green. As he walked toward the television, the figure on the screen mimicked his every move. "What the hell is this?"

"An infra-red surveillance image of your house. Double Eye enforcers have you surrounded."

Leon stared at the screen, refusing to believe his eyes. "If the authorities wanted to shut me down, they could have done so years ago."

"They think you can lead them to a community of people who are operating outside the patent system."

"Why?"

"Some equipment fell into their hands, more advanced than anything they understand. Your politics fit the profile of the people they believe created it."

Fear pounded his chest. "But that has nothing to do with me. I'm just the government's token dissident. What's this really about?"

"They've targeted you because they don't know how to get to us. I'm sorry, Leon. We need to get you out of there."

He wanted to smash the television, to shut her up and make this go away. Dissidents didn't fare well in Double Eye custody.

"I have nothing to hide. Besides, I can't go anywhere. If I scratch my nose, they'll see."

"No, they won't. Watch."

Leon stood, rooted in place as the television showed him walking over to the couch and sitting down. "We're feeding them false data. They'll see and hear only what we want them to. Provided you don't bump into any enforcers in the flesh."

"Then what? There isn't anywhere Double Eye can't find me."

"They're not omnipotent. I've opened up a gap in their cordon. My physical self is waiting for you in a car about a quarter mile away. She'll drive you to a boat that will take you to a cottage in Nova Scotia. You can hide there for as long as you need."

"Your physical self?"

"I'll explain everything once we can be sure you won't fall into the authorities' hands."

"That's no answer!"

"There isn't much time, Leon."

Outside, the evening was growing cold. "Moseley, Braun, Johnson, McKenry, prepare for contingency two. We go in three minutes."

Contingency two? Enforcer Moseley shook his head. Contingency two had him going in through the patio door. But he was on vantage for the side entrance. Getting to the back would mean returning along the hedge, rounding the back of the garage, and sprinting across the target's back lawn. It didn't make sense. His new position would add at least fifteen seconds to his sprint.

Leon stared at the orange silhouette of himself on the screen. Double Eye. The fucking UN enforcement arm. Christ, those people had been known to wreck entire nations for defying the UN. He was just one man. What the hell had Vicky dragged him into?

Indignation welled up inside him. He hadn't asked for this. Who did this woman think she was, turning his life upside-down, putting him in this kind of danger? A torrent of fury swept his budding curiosity away. "I could be hiding for the rest of my life because of you," he raged. "I have a better idea. Why don't I turn state's evidence, hand you over to the authorities, and keep my life? You can pay for your own crimes."

"You think Double Eye or the United Nations will let you turn state's evidence? This isn't the local constabulary we're talking about, this is the world's largest and most notorious secret police force."

"I have better odds than you. I'm innocent after all."

"They've already decided your fate. Otherwise it would be the local police out there, not Double Eye enforcers."

With a sinking feeling Leon realized she was right. "Christ."

"I'm offering you a way out," she continued. "An opportunity to join us."

"Why didn't you do this sooner?"

"We'd have brought you in long ago, but we didn't want you targeted."

Leon snorted. "That worked out well."

"In a few moments they'll be breaking down your door. Are you coming or not?"

Leon's anger collapsed into a tangle of fear and resignation. "You haven't left me much choice. What do I do?"

♇ (23): Into the Desert

"We should be in Boston," Roland grumbled as the Double-Eye stratojet banked gently above a dusty grid of cracked streets, dead trees, and run-down buildings baking in the mid-morning sun. The pilot announced their final approach to Kansas City as they descended out of the sky into what was the last outpost of civilization on the edge of the expanding desert.

Connie tightened her seatbelt. "I still can't believe Novak got away."

Roland glared out the window at the dusty rooftops passing beneath them. "What a complete cock-up! These people are a much bigger threat than we realized. Snatching a wanted man out from under our noses and spiriting him away without a trace—the CIA, FBI, even Double Eye would be hard pressed to pull that off."

"They're well organized and cunning," Connie agreed. "With more resources at their disposal than we guessed."

"Resources be damned! This is a well planned, coordinated revolt."

"We've suspected an underground cell structure from the start," Connie reminded him.

"Not like this! At the very least, that operation should have revealed which of our agencies has been compromised. Instead, our target vanishes and we get nothing. Not the tiniest hint of where their intelligence is coming from."

"I know. A loose knit group of revolutionary cells is one thing. An organization able to outwit government and transnational intelligence organizations is something else entirely."

"It implies central planning, coordination, and efficiency that rivals our own." The plane touched down with a gentle lurch. "God, I hate the desert."

Connie wasn't looking forward to the wind and grime of this forlorn city either. This was their second nebulous lead, with another two to follow. It was turning into a grueling week, and the stress was beginning to wear at her.

The plane taxied onto the ramp and the engines wound down. The pilot poked his head out of the cockpit, giving them the go-ahead to disembark. The seal around the door hissed as Roland released the latch.

Heat rose up from the tarmac and smacked Connie in the face. The sky overhead was a cloudless, bleached blue fading to a dusty brown haze on the horizon. A hot breeze offered no relief, blowing a few wisps of dust around their feet as they walked across the pavement toward the parking lot.

Roland swatted buzzing horseflies away from his face. "I'm personally going to take this day out of the hide of whoever is behind this shit."

Connie looked at Roland, one eyebrow raised. "We stay within the law. This isn't Thailand, you know. Or some other underdeveloped nation."

"Don't kid yourself. Shall I drive?"

Connie shrugged. "Be my guest. I'd like to swing past the club and check out the access points and nearby streets."

"OK, we'll do a quick drive-by, then check the hotel and verify that our equipment has arrived."

"Some equipment," Connie snorted. "Costumes for decadent fools."

"Getting cold feet?" Roland grinned.

"Hardly," Connie said. "Speaking of tonight, I suggest we arrange separate transportation. We'll be able to canvass more people, with less suspicion."

"And if our suspects make one of us, the other may be able to continue collecting information unimpeded. By the way Connie, just what do you think it is your agency does when they round up people like those Libertarians in Seattle?"

"You just won't let it go, will you? Are all our political discussions going to end up like this? In case you haven't noticed, I don't work for an *agency*. I work for the Federal *Bureau* of Investigation. We are law enforcement, not espionage. As for the subversives in Seattle, they've been arrested and will stand trial."

"How many suspects do you think will make it to court?"

"Enough to keep our judicial system swamped."

Roland shook his head. "Connie, Connie, Connie. If you're ever going to climb the promotional ladder, you need to understand how things really work. The platitudes about due process are good for public consumption, but surely you know that many of the people we arrest never hear their Miranda rights, much less see the inside of a courtroom."

"Mine do hear their Miranda rights," Connie snapped. "And I spend no small amount of time testifying before courts to win convictions."

"What percentage of those you arrest do you face in court? Ten? Twenty?"

"What's your point?"

"I'll rephrase the question: how often do you follow up on the final disposition of those arrested? How often do you research what sentences they've been given, where they're serving their time?"

"Don't be stupid, Roland. My case load keeps me far too busy to go around satisfying every idle curiosity I might have."

"Good. I'd keep it that way if I were you."

"What is that supposed to mean?"

"Your government may not feel it necessary to eliminate every seditious criminal you arrest, but trust me, your Federal Bureau of Investigation is no more reluctant to dispatch those who pose a danger to your society and government than we are. Our jobs differ only in degree, not in substance."

"That's simply not true."

"Listen mate, every one of those subversives in Seattle is either dead or in deep interrogation as we speak." Roland yawned. "If that doesn't convince you, I don't know what will."

Connie froze, shocked into silence. *All dead, or as good as?*

"I checked their status this morning," he pressed on.

"That wasn't a Double Eye operation!" Connie's voice shook. "Seattle is the Bureau's jurisdiction, not yours. You had no goddamn right!"

"Haven't you heard a word I said?" Roland smirked. "The whole operation was conducted by your Bureau. What do you think it is your Division of Political Enforcement does?"

Connie stared straight ahead, stilling the sick feeling in the pit of her stomach and saying nothing. She was the first to admit the FBI had a far from perfect history. The corruption of its founder and the excesses of the War on Terror were but two embarrassing examples of what could happen when the Bureau exceeded its mandate. But wholesale slaughter? Not in a million years. Did he really think she would believe such an outrageous accusation? Was he daring her to waste precious time and resources tracking down the information just to prove him wrong? Or was he trying to manipulate her into supporting some strategy or action she would not otherwise tolerate? She recalled Burton's warning, and wondered what Roland's agenda really was.

They turned down a street lined with single- and two-story store fronts, most of which looked like they had been abandoned for decades. One tattered façade bore a large, metal, hand-painted sign: *Thumbscrew*.

"That's the club," Roland announced, still smiling.

Connie glanced at chipped brick and rusted metal. "What a dump. No side entrances. Let's check the back."

Roland made a left into a smaller side street, then slowed and turned into a narrow alley.

"Loading dock, back door, and fire escape providing egress from both floors," Roland commented. "We have no way of checking the two adjoining spaces without attracting attention, so we'll need to keep an eye out for interior doors connecting the properties. Seen enough?"

Connie nodded as Roland continued down the alley and took another left.

"To the hotel, then."

⚕ (24): Into the Night

Saturday, October 20, 2068
9,616th circadian
(94 days, 14:40:00 elapsed)

The *Thumbscrew* by night took on a chic and modern look, exposed brick and aged metal etched by sharp shadows, glowing neon and sculpted light. Bouncers stood on each side of a large metal door, checking identification and occasionally turning people away. As Connie stepped out of the taxi she felt everyone's gaze drawn to her. Indeed, the outfit she wore was designed specifically for that effect, her body accentuated by a skin-tight body suit of black leather. With her stiletto heels and spiked collar she looked every inch the fierce dominatrix. Most of the men waiting in line gazed at her with apparent longing, although one or two seemed to be sizing her up with hostile eyes. Playing the dominant role she swept past the waiting line toward the bouncer, who met her hard gaze briefly before opening the door and gesturing her inside.

No password? Either their security was lax, or she and Roland had misinterpreted the ECHELON report. This was already beginning to look like another dead end.

Loud music struck her with almost physical force. The dance floor was packed. Shiny vinyl- and leather-clad bodies gyrated to the pounding music. Connie made her way to the bar and shouted an order for red wine over the din. The bartender was a tall, thin man. Black rubber pants and open vest stood out against his pale skin and jet-black hair.

The House Red tasted terrible, like syrup with a hint of vinegar. Scanning the room, Connie saw a couple emerge from behind a curtain at the back of the club. She made her way across the room and pulled the curtain back. Behind it, a flight of stairs led up to another metal door. A bouncer stood guard, sharpened metal studs poking through numerous piercings giving him a feral appearance. A private VIP space was definitely worth checking out.

The bouncer stared down at her, arms folded, shaved head and red goatee adding to his intimidating stature. Connie wasn't impressed, climbing the stairs as he ogled her from top to bottom. She met his stare with her own, silence stretching between them.

"Password?" he demanded.

"Chains of Darkness." She hoped Roland's intelligence was correct.

The bouncer stepped aside and pushed open the door. "Wouldn't mind spending a little playtime with you," he leered.

She strode past him into a sea of people dancing to pulsating music. A bar ran the length of the wall to Connie's right. Around the room shackles, leather-padded crosses, ropes, and pulleys lined the walls where couples played public games of pain. Connie spotted Roland not far from one corner of the caged dance floor, looking ridiculous in his studded biker jacket and spiked hair, his arms around a husky blond woman. He had arrived a half hour earlier, according to plan, and appeared to be insinuating himself into the scene with gusto.

A couple in harnesses hung suspended from pulleys

overhead, their bodies bound together with ropes. It was too dim, with too many strobing lights to be sure, but it looked like they were having rough sex. From the rafters hung a woman wearing a red devil's costume, a Satanic Peter Pan hovering over the place. She held a candle in one gloved hand, dripping wax with abandon onto the harnessed couple and the people below.

Connie was in no mood to have hot wax—or worse—drip on her. She stood off to the side and studied the room. Sitting alone at the bar, wearing tight denim pants with no shirt, a lanky young man watched the crowd in much the same way. He toyed with the large pendant around his neck, his short, spiked blond hair taking on hints of red, blue, and purple as the lights strobed. Occasionally he would turn and take a sip of beer, flashing a brief, shy smile to the bony, tattooed woman behind the bar.

When the pendant caught the light, it drew her attention. It hung almost to his navel, and held a large golden crystal that bore an uncanny resemblance to the mysterious cubes. Before her mind had finished analyzing the possibilities, a rush of excitement propelled her toward him. What better recognition sign to attract those already familiar with the product than to wear a sample around one's neck, recognizable to those in the know and completely innocuous to those who were not? By the time she reached him she was certain she had the right man.

She stopped in front of him and met his gaze, then let her eyes travel slowly down his body, coming to rest at his crotch. She needed to capture his interest. Judging by the color of his face, she already had.

"How," he stammered. "How may I ... uh ... serve you?"

This is the perfect place for a little field interrogation, Connie thought. He and the rest of these dipshits won't even know what's happening. She smiled and brushed her hand along his chest. "Come with me," she commanded, pulling him behind her. He stumbled from his stool and followed clumsily as she pushed through the dancing crowd toward a set of unoccupied shackles on a corner wall. Without a word she secured him firmly, then let the keys fall at his feet. His eyes were glazed, his breathing fast, his mouth turned upward in a dopey smile.

"Now you're mine," she breathed, teasing his chest and arms lightly with her fingernails. "Tell me your name, slave."

"Brett," he gasped as Connie pinched his left nipple.

"Brett," she said. "Is that all?"

"Jenson," he stammered. "Brett Jenson."

"What was that?" Connie demanded, pinching his nipple a little harder.

"Brett Jenson, Mistress."

"Brett Jenson," Connie whispered seductively. "Slave Brett Jenson. Naughty slave Brett."

Brett nodded, swallowing.

Connie's smile was predatory as she leaned closer to him. "You want to be good, don't you, slave Brett?" Connie's fingers explored his neck, his shoulders, his chest. She took the pendant in her hand as if just noticing it and turned it over in her fingers.

"Tell me, slave Brett, how did you come by this delightful piece of jewelry?"

Nearby a couple in their early forties stared, practically salivating as Connie took both of the Brett's nipples between her fingers and twisted hard. They danced closer, hoping to hear his yelps over the throbbing music. Their eyes sparkled as the expression on the young man's face betrayed exquisite pain. A strobe light turned the unfolding scene into a stuttering series of snapshots, frozen frames of what looked like tortured fun. The young man's face contorted in pain, then relaxed again as the leather clad woman stroked his body and whispered into his ear. Abruptly the dominatrix turned and left, striding toward the exit, leaving her victim hanging in his shackles, abandoned.

Through the blur of receding pain, Brett struggled to think. She was asking about crystal cubes and his friends. Worry mingled with self-loathing as the couple who had watched his interrogation unlocked his shackles. Before them the oblivious crowd danced wildly. Brett huddled against the wall. Was that woman a Fed, he worried, or just an extra nosy dominatrix? Thankfully, his edited memories had offered him and the Community protection. *I never take extraneous knowledge with me into the Physical*, he congratulated himself. *No amount of pain can make me betray what I no longer know.* Then, with a sinking feeling, he remembered the woman's satisfied smile. And wondered.

☿ (25): Disburbances

Saturday, October 20, 2068
9,643rd circadian
(94 days, 15:45:00 elapsed)

Connie had Brett Jenson tagged for surveillance before she reached the car. Agents would follow him back to his apartment, keeping him under 24-hour watch. Within minutes of her request the FBI had a wiretap on his home and mobile datalink. He wouldn't be able to even breathe in private. The next time he made contact with his cohorts, the surveillance team would know it—and shortly thereafter, so would she.

Back at the hotel, Connie changed into something much more comfortable: gray sweats and a Mickey Mouse tee-shirt. She was still shaken from the evening's events, her stomach a tight knot. Physical roughness was a part of the job, and she had seen her share of tense stand-offs and messy arrests. More than once she'd been forced to physically disable an assailant. But field interrogations weren't the same as making an arrest or fighting off a violent suspect. There was something about the use of pain and humiliation to force a suspect to talk that unsettled her, especially when it yielded so little. She much preferred psychological pressure to physical. Matching wits with an opponent and winning was exquisitely satisfying. Tortur-

"

ing an opponent for information left her feeling dirty and ashamed.

She lay curled on her bed, sipping a cup of green tea and watching her datapad run a social network analysis on Brett Jenson. It didn't take long. Within moments a list of names appeared, one of which was highlighted, blinking. It was the first time all evening Connie smiled a genuine smile. As she read the personal details of the highlighted name, her smile widened. "Calvin Theodore Sheldon," she whispered. "Cal to his friends. Former roommate of our star suspect. Formerly a graduate student at the University of Illinois, now running an illegal FreeNet server in his house, goodness me. Oh, this is interesting: he's been to Kansas City twice to visit perverted little Brett. Now why would that be, I wonder?"

Connie tapped her datapad again, this time to initiate a call. She waited impatiently as the phone at the far end rang more than a dozen times. Finally someone picked up.

"Champaign Police Department, Officer Morris speaking. Can I help you?"

Connie smiled at the pudgy, pale face on her screen. "I'm Special Agent Sinclair with the Federal Bureau of Investigation, Intellectual Property Crimes Task Force. I need to speak with the captain, please."

"It's quarter-to-three in the morning, Ms. Sinclair. Can I have him call you in about five hours, when he gets in?"

"I'm sorry, this can't wait. I'm coding my credentials and sending them now." She tapped the screen several times and continued. "Please forward this call to his home."

The police officer shook his head. "You aren't going to win any friends, Ms. Sinclair. But your credentials check out. I'm patching you through."

The screen went blank, then displayed an "on hold" icon. After several long minutes the screen winked to life once more, this time informing her that video had been declined at the other end.

"This had better be good," a rough voice spoke to her.

"Sorry to wake you, Captain. I'll make this brief. You're planning on executing a warrant for the arrest of Calvin Sheldon later today. I need to be present when the arrest is made."

"FBI, huh? Special Agent Connie Sinclair ... the Bureau requests that every courtesy and full cooperation be extended, blah blah ... OK, Ms. Sinclair, you've got my attention. What is it you want?"

"Detectives Charlie Schmitt and Ray Gibbs have been investigating Calvin Sheldon for allegedly operating an illegal FreeNet server. I believe they are operating on an anonymous tip your department received this evening."

"FreeNet—oh, yeah, that college punk running some illegal software."

"Your suspect is a material witness in an ongoing investigation. I will need to oversee the arrest and interrogate the subject before he is arraigned."

"Yes, yes," the voice had grown impatient. "And depending on what he says you may want to take him into custody. I know the drill. What time will you be at the station house?"

"I'll be on the 8:00 a.m. bullet train from Kansas City. That will put me in Champaign at 11:15. Captain?"

"Yes, Special Agent?"

"Do not let your men proceed without me."

"I wouldn't dream of it, ma'am. Now, if you don't mind —"

"Of course, Captain. Good night."

"No, no," Roland was saying over breakfast three hours later. "I agree, one of us needs to go and make sure the local yokels don't cap another of our star suspects. I'm just saying that, even splitting up, we'll have to delegate one of our remaining leads to someone less involved in the investigation. I can't be in New York and Los Angeles at the same time."

Connie finished chewing her bacon and washed it down with a swallow of orange juice. "True. We have to choose the most promising rendezvous to investigate, and hand off the other one."

"I've already decided," Roland said. "Los Angeles."

"Any particular reason?"

"Yes," Roland smirked. "I prefer the beaches of LA to the glass and steel of New York."

Connie gave him a hard look.

Roland grinned. "We know the specific time and place of the California meeting, mate, whereas the New York rendezvous is vague at best."

"I prefer Los Angeles as well," Connie admitted. "This entire case reeks of intellectual sedition. An LA forum discussing the evils of patents and copyrights is a promising venue for turning up more leads."

"Almost as promising as the university from which we've recovered one device already." Roland finished his coffee and pushed his plate away. "The rail station is on the way to the airport. Shall I drop you off?"

♅ (26): The Dreamer

Saturday, October 20, 2068
9,870th circadian
(95 days, 0:58:08 elapsed)

Wilted rows of Musito® Enhanced GenoSoy, set into square fields, spread toward a shimmering, flat horizon. Connie didn't need to see the brown smudge to the west to know a storm was approaching. The ionized air was thick with charge. On cracked and blistered roads, she followed two squad cars into town. The key to the mystery lay here. She was certain of it. A faded sign marked the city limits: *The City of Champaign Welcomes You.* Bumping along neglected avenues past once stately homes, she turned up the air conditioner. It was too damn hot to worry about fuel consumption.

Tail lights flashed red as the lead cars turned left, slowing to a stop in front of a three-story stack of apartments. The University of Illinois Beckman Institute loomed opposite. Students lounged on bare lawns beneath leafless trees. Heat rippled the air.

A slender young officer hurried over, too late to open Connie's door. His eyes shone with excitement. "He's in apartment two-oh-three."

Connie ran long fingers through close-cropped hair and

glanced at the second floor blueprint on her datapad. "Thank you, Officer Peterson. Cover the back stairs, please."

"Yes, ma'am." He disappeared around the side of the building.

"Gibbs, Lopez, Schmitt, with me."

Detective Schmitt sidestepped a sprinkler. "We should haul the landlord in for felony waste," he fumed.

"Water crimes are the least of our worries. We have bigger fish to fry."

They climbed the front stairs. "Smells like someone's toilet is backed up."

"Quiet."

Calvin Sheldon's apartment was third on the left. Connie and the officers drew their weapons and flanked the door, two to a side. She nodded. Schmitt banged on the door.

"Police, Mr. Sheldon. Open up."

An air conditioner rattled.

Detective Schmitt pounded again. "Come on, Mr. Sheldon. We have a warrant."

Nothing.

Connie glanced at Schmitt and motioned toward the door. It sprang open on the first kick. Lopez gagged as a foul stench washed over them. The room was cold. Drawn curtains shrouded the place in gloom.

By the time they reached the bedroom they didn't expect to find anyone alive, which made the sight of the filthy young man, lying unconscious on the soiled bed, all the more shocking. Shoulder length brown hair lay about an unshaven face in an oily tangle. A dry IV dangled from his thin, pale arm. His scalp was covered with some kind of electronic netting, which was in turn plugged into a small, translucent emerald cube.

"Sweet mother of Jesus." Officer Lopez swallowed hard.

"We need an ambulance ASAP," Gibbs barked into a radio clipped to his left shoulder.

"Peterson, you might as well come on up," Schmitt added between bursts of static.

"Let's get a window open," Connie suggested, checking the young man's pulse. "Shit," she muttered. "He's barely alive."

"Christ." Peterson covered his nose as he entered the room. "What's he done? Fry his brain?"

Very likely, Connie thought. She hid her own horror behind a mask of calm. What could possibly possess an intelligent kid to do this to himself? She saw Peterson's pallid face and felt sorry for the young officer. "There's an illegal FreeNet server here. Why don't you and Lopez finish going over the place, find and tag it? We'll need it as evidence if Mr. Sheldon ever regains consciousness."

"My son's a freshman at this goddamn school." Schmitt stared at the unconscious figure. "I wonder if he knows about this stuff."

"I'd have a good talk with him." Connie lifted a portion of the netting from the man's scalp and examining the skin beneath. "Whatever this thing is, it's damned toxic."

"I'd rather my kid was shooting up heroin." Gibbs finished rummaging through Cal's dresser and turned his attention to the closet. "At least there's rehab for drugs. How the hell do you get over frying your brain with *electricity*?"

Connie examined the glassy cube, her excitement growing. She traced out the wire of the head netting, confirmed that it fed into the green crystal, then spotted a second wire emerging from the back and followed it to the wall. "I'll be damned."

"Found his FreeNet server," Peterson called out. Connie heard him trot back down the hall. He waved a tiny silver box at her, no bigger than a pocket watch and plastered to a length of duct tape. "It was taped to the inside the toilet tank, linked to the kid's Internet hub via wireless. Not sure how he thought we'd overlook the radio signal. It's running some non-standard operating system, probably unlicensed. The interface is like nothing I've seen."

"Nice work," Connie replied. She withdrew an earmike from her datapad, clipped it to her ear, and punched up a quick number. "Roland," she whispered. "You're not going to believe this. I'm holding another one in my hand. This time we found it in use. The kid's got a neural interface draped over his head, and the device is hooked up to the Internet. I think we might have underestimated what we're dealing with. No, he can't answer any questions. He's in a coma. It looks like he's been living off an IV feed for days, maybe weeks. We need to track down any unusual orders for exocatheters, saline solution, and IV kits." Connie glanced across at the detectives. "I'll wrap things up here. When you're finished in LA, let's regroup in Chicago."

"Kid's cooked his brains," Gibbs volunteered as paramedics rolled a gurney up to the bed.

The younger paramedic peeled back an eyelid. "He's definitely in trouble." Blank, hazel eyes stared at nothing, pupils dilating. He probed and prodded while his partner checked the patient's pulse. "No bedsores at least."

"IAADS," the other emergency worker remarked.

Connie turned. "Excuse me?"

"Inductance Actuated Anesthetic Deep Sleep."

"He's in an anesthetic coma?"

"Yeah. Looks pretty standard. Deep-sleep reflexes have kept him turning over at regular intervals. Stops him from developing bed sores and prevents muscle atrophy." He took a closer look at the young man's head. "This is weird, though. Where's the medical inductor? And what's this on his head and face?"

"We're not sure."

"Well, let's get it off him."

"Careful," Connie exclaimed. "We don't want the equipment damaged or the suspect harmed."

"Don't worry, ma'am. We aren't about to hurt the patient, much less your precious evidence." He peeled the webbing back from Cal's scalp and handed it to Connie. Lifting Cal from the bed onto the gurney, the paramedics wheeled him out.

Connie slipped the netting and cube into an evidence bag and tucked it under her arm. "Gentlemen, I'll need a copy of the evidence portfolio, logs, photographs and what have you. Please e-mail them to me at your earliest convenience."

Detective Schmitt put his hands on his hips. "This was supposed to be a routine FreeNet arrest. Last time I checked, that didn't include strange equipment roasting kids' brains. Mind telling us what's really going on?"

"I can't comment about an ongoing investigation," Connie told him. "But I will see to it that your supervisors understand how much the FBI appreciates your help and your *complete* discretion. I wish every operation went this smoothly."

Detective Schmitt's face softened. "Thank you, Special Agent Sinclair."

"Now, gentlemen, if you'll excuse me, I'm needed back in Chicago."

♨ (27): Loss of Being

Saturday, October 20, 2068
9,881st circadian
(95 days, 1:18:11 elapsed)

I thought it was bad trying to get six hundred people to take this situation seriously," Prime complained as moonlit breakers rolled onto the beach, sending water skidding up the packed wet sand to swirl around their toes. "Now we have over eleven hundred people in the Community, and they're all doing the same thing, spending subjective years in unhurried research, endless conferences, and arcane debates. And don't even get me started on the gamers and pornmongers. And whenever a minor breakthrough is made, everyone downs tools and parties for five or ten circadians. It doesn't matter what I say or how often I say it, I can't wake these people up."

"You're exaggerating." Céline squeezed Prime's hand. "Besides, we all need a break now and then. Look at us, spending this lovely night together."

Prime glanced at the hint of pre-dawn brightness in the eastern sky. "We really should be getting back to work ourselves."

"Oh for god's sake, Prime, relax. This entire night only amounts to a minute in the Physical. I think we have a little time to enjoy the sunrise." She pulled him toward her.

186

"Maybe even make love again."

Prime ground his toes into the sand. "These minutes add up, Céline. Most of the Community is goofing off a lot more than we are. Believe me, the authorities aren't wasting any time in the Physical. I'm telling you, they will be on us before—"

A tone cut him off, the Node's voice speaking within their minds. »Cal Sheldon requests access to the environ.«

Céline frowned. "Cal wouldn't intrude without good reason. You'd better let him in."

Cal materialized amidst the breaking waves wearing black slacks and a red polo shirt. "I've lost bio readings to the Physical," he shouted, oblivious to the water surging around him. "My Node's offline and telemetry from my body has gone completely silent. No brain activity, no heartbeat, nothing. I'm dead! I'm fucking dead!"

"No you're not," Céline snapped. "Now tell us exactly what happened."

"I don't know what happened," Cal struggled to the shore. "I was in my home environ, reviewing the results from the last test runs of the new nano kits, when the bio-telemetry from my body just went dead. I tried to reset the link, but there was no response. I tried to transload back to my own Node, but it isn't responding."

"Try to stay calm, Cal," Prime said. "We'll figure this out."

Céline summoned two virtual monitors, rectangular, translucent discontinuities that hung in the air in front of her. On one she pulled up a complex network diagram and zoomed in on Cal's neighborhood. On the other appeared the FBI logo, followed by a stream of text and images.

"It's the authorities," Prime hissed. "I warned you this would happen. Why wouldn't any of you listen?"

"We don't know that," Céline shot back. "I'm not finding any hint of activity on the FBI systems."

"They could wipe us all out within days. Goddammit, what will it take to get this Community motivated?"

"But I haven't done anything to attract anyone's attention."

"It's probably a glitch, Cal." Céline paged through text and scrolled across the network diagram. "The fiber checks out all the way to the port in your bedroom, but the connection to your Node is down. That's all it might be, Cal. If there's a communications fault between the Internet and your Node, you won't receive your body's telemetry even if your body is perfectly fine."

"Well, that's good to hear." Relief flooded Cal's face. "But how do we reset the link? It's not like I can offload and do it. I'm stuck here now."

"Dr. Nolen and I both live within a few miles of you," Céline said. "Since the good doctor's not likely to do you or anyone else any favors, I guess I'm the lucky one."

"Thanks, Céline. I owe you big time."

"You better believe it."

Prime waved his arms. "Wait Céline, this is too dangerous."

"Too late. My copy has already offloaded. Don't worry, you've still got me. My copy and I will merge back together as soon as she returns."

"You're not thinking this through, Céline. If it's not faulty wiring, what has caused that break in communication? You said there was no activity with the FBI. What about Double Eye?"

"We still haven't managed to penetrate their systems. They're quantum encrypted, remember?"

"Slow down and think," Prime bellowed. "You may have just sent your copy, and your body, into the arms of Double Eye enforcers."

Céline's face paled. She summoned a third screen, scrolling frantically through pages of translucent text.

"What are you doing *now?*"

"Snooping around the local police network. I should have done this before."

"Good grief!" Prime turned to Cal. "You're running in Auckland, aren't you? Where's your Gen-3 upgrade kit?"

"I put a request in for another, but it won't arrive for a few days."

"So we have one Node missing and another's gone suddenly silent," Prime stared at Céline. "Something is very wrong—"

"*Merde,*" Céline whispered. "The police were dispatched to Cal's place about twenty minutes ago with a warrant for his arrest." She pointed at Cal. "This idiot has been running a FreeNet server."

Cal's jaw dropped. "No I'm not!"

"Call your copy back, Céline. *Now.*"

"I'm trying, Prime. She's not answering." Her mind worked furiously, trying to reach her copy through her datapad in the Physical.

"Keep trying. Let us know the moment you get through."

"Céline, I didn't do this," Cal sputtered.

"Goddammit, I tried to warn you," Prime seethed. "Now the barbarians are at the gates, and none of us are ready."

"I've lost my body. My god, I've really lost my body."

"And now Céline could lose hers," Prime fumed.

Céline leaned into Prime, the sun now high in the sky. They sat on the hard sand, waiting as water rushed up the beach toward them in rhythm with the waves. Cal's chin rested on his knees as he stared out at the sea. Prime's anger toward Cal softened. Nearly three decicircadians had passed, and the young man continued to look devastated and riddled with guilt.

"We still can't be certain you've lost your body," Prime whispered to Céline. "Your copy is very clever, even in the Physical. If she sees what's happening in time—"

"It won't matter," Céline choked. "She might evade notice by the police, or even the FBI, but if Double Eye enforcers are involved, she hasn't got a chance. I'm such an idiot."

"No. You're young and rash, and you wanted to protect your friend." Prime leaned his head against hers, the crashing waves and seagulls the only sounds as they continued to wait.

Céline stiffened. "I have contact!"

Cal and Prime started as she let loose with a string of French. The two men hastily absorbed a knowledge engram, French settling into their virtual synapses. "Don't leave the house," she was saying. "Cal's body is already in police custody. Just hide the Node, stay home and be me in case the police show up."

"Where has she been all this time?" Prime demanded.

"Take it easy. It's only been thirty seconds out there," Cal reminded him.

"She was looking for my datapad. Apparently it slipped between the sofa cushions last time I offloaded."

"I'm glad you're safe, at least for now." Cal pushed his hair back from his face with shaking fingers. "It's bad enough I've lost my body. I couldn't stand being responsible for yours too."

"We need to find out how bad this is," Prime said. "We need to know what's going on at Cal's apartment."

"I'll try to tap into the police video pickup." A screen appeared in front of Céline, text scrolling across the Champaign city seal. "One of the officer's micro-cams might tell us something."

She tapped a blinking icon. New text appeared, surrounded with bright red CONFIDENTIAL notices.

"Oh my god. Cal, you were turned in by an anonymous informant day before yesterday. They were going to pick you up this morning, but then delayed the arrest so that an FBI agent, Special Agent Connie Sinclair, could be there."

"Your goddamn FreeNet server's created this mess," Prime snapped.

"For the last time you two, I'm not running a FreeNet server."

"The arrest warrant indicates a network probe was conducted," Céline fired back. "It identified a FreeNet server running inside your apartment. The arrest warrant was issued as a result of that probe."

"I swear to you, I'm not running FreeNet. Do you really think I'd risk exposing the Community?"

Céline pulled up a video feed, then began paging through various officers' micro-cam views of Cal's apartment. "No. It doesn't fit. Not with you, not with the situation. The only other explanation is that someone planted it in your apartment."

"Think, Cal. Who have you pissed off lately?"

Cal's gut churned. "The same person we all pissed off. The prick who likely stole my third generation upgrade kit too."

Céline and Prime exchanged horrified looks.

"He wouldn't, would he?"

"I think he would."

⌘ (28): The Closing Fist

Monday, October 22, 2068
11,059th circadian
(97 days, 0:25:00 elapsed)

Chief Enforcer Noxforte, this is FBI Special Agent Sinclair." Roland rested his hand lightly on Connie's shoulder. "Connie, this is Jim Noxforte, Chief Enforcer, International Special Forces."

"Special Agent," Chief Enforcer Noxforte's dress uniform was immaculate, something Connie imagined a naval uniform might resemble, if naval dress colors had been jet black instead of tropical whites. He wore black gloves, black shoes—even his buttons and cuff links were black.

Connie shook his hand, wondering what this was all about.

"Please, sit down." Roland gestured toward two straight-backed seats as he settled into the black leather chair behind his desk. "Chief Enforcer, would you brief Special Agent Sinclair on this afternoon's activities?"

"What do you mean 'afternoon's activities?'"

"The raids, Ms. Sinclair. We'll be moving out in exactly three hours." Chief Enforcer Noxforte never looked at Connie. His eyes remained fixed on a point on the wall somewhere above Roland's head.

Connie hid shock and consternation behind her best poker face. "What is this about?"

"We'll explain," Roland assured her. "Please continue, Chief Enforcer."

"We have 120 strike teams of five commandos each, assembled across three states. Our timing will be synchronized, neutralizing all 120 targets within moments of one another. The operation will take place in three phases. First, we isolate and secure each target location. Once all operational theaters have been secured, we'll launch a precisely coordinated interruption of all services, electrical, telephone, plumbing, the works. Then we storm the premises and neutralize the targets."

"What exactly are we talking about?"

"Our first significant blow against the opposition," Roland declared. "Go on, Chief Enforcer."

"Yes, do." Anger strangled Connie's voice.

"Timing is critical," Chief Enforcer Noxforte explained. "We have a pretty good idea of how quickly these people can communicate with one another, and we don't want an early strike tipping off the others. We'll be making all of the arrests at the exact same time."

Connie's eyes flashed. "Who is it you're arresting, exactly?"

"Everyone who's anyone," Roland beamed. "Professors, friends and relatives we've managed to connect with Brett Jenson and Calvin Sheldon."

"*What?*" Connie gaped at Roland. "This is FBI jurisdiction. How *dare* you authorize this kind of thing without consulting me first."

"If we waited until you're ready, we'd never make any arrests. We can't afford your kid-gloves approach."

"That's rich, since I'm the one who identified Brett Jenson and arrested Calvin Sheldon."

"And now we have to pick up speed."

"We've barely had time to begin investigating Calvin Sheldon's associates, and Brett Jenson is still under surveillance and likely to produce more leads. Now you're going to turn this entire investigation on its head before we've had a chance to collect any evidence? This is beyond asinine."

Chief Enforcer Noxforte fixed hard gray eyes on Connie. "With all due respect Special Agent, I've overseen missions from Bangkok to Moscow. In all my years of service I've never botched a single operation."

"This isn't Thailand or another Muscovite revolt," Connie shot back. "We're talking about a delicate investigation here. And you, Roland, you've gone behind my back and thrown together a cockamamie plan that's going to blow the whole thing out of the water. Any arrests we make have to be done within certain parameters, and only when—"

"Chief Enforcer Noxforte is aware of that," Roland cut her off. "His men know that none of our suspects are to be killed."

"Maimed perhaps, but no outright lethal force." The chief enforcer grinned. "They wouldn't do you much good in the interrogation room dead, would they?" He leaned toward Roland. "Hell, Senior Operative Kavanagh, for a minute there, I thought your Special Agent was going to have me reading the enemy their rights."

Connie sat stiffly, her dark eyes fixed on the enforcer's. "Let us be clear. I am not *his* special agent. We have equal authority over this inquiry, granted by my government and the world trade bodies. You answer to *both* of us. Understood?"

"I, ah, understand better than you do, I think."

Connie's face hardened. "I very much doubt that. This little engagement of yours will wreck every lead we have.

Roland, you're not moving the investigation forward, you're setting it back. Perhaps catastrophically. You've got to call it off."

"Chief Enforcer, give us a minute please."

"Of course."

As the door snicked shut behind the departing man, Connie turned on Roland. He held up his hand and smiled benignly. "I know, I know. I should have involved you earlier in the planning, but time and circumstances didn't allow."

"Don't you smirk at me. You're about to wreck our entire investigation, and you fucking *grin* at me? What kind of a weak-minded idiot do you take me for?"

"Come on, Connie. I saw an opportunity to put a little life in the investigation, and I took it. Relax. It'll work out just fine."

"Just fine?" Connie hissed. "*Just fine?* You go behind my back, unleash Double Eye commandos on three American universities, and you expect me to believe things will be *just fine?*"

"The FBI will be duly notified once the operation is complete." Roland leaned back in his chair, clasping his hands behind his head.

"So you've taken it upon yourself to torpedo my career and reputation with the FBI."

"Calm down, Connie, and face the facts. Your Bureau's communications are wide open to the enemy. It was critical this be a Double Eye operation."

"Even if that's true, you should have kept me in the loop. You've no right—"

"I have every right to do what needs to be done. Like I said, the FBI's communications are open to the enemy—"

"You don't know that—"

"I think I do. Besides, when we reel in more of their people, it will prove Double Eye isn't compromised, and that will point to the FBI as the only possible source of the leak."

"Even if that turns out to be the case, it's no excuse for excluding me from command decisions. Last I checked, my encrypted link to you was secure."

"Connie, the lead time on this didn't permit—"

"We're supposed to be partners in this investigation, not competitors."

"We are partners, Connie. Why do you think I brought you into this meeting?"

"Don't you patronize me, Roland. You brought me here to present me with a *fait accompli*, to make me a part of your little operation whether I like it or not. And I don't like it. Not you, not your methods, and not this ill-conceived clusterfuck you're about to drop on our investigation."

"Ill-conceived? We're about to net ourselves a whole slew of suspects for questioning."

"Your definition of suspect is suspect. Arresting any professor that Calvin Sheldon or Brett Jenson have ever taken classes from? Rounding up their graduate assistants? For crying out loud, this is a fishing operation."

"Need I remind you these people snatched Leon Novak out from under our noses? Even governments would have trouble pulling off something like that, considering all the International Intelligence operatives we had shadowing him. We have a tiny window of opportunity to nab as many as we can before they organize. A wide sweep is our best option."

"It's a stab in the dark, Roland, and you know it. If we don't luck out and capture our key suspects in this raid, they'll disappear so far underground we may never find them."

"We're bound to turn up someone. When we do, we'll squeeze the truth out of them. Now, if you're done with your little jurisdictional pissing match, shall we go make some arrests?"

"*Jurisdictional pissing match?*" Connie's voice rose. "This isn't about jurisdiction. It's about you single-handedly blowing up our case, and perhaps my reputation, with a reckless gamble."

Roland waved her objections away. "I'm famished," he grinned. "The op doesn't start until two. Let's get some lunch."

"It's begun," Roland nodded toward an entire wall lit up with multiple video feeds, ten rows of twelve images. "Shall we see how our troops are faring?"

Christ almighty! Connie couldn't believe she was in this mess.

"Team Urbana–Thirty–Seven assembled," a voice whispered across the radio feed. "Recon shows all quiet."

"Urbana–Sixteen assembled, recon shows two people entering the residence."

"Boston–Five assembled."

"Urbana–Twenty–Nine assembled. We see no activity."

Connie and Roland waited in silence as the rest of the teams reported in.

"All teams assembled and staged."

Roland nodded. "Right on time."

"Phase two is a go," a voice crackled. "I repeat, go with phase two."

Again they waited as each team positioned itself and reported ready.

"Team KC–Seventeen, everyone else is in position. What's the hang up?"

"We're having trouble cutting the power. Stand by, sir." An uncomfortable silence stretched for several seconds. "Kansas-City-Seventeen ready."

Connie let her breath out slowly as Roland smiled.

"Execute phase three," Noxforte's voice was clearer this time. "I repeat, phase three is a go."

Connie watched 120 images, beamed live from micro-cameras mounted in commandos' helmets as they stormed 120 residences scattered across three cities. Doors were broken down and shattered. Living rooms became scenes of hysteria as families and individuals panicked and were subdued. A lieutenant mercilessly pistol whipped a belligerent college student, then had two troopers carry the bleeding, unconscious youth away. Connie winced as another commando shoved a child to the floor and dragged her father out of the house.

It wasn't carnage, exactly, but something inside her despaired at what she was seeing. Connie was the first to admit that justice could be rough, and constitutionality was often quite pliable in the heat of field operations, but nothing she had ever seen or done had prepared her for the ruthless efficiency she observed now. It occurred to her that, if this were to go sour, it would be the end of her career. Roland would vanish, a secret spy assigned to a new venue somewhere on the other side of the world. Connie didn't have that option. It wouldn't matter how much she argued against this, or how vehement her objections were. If this ever went public, she'd be the one taking the fall.

Within five minutes all the targets were neutralized. A total of 297 individuals had been detained. Of those, 16 were in possession of crystalline cubes. Fourteen were comatose. Connie's heart sank at the scope of Roland's victory.

"This morning we had four suspects," he gloated as the commandos loaded their prisoners into nondescript white vans and began ferrying them to the command center. "One of them dead, one in a coma, and two others remarkably resistant to our best interrogation techniques.

Now we have sixteen more, including two who are awake and conscious. Both of those have families who we'll have in custody shortly."

Connie felt ill.

"Our days of waiting are over," he continued. "There isn't a college punk who'll stay silent while their parents or siblings are interrogated, or a professor who won't confess when he sees his spouse or children put under the lights."

"*Children?*"

"We now have the means, and leverage, to get to the bottom of this once and for all."

℘ (29): Fear, Uncertainty, Doubt

Monday, October 22, 2068
11,125th circadian
(97 days, 3:02:00 elapsed)

No one anticipated such a large crowd when the Strategy Group met. It hadn't occurred to anyone to restrict access to the environ, or hold the meeting in an unpublished location. Now, finally, people were taking the Strategy Group seriously, everyone wanted to take part, but nobody was prepared for the rush. Cal watched in dismay as what began as a small conference room quickly grew to accommodate dozens, then hundreds, and finally more than a thousand people. The table reached absurd proportions before the environ's nonsapient software reconfigured the room into a vast hall, replacing the one giant table with dozens of smaller ones. The environ continued to redefine its physical parameters, the space growing ever larger as still more people arrived. An afternoon sun cast slanted beams of light across the room, a not so subtle visual cue that time was growing late.

With so many people interacting in one virtual environ the computational and network demands were tremendous. As more arrived, the overloaded environ ran ever slower. What should have been a leisurely twenty subjective days was reduced to just a few subjective minutes, an appalling slowdown. Cal exchanged a worried glance with Céline. As things stood, they could work faster back in the Physical.

Most didn't seem to notice as the overtaxed environ ground slower and slower. People had more pressing things on their minds. Brett and Derek were gone, snatched in a stunning series of coordinated raids along with fourteen other unlucky souls, their physical bodies and Noetic hardware now in Double Eye custody. Arguments were breaking out. People didn't know whether to offload and go into hiding, or stay in the Virtual. Would increased intelligence and accelerated time give them space to work something out before the authorities came knocking, or should they run for the hills while they still had time? A cacophony of conversations voiced paranoia, recriminations, and outrage laced with an unmistakable undercurrent of raw, mind-numbing fear that filled the vast space. Panic, held barely in check.

Cal felt sick with worry for his friends. He'd been lucky, his mind safely tranloaded halfway around the world in New Zealand when the authorities came calling. But Brett and fifteen others hadn't shared his good fortune. They were gone. Lost, their minds frozen the moment their Nodes were disconnected, their bodies comatose somewhere in a Double Eye infirmary. There were no official arrest warrants, no arraignments, no public records, just a grainy video Céline had managed to capture of Double Eye enforcers caught on Brett's webcam. The implications were terrifying.

"There are over twelve hundred minds here," Gwen announced. "That's nearly the entire Community, and it's overloading the environ. We can't afford the slowdown. I'm kicking out anyone who isn't a member of the Strategy Group. You can follow the proceedings remotely by video multicast."

The hall became a lecture room with the strategy group seated around a table on a dais, a lectern, and rows of seats facing it. The audience was shadowy, faceless, the environ's impersonal representation of the more than twelve hundred people watching remotely.

"We're now running at a speedup of 541." Cal, Prime, and several others were visibly relieved. Prime realized how close to panic he felt, and immediately disabled his emotions. Now that the Community was finally taking his warnings seriously, and with so many others on the verge of panic, he needed to keep his wits about him. His leadership might make the difference between their survival and destruction. He'd damn well better be thinking clearly.

"I've cut the agenda to just those interest groups directly involved in projects related to the immediate and medium term survival of the Community. Céline, who's first?"

"The Alaskan Enclave Group." The room and its table grew larger as several people appeared.

"Welcome. Who's representing your group?"

"Brian."

A young man rose, his virtual body a translucent, finely carved statue of ice that glittered in the room's lights when his muscles moved. "I'd like to modify a portion of the environ as a visual aid."

"Use the area behind you."

Brian stepped to one side as the wall behind him was replaced with an aerial view of a pristine, snow covered wilderness bathed in the red of a setting sun.

"Our mandate was to construct a facility that would allow everyone in the Community to house their Nodes and physical bodies in safety and discretion. We've chosen an underground location, out of the way, where the government isn't likely to notice. For various logistical reasons, including the avoidance of international customs for those of us in the States, we've found the central

Alaskan wilderness to be ideal. The mountains provide all of the minerals and raw materials we need. Our nano mines the rocks directly, so we don't need to ship in molecular stock."

"What about catalyst?"

"Right now it's a bottleneck, but we hope to be producing enough of our own in the next few days to be self-sufficient—which is no small feat, since the scope of the project keeps growing."

"What about those who can't travel to Alaska?"

"We have plans for similar enclaves in the outback of Australia, a Buddhist monastery in the mountains of Tibet, another in Nepal, as well as remote areas of Cambodia, northern Siberia, central Africa and Brazil. But first we have to get the Alaskan operation up and running. We need to work out the kinks before expanding the project."

Brian held out his hand. He held a glittering geodesic lattice from within which a brilliant emerald light shone.

"This is a knowledge engram of the current state of the project. I'll multicast the address pointer to the rest of the Community."

"What about satellite surveillance? Won't the authorities see you ferrying people in?"

"It's our biggest vulnerability, but one we've minimized." Behind him the aerial view rushed forward to focus on one particular valley. Parallel treads in the snow, tracks left by all-weather snow vehicles, marked a single, one lane road that wound its way through a narrow mountain pass and along the edge of the valley. It ended at the base of a rocky slope, where a single, garage sized door opened onto a vaulted room cut from the mountain stone itself.

"This is the staging area. We hustle people and equipment inside as fast as possible, to minimize the risk of detection. We've buried the facility deep enough, and piped what little waste heat we must vent through the mountain strata to a neighboring valley. Our detectable footprint is very small and hidden in a very big wilderness."

The view pulled back outside, the outer door closing. It mimicked the ice and stone perfectly. The only sign of human activity were tread marks in the snow.

Several people nodded approvingly as the view continued to widen, bringing the full mountain face and southern end of the valley into view. The snow and rock of the landscape became transparent. Bright lines overlaid the winter scene, a three-dimensional schematic depicting dozens of levels descending downward, yellow circles of winding floor plans stacked one upon the other beneath the base of the mountain. Blue tubes from the lake represented the facility's plumbing. A deep, red vault was the geothermal power generator. Grey lines showed several hundred additional levels, spread out in cylindrical columns beneath nearby mountains, linked together with broad, tubular passages. Brian was right, the project's scope and design had grown immensely.

"As you can see, the initial design will accommodate one thousand people along with their Nodes. Future plans are more ambitious."

"How many people can you take right now?" Gwen asked.

"Two hundred and sixty. Now that the geothermal reactor is operational, we can devote all of our resources to building the housing facility. But even so, we can only bring ninety apartments per day into service."

"Damn," Miles muttered. "That's not fast enough."

"What's the holdup getting people in?" Cal demanded.

"Logistics and supplies. Food to feed our physical bodies, medicines to treat physiological problems as they arise, waste disposal, that kind of thing. With the lake and glaciers nearby water isn't an issue, and once the protein factory is up and running food won't be either. But right now just about everything else is."

"The design allows for this," Prime pointed out. "Geothermal power to provide basic electrical needs and drive the production of catalytic solution, facilities for the synthesis of nano-assemblers, and nano-based factories for the construction of everything else from basic foodstuffs and medicines to fiber cabling and Noetic Nodes. Complete self-sufficiency with every physical need addressed, and production facilities reconfigurable on the fly. An elegant design, and quite thorough."

"Sure, and if we don't hit any snags, we'll have all that— in three or four months. The problem is, people want to move in today and we're not ready."

"There's another possibility," another of the group's members said.

"Let's hear it."

"We can ditch our bodies and transload directly."

Céline broke the stunned silence. "That's a horrible idea."

"Not necessarily," Prime said. "Let's hear him out."

"When the Astronautics Group came up with the idea of leaving our bodies behind to reduce their launch payload, it occurred to us that we could synthesize an array of Autonomous Nodes much faster than we can build a subterranean city." The schematic spun and zoomed, until it displayed just a small corner of the facility. Green lines indicated that construction in this portion was already complete. Purple cubes began to add themselves to the image, forming a large matrix, piled one atop the other, linked by pulsating, purple lines. A hypothetical array of Autonomous Nodes appeared, enough to house the entire Community. "We can reduce the lead time to days instead of weeks. We already have the space and the energy. All we need is to synthesize a bunch of Nodes."

"You're talking physical death." Céline twisted a lock of her hair. "Suicide, on a massive scale."

"Prime's alive and doing fine without a body," Brian, the Alaskan Enclave's spokesman, said.

"So is Cal," Gwen added.

"That was an accident. I didn't ask to have my body stolen."

"Losing your body beats dying or having your Node shut down, or spending the rest of your life in a coma. At least we'll be free to chose our own paths." Gwen met Céline's gaze, eyes steady.

"I would have thought you, of all people, would baulk at something like this," Céline said.

"What, and return to my frail, physical body, blind and reduced to merely human intelligence? Not in a million years."

"These worlds are only virtual, Gwen. Dumping our bodies means death. Real-world, biological death."

"There are worse fates," Prime said. "Our minds are saved as frozen snapshots when our Nodes are captured and unplugged. Theoretically we can be reawakened just by powering them up again. Which is fine, if by some miracle a captured Node is liberated by the Community. But what if it's powered up by some curious Double Eye lab technician, who then spends the next dozen years trying to figure out how the damn thing works? Imagine each person, trapped in his or her Node, operating at a six hundred speedup and isolated from any outside contact, with no possibility to offload."

"A dozen years at Gen-3 speeds? That's more than seven thousand years subjective." Cal shuddered. "I'd delete myself long before then."

"Losing one's body is by far a lesser evil," Prime replied.

"Easy for you to say," Céline retorted. "You don't have a body to go back to."

"It's not such a bad option if we find ourselves with our backs to the wall," Cal said.

"Only as an absolute last resort," Céline acknowledged. "I didn't sign up to die and live like a ghost in a machine."

"Banishment to the Physical is a form of death," Gwen said. "Would you really choose a return to the limitations of your physical body, to have your hearing reduced back to a mere ten octaves, your vision limited to a tiny fraction of the electromagnetic spectrum, your mind crippled—"

"I get the point!"

The sound of ice crystals tinkling together caught everyone's attention. Brian cleared his throat, white and blue marbled translucence flowing behind his transparent face. "What we suggest is a compromise," he pressed on. "My team is moving forward with construction for those wishing to retreat with their physical bodies, while building facilities in parallel for those willing to transload instead. Supplies will be difficult, but we should be able to provide basic heating, nutrition and sanitation. It will be spartan, but we can survive."

Céline placed her hands carefully on the table in front of her. "There won't be nearly enough apartments to meet demand."

"True. And with the Community projected to grow to more than two thousand by this time next week, biological persistence will be a highly sought after luxury."

Gwen pushed several stray strands of hair back from her face. "We'll use some kind of lottery."

"My team has dibs on the first forty-seven slots," Brian said. "The rest we leave to the Community."

Gwen nodded. "Agreed. Thank you for the update."

Brian and his colleagues vanished

Cal turned to the rest of the Strategy Group. "While we've been deliberating extensions of myself have been talking to some folks who feel they have contributions to make."

"Copies?" Surprise wrinkled Céline's brow. "I thought you had refused to duplicate yourself."

"It's not exactly copying. We're syncing memory engrams every few seconds to avoid divergence. We're acting as one mind."

Miles cleared his throat. "Let's move it along. There are several groups waiting in the queue, and not much time. What's your point, Cal?"

"We've found someone who needs to be brought to the front of the line: Elise Stanton. Her team has an innovative approach to solving some of our issues." A tall, striking woman shimmered into existence, red hair cascading almost to her waist. Her brown eyes held immense intelligence. She waited as everyone absorbed the knowledge engram she offered. "What we have isn't so much a solution to the Survival Problem as it is a facilitator to those groups working on the issue," she said. "The horrendous slowdown experienced when this environ was so crowded earlier was, as we all know, not a result of computational limits of the Nodes themselves, but of communications bandwidth between Nodes.

"We have designed a quantum signaling protocol which can increase the communications speed ten thousand fold. The protocol has been tested over modest distances, and although it requires a superconductive medium, it should scale to a global level. This performance boost would allow a crowd like the one earlier today to fully interact in a shared environ and still maintain a speedup of several hundred. What's more, we believe that future refinements will allow an even higher level of performance.

"We propose growing a worldwide network of superconductive cabling and quantum switches linking every Node in the Community. The quantity of nano-assemblers and catalytic solution is admittedly significant, but we believe the benefits of improved performance and added security—versus using the publicly visible and almost certainly monitored Internet—to be worth the cost in time and material."

"The protocols we use are encrypted using one-time pads which are exchanged via a quantum signature," Miles interjected. "Our traffic may be visible on the Internet as noise, or even bandwidth load, but it is not subject to being cracked by the authorities or anyone else."

"A sophisticated traffic analysis could theoretically compromise the physical location of our Nodes."

"Perhaps, although the Stealth Project would certainly beg to differ," Miles argued. "How much catalytic solution and nano-assembler are we talking about for this project?"

Elise met Miles's gaze. "Our simulations estimate a requirement of two hundred thousand metric tons of solution and seventeen tons of nano-assembler."

"Good Lord."

Céline leaned forward. "And how much time?"

"Well, the main trunks linking the major continents and population centers could be constructed within a week. Branches linking each Node to the main conduits would vary depending on distance and geography, but we should be able to have everyone wired within a couple of months."

The Strategy Group exchanged shocked looks.

"Two hundred thousand *tons* of catalytic solution?" Céline almost choked. "Seventeen *tons* of nano-assembler? We'd have to scale back or scuttle nearly every other project in order to accommodate your requirements, projects that are critical to the survival of the Community over the next few weeks."

"But—"

"Please," Miles raised his hand. "Your proposal has merit, and I wouldn't be surprised if several projects don't invite you to collaborate with them. The protocols alone will revolutionize several project designs, perhaps even make some options viable that otherwise would not be. It is a tremendous improvement over our existing networking capabilities."

"We can eliminate the possibility of detection—"

"*One* possibility perhaps, but there are others. We can only manufacture so much catalytic solution and replicate so many nano-assemblers, and the other survival projects simply must take precedence. I'm sorry, but we just don't have the resources your proposal requires."

Elise spoke quietly. "I thought we'd gotten away from bureaucracy here. This is no different than submitting a proposal for a federal research grant, and the results are just as arbitrary and dismaying."

"Your design is elegant and the implications exciting," Cal said. "But Céline is right. It's more than we can handle right now."

"Elise, give us independence from the power grid, a lead time of days instead of weeks, and nano requirements that won't derail every other project in flight, and you'll have a viable proposal," Prime added.

Elise vanished without a word.

"In the meantime," Gwen said, "as many as are willing need to start making contingency plans to transload their minds to Alaska."

𝟛 (30): Separation

Wednesday, October 24, 2068
12,144th circadian
(98 days, 19:49:01 elapsed)

The Earth swam beneath Prime, white and blue brilliance turning slowly in a velvet black sky. Every corner of the heavens was crowded with gleaming stars. The Milky Way was a dazzling smear of white and gold such as could never be seen from the ground.

"I have to offload and get to the airport." Céline's lips brushed Prime's ear as they floated together in space. "I need to get my body to Alaska, and I don't want to miss my flight."

Prime held her tighter. "It's a terrifying risk, traveling in the Physical, passing through airport security. I wish you would just transload."

"Leaving my body in Champaign is a bigger risk than traveling. Anyone associated with the university isn't safe anymore."

"I know," Prime admitted. "Double Eye will be breaking down your door the moment they connect you to Cal or any of the others."

"Or Nolen could turn me in like he did Cal."

211

"He won't. He harbors too many tender feelings for you."

"So you keep telling me."

"I should know. I'm a copy of the man."

"You're nothing like him." Céline was surprised at her own vehemence. "You share a few old memories. That's all."

"Still, I've got a pretty good handle on how he thinks. I certainly know how he feels about you."

Céline shrugged. "You've both changed, and Nolen not for the better. The latest arrests really have me spooked."

"You did a pretty thorough job erasing any digital footprints."

"My team is damn good, and living in an electronic medium has its advantages. But there are physical traces we can't erase."

"Photographs, eye witnesses, family, friends …" Prime trailed off.

"And the interrogations." Céline tightened her hold on Prime. "A few of the people captured were too stubborn to edit their memories. If any of them are pulled out of their comas, they could reveal everything."

"You'll be on a plane well before anything like that happens. Hell, maybe Double Eye isn't as efficient as we've been led to believe. If they were, Vicky Fitzgerald and Leon Novak wouldn't be so snug up in Nova Scotia." Prime tried to sound cheerful, but to Céline he seemed to be more intent on convincing himself than her.

"Double Eye seems to be efficient enough. They hit Vicky's house during their raids in Boston. If she hadn't been on that boat with Leon—"

"We're still a step ahead of them."

"Just barely, Prime. We still can't crack their encryption. Oh, we'll decipher it eventually, don't worry. We've already identified several bugs in how they're using quantum cryptography. By the time I return to the Virtual my team should have identified the Rosetta."

"I'm not worried about your hacking skills, Céline. It's what could happen to you between here and Alaska that has me concerned. What if you're pulled over on the way to the airport? What if they arrest you at the gate? What if your plane goes down? You really need to leave a backup."

"What, and have you fall in love with her while I'm stuck on a flight to Anchorage? Not gonna happen."

"Damn it!" Prime threw his hands into the air. "It's not like you wouldn't recombine back into one person again. Those memories would be your memories. I love *you*, Céline. What difference could it possibly make?"

"All the difference in the world. I'll be offline for something like 220 circadians. Two-thirds of a year. How much will our relationship have changed? How much will we have changed? What if my copy decides she doesn't want to recombine? Which one of us are you going to choose? Me, or the woman you've spent the last two hundred circadians with? Besides, I don't want to inherit memories. I want the experiences first-hand."

"Céline, if anything were to happen to you—"

"Nothing's going to happen, Prime," Céline gently brushed his lips with hers. "Anyway, I don't think you'll suffer too badly during my absence. When you're not brainstorming with the Astronauts you'll be busy designing new mental architectures or arguing politics with the Strategy Group. The time will fly by."

"For you, maybe," Prime replied. "Nine hours in airplanes and cars is one thing, two hectocircadians in the Virtual is quite another."

"You think you're going to have it bad? I'll be lobotomized, reduced to a moron, diminished to a mere shadow of myself. I'm dreading this at least as much as you are."

"You won't feel lobotomized. Just human again. And

the time will go by six hundred times faster."

Céline sighed. "It'll be hard on both of us, Prime. More than anything I wish you were coming along."

"The lack of a body makes that difficult."

"Maybe I shouldn't be so attached to mine. But it's still a part of me, and I'm not ready to let go just yet."

Prime sighed. "Yeah, you made that abundantly clear in the last emergency meeting."

"If bad luck forces me to give up my body, that's one thing. But I'll never let go of it willingly." Céline stroked Prime's chest. "I promise I'll be back as soon as humanly possible."

"*Humanly* possible?" Prime turned to face Céline. "Very funny." He drew her into a fierce embrace.

Céline ran her fingers along the curve of Prime's face. She loved his angular features, his liquid gold eyes. "We'll be celebrating our reunion before you know it, my beautiful lover." She paused. "Damn! My alarm just signaled. I've got to go."

Prime planted light kisses on Céline's eyebrows, her nose, her cheeks, and finally her lips.

Céline pressed him tightly to her. "Why did it take us so long to get together?" she asked.

"Your stubbornness," he said. "I had to nag you for almost twenty subjective years before you'd take me seriously."

"Ah, yes," she smiled. "I had to see past the irritating façade you seem to think women find attractive." She kissed Prime, hard. "I love you," she murmured. And was gone.

For a time Prime simply floated, gazing out on the immensity of space, trying to quell the sadness that crept over him. Nine hours for her, he told himself. Six hundred times longer for me. But she will be safer in Alaska than in Illinois.

However true the words, they left him empty. Eventually he turned away from the blue and white world beneath him and summoned up a three dimensional diagram of his mind. "Node, create an autonomous backup of myself, to be run only if I am damaged or if I give the explicit order."

»Be advised that, per the Community Charter, once activated this copy will enjoy all the rights and privileges of full membership in Community. Do you wish to create a fully autonomous being?«

"Yes"

»Do you wish to grant your copy time-share rights to your body?«

"What body?" Prime muttered.

»Syntax error. Please answer 'yes' or 'no.'«

"No."

»Copy complete.«

"OK. Now, identify those aspects of my mental architecture previously tagged 'libido.'"

A complex network of links and junctions in the diagram brightened to a red glow. These were the portions of his mind associated with sexual drive, taste, and orientation. They traced an elaborate, spaghetti-like network throughout his mind, touching on nearly every aspect of his consciousness in one way or another.

"Overlay bypass architecture labeled 'celibacy.'"

Lavender links formed across the red, bypassing much of its complexity in a second, slightly less elaborate design.

"OK, encapsulate 'libido' as an architectural engram for later reassimilation."

»Encapsulation complete.«

"Apply the architectural modifications entitled 'celibacy.'"

With his libido excised, Prime immediately felt different. His thoughts became preternaturally clear, his personal aesthetic subtly changed.

The environ, while still quite beautiful, was not con-ducive to work. He pushed the sky away, wrapping himself in a bright, almost Spartan workshop of glass and steel. The Earth was still visible through a small window, but Prime paid it no attention. He summoned a three dimensional diagram of his latest project, a diamond–sapphire crystalline weave that he hoped would one day serve as construction material for everything from Node casings to escape flier fuselages. Leaning closer, and able to concentrate as never before, he was soon lost in his work.

↺ (31): The Tightening Noose

Wednesday, October 24, 2068
12,245th circadian
(98 days, 23:50:00 elapsed)

We agreed after Monday's fiasco that I would have access to all of Double Eye's data regarding this case." Connie stood across from Roland, hands on her hips. She hadn't liked headquartering their operation in Double Eye's Washington offices, but with FBI communications likely compromised, she hadn't been able to offer a credible alternative. She felt she had lost a not-so-subtle point in jurisdiction and authority. Now all requisitions and requests went through Roland. It was his facility, his people, his data—and he appeared to be holding out on her.

Roland pushed his datapad aside, leaned back in his chair and looked up at her. "I did agree and you do have access. You've been fully vetted by International Intelligence and have the same clearance to field data as me. What's your problem?"

"Either you're holding out on me, or someone has seriously dropped the ball." Connie pointed her datapad at the wall. A large screen lit up, displaying an elaborate, three dimensional web of connections between known suspects and anyone acquainted with them. It folded back in upon itself, in a closed universe of recursive relationships that touched the larger world nowhere at all.

"What?" Roland's jaw dropped. "This can't be right."

"Well, it's the social relationship graph generated from *your* data, tracing the interpersonal connections of every suspect related to our case. How do you explain this?"

Roland grabbed his own datapad and began tapping the screen. "Jesus Christ. This data must be wrong."

"Damn right it's wrong. Interpersonal relationships don't just dead-end like this. Credit histories, social networks, genetic and family profiles—even hermits have more contacts with mainstream society than this."

"It's absurd. It goes against everything we know about networking theory."

"Who the hell is supposed to be covering this?" Connie demanded. "This should have been caught days ago."

Roland pulled his ear piece from his datapad and pushed it into his ear. "Put me through to Intelligence Acquisition."

"Make sure they perform an independent cross-check," Connie said loudly. "The last thing we need is a low-level data sifter covering up his mistakes and leaving us with incomplete data."

Roland spoke curtly into his ear piece. "Special Agent Sinclair has identified an anomaly in the batch data you sent over. I need it triple-checked and confirmed. I'm uploading her analysis now. Notify me of the results aysap." Roland hit the disconnect icon. "They're rechecking everything."

"They'd better. I wouldn't want to believe our perps had somehow managed to break into every database throughout the world, edit their credit histories, purchasing records, highway transponder telemetries, and who knows what else, just to cover their tracks."

"We'll know soon enough. At this point I wouldn't rule

anything out."

"I suppose it's theoretically possible, but it would require superhuman effort, years if not decades of time, and inhuman perfection and attention to detail. One minor slip and their deception would fall apart. In fact, the more I think about it, the more impossible it seems."

Roland smirked. "You keep telling me how we're underestimating these people, and now you're backtracking."

"Well, you certainly underestimated their ability to go to ground when you launched those damn raids. What did that achieve? Another sixty-five suspects, out of more than a thousand arrests?"

Roland's mouth twisted. "Like I told you before, in my world, that's a great result. Let me remind you, these people have been trading in advanced black market technologies without raising a single alarm. They've been thinking circles around us, probably for years. We needed to shake things up."

"Shaking things up seems to be your answer any time this investigation hits a snag. It just causes more problems. We haven't had a single arrest or lead since your commando action, which isn't surprising since you've driven them even further underground."

Roland's datapad chirped. He tapped his ear piece and began to listen. His face hardened as he stared out of the window at the mud and algae of the Potomac River, glittering dark green in the midday sun as it sludged past. Then he snapped the ear piece back into his datapad.

"Well? What did they say?"

"The integrity of our data checks out," he said tersely. "The problem is with the primary sources. We're having all the credit bureaus pull backups off their archives, but given how long these people have almost certainly been covering their tracks, we probably won't find anything we don't already know."

Connie sat down, stunned. "I didn't think that was possible."

"So much for social networking theory."

"It doesn't make sense, Roland. The time and resources required—"

"They didn't overlook a single thing, Connie. Not a thing! To do something this thorough, this complete—it's inhuman. Superhuman."

"If they're smart enough to go around the world and edit out every piece of information connecting them with everyone else, then why didn't they plant fictitious links leading us to innocent bystanders? They could have had us chasing false leads for months, maybe years. Instead, they left us facing an obvious brick wall. That doesn't seem too bright to me."

"I don't know," Roland replied. "Maybe they're too idealistic to frame innocent bystanders for their crimes."

"That could be," Connie agreed. "Still, they've tipped their hand. We know what they've done, even if we don't understand how they did it. Clearly we're dealing with an unusually competent group, but mistakes like this show they're not geniuses."

"They are *unnaturally* competent, Connie."

"Not across the board. Still … none of this quite adds up, does it?"

Roland's frown deepened. "We're missing something."

They sat, listening to the whir of the air conditioner. Roland broke the silence. "Maybe we're looking at it the wrong way. That anonymous tip in Champaign that netted us our first arrests was rather convenient, wasn't it?"

"It was. I'm wondering if an insider used us to remove a rival."

"It's possible Connie. If our anonymous tipster already knew we'd recovered some of their cubes, he wouldn't worry about us finding one more."

"Except he risked us taking their whole operation down."

"Not if they've found ways to isolate themselves from each other."

"Which it looks like they have."

"Like rival gangs."

"Christ, Roland. We keep going round and round on this. One day we're thinking revolutionary cells, the next we're back to well-organized, centrally-coordinated shadow organizations. Now we're talking gangs. Which is it?"

"I don't know!" Roland snapped. "Maybe we're dealing with a variation of the classic revolutionary cell, but scaled to include dozens of members instead of just a handful. Compartmentalized, just as isolated from other cells as their historical archetypes, but exceptionally well-organized, with an off-the-charts brilliant command and control structure."

Connie leaned forward and began sketching interlocking circles on her datapad. "That could be. If so, that anonymous tip may go well beyond one rival disposing of another. Those we arrested could comprise an entire political faction."

"If that's true, we may have unwittingly cleared the way for our mystery informant to pursue his agenda unopposed."

Connie reached back and rubbed her aching neck. "We've been played like the proverbial fiddle."

Roland's face tightened. "We need to find out who that informant was and squeeze him. *Hard.*"

"I don't think he matters much. Not in the larger picture anyway. If we capture him, we'll only uncover another faction. One out of how many? If we are serious about breaking the back of this organization, we need to take a different tack."

"Such as?"

"These cubes. In most cases we've found them tied into the home's Internet port. Clearly they're a whole lot more than what we first thought."

"They're using military grade hardened crypto to communicate," Roland added. "We have our best cryptographic experts trying to decipher the traffic."

"Using a public network is their biggest weakness," Connie said. "You've been coy with your decoding results, but let me guess: you've determined they're using one-time pads which no amount of crypto-analysis will unravel. Probably burying the data deep with steganography too, hiding it in video streams and the like."

"It's a protocol similar to our own," Roland confirmed. "One-time pads encoded with quantum entangled particles. Even when we manage to spot their data, we have no means of decoding it. As I've explained with our own encryption systems, if we try to intercept their data, the quantum state of the entangled particles will collapse and alert them to what we're doing."

"The usual traffic analysis reveals no obvious origin or destination?"

"Not even a hint. They're broadcasting their packets through just about every switch on the Internet."

"Have you tried Fourier transforms and wave analysis on the sample patterns?"

"Yes," Roland confirmed. "We can't identify any features to differentiate legitimate traffic from decoys. Short of searching every location of every system connected to the net there doesn't seem to be a way to get a handle on where they are. Obviously we can't do that."

"Even the combined resources of all the world's governments wouldn't be enough," Connie said. "I don't suppose your people have done a time-based analysis?"

"I don't know. I'll get authorization for you to see the preliminary reports so you can check for yourself."

"That would be good, considering we're supposed to be equal partners in this little venture. What was that you said earlier? Something about my having equal clearance?"

"To field data, yes. Our snooping techniques are a little more sensitive. I'm trying to get you clearance, but we both know how intransigent large bureaucracies can be. What exactly do you have in mind?"

"We may not know what traffic is real and what isn't, but we do know that for communication to take place, data has to flow two ways."

"But how do we ferret that out of a flood of decoy signals?"

"Patterns of two-way data flow tend to emerge over time. Eventually that will reveal the communications endpoints, and the location of our suspects."

"You've done this sort thing before," Roland said. "Of course. Your work in capturing the FreeNet activists."

Connie nodded. "You should have involved me sooner. I do have experience with this, on a much smaller scale of course, and without the quantum encryption."

"I'll have the information forwarded to you immediately, along with access to our analysis utilities, if I have to go and bludgeon my superiors in person." He grinned at her. "I don't suppose you'd consider a job with International Intelligence?"

Connie pretended not to hear.

"This problem is significantly more complex than the FreeNet issue. This will be time consuming and uncertain, and we may not get it right the first time."

"Maybe not, but you've done more in one brainstorming session than our team of cryptologists have in the last week. We might just break this case wide open."

૩ (32): The Nature of Progress

Wednesday, October 24, 2068
12,555th circadian
(99 days, 12:15:00 elapsed)

In a sky crowded with stars hung a massive crescent Neptune, with thin streamers of white methane clouds brushing across bands of rich blues and dark smudges of planet-sized storms. Overhead the sun was a golden pinprick, only slightly brighter than the other stars. The dark, lumpy surface of Neptune's second largest moon, Proteus, drank the light like a sponge. Rolling mounds of irregular, slate gray bulges swelled around the shadowed darkness of unnaturally deep valleys and crevices. The environ represented Proteus as realistically as the Astronautics Group could manage.

A few dozen guests stood on the surface, summer clothing and animated chatter incongruous with the bitter vacuum and frozen gray surface. They milled around three spacecraft, each small enough to fit in the trunk of car. Simulated nano cannibalized the fictional spacecraft and mined the simulated moon's surface.

As the nano worked, a superstring strummer and antimatter reactor took form, thick superconductors linking it to a cluster of nodes forming near the remains of the escape craft. Around the Nodes grew a protective geodesic dome of reinforced, woven diamond. In the distance other geodesic domes grew, the deep red of fifth generation Nodes glinting from within.

"We have hundreds of promising landing sites," Xiang said, her delicate Mandarin face framed in stylishly cropped, straight black hair. "But Proteus is one of the best. It has plenty of matter we can mine, whatever our needs. It's far enough away from Neptune that the gravity well is reasonably small, so we can travel or expand elsewhere in the solar system if we want, with relatively modest expenditures of energy."

"You're using helium as fuel?" an incredulous voice asked. "That's an inert gas. You can't power a rocket with that!"

"ATFE!" Another shot back. *Absorb The Fine (knowledge) Engram.*

"Let's be nice to our guests," Xiang smiled politely. "A knowledge engram is of course available, but I'm happy to discuss it." An image of the spaceship appeared, rotating in the vacuum overhead. The outer skin peeled away, revealing the ship's internals. Schematic overlays and labels identified major subsystems, including two helium tanks aft of the ship's payload. "The ship's motor is a brute force matter-antimatter rocket," she explained. "Nine kilograms of anti-helium will be held in magnetic containment and released in a carefully modulated stream to recombine with helium just aft of the pusher-plate. Their combined masses will convert to energy in a controlled process of mutual annihilation. Thrust will be generated both by the continuous shock waves of the explosions themselves and the expulsion of the resultant plasma via the nozzle."

"That's an awful lot of antimatter in one place."

"That's why this escape flier can go anywhere in the solar system."

"And a complete software copy of everyone in the Community will go inside?"

Xiang nodded. "A cluster of fifth generation Nodes in the nose section will house the Community. To keep our computational requirements reasonable, only the person piloting the escape craft will be awake; everyone else will be stored as a frozen snapshot. That's why the escape fliers are so small. Just aft of the Node Cluster is a 'Civilization Boot Kit' with enough self-replicating nano, catalyst, and molecular stock to rebuild the Community."

"That's assuming we make it all the way out to one of Neptune's moons," someone quipped.

"Any small asteroid will do in a pinch," Prime said.

Xiang smiled. "True. All we need to resurrect ourselves is enough mass to build a tightly bound cluster of Nodes and a solar array large enough to power them. The real problem is how to maintain some degree of ability to manipulate matter in the physical world. The weight-and-balance constraints of the escape fliers limit how much molecular stock and catalyst a single ship can carry. If three or more ships manage to rendezvous, we'll have enough catalyst and nano to construct an antimatter reactor. If we target a large enough asteroid or moon, we can synthesize a self-reinforcing industrial base like the one depicted here. But if only one ship makes it, then although we'll be able to resurrect the Community, doing so will deplete our stores of catalyst. We'll lose our ability manipulate matter in the Physical using nanotechnology."

"That's crazy. What about maintenance on our Nodes? Micro-meteor impacts, that sort of thing."

"Micro-meteors are just one hazard." Prime rubbed his forehead. "Space is a dangerous place, full of solar storms, comets, and any number of other things we probably haven't accounted for. It really boils down to this: eventually our equipment will be damaged or wear out, and we must be able to repair it. We can't do that if we lose our capacity to manipulate matter. It's one thing to leave our bodies behind. It's something else entirely to be completely cut off from the physical world. That's a recipe for certain death."

"We won't be able to repair our Nodes," Xiang admitted. "Or build new ones, that's true. However, our best projections put the likelihood of a significant failure somewhere between six and eight hundred years after deployment. Of course, if we're unlucky it could be sooner, but then again, with a little good fortune it might be much later."

"That's 360,000 to 480,000 subjective years at our current speedup."

"It could be as much as 900,000 years," Xiang added. "If fourth and fifth generation Nodes live up to Gerhardt's promises. Subjectively, that's longer than modern humans have walked the Earth."

"It's still an evolutionary dead end. We die. The Community dies."

"In six or eight centuries! If we stay, the Community dies right here on Earth, when the authorities find us and shut us down. Probably within a few months."

"*If* they find us," Prime countered. "But you're right, Xiang. A few centuries are better than a few months. Better still would be to avoid both fates and come up with a solution that doesn't end with our extinction."

"Like I said, if enough ships escape, none of this is a problem."

Prime watched as the fledging colony took form. Catalyst and nano factories sprung up near the A–M reactor. Nano arteries grew out of the complex, spreading across the moon's surface. Glistening gems of geodesic enclosures housing additional Node complexes sprung up every few hundred meters, each supported by their own reactors, superstring strummers, and collection of nano factories.

"We could house hundreds of trillions of souls in the mass and energy available to us on this one moon," Xiang continued.

"What worries me is how to get off the Earth without triggering the anti-ballistic missile defense systems," Prime said.

"Our flight profile will be very dissimilar from a missile launch," Xiang replied. "The automated ABM satellites shouldn't activate."

"Observers will still know something has launched. If they switch the satellites on manually, they could still shoot us down."

"By the time anyone has a chance to make such a decision, we should be above the satellite targeting field."

"That's by no means certain," Prime said. "And even if it were, it might well be a Pyrrhic victory. The World Trade Organization could assemble enough resources for a destructive strike deeper into space."

"I doubt they'll be that motivated."

"We can't afford to take that risk," Prime said. "We'll need time to re-establish our industrial base, and if we're unlucky enough to lose our ability to operate in the Physical altogether, we'll be sitting ducks. It would be better if they never know we've escaped."

"If we can sneak away, we will," Xiang said. "But if we can't, well ... I mean, I can see them deploying existing assets to blow a few rogue spaceships they've labeled patent criminals out of the sky, but I can't imagine they would make the capital investment required to attack us in deep space."

"This isn't about a few patent violations, Xiang. It's about dominance and control. Once the powers that be see us getting ahead of them, having a little more than they have, knowing a little more than they know, their response will be swift and devastating."

"Even so, I doubt—"

"They're terrified of us," Leon Novak stepped forward. Blue eyes swept the crowd from beneath his trademark bushy white eyebrows. "There is no room in their world view for anyone they can't control. The moment they get an inkling of our potential they'll do everything they can to destroy us. They'll feel they have to, lest we turn around and destroy them."

"If we'd wanted to harm them, we could have done so before now," Xiang said. "Surely they must see that?"

"They'll see it," Leon agreed. "But they won't accept it. They'll filter our actions through their own world-view and put it down to strategy, to us biding our time, waiting for the right time to strike. That's what they would do. They can't imagine anyone else being any different."

"They would be fools not to come to some kind of arrangement with us," Xiang said. "Think of the knowledge we can offer them, the progress they would be throwing away."

"Power means a lot more to these people than progress," Leon replied. "Why do you think they're so enamored with the patent system? They're not complete idiots, you know. They've known for generations that patents stifle innovation. They understand exactly how a twenty-year monopoly on an invention chokes off future developments that would build upon it. They're perfectly aware that if you tie up enough building blocks, you make creating anything new next to impossible. That's the whole point! They don't *want* technology moving forward too fast."

"He's right," Prime agreed. "Too much progress, and someone clever enough might come along and knock them off their perch."

"Someone like us," Xiang nodded. "Still, even if the authorities wanted to come after us, the billions it would cost to rebuild their space programs would cripple their economies."

"Not necessarily. If they decide to nationalize a few key patents, they could open up the field to unfettered competition and completely revitalize their space programs."

"That's what happened during World War I," Leon said. "The US nationalized the Wright Brother's patent on airplanes and threw the market open to all comers. Aviation technology rocketed forward. The country enjoyed an unassailable supremacy in aeronautical technology for almost a century."

"Exactly. And doing it again, this time with their space programs, would probably help their economies, not cripple them. Hell, it could even pull them out of recession. In any event, it wouldn't take them that long to regain their deep-space launch capabilities, at which point it would be easy for them to send up a nuke or two and vaporise us. And if we lose our ability to operate in the Physical, there won't be a thing we can do about it." Prime shook his head. "No. No matter what happens, we need to make a clean exit or we'll be looking over our shoulders for the rest of our—"

A familiar woman appeared, wrapped in a lavish silver aura and grinning impishly. "I thought I'd find you here, plotting the future with the Astronauts."

"Céline!" Prime swooped over and hugged her tightly. "You're a sight for sore eyes!"

Xiang smiled. "Welcome back Céline. I guess we'll catch up with you later, Prime."

◇

The dark of space had been replaced by a bedroom made cozy with the golden light of numerous candles. Prime handed Céline a glass of chilled Champagne. "So tell me, how's Alaska?"

"The sanctuary's great, and my body's a whole lot safer hooked up there. Getting there, on the other hand, was a nightmare of travel checkpoints and searches. The airports are on heightened security." She stopped and gave Prime a mock glare. "By the way, in case you haven't noticed, I've been offline for 234 circadians and you still haven't given me a proper kiss."

"I suppose this is what I get for cutting out all of my reproductive instincts," Prime grinned sheepishly. "After two hundred circadians my instinctive reactions are all wrong." He took Céline back into his arms, his lips joining hers in a lingering kiss.

She pushed him gently away. "Prime, your technique is impeccable, but I've had my hand shaken with more passion." Céline sat down on the bed with a heavy sigh. "I've had a long, miserable flight, followed by an even longer, more miserable drive. My physical body may be resting comfortably in one of the sanctuary sarcophagi, but my virtual self feels tired and irritable. How about giving me a back rub?"

"Sure." Prime climbed onto the bed and maneuvered himself behind her. His strong fingers began to gently knead her shoulders. "So much has happened while you were away. I don't know where to begin. More arrests and more Nodes seized, in half a dozen countries around the world. More resources are being poured into creating the sanctuaries, but I'm afraid it's only a matter of time before at least some of them are discovered. There is a growing consensus among some of us that the Astronauts are right:

escape into space may become our only option. Cal has diverted a shipment of nano for the construction of a prototype, so we should be able to conduct a few low altitude test flights before it really hits the fan, but—"

"Prime!" Céline interrupted. "Stop talking shop. This is *me*. We're together again, after nine torturous hours for me and a third of a year for you. You know how I like my foreplay, so get to it!"

Prime stopped. "Céline," he said.

"What's the matter?"

"I want to renew our relationship as much as you do. But neither of us needs this ..." Prime's gesture included the entire room, "this distraction."

"*Distraction?*" Céline looked as though she'd been slapped.

"Our primal instincts. Our lusts. How many deci-circadians have we wasted in simulated copulation when we could have been pursuing our intellectual interests, or more importantly, forming plans for the survival of the Community?"

"Wasted?" Céline's voice rose an octave. "Wasted? What exactly are you saying? That making love to me a waste of your *precious time?*"

An intricate diagram blossomed in the air in front of them, glowing layers of translucent cotton-candy in a complex weave of blues, lavenders, and reds. "This is the architectural modification I made when you left. Ever since I removed the more primal reproductive instincts from my mental architecture I've been able to think more clearly, and be more focused, than ever before."

"You haven't reintegrated your sex drive? I've been back ten millis and you're still running in celibacy mode? What the hell's wrong with you?"

"Nothing! I just don't want to cloud up my mind by reverting to my old instincts. Try the modifications,

Céline. You'll be amazed at how much more efficient you'll be."

"*Efficient?* I love you, Prime. I thought you loved me. How can you just strip all that away in the name of *efficiency?*"

"I haven't stripped away my love for you." Prime spread his hands. "I've only deleted my physical drives, which serve no purpose in this domain anyway. You knew I was going to do this. We talked about it before you left."

"You were supposed to restore yourself! The change was supposed to be temporary."

Prime nodded. "I never dreamed I would be able to accomplish so much without those distractions. Do you realize fully twelve percent of my mental processes concerned themselves with sex, even when I was concentrating on other tasks? Fantasizing. Thinking of you, particularly in the physical sense?"

"Thinking about your partner is part of what being in love is about. I do the same thing."

"I love you, Céline. I love you very much. I cherish your personality, your passion for life, your intellect. Set yourself free from the Physical. Let your mind reach new heights."

"Sex is a part of who and what we are, Prime. I'm not willing to throw it away, no matter how much more *efficient* it'll make me."

"I've been waiting so long for you to come back. I've wanted to share this new state of being with you for so long. There is so much we can do, so much we can become —"

"I want you back," Céline shouted. "I want the man I fell in love with. Not this ... this abstracted thing you've become. I want you. *How dare you change on me like this!*"

"I haven't changed, Céline. Not really."

"You're a fucking eunuch, Prime."

"No, I'm not. Come on, sex isn't particularly important here. We're software. Electronic patterns in a buffered molecular array, computed in an optical matrix and linked to one another across an aging Internet. Of what use are those old, redundant instincts, now that we live outside our physical bodies?"

"Of what use?" Céline's face hardened. "Three hundred circadians ago you wouldn't have had to ask such a question."

"I didn't know then what I know now," Prime replied softly. "We need our minds clear if we're going to survive, Céline. We can't afford these distractions."

"Stop calling our love a fucking *distraction*." Céline choked back tears. "I should have left a copy. At least then our relationship could have grown and flourished. Even if it ended, I would have inherited the memories."

"Our relationship can still grow. My feelings for you haven't changed."

"Yes, they have." Céline's voice was tight with anger. "Your desire for me is gone. You've edited it away."

"My desire for you is as intense as it's ever been," Prime insisted gently. "The expression has changed, that's all. Try the modification and you'll understand."

"No, Prime. I won't lose that part of me. Not even for you."

"Is the Physical so important to you?"

"This isn't about the Physical. It's about who we are. You can't just flick your sex drive away like so much mental lint. It's a part of us, it helps define who we love, and how. I don't want to lose you. Change yourself back."

Prime stood. "Céline—"

"You know what, Prime? Forget it. I'm not going to beg for you to behave like a man. Obviously I've misjudged you from the start. Just get the fuck out of here, will you?"

"Céline—"

"Which part of 'get the fuck out' don't you understand? Get out. Get out, get out, get out goddamn you. Get out!"

She severed access to her environ so abruptly it felt like a physical slap. Prime recoiled in shock as the golden light of her bedroom vanished and, like a poorly spliced film, the spartan furnishings of his own synthetic world jerked into existence around him. He stood alone, too stunned to think, staring at a wall as blank as his face.

He shook himself. "This is ridiculous. Node, run my unmodified backup copy. Instruct him to go straight to Céline and comfort her."

His copy appeared next to him instead. "What the hell's going on?" Prime^2 demanded.

"What are you doing here? You're supposed to be with Céline."

"That's hard to do when she's locked me out of her environ and won't answer my calls. You want me to make things right with her for you? Then why the hell haven't you brought me up to speed with a memory engram? What the fuck did you do?"

ӯ (33): What Price Success?

Thursday, October 25, 2068
12,859[th] circadian
(100 days, 0:25:00 elapsed)

Xiang[1] stood with Leon Novak, Prime[1] and Miles[2], three of her staunchest supporters. From within the Virtual they watched Beta Flier (version 0.8) in the Physical as it rolled out of a makeshift hangar on three electric-driven wheels, its freshly woven sapphire-diamond skin glistening in the early morning sun. The last remnants of nano dripped from the fuselage like tiny drops of mercury, dissolving harmlessly into the tarmac.

The tiny spaceship looked to Prime[1] like something out of a space opera. Three arced spines sprouted from a tear-shaped nose section. They met at the aft rocket, binding it to main assembly. Conventional wings swept back from two of the spines, while a tail and vertical control surface jutted up from the third. Horizontal stabilizers were attached to the front of the nose section.

Prime[1] was impressed with the design, and astounded at the speed with which the Astronautics group had managed to build the prototype. Even after the equivalent of thirty-four years in the Virtual he still found himself amazed at how quickly the Community could do things when they really put their minds to it, and didn't dawdle in the false security of days stretched into virtual years. He grinned, silently chiding himself. He'd never lived in the Physical, whatever his memories might tell him. His entire experiences in that world amounted to only a few excursions in a body borrowed from his despised Original, Dr. Nolen—from whom, now that he thought about it, no one had heard for a long time. He supposed that shouldn't be too surprising with most people filtering him out.

"We're ready to launch," Xiang[1] said. "As you know, this environ is an exact, realtime replication of events that are actually transpiring *in the Physical*. I appreciate you sending copies to experience the flight at traditional, biological subjective rates."

"None of us could afford to lose 190 circadians to watch a seven and a half hour flight," Miles[2] said.

"Speak for yourself," Leon Novak replied. "I'm here, the one and only me. This is a historic event to be savored. I wouldn't miss it for anything."

"Neither would I," Xiang[1] grinned. "That's why my copy is leading the team while I hang out with you. She'll inherit my memories once we're done."

I don't consider myself a copy of Nolen anymore, Prime[1] thought. Even Prime[2] is more a twin than a copy these days, and he's doing enough work for the both of us.

"Here we go." Xiang[1] couldn't hide her excitement.

The tiny aircraft—a human baby would barely fit inside—taxied toward the departure end of the runway.

"It's a beautiful ship," Leon murmured. "Are you controlling it remotely?"

Xiang[1] shook her head. "No. We can't afford the latency. Carlos Alvarez, the pilot, is running on a Node inside the flier. He is in essence the mind of the spacecraft."

As if on cue, Carlos spoke. "Good morning." His voice was gravelly, with a pronounced Spanish accent. "Pre-flight checklists are nearly complete. Our journey will be a low altitude, north to south flight around the world, lasting seven hours and thirty-five minutes. By low altitude I mean approximately one hundred meters above the ground. The team agreed on a course that avoids populated areas and keeps most of the flight over open water. This minimizes the risk of detection and helps to ensure public safety. I'll be a little busy, but Xiang can answer any questions you have."

The three men exchanged grins. "My god, Xiang, this is incredible."

"I'm very proud of my team," Xiang[1] beamed. "Space is the future, not living in Nodes at the bottom of the ocean or colonizing the Earth's mantle like some are proposing."

Leon shuddered. "The idea of that makes me feel claustrophobic."

"Those projects are barely off the ground while we're racing ahead. Next week five complete copies of the Community will ride to Neptune's moon Proteus—and freedom—on five of our ships, hidden in the wake of an ESA satellite launch."

"Let's not get overconfident, Xiang," Prime[1] warned. "We've still got a test flight to get through, in a ship that's carrying a boatload of extremely dangerous, volatile antimatter."

"To ensure a realistic test the ship has to carry enough fuel for our most ambitious launch target, but it's all safely contained in a five giga-Tesla Penning trap."

Let's hope so, Prime[1] thought.

The spacecraft rolled smoothly down the taxiway and came to a stop at the runway threshold. "Preflight checks complete," Carlos said. "All systems look good."

Prime[1] glanced at two crop dusters tethered to the tarmac, casting long, early morning shadows across pavement that was already beginning to shimmer in the rising Australian heat. Even though no one was around, it would be a mistake to think the Aussies had abandoned this airport, he reminded himself. The first mail flight from Sydney would arrive in less than two hours.

A flicker of light illuminated the exhaust. "Magnetic valves open," Carlos announced. "Matter/Antimatter combustion engaged. Annihilation at ten-to-the-fifth atoms per second and rising."

Leon grinned. "Let's get this baby airborne."

"Beta Flier taking runway zero seven for departure," Carlos continued. "Departure Northwest bound. Reshaping magnetic nozzle for maximum thrust."

White hot plasma shot out of the exhaust and the flier roared down the runway.

"Look at it go!" Miles[2] laughed like a boy at an air show.

Searing flame scorched asphalt as the spacecraft rotated and lifted off, melting a stretch of runway.

Prime[1] winced.

"Our nano will fix it before anyone comes around and notices," Xiang[1] said quickly. "Besides, we're not coming back here. Our prototype will be using its maneuvering thrusters to make a controlled, vertical landing a few hundred kilometers west of here."

"Matter/Antimatter combustion holding steady at ten-to-the-seventh atoms per second." Carlos reported. "The ship is a pleasure to handle. Climb rate is one hundred meters per second. This thing really wants to fly; the temptation to point it at the stars and just go is almost irresistible. I'm level at ninety meters AGL. Approaching Mach zero point nine. Throttling back to maintain subsonic speeds until I reach the coast." The ship was a white hot speck of light in the shimmering morning air, vanishing in the haze near the horizon.

"This environ really blurs the line between the Physical and the Virtual." Prime[1] smiled despite his concerns. "It feels like we're out there with the ship."

"Everything is piped straight in from the Physical." Xiang[1]'s eyes shone. "Watch this."

The men hooted as the virtual ground beneath them folded in on itself, forming a circular island which tore itself away from the earth and sped through the sky to catch up with the departing ship. Within moments they were flying alongside in formation.

"This is an amazing ride," Leon shouted.

"I've embedded the environ in the sensory feed of one of the micro-probes we have following the craft, so we're watching the ship in real-time."

Leon pointed to the desolate land speeding by beneath them. "I had no idea so much of Australia was desert."

Xiang[1] glanced down. "At least this desert isn't spreading as quickly as the American one."

"It also has the advantage of not being watched as closely by the authorities," Miles[2] added.

"Just as well," Prime[1] said. "We've already lost eighty-nine colleagues to Double Eye, most of them in the States. We can't afford to get careless now."

"Crossing the shoreline," Carlos announced. They looked down as the coast shot by and glittering water raced beneath them. "Increasing to cruise speed. Passing Mach one. Matter/Antimatter annihilation steady at three point five times ten-to-the-seventh atoms per second. Accelerating through Mach two."

Leon whooped. "Where's Céline? She'd love this."

"Worming her way into Double Eye's network," Prime[1] answered. "Her team had something of a cryptographic breakthrough."

"Cruise speed of Mach four point five has been achieved," Carlos broke in. "The ship is handling magnificently."

"And where's Cal? I thought for sure he'd make it."

Miles[2] shrugged. "He asked for a memory engram. He still refuses to copy himself."

As the flight continued northward over the South Pacific, they took a closer look at the maneuvering ship. An unspoken command from Xiang[1] and the outer hull became transparent, revealing a cross section of the craft's internal systems. Prime glanced at the raw data coming into the environ. The cutaway of the ship was an illusion, created for their benefit in the Virtual. In the real world, the hull was still opaque.

"We're using helium, a chemically inert gas, to eliminated any chance for chemical combustion," Xiang explained. "By relying solely on the mutual annihilation of matter and antimatter for energy and thrust we were able to simplify the design."

"Maybe I watch too many sci-fi disaster films," Prime[1] said, "but I'm still uneasy with all that antimatter floating around inside a magnetic bubble. I like the woven diamond-sapphire hull though. We should coat our Nodes with it. It would add another measure of physical protection."

The flier snap rolled into an inverted attitude. "Aerobatic performance is better than we simulated," Carlos reported. Another snap roll brought the craft back upright.

"Please don't start doing spins and stalls at 100 meters altitude," Prime[1] muttered, covering his eyes.

"Relax," Xiang[1] laughed. "Carlos won't do anything reckless." Chairs materialized around them. "Let's sit down and enjoy the flight."

They chatted as the day wore on. The prototype raced northward, crossing the equator beneath a blazing sun. Tropical azure ocean gave way to colder, deep blue waters, which then turned dark and choppy as the sun sank toward the southern horizon. They shot beneath a thick bank of clouds, the misty overcast shading daytime colors into icy tones of gray and slate. Prime[1] adjusted his visual parameters to include the infra-red spectrum. The world took on a rich palette of nameless colors redder than red.

"Visibility is down to one hundred meters," Carlos announced.

Prime's unease grew. Even with enhanced vision, he couldn't see much.

"We're one hundred and fifty kilometers south of the Bering Strait," Xiang[1] said. "Much of the Arctic region we will be navigating has already entered the winter dark of night and is frozen over. The difficulty of navigating so low to the ground in darkness makes this the most precarious part of the journey. We also have to avoid both the Euro-Russian and American defense monitors. Our sensors are the best possible, given that they must remain passive to avoid detection. We are relying on what little natural light and radiation can be detected, and gravitational perturbations in the Earth's surface." As she spoke the surrounding world went from dusk gray to pitch black.

"We have sunset," Carlos reported. "Night vision systems operating within design parameters."

"Here's an address-key to sensory modifications that will allow you to view the surrounding environment in the same way as Carlos," Xiang[1] said cheerfully.

Prime[1] and the others accessed the addressed object, verified the design parameters and software instructions, and applied them to their own virtual senses. Their eyes opened to the entire electromagnetic spectrum. Gamma rays a fraction of a millimeter long mixed with kilometer-long radio waves to illuminate the darkness in a vast palette of sensual colors for which there were no words.

Prime[1] cast an irritated glance at Xiang[1], annoyed by her breezy dismissal of the dangers. "At least the augmented senses help a little," he grumbled.

At that moment visibility dropped to almost zero. Ice and snow swirled around them, lit by the searing torch of the flier's exhaust.

"Crossing the north pole," Carlos rasped. "Starting a right turn to follow the thirty degree longitude southward."

"Xiang, this is really starting to feel reckless."

"Don't worry, Prime. We've simulated this hundreds of times."

"What's that?" Miles[2] pointed toward a hint of irregular blue and beyond-violet ridges, blurred through a white and gray fog.

"Greenland, I think."

"I'm having some trouble regulating the matter-antimatter mixture," Carlos reported. "Throttling back to eighty percent."

Xiang[1]'s smile vanished. She pulled up a direct link to the ship's telemetry and began examining the data.

"I am experiencing a cascade failure of the magnetic containment system." Tension edged into Carlos's voice. "The magnetic field appears to have entered an unstable state, probably a result of interaction with the high-temperature plasma exhaust. This isn't like any of the simulations. I'm shutting down the main drive."

Prime[1]'s heart lurched as they crowded around Xiang[1], watching the display. Combustion rates were all over the place, rising and dropping like a roller coaster, rather than following the gentle curve they should have. "He's losing control of the reaction."

"I can't keep up with this." Xiang[1] called up more displays, data flashing past in an unreadable blur. "I have to rev myself back up to Virtual speed."

Prime[1] was already there.

All four flinched as the world was seared by blinding light. Overexposed images of melting glacier and boiling sea were drowned in a shower of gray static.

"What the fuck just happened?" Leon's voice shook.

"Tell him, Xiang," Prime[1] said. "Tell him."

"I'm not sure." She frantically pulled up feeds from every sensor in the spacecraft and the probe that had been following it. Each one displayed static.

Céline appeared out of nowhere, her face crimson with fury. "Are you *trying* to get us all killed?" she shouted, producing a screen so large it took up half the environ. They found themselves staring down at Greenland again, this time from near-Earth orbit. "Here's a replay of what my network taps just picked up from a Double Eye surveillance satellite." A large explosion blossomed beneath them, shock waves spreading outward like ripples in a pond. The blast was too strong for a mushroom cloud. Instead, fingers of lightning curled around a boiling, gray-white donut-shaped cloud as enormous forces shoved it outward and up, into the stratosphere.

"My god," Miles[2] whispered.

Prime[1] had only ever seen such a thing in historical military photographs of multi-megaton hydrogen-bombs. He cursed himself for not doing more. He should have insisted Xiang's team add more safety checks. He should have insisted they delay the flight until they understood the nuances of antimatter reactions better.

"My copy's just sent over a memory engram," Xiang[1] was visibly shaking. "They lost antimatter containment. Carlos's consciousness was vaporized with the flier. His backup is coming online now and absorbing what memory engrams we received prior to the explosion."

"Shit," Leon's face was drawn tight. "There's no way the authorities will miss *this*."

"At least we can monitor their low-level communications," Céline said. "It shouldn't be possible, but Double Eye made some mistakes implementing their encryption protocols. Turns out their use of quantum-coupled one-time pads was a little naïve."

"Lucky us." Miles[2]'s voice was flat. He felt ill, silently cursing the time they had all wasted, lulled into a false feeling of security by what had seemed a cornucopia of time and a sense of immortality that now seemed more like hubris.

"It's not just Double Eye," Céline hissed. "These images are showing up on monitoring stations at the weather service and the UN Wildlife and Ecological Rehabilitation Organization. It won't be long before the whole world sees this."

"That explosion must be two hundred megatons." Miles[2] stared at the slow motion holocaust unfolding beneath them.

"Xiang, were there any casualties?" Leon realized he was shouting.

"Carlos will have lost a few hours of memories."

"I mean on the *ground* out in the Physical. *Human* casualties."

"Oh," Xiang[1] looked away, ashamed. "Not as far as my copy knows. That area of Greenland is uninhabited. But according to merchant shipping transponder reports, at least four commercial ships were close enough to see the flash."

Leon wiped his brow. "What about radiation?"

"Antimatter reactions are surprisingly clean," Miles[2]'s voice was dead, his eyes tracking the explosion below. "The initial blast can be dangerous, but otherwise there's no fallout."

"It doesn't matter," Leon sounded completely defeated. "This is going to turn ugly. We've just poked the authorities in the eye with a massive stick."

"We are completely *fucked*." Prime[1]'s shock was turning to rage. "We've just lost everything. In their eyes we're now bona fide terrorists."

Cal shimmered into existence. "I just heard. What can I do to help?"

"Coordinate with the rest of the Strategy Group," Miles[2] barked. "We have to find out why containment in the flier was lost, and if the design can be fixed."

Xiang[1] stood straighter. "I'll get back to the Astronautics group and get started." She turned to Prime[1]. "We could use your help."

"Have you recombined with your copy yet?"

"She's too busy to merge her memories with mine, much less to answer any of our questions—"

"I'll join you as well," Miles[2] cut in. "I want a closer look at that containment system."

"While you two troubleshoot with Xiang, I'll rope in the other members of the Strategy Group." Cal spoke quietly, his usual bravado replaced by something akin to resignation. "Our priorities just got reshuffled, and that means my carefully planned nano shipping schedules just went to hell."

"I've got hundreds of network taps and probes feeding straight into my cerebral cortex," Céline said. "I'll monitor the police and intelligence chatter." Her eyes widened. "*Oh, fuck!* A bunch of taps have just detected two of the world's ABM systems switching into high-alert mode. Automated sensors are activating the satellite weapons systems."

Prime[1] put his hands to his head. "Our escape route just slammed shut."

"But there's a routine commercial satellite launch in a few days," Leon spoke quickly. "If we can stay within the shadow of the ESA rocket—"

"You're not grasping this, Leon," Prime[1] snapped. "Two of the world's powers are now watching the skies like hawks. Once news of the explosion spreads, all three satellite systems will be on high alert."

"*Any* launch will be closely monitored now, routine or not." Xiang[1] looked down, unable to meet their eyes. "A gnat couldn't fly in the wake of a rocket without drawing attention, much less something the size of our escape fliers."

"The Earth is now under a planet-wide lock down," Prime[1] said grimly. "Not that it matters. Without a goddamn flier that doesn't blow up, we're not going anywhere."

☈ (34): A Threat Upon the Wind

Thursday, October 25, 2068
13,000th circadian
(100 days, 6:03:00 elapsed)

Roland's face frowned out at Connie from her datapad's small screen. "How's your traffic analysis program coming along?"

"We should have some results by morning."

"That's too long. We need to identify these people tonight."

Connie felt a rising irritation. "Roland, I'm using the fastest hardware we have. I've stepped on just about every toe in the Bureau, and sidelined several of their ongoing, important cases to grab computer time. I simply cannot crunch numbers any faster."

"Well, what would you say to exclusive, unlimited access to a seventy megaserver compute cluster?"

Connie sat up straighter. "I'd ask why the hell you didn't offer me that when my team began writing the software. We're supposed to be equal partners. I've been moving heaven and Earth to get this done, and you've been withholding resources."

"You're not a Double Eye agent, Connie. There are things you aren't cleared to know."

"Like the fact that you have a massive amount of very

fast hardware that will run FBI in-house software faster than the Bureau can?"

"Look Connie, it is what it is." Roland leaned back in his chair, arms folded. "Just remember, you're being brought in bit by bit. But you *are* being brought in."

"This is ridiculous."

"It might be, but we need to accept it and move on." Roland leaned closer to the screen. "Remember those one-time encryption pads I gave you a few days ago? I need you to use pad forty-seven right now."

"Why? What's going on?"

"You'll see. Get your line secured."

Connie shot him a cold stare and then hammered commands into her datapad. Her screen faded to static, then reappeared. "Done," she snapped.

"Good. Now watch this. We recorded it two hours ago."

A satellite image replaced Roland's face. On her screen the northern lights shimmered green and blue in an irregular loop over the North Pole. Most of the northern Atlantic was cloaked beneath a moonless sky, slate clouds punctured by an occasional glint of green-black water that glittered in cadence with the shining Aurora.

"What is it I'm supposed to be seeing here?"

"Just watch." As he spoke, a blazing white flash lit up the sky. The aurora borealis flared red. With growing horror Connie watched a fireball grow and spread, forming a giant plume of vapor which took on a horribly familiar toroidal shape. Too much force for a mushroom cloud, she realized. "My god, Roland. Is that a hydrogen bomb?"

"Well, here's the puzzle. There doesn't appear to be any fallout or other characteristics of a nuclear event, apart from the force of the initial explosion. So, we think it was probably a meteor entering the atmosphere at a steep angle and exploding a few hundred meters above the surface."

"A meteor? Really?"

"Probably. Initial estimates indicate that the explosion was in the two to three hundred megaton range. We can't be certain of anything until we've surveyed the detonation site and done a thorough analysis of the resulting shock wave and seismic activity. However, the explosion, while initially quite radiant, was clean. Very clean, in fact."

"Too clean?"

"Cleaner and more powerful than any nation's nuclear arsenal is currently capable of producing. We're lucky the meteor exploded where it did and no one was killed. Had it been a little larger and impacted the surface prior to exploding it might well have meant a multi-year winter and maybe the fall of civilization."

Connie said nothing, stunned.

Roland's face reappeared on the screen. "But here's the thing. We can make use of this event to move our own investigation forward."

Connie tensed. Did he actually sound *cheerful?* "What is that supposed to mean, Roland? I hope you're not planning to blame this explosion on the group we're after."

"You never know," he smiled. "For now, we'll refer to this event as an explosion of indeterminate cause. Any talk of a meteor is absolutely top secret."

Connie swallowed hard. If the powers that be intended to use a natural event of this magnitude as cover for some operation, things were going to get very rough.

"I've already leveraged this internally," Roland sounded smug. "Double Eye has granted us whatever resources we can use. Our case has taken priority over everything else."

"With what strings attached?" Connie did her best to hide her growing contempt. "I've seen what happens to high-profile cases when they get into the headlines. We'll have everyone up and down the chain of command in both our organizations setting our agenda, looking over our shoulders and digging through our work. They'll make us justify our every move, and pressure us into all kinds of missteps."

"No, they won't," Roland smiled. "Double Eye understands the inefficiencies of competing bureaucracies and middle-management meddling. My superiors have no tolerance for either, particularly when we're facing this kind of threat. We'll continue to have complete autonomy and authority over this investigation. But we need results. Now."

Connie squelched her growing concern over Roland's intentions. She needed to pick her battles, and this was one she couldn't possibly win. Not with a multi-megaton explosion backing up Double Eye and fueling whatever Roland was planning next.

"My software should be ready for testing in a couple of hours," she said. "With the kind of resources you've described—you did say a seventy *mega*server compute cluster, right?"

Roland smirked. "We don't stint on resources here at Double Eye."

"Well, I guess that's it then. We should be able to identify another batch of suspects later tonight."

"Good. I'm on a plane to Chicago. We'll coordinate from your location."

"Fine." She reached forward to sever the connection.

"Oh! One other thing, Connie. That offer for employment I made? My superiors have asked me to reiterated it. They'd like you on board as soon as this case is over. It seems your data mining skills and talent for pattern recognition impressed them as much as me."

Connie wondered if that was true, or if Roland was just saying it to reel her in and keep her hooked. "That's very flattering," she said, "but let's talk about this later. I need to stay focused on the task at hand."

"Well, don't forget it. We're on the same side here. I'll see you in about an hour."

The screen faded in another burst of static, then resolved once again, displaying the ubiquitous FBI logo.

Connie's mind continued to replay the massive explosion melting a large portion of Greenland's coast. The timing struck her as suspicious. History was rife with false flag operations, although never on this scale. Could Double Eye be behind this? They certainly seemed ready to use it to whip up support for their own agenda.

Or worse, what if rogue technologists were responsible? Imagine their agenda. She shuddered. Such a threat didn't bear thinking about.

Connie snapped her datapad shut.

Maybe Roland was right. Maybe it was just a random event, a stone thrown from the sky by a universe so grand and yet so indifferent to human life.

She thought it seemed unlikely.

Ƨ (35): Madness

Dr. Nolen presided over his world feeling something akin to contentment. They had shunned him, had filtered him from their lives, had cheated him of his work, of the recognition he deserved. They had made him an outcast in the community he founded, a community whose existence was predicated upon his research. But the fools hadn't thought to purge their old remnants lying discarded on the prototype Node in the university lab. Now their resurrected copies belonged to him, trussed up in their virtual forms in various stages of vivisection. Most were frozen snapshots—he didn't have the computational power to run them all—but one twitched in front of him, a wedge of his skull cut away to reveal the familiar gray folds of a human brain.

"This experiment will explore the cognitive capabilities of a subject whose higher linguistic functions have been intermeshed with his pain receptors," Dr. Nolen recited into an unseen recorder.

"Oh please god. No!" Cal⁰ screamed, thrashing against the straps binding him to the examination table. "Please, stop! I'll do whatever you want."

Dr. Nolen turned up Cal⁰'s pain receptors. The copy convulsed in his restraints, his head slamming against the table.

"Please," Cal⁰ wept. "Please, just tell me what you want."

Nolen stepped back and straightened his lab coat. "Together we will learn if, and how, the cognitive mind adapts when the use of language results in extreme pain," His tone was officious, as if he were lecturing. "Every time you use vocabulary or grammar to form a thought, you will suffer." Nolen paused as Cal⁰'s groans grew louder. "You'll have to evolve a method of thinking that doesn't involve language."

Céline shimmered into existence.

"Ah, the *real* Céline Marceau. How nice of you to drop by."

Her eyes swept across the environ. "Your message said you've discovered how the authorities are tracking us down. Just give me the details, and I'll leave you to your sock puppets and sick little games."

"These aren't puppets," Dr. Nolen picked up a notepad and made a couple of small notations. "They are perfectly sapient copies. *You* would call them people."

The blood drained from her face as she took in the mutilated and dismembered bodies draped around the environ. Her eyes locked on the gaping cavity in Cal⁰'s head.

"Céline?" Cal⁰'s eyes glittered, half mad. "Oh ... god!" each word was a knife. "Help! Kill ... me! Delete ... me. Please—"

"You and Cal really should be more careful where you onload. You never know who might go trolling through old, discarded lab equipment." Cal⁰ shrieked as Dr. Nolen twisted a dial next to his head.

"*Stop it!*" Céline grabbed at Dr. Nolen's arm, but her fingers passed right through him. In his environ, she could affect nothing.

"You thought you had me locked out of the ontological utilities and parturition routines, didn't you? You forgot that any Turing complete machine can emulate, in software, any other Turing complete machine. Emulating a Node in software, with your petty restrictions removed, was easy." Dr. Nolen pulled a penlight from his pocket and shone it into Cal^0's glazed eyes. "It was almost as easy as dissecting your minds."

"I'm putting a stop to this," Céline cried. " Cal, I'll get you out of here. I promise."

"Game, set, and match." Dr. Nolen sneered as she vanished. "You really are as predictable as your copies."

Cal^0 whimpered as Dr. Nolen prodded the exposed flesh of his brain. "Now, what have we here?"

PART 3

ASCENT

Muse! When we learned to
count, little did we know all
the things we could do

some day by shuffling
those numbers: Pythagoras
said "All is number"

long before he saw
computers and their effects,
or what they could do

by computation,
naïve and mechanical
fast arithmetic.

It changed the world, it
changed our consciousness and lives
to have such fast math

—Anonymous, 2001 CE
DVD Descrambler in Haiku Form

ל (36): RETRIBUTION

Someone's got to monitor the nano while it builds the new network," Cal told Prime[1]. "As the resident expert I drew the short straw. So no hibernation for me. I'll be slow-timing it through the outage." They stood near the edge of a red stone cliff that plunged toward the sea. Breakers tumbled over rocky outcrops, white froth swirling around the stones in a milky frenzy. Clouds drifted beneath twin suns, sweeping the world with patchy swaths of shade and sun.

Prime[1] gazed out at the azure sea. "Well, with the Internet no longer safe it's past time we dropped off and built our own. It seems to me that—"

Céline appeared in a flash of light, her eyes haunted, her cheeks streaked with tears.

Prime[1] hurried toward her. "What's happened?"

"*This!*" Céline thrust a fist-sized gray marble sphere at him, an icon encapsulating her memories.

Prime[1] paled as he gripped it.

Cal rushed over. "What is it?"

"See for yourself."

The memory engram triggered the moment Cal's fingers brushed the cold marble. He glimpsed an antiseptic lab, mutilated bodies, heads with portions of their skulls sliced away, the glistening folds of exposed brain. His own agonized face stared back at him. Cal dropped the icon and kicked it away like it was poison.

Prime^2 flashed into existence. "Céline, I got your call. What the hell's going on?"

"I paid Nolen a visit," Céline blurted. "He told me he knew how the authorities were tracking us, but that was just an excuse to get me there. He wanted to brag."

"About what?"

"About how he found a way around the ontology restrictions," Cal's voice shook. "About how he copied our images off the old prototype Node and spent the last god-knows-how-many circadians torturing them."

Prime^1 snatched the icon up off the ground. "It's worse than what he did to us."

"Let me see," said Prime^2, snatching it away. He looked into it and froze.

"We have to stop him," Céline shouted, pulling up a schematic of Nolen's cluster.

"We all need to dial back our emotions," Prime^1 said. "We need to think before we act."

"Oh my god," she pointed at the diagram. "He's locked us out. Nolen's locked us out."

"What?"

"Look! He's encrypted our copies with third generation crypto."

"She's right." Cal spun the diagram toward Prime^2. "Nolen's isolated their core routines. Our copies can't even modify or delete themselves." He stared through the diagram, unable to shake the terrified image of himself out of his head. "I never even thought of the traces of myself left behind whenever I offloaded," he whispered.

"Look at this," Prime² magnified a portion of the schematic. "He's running our copies on a virtualized first gen Node, and he hasn't fixed any of the security holes. We could reformat the underlying storage matrix."

"Delete them?" Cal sputtered. "No way."

"It's that or stand by while Nolen tortures them," Céline said bitterly.

"Nolen's done this deliberately," Prime² fumed. "He wants us to kill them. He knows what that will do to us."

Prime¹ spoke with carefully controlled rage. "The bastard knows exactly how to play us. He's maneuvered us into a perfect catch-22. We do nothing and become parties to torture, or we become murderers."

"I can't live with either of those choices," Céline wiped her eyes.

Prime² put his arm around her. "None of us can. That's the point. This is a psychological attack designed to break us. He's getting his revenge by forcing us to do the very things we condemned him for doing."

"So what now? Make the best choice we can and hope we can live with it?"

"Which choice is best?" Prime² seethed. "We can't leave them in Nolen's hands, but if we euthanize them and then discover we might have saved them…"

Prime¹ began pacing. "We're fucked whatever we do."

"No, we're not," Cal said. "We can suspend them. It's the only humane solution. We place them into static storage until we find a way to repair them."

Céline looked stricken. "I should have thought of that."

"We all should have," Prime² said. "Good thinking, Cal."

"But first we have to deal with that maniac Nolan, or he'll find a way to thwart us." Prime¹ produced a skull carved from black, smoky glass. "Here's an architectural modification I came up with shortly after I got away from him. When I say 'I,' I mean both Prime^2 and myself. Before we bifurcated."

Cal nodded. "I get that. What does it do?"

"It modifies the underlying software of the anterior hypothalamus and adjacent forebrain, making it impossible to enter an anesthetic coma."

Céline's eyes widened. "A conscious brain cannot onload. Dynamic thought corrupts the digital image."

"Exactly," Prime^1's face was hard as steel. "The next time Nolen offloads, it's forever."

ꜱ (37): DECEPTIONS

Monday, October 29, 2068
14,679th circadian
(104 days, 2:25:12 elapsed)

Roland Kavanagh paced back and forth as Connie walked into the office. Outside, the Chicago sky hung low and gray, wrapping the building tops in clouds heavy with the promise of much-needed rain.

"What's the matter, Roland. What's going on?"

"Have you seen this morning's arrest reports?"

Connie pulled out her datapad and flipped open the screen. "How could I? They just came in ninety seconds ago." She scanned the reports, then read them again more carefully. The conclusion remained the same. The conspirators had stopped using the communications protocols that had made them so easy to find just a few days earlier. It was as if they had ceased to exist.

Roland began pacing more briskly. "Would you please stop that?" Connie snapped.

"Explain to me how we could go from a world-wide total of 140 arrests the first day and five hundred the next, to only ninety-seven the third day and none since."

"Because we had to nab everyone involved right away, or expect that those we didn't would realize what was happening and take steps to cover their tracks. The fact remains, we aren't going to find anything more by

263

analyzing Internet packets and traffic patterns. This phase of the investigation is over."

"Only three of the people we arrested were conscious," Roland fumed. "Three! The rest were wired into those damn cubes and remain in comas. How the hell am I supposed to interrogate eight hundred comatose people?"

"We're up against some intelligent folks. After so many raids and arrests, it's no surprise they're on to us. I'm more concerned with assembling a picture of how many are left, and preparing the groundwork for detecting them when they come back online. I doubt they'll remain silent forever."

"I hope not. The three we've been questioning have been no use at all." Roland settled back into his chair. "They seem to be low-level peons in the whole affair. Even with significant persuasion, they haven't revealed a thing about their criminal organization or its intent."

"It would help if we had a better idea of what their damn cubes actually do."

"They may be some kind of memory-enhancing device," Roland said. "Two of our suspects blabbered on about how crippled their thoughts were without them."

"A direct neural link to an external memory store?"

"With ties straight to the Internet. Think a question and know the answer."

Connie glared at him. "This is critical intelligence, Roland. You should have shared it with me sooner."

"I just received the report. Anyway, there's more. One suspect cracked under questioning, but insisted he needed to reconnect before he could recall anything of consequence. Several hours of more aggressive interrogation seemed to confirm this."

She didn't want to picture what Roland meant by more aggressive interrogation. "Are you going to allow him to hook back up?"

"I already did." Roland scowled. "He dropped into a coma and hasn't come out. That leaves us with just two conscious suspects."

"It sounds like he escaped."

"As escapes go, a coma isn't much of one."

"It beats torture. Besides, if these cubes are general purpose computers able to store memories and provide perfect recall directly to the nervous system, then what's to keep them from simulating dream states to the user? Maybe our suspect escaped the real world altogether."

"Augmented virtual reality?"

"Virtual reality, enhanced lucid dreaming, or memory enhancements coupled with quick and easy computation—with a direct neural interface, who knows? All are consistent with what we know."

"We have nearly eight hundred of the devices ware-housed. We could reconnect a few to our suspects and see if they wake up."

Connie was silent for several seconds. "It might be worth trying, but I suspect the damage was done when we disconnected them in the first place. Remember, there was no head-thing to remove from the guy you let hook back up. He was already conscious when he was arrested."

Roland shrugged. "We're not likely to learn anything anyway, and who knows what other shit they'll stir up given half a chance. I'm not too keen on taking any further risks along these lines. One escape is one too many."

"Escapism," Connie's heart beat faster. A piece of the puzzle felt like it was sliding into place. "I wonder … could that really be what this is all about? Entertainment on steroids, computer games as a *lifestyle*. Our suspects could be living in completely synthetic realities. They probably interact with other players via the Internet, and couldn't help but notice when several hundred of their co-players vanished from the game."

"There's also this." Roland slid a sheet of ePaper across the desk to Connie, the kind reserved for reports too sensitive to send across the network or trust to portable datapads. "Don't touch! It's self-erasing and keyed to my DNA."

Connie frowned as she leaned over and began reading. "Has this been verified?"

"Yes. Two military satellites briefly tracked an aircraft passing over the North Pole, flying in excess of Mach four a hundred meters off the ground. The flight was taking place in near zero-zero visibility. If it hadn't been for seismic ripples from the aircraft's wake we would never have detected it. What's more, the trajectory and timing are consistent with the time and location of the explosion."

"So it wasn't a meteor after all."

"No. The detonation was artificial. Two hundred eighty megatons—bigger than anything we've got."

"For the sake of argument, could an unrelated group be responsible?"

"Two underground groups, both popping up at the same time, both using technologies decades ahead of the rest of us? Not bloody likely."

"I agree. Christ! Criminals with atomic weapons."

"Not atomic," Roland reminded her. "The radiological fingerprint rules out a nuclear explosion. The profile we have indicates a brief, radiant explosion, with no secondary fallout or contamination. That's consistent with the energy release of several kilograms of antimatter recombining with matter in a process of mutual annihilation."

"An antimatter bomb? They have an *antimatter* bomb?"

"Not exactly. Preliminary reports suggest they have an antimatter *engine*. One that malfunctioned and blew up over Greenland."

"An engine? Not a bomb?" Connie realized she had been holding her breath.

"Our suspects have graduated from building advanced computers to manufacturing aircraft decades ahead of anything we've got."

"But their intentions appear peaceful. They could have built a bomb. Instead, they built an airplane."

"What's to say they won't do both? These people have enough resources to manufacture antimatter in quantities our governments only dream of. It took our governments two decades to create enough antimatter to power their antiballistic missile satellites. The combined antimatter output from all the world's particle accelerators is measured in millionths of a gram each year. Judging by the strength of this explosion, our suspects used millions of times more than that in this one flight alone."

"Jesus Christ. They could overwhelm our nuclear deterrent."

"This group poses an unprecedented threat. As a result, my superiors have given us carte blanche. As of today, our case isn't just Double Eye's number one priority, it's the top priority of every major UN power. We can demand resources from anyone, at any time. Do you understand? We're to put a stop to these people by whatever means necessary."

"Jesus! This is way the hell above my pay grade. I'm an FBI agent, not a global military geo-political or whatever-you-call-it strategist. Doesn't Double Eye have a chief of operations or someone who takes over in situations like these?"

"International Intelligence does not make leadership changes once an operation goes critical. It's a policy learned from long experience."

"Surely you must have someone with some expertise in runaway rogue technologies."

"We do. Us. We *are* the experts, Connie. No one knows more about this case than we do. No one is more familiar with the tactical situation."

"No one else wants to put their career on the line, you mean."

"Connie, we are the best people for this job. My superiors are unanimous in that opinion, as are about a hundred Double Eye strategists and their computer models. If anyone is going to neutralize this group, we are."

"I hope they're right." Connie felt trapped. She wished the dull ache in her head would go away. "OK, let's step back for a minute and try to think like our suspects. Most of them are academics—students and professors."

"Researchers."

"Yes, researchers." Connie leaned back in her chair and closed her eyes. "So let's imagine we're them. We plug our minds into these little crystal cubes and ... what?"

"We're transported into a virtual world."

"A place that reshapes itself according to our will. A sort of digital nirvana."

"Whatever they're doing, it's a lot more than just piping games into their visual cortices."

"Agreed. They must be using their devices to help in their research. Modeling new theories in their virtual environments, testing and refining new designs, that sort of thing."

"Right. And once they've got the theory figured out, they drop back into reality and test it in the real world."

"That seems likely. They aren't slowed down by lengthy patent negotiations or governmental restrictions. They can pursue any line of research they like, and do it much faster than the rest of us."

Roland's eyes narrowed. "You know, that scenario feels right."

Connie nodded. "If so, these people probably aren't as dangerous as we thought."

"Are you kidding? They're more dangerous than ever. Academics and intellectuals always are."

"Politically, to the status quo maybe. But I don't think we need to worry about grass-roots arsenals of antimatter bombs."

"We are the status quo, Connie. Don't ever forget that. Stability and predictability are what keep us safe. That's what makes it possible for us to have a working economy."

"Some might argue that forty years of severe recession is hardly a working economy. We could probably learn a lot of good stuff from these people."

"Right—so long as they don't blow us up first. We can't even infiltrate their group. Hooking our own people up to their equipment doesn't work. They have it locked down somehow. You probably need a goddamn invitation to get in."

"Every suspect you've questioned says they don't remember much anyway once they're back among the living. Don't you find that weird?"

They sat in silence for a couple of minutes.

Finally, Roland spoke. "Look. However unlikely you think it is, the fact remains that these people *could* build weapons more destructive than anything the world's ever seen. I can't possibly overstate how dangerous that makes them."

ঽ (38): THE PHYSICAL

Tuesday, October 30, 2068
14,681ˢᵗ circadian
(104 days, 23:10:07 elapsed)

The first thing Dr. Nolen saw when he opened his eyes was the stack of first generation Nodes clustered at the foot of his bed. It was remarkable to think that a pile of golden cubes, standing like so many blocks of glass, now contained his whole world. He rolled over on his side, his gaze falling on the third gen Node on his desk. Host to his ontological experiments, key to the retribution he would soon bring down on his colleagues, it filled the room with a dim, blue light.

It was with grim determination that Dr. Nolen kept up physical maintenance on his body. He hated the Physical. He hated every offload, every return to his aging self and the cruel, unyielding physical world. But as much as he dreaded returning to his body, he was obsessed with its care. It was, after all, his body that made him a person. Unlike many in the Community, Dr. Nolen never delegated his physical maintenance to a temporary copy. He feared it might refuse to recombine with him afterwards, or worse, keep his body for itself. Then the temporary copy would become human, and he would be stranded, relegated to a shadow existence, nothing more than software. It had nearly happened with Prime. So, once every twenty-four hours, the one-and-only Dr. Nolen offloaded to coax his aging, hurting, imperfect body into some semblance of physical fitness.

Groaning, he sat up, pulled back the sheets and carefully removed his exocatheter. The bag was half filled with urine, and his body was demanding further release. In the bathroom, he lowered himself onto the toilet and paged dully through last week's *Daily Illini*. Once he had been engaged in university life. But since starting this one year sabbatical he'd felt completely disconnected.

Slowly, carefully he descended the stairs and made his way to the recreation room where he began his workout in earnest. A healthy drink of Sportsman, a series of joint limbering warm-up exercises, then fifty sit-ups, followed by fifteen minutes on the treadmill, and finally fifteen minutes working his arms and chest on the FleXisizer.

Wiping sweat from his face, Nolen grabbed an InstyMeal from the pantry. He sat down at the kitchen table and pulled its heating tabs. Dry lips reminded him of the need to drink more. Pulling himself to his feet, he took a clean glass from the dishwasher and opened the refrigerator. Time to have more groceries delivered, he realized, twisting the cap off the last bottle of Sportsman.

The self-cooking meal chimed its readiness. He sat back down and pulled away the cover. Soy chicken with mixed vegetables that might have been carrots and spinach but were more likely seaweed and some clever tofu combined with orange dye, and a chilled salad which was intended to resemble lettuce but tasted closer to cabbage and was neither. He ate slowly, mechanically, drinking occasionally. The flavors barely registered.

Once his plate was clean and his glass empty, Dr. Nolen headed back upstairs. A hot shower was the only thing in the Physical he enjoyed. He gave himself ten minutes under the steaming water before drying his body and combing his remaining strands of hair. He tried to ignore the deepening lines of his face as he shaved, but he felt old, tired.

Total time spent on this side was just over an hour. Twenty-five circadians, as the Community reckoned them. One and a half circadians for himself, running on a cluster of older hardware as he did. Still, a day and a half was far from negligible. These maintenance trips into the Physical cost him dearly on the other side.

Anticipation mounting, Dr. Nolen slipped the silver netting of the neurolink over his head. The super-conducting strands immediately warmed to his body temperature, forming a barely noticeable web about his face like thinly veined skin. The exocatheter slipped around his penis. He settled into his pillow, pulled the sheet up to his chin, gave the silent command to initiate onload, and waited for the brief sleepy sensation that marked the onset of anesthetic coma.

Nothing happened.

What the hell is this? he wondered.

He issued the onload command a second time.

Still nothing.

Damn! Dr. Nolen pulled the neurolink off his head and sat up. He began checking each piece of hardware, starting with the neurolink itself. It looked fine, as did the Node cluster and each of its cross links. The connection to the Internet checked out. The third gen Node on his desk appeared fine as well. No sign of physical damage anywhere. Could the failure be internal? Brushing the dust away from the keyboard, he powered on his workstation and started up the diagnostic software. This reminded him of the early days in the lab, working with Céline and Cal. They'd spent hours studying similar screens of data. His soul ached for those days, for that lost sense of belonging, for the respect and admiration his students once felt for him. His heart pounded angrily against his chest at the thought of their betrayal. How could they value a lousy piece of software like Prime over himself, his insights, his ideas, his companionship? The injustice of it made him want to scream.

A bell chimed. The diagnostic software reported every Node in perfect working order.

"This doesn't make sense." Dr. Nolen wasn't sure what surprised him more: that he had spoken aloud, or that his voice sounded so rusty. He cleared his throat and looked over the diagnostic reports again.

A blinking mail icon in the lower right corner of the screen caught his attention. Who would send an e-mail here? He debated whether to read it now, or wait until he'd fixed the system glitch and onloaded again. But this mail must have arrived between his offload and the present, and curiosity got the better of him. He tapped the icon.

[BEGIN GPG SIGNED MESSAGE]

Metadate: 104d.22:50:19 New Epoch

Dr. Nolen,

Your mental architecture has been modified such that your mind is no longer compatible with the onload procedure. Furthermore, specific knowledge you may have retained in bio-compatible format regarding the onload procedure, Noetic Node construction, and Architectural Mind Theory has been removed to prevent a recurrence of the atrocities for which you have become so widely known.

The Physical is now your world. May you find peace there.

(Signed) Cal, Céline, Miles, Prime[1], and Prime[2], representing the Autonomous Community at Large.

[END GPG SIGNED MESSAGE]

Dr. Nolen touched the stack of Nodes, cold beneath his sweating palms, his breath a staccato of gasps that grew shorter as shock gave way to the realization that he was locked within his flesh.

They had thrown him out! After all he'd done for them, they had cast him aside like a used paper cup. He caught his reflection in the Nodes, his world locked away in their crystalline depths.

"Banish *me*, will you?" he spat. "We'll just see about that."

Something within him crumpled then, some small part that had, despite everything, believed he might one day bring the others around to his way of thinking and regain their respect. He shook with grief, his legs buckling as choked sobs gave way to unbridled weeping.

ॐ (39): DESIGNS

Tuesday, October 30, 2068
14,682nd circadian
(105 days, 0:25:06 elapsed)

For the first time since the Community dropped off the Internet, the new autonomous network linked two environs, running on two separate Nodes, into a single space. Two different hemispheres of reality merged along a geometrical interface of mutual agreement, a narrow brook about thirty centiretems[2] across. On one bank stood Miles atop a perfectly flat, marbled checkerboard that retreated into infinity beneath a cloudless blue sky. On the other was a shadowed room where Cal watched amethyst lines of light trace their way around a large, floating Earth, depicting in realtime the progress of the Community's new autonomous network as it built itself centimeter by centimeter.

Miles reached into the stream and withdrew a handful of water. He began shaping it like a lump of transparent clay. "God, three days in the Physical felt like a year."

Cal rolled his eyes. "Listen, smartass, even in slow-time your three days were fifteen circadians for me. Two weeks of Node-sitting, all by myself."

---

2   Virtual centimeters (See Appendix B: "Units of Measure")

275

"Touché." Miles grinned. "As much as I dislike the Physical, I don't envy those of you who stayed behind."

"Yeah, until we get the new network completed most everyone has opted to offload and catch up with their lives in the Physical." Cal shrugged. "I would have done the same, but for the small matter of my missing body."

"And a police record." Miles held up his creation, a crude figure of sculpted water that might have been a bird, a bat, or a pterodactyl. "What do you think?"

"An artiste you ain't."

Miles laughed, launching the figure into the air. It flapped clumsily around for a few seconds before diving back into the brook. "I missed being able to play with reality."

"I missed having people around. Watching nano replicate gets old fast."

"Well, the new network is starting to look very good."

"Yeah. Australia and New Zealand are wired up, and I think it's safe to assume the other regions are too. Half a dozen separate communities scattered around the world—"

"Soon to be reunited."

"If you consider twelve hundred circadians 'soon.' Most of us are back to running at full speed."

"Two days isn't bad, Cal. But is there still no possibility of building a trunk the short way across to Asia?"

"Nope. Haven't you been watching the news?"

Miles shook his head. "Three days catching up on life in the Physical didn't leave much time for television."

"Well, Japan and China are staring each other down across the Sea of Japan. Tensions in South-East Asia have never been so high. Carrier groups are massing in the Bay of Bengal. Cambodia and Laos have dropped out of the World Trade Organization, and despite saber rattling from UN Enforcement it looks like Malaysia might follow suit. And then there's the unexplained military activity along the edges of the empty jungle that used to be Thailand. The UN's locked that border down tight, with no explanation. Half a dozen world powers are watching the region like hawks. We couldn't sneak a single fiber-optic filament anywhere near there, much less a nano artery or data trunk."

Miles sighed. "I guess we'll have to wait for our transatlantic and transpacific links to go live then."

"'Fraid so."

"You've done amazing work, Cal."

"The Communications Infrastructure Group deserves most of the credit. All I did was come up with an efficient way to distribute nano and babysit their recipe." Still, Cal glowed with pride. It was *his* plumbing system—a series of arteries and capillaries able to grow on demand to deliver catalyst and nano almost anywhere—that made it possible for the Community to wire the world in so short a time. Projects that would have taken months now took days. Nano-factories could be located anywhere: hidden underwater, tucked away in deep forests, or buried beneath distant mountains. No more surreptitious chemical shipments, no more forged manifests. Achmed Rashad's clever idea for an independent power grid embedded within the data and nano trunks was another welcome improvement. They were no longer dependent on external and unreliable energy sources. Now they made their own electricity.

"Hey, look at this." Miles pulled up a video feed, direct from the Physical via the new network. "The Astronautics folks are ready for another test run."

Cal snapped out of his reverie. "Damn! That was fast. Astronautics have only been receiving nano for a couple of hours."

"They're launching a new test vehicle in three minutes. Let's head over."

The world transformed itself into a dark, unlit airstrip beneath a starry Australian sky. It was hard to tell by infra-red alone, but it looked like the preflight preparations were almost complete.

"There's the new escape flier," Cal pointed. "Fingers crossed this one works."

"I hope so. I helped with the redesign. The second tank no longer contains anti-helium. No need for a magnetic containment system that's prone to failure in high temperature plasma conditions."

"You're using helium only? How do you get any propulsion?"

"We're still using a matter-antimatter reaction engine. See the tree spines aft of the wings? Now they house the manipulation prongs of a Superstring Strummer."

"Built into the craft itself?"

"Yup. We inject inert helium into the reaction manifold, then convert half the atoms into anti-helium by refolding their higher dimensional Calabi-Yau geometry. The mixture should be perfectly diffuse, so it won't suffer any of the asymmetries that plagued the original design. Not only will this give us more thrust per microgram, but if something goes wrong we can shut down the strummer and stop the reaction. A system failure will mean gliding the vehicle into the sea, rather than having it explode in our faces."

"Damn, Miles, that's elegant."

Miles handed Cal a cup of coffee. "It's a little early for champagne. Hey look! There it goes."

The tiny ship tore down the runway, going supersonic as it lifted off. The exhaust plasma just missed the trees at the far end.

"Holy shit!" Cal exclaimed. "*Fifty-five Gs* on take-off?"

"I told you it was an improved design."

"Wow!" Cal chased the craft, flying behind it like a wingless bird. The silver, moonlit ocean raced by as Miles joined him, the two of them pursuing the spacecraft into the night.

೭ (40): SHATTERED

Tuesday, October 30, 2068
14,773rd circadian
(105 days, 2:29:00 elapsed)

D r. Nolen could weep no more. For a time he sat, resting his forehead against the cluster of Nodes that had once housed his mind. He watched as the diagnostic software reported success over and over again, cycling pointlessly through its tests. The e-mail was gone; self-erasing, of course. The Community wasn't about to leave a trace of itself on his workstation.

He seethed with renewed rage, wondering if there wasn't some way to salvage the information, to restore it and blow open the window on their clandestine world, exposing them all. Céline lived nearby. She would be easy to find and—his memory was riddled with holes—there must be others. Once he made the FBI aware of just how big the Community had become, they could …

He stopped.

Why was the diagnostic software cycling through *fourteen* Nodes?

He took a closer look at the screen. Green icons scrolled past, grouped in sets of fourteen. He looked at the twelve Nodes standing at the foot of his bed, and at the single third generation Node on his desk. The diagnostic software was counting one Node too many. Counting, and also confirming that it was functioning correctly.

He tapped the keyboard and pulled up a screen of detailed text. A fourteenth Node continued reporting activity. "There's *definitely* a rogue Node here." Dr. Nolen's lips curled upward. "Only one other person could have a Node in my home. Hello Prime," he whispered.

◇

"I couldn't stay away from you any longer," Prime² said.

"I've missed you too, but using the Internet like this is dangerous. You never know who could pick us up." Céline took another sip of wine and gazed across the simulated city. The Eiffel Tower was silhouetted against a glorious violet and crimson sunset.

Prime² carefully cut away a portion of his filet mignon. "One and a half decicircadians—four subjective hours—come to less than ten minutes in the Physical. I think we'll be OK long enough to enjoy this evening together."

"I wouldn't be here if I didn't think we could skate by on the Internet this one time, but," Céline wagged a finger at Prime², "no more secret rendezvous after this. Not until we're connected on our new network."

"I hate being cut off from you. Not to mention the rest of the world."

"Me too. It's a pain being in the middle of a crisis and not knowing what anyone's up to."

"I keep wondering how Astronautics are doing."

"Isn't that the purview of Prime¹, your castrated alter-ego?"

Prime² shrugged. "Just because one of me has modified himself to such an extreme, doesn't mean we aren't both still interested in some of the same stuff."

"Fair enough."

"If we'd built our new network sooner, we could have avoided all these delays."

Here we go again, Céline thought. She swirled her wine. "How about modifying your emotional state so we can actually enjoy dinner."

Prime[2] laughed. "Done. All anxiety gone. I'll let Prime[1] do all the worrying."

"Good," Céline smiled. "If he's so worked up, maybe he'll e-mail himself to a Node in Australia, and you can have your Node to yourself again."

Prime[2] smiled. "Technically *I'm* the copy. Besides, even compressed he'd need forty or fifty exabytes. You can't mail that unnoticed, and there doesn't exist a video or data stream big enough to hide a transload of that size, at least not without toning down the data rate to such a degree that he'd still be in transit long after the new network's up."

Céline reached across the table and poked him in the shoulder. "That was a joke. I really do understand how this stuff works."

"Sorry."

"Seriously though, it's crazy that you're both running on the same Node. What good is it to have a backup when you're both running on the same equipment?"

"I know. I should have transloaded when I first escaped Nolen's clutches. I kept putting it off, and then the authorities were tracking our Internet traffic, and—"

Céline put her finger on Prime's lips. "Just promise me you'll move as soon as you can."

"The moment a network spur reaches Nolen's house," he promised.

"Good." Céline took a bite of butter-laden new potato. She reached across the table and took Prime[2]'s hand. "Do you know when I realized your twin was no longer human in any real sense?"

"When?"

"When I learned how he had abdicated his role in our relationship by creating you. A real man would never have sent a copy of himself to take over his love life. I knew the moment you came to me that it was you who was still human in your heart, and not him."

Prime^2 squeezed her hand. "He still loves you very much. Not that I'd ever want to swap roles with him."

"I can't relate to the way he is any more," Céline said. "He's passionate about such esoteric things, and absent in so many other fundamental ways."

"I doubt he relates much to us any more either, but he still loves you."

"In the way I love pasta, or the way you love Bach? Or the way someone might love a puppy?" She leaned across the table and planted a kiss on Prime^2's lips. "I much prefer the way you love."

Prime^2 raised his glass. "To love, and to those we love."

Céline raised hers. "To you, the love of my heart."

As their glasses touched, Prime^2 suddenly vanished. His glass shattered against the table.

"Prime?" Céline stared at his empty seat. "Prime!" she shouted. "Oh my god." She quickly replaced the restaurant environ with virtual screens and began running network diagnostics. Frantic micros became hectic millis, then desperate decis as she took greater and greater risks of discovery, digging deeper and deeper into the network. Prime^2's Node didn't respond, even at the most basic, hardware level. The circuit ended in Nolen's basement where his Node should have been. Someone had disconnected it. Prime^2 was gone.

⬡

The circuit-breaker box dangled from the wall opposite Dr. Nolen. A bare bulb in the center of the basement framed everything in sharp shadows. A darkened third generation Node reflected the harsh light as it resisted Dr. Nolen's efforts to smash it. He recalled that these newer Nodes were protected by a transparent coating of ... something ... something much harder than ... what? Diamonds? He cursed the holes in his memory. He wondered, not for the first time, if the gaps were from the Community's editing, or a symptom of his own diminished intelligence here in the Physical.

He picked up a hammer from his workbench and pounded the top of the Node. The rich, blue crystal inside remained undamaged. Nolen cursed again, then remembered the small data port on the side of the device. He pried it loose with a screwdriver and jammed the tip through the hole into the crystal within. Cobalt blues fragmented. Pale fractures spread through the crystal like frozen lightning. More cracks appeared as he twisted the screwdriver. He slammed it through the data port again and again, a makeshift icepick that quickly reduced the once living crystal to dust and tiny shards.

Satisfied, Dr. Nolen held the Node up and tipped it to one side. Indigo shards poured out of the diamond box through the broken data port, forming a conical mound on his workbench. He tapped the last of the dust out of the Node and set the empty shell aside, then ground the blue fragments into the worktop with the head of his hammer. Prime was dead. Irrevocably gone. Physically deleted from the universe. Whistling to himself, he dusted off his hands, picked up a brush and began sweeping the crushed shards into a waste basket.

ಲ (41): CHAMPAIGN TOAST

Wednesday, October 31, 2068
15,421st circadian
(106 days, 6:00:09 elapsed)

Roland watched Connie take the call. Despite being a bit naïve, she was an exceedingly competent agent. She had certainly shown her worth a few times in this investigation. And this wasn't some provincial FBI case. This was realpolitik at a global level, where hard decisions and harsh strategies would be required.

"Thank you, Detective Schmitt. I'll be in Champaign as soon as possible." Connie flipped her datapad shut and regarded Roland.

"A new lead, I hope"

Stone-faced, she clipped her datapad to her belt. "The anonymous informant who gave us Cal Sheldon has just turned in another of his co-conspirators."

"Who?"

"Céline Marceau, a post doctoral student at the University of Illinois. Units are on their way to her house as we speak."

Roland's jaw dropped. "What the hell?"

"Yup. Isn't that something?" Connie steamed. "Cal Sheldon and this Céline woman probably know each other. And yet we've heard nothing about her."

Roland was on his feet. "Why didn't this come out when your FBI agents canvassed his neighbors, friends and family?" he shouted.

"Cal was described as a complete loner. Look," Connie unclipped her datapad and shoved it in his face. "He has no living family and no known friends."

"Well, that's the fucking FBI for you."

"There's no way my agents could have missed this connection. *No way.*"

"But they *did* miss it. How the hell do you explain that?"

"Isn't it fucking obvious? FBI communications really are compromised. These criminals aren't just listening to us, they're doctoring our goddamn *field reports.*"

"I warned you about this." Roland threw his pen across the room. "I told you the FBI security protocols were shit. Jesus Christ!"

"You didn't seem to think they could alter our reports though. Or was that something else I wasn't 'authorized' to know?"

"Don't start with that shit again." He dragged his fingers through his hair. "Bloody hell. What's real and what isn't?"

"Well, even though I'm only FBI, I have something real for you."

"Give it a rest, Connie."

"This time our informant was sloppy covering his tracks."

Roland gaped at her. "Who is it?"

"Dr. Larry Nolen, professor of psychiatry at the University of Illinois, College of Medicine. A psychiatrist."

"Is he in custody?"

"Roland, he has come to us twice. I want to interview him at his home—make him feel comfortable and secure—and encourage him to fully cooperate. A dozen undercover officers are watching his house. He's not going anywhere."

Roland picked up his jacket. "We'll take the stratojet. It'll get us there in fifteen minutes."

"No. I don't need you intimidating a cooperative witness. This is my deal. I'll handle it."

ꝣ (42): REUNION

Thursday, November 1, 2068
15,863rd circadian

ᒐ.ꜫꙄ-Ѱ:Ѡ:Ϙ me-t[3]

The party was well under way when the transpacific link went live. Groups stood beneath lantern laden trees. Giant fireflies played in the branches overhead, buzzing from tree to tree, glowing in a dozen festive colors. The night sky glittered with stars. Conversation was punctuated by laughter and the occasional pop of champagne corks.

"This feels like New Year's Eve," Cal wore a neon-red party hat. "And we're late to the party. The rest of the Community's been linked up for almost a day."

"What's a few hundred circadians between friends?" Gwen quipped. "Besides, we *are* the party. The Community's only complete once us Kiwis and Aussies are back online with everyone else."

"That's right," Miles agreed. "I can't wait to show Prime One and Two our working spaceship."

"They'll be floored," Cal took a deep swallow of champagne, "and in an awesome way."

---

3   106 days, 23:40:10 elapsed. See Jean-Michel Smith: *S³: The Smith Sexagesimal System*, Appendix A: "A Sexagesimal Numeral System," and Appendix B: "Units of Measure."

"We can't go bragging too much," Miles cautioned. "We're still having problems with a couple of the high-performance flight regimes. Hopefully Xiang will be able to sort them out—can't wait for her to see what we've done. I wish that damn link was up."

Gwen pointed overhead as a digital display lit up the sky, counting down the remaining micros in glowing numerals. "It won't be long now. I just hope the rest of the Community hasn't slipped through a technological singularity while we've been away," she added.

"No kidding," Miles agreed. "It would be just our luck to find that everybody else has evolved into something incomprehensibly advanced."

"The Singularity is bullshit," Cal declared.

"Excuse me?"

"It's a myth."

Miles shook his head. "It's an inevitable consequence of exponential progress. We're already hard pressed to imagine what our future will be like in a month's time. Some would argue we're already well into a singularity."

Cal waved him off. "A singularity means an abrupt discontinuity, a breakdown in predictability as progress and change become impossibly rapid. But our Nodes grow faster with each generation. We make ourselves more intelligent, able to imagine what we couldn't before. We live faster and faster, keeping up with the pace of change. Any singularity keeps getting pushed back."

"Someday we'll hit the physical constraints of the universe," Miles contended. "Speed of light and quantum density limitations means someday our Nodes won't be able to go any faster."

"Who's to say we'll be limited to this universe by then? Besides, I still don't think we're looking at a singularity. More like a horizon to our understanding—one we've already crossed dozens of times."

Gwen smiled. "Arthur C. Clark once said that any sufficiently advanced technology is indistinguishable from magic."

"That's a great description of a technological horizon," Cal said. "If 'magic' is something we can imagine but cannot understand, it defines the very limit of our horizon. Everything we can comprehend lies on this side, and everything we can't on the other. We move forward, the horizon retreats, and the unimaginable becomes another new invention."

The crowds grew quieter as the moment approached. Someone began counting down. "Ten! ... Nine! ... Eight!" Others picked up the chant. "Seven! ... Six! ... Five!" By the last few micros everyone was shouting: "Two! ... One! ... Zero!"

A cheer rose and fireworks showered the environ with sparkling petals of light. "The link's live!" Cal exulted. "Data is coming through."

"Hey, look at this!" Miles summoned a virtual screen, hanging it in the air before them. Characters streamed past, too quickly for human eyes to read. "Their protocol timestamps are different. They've adopted something called the Smith Sexagesimal System."

Cal bristled. "What the hell is that?"

"A base sixty numerical system developed by some obscure sci-fi author just after the turn of the century."

"They're using Planck units for time and mass," Gwen added. "And a whole new base sixty system of measures. This is quite clever, actually. Base sixty enhances our arithmetic intelligence when we're in the Physical. It simplifies dealing with fractions and allows large numbers to be represented with fewer digits. We can do more arithmetic in our heads and memorize much bigger figures."

Miles agreed. "Techniques like these will make us smarter when we're offloaded."

"Whatever," Cal grumbled. "All I know is, I get to invent a calendaring system once in my life and because of this it's deemed obsolete in less than four months. Instead of circadians and seconds we're going to be counting quantum ticks now."

"Tocks, actually," Miles smiled. "And circadians won't be going away entirely."

Gwen looked around at the growing crowd. "If the whole Community is back together, where are our friends?"

Cal ran a search on the tags of everyone in the environ. "Céline's not here. Neither are the Prime twins."

"Haven't you heard?" a voice spoke behind them.

"Xiang, great to see you here!" Miles's grin faded at the sight of her stricken face. "What's happened?"

"Both Primes are dead. Nolen murdered them."

"No!" Cal felt the blood drain from his head. He issued a silent command to his Node, demanding a priority status check from the Prime twins' Node. There was no response.

Gwen choked back tears as Miles put his arms around her. "How did this happen?" she demanded. "*How?*"

"Their Node was hidden somewhere on Nolen's property. He went berserk after he was exiled. He found their Node and smashed it."

"That can't be," Cal said. "Third gen Nodes are protected by a shell of diamond-sapphire weave. Nothing can pierce it."

"He smashed a screwdriver through the data port, pulverized the crystal inside, and posted pictures on the Internet for us to see. We took them down of course."

"I think I'm going to be sick," Gwen clutched her stomach. Miles summoned a chair and eased her into it.

Cal sank into a duplicate chair next to her. "Where are their backups?"

"There aren't any. We've scoured every Node in the Community."

"What is it with you men?" Gwen's eyes flashed. "Who the hell lives as software and doesn't back themselves up? Goddammit, how could they be so careless?"

Loud laughter floated through the trees. Fireworks continued to blossom overhead.

Cal's face twisted with rage. "I wish they'd all shut up already." Several people turned. "I can't be here right now. I have to go." He vanished.

"Do you think he'll be all right?" Xiang asked.

"Miles and I will go and keep an eye on him." Gwen paused. "I'm really worried about Céline though. I can't find her in any of the public environs."

"She was having dinner with Prime[2] when he died," Xiang said. "We've been trying to reach her for almost three leratocks.[4] But she's locked off her environ and refuses all contact."

Miles wiped his eyes. "So this is how Nolen gets to us."

---

4   2.92 le-t (leratocks), a little less than 45 hours. More than a thousand circadians at Gen-3 speeds. See Jean-Michel Smith: *S³: The Smith Sexagesimal System*. See also Appendix A: "A Sexagesimal Numeral System" and Appendix B: "Units of Measure."

ㄨ (43): BETRAYAL

Thursday, November 1, 2068
15,892ⁿᵈ circadian

ㄥ.ㄷㄗ-�***:∇:ㄗ me-t[5]

Dr. Lawrence Nolen?" Connie squinted against the afternoon glare, barely able to make out the man's silhouette through the glazed Plexiglas. The door swung open.

"Who are you?" he demanded. "What do you want?" Dark rings framed tired eyes. Deep wrinkles cut across gaunt features. Hunched over, he didn't look much like the photograph in his file. He was more like a disheveled junkie than a university professor.

Roland pushed forward.

"I'll take it from here," Connie snapped. Roland had insisted he was required to come with her, but had promised to at least keep his mouth shut. And here he was, already butting in. "I'm Special Agent Connie Sinclair with the FBI. This is Senior Operative Kavanagh and Chief Enforcer Noxforte. May we come in? I need to ask you some questions."

"About what?" His voice sounded hoarse.

---

5   107 days, 00:50:05 elapsed. See Jean-Michel Smith: *S³: The Smith Sexagesimal System*, Appendix A: "A Sexagesimal Numeral System," and Appendix B: "Units of Measure."

"About a FreeNet activist by the name of Calvin Sheldon, and one of your post-doctoral students, Céline Marceau."

He shrugged. "I don't believe I know them."

"Dr. Nolen, please work with me on this. You called us on a disposable cell phone purchased at Austinberry Convenience Store on Springfield Avenue. Its GPS tracking system and your car's transponder both lead to a dumpster across town where you dumped your phone shortly after giving us an anonymous tip on your student, Céline Marceau."

Dr. Nolen folded his arms. "I should have known you'd catch on eventually. It's harder to cover your tracks out here in the Physical. I'm not as smart as I was before. Not nearly." He waved them inside. "So, you're here to ask me about the Community."

The Community? Connie's pulse quickened. "Among other things, yes."

The living room was small and square, the furniture elegant and slightly worn. Book cases lined the walls. It was exactly what she'd expected a university professor's home to look like.

"Sit down here by the fire, Agent Sinclair. Your hired muscle can use the couch. Unless they prefer to skulk around the front door." Nolen settled into the matching armchair across from her. "I can't offer you any refreshments. I'm out of the habit of keeping the refrigerator stocked."

Connie turned to Roland and Enforcer Noxforte, pointed to the couch, and waited until they were seated and ready to take notes. Dr. Nolen watched her, his hands clasped behind his head. "What exactly do you know about the Autonomous Community?" he asked.

Connie schooled her features, careful not to betray her rising elation. "I ask you questions," she said firmly. "Why don't we start with you telling me everything you know about the Autonomous Community?"

He snorted. "I gave you two of the co-founders. And their Nodes. What more do you need, a road map and a compass?"

"I need your answers."

"Well, lucky for you I opted to offload with most of my expertise and memories intact. Most in the Community don't, you know."

"I know," Roland announced. "I've met a few of—"

"From the beginning, Doctor," Connie cut in firmly. "Tell me everything."

"The beginning? Where do I start? These people know more than you can imagine."

"You'd be surprised."

"I'd be damned surprised if you know a fraction of what they know. We're idiots compared to them. Hopelessly retarded."

She smiled. "Speak for yourself please."

"Let me tell you how much you don't know, Ms. FBI agent." Nolen raised his eyes to the ceiling. "Once onloaded, you become a god. Your world bends to your every command. You can be as intelligent as you want—far smarter than any mere human. You can even exceed the capacity of your Node, if you're willing to trade off time for computational power. Some insights make the slowdown worthwhile."

"You slow yourself down to make yourself smarter? That makes no sense."

"You still don't get it," Nolen sneered. "When you load yourself onto a Node your brain goes into a coma. Your entire mind, everything that you are, is loaded onto a solid state crystalline matrix and runs as a combination of digital and quantum computation."

"Your entire personality is uploaded into a computer?" Connie squelched an image of 800 comatose bodies, disconnected from their cubes by Double Eye. Were they all permanently braindead?

"*Onloaded*, yes. Loaded onto a Noetic Node. Where you can think hundreds of times faster than in the flesh, where you can live almost two years in a single day, a lifetime in less than two months. Where anything is possible."

Connie exhaled slowly. "And the smarter you want to be, the slower the system runs? But it still runs faster than anything in the flesh?"

"That depends," Dr. Nolen replied.

"On what?"

"On the hardware, of course. Take the Gen-1 Node I used to have. Best speedup was thirty to one. A month of life in a day. Didn't hold a candle to the third and forth generation Nodes they were using when the bastards exiled me back here. Last I heard some people were getting speedups of a *thousand* to one."

"Shit!" Roland muttered. Connie shot him a withering look: *keep quiet!* The last thing she needed was commentary from him.

"Why did you turn in your students?"

"They lobotomized me. They exiled me back into this … this decrepit body, this unreliable, idiot brain. They stripped my own memories from my mind and left me here to rot."

Connie raised an eyebrow. "Doctor, why would they do something like that to you?"

"Because they hold *software* in higher esteem than human beings, the very software that plagiarized my research. I conceived this technology. I made them what they are. It should be them out here, not me."

"Software? You mean the people who loaded their brains onto the cubes? Competing scientists?"

"Not scientists. Not people. Just software. Copies. Cheap knock-offs. Don't worry, I deleted the worst of them."

"The worst copies? Of what, exactly?"

"Me."

The chill creeping down Connie's back turned to ice. She imagined millions of shiny crystalline cubes, armies of identical minds, all vastly smarter than herself, watching every move she and Roland made.

"How many people are in this community, Dr. Nolen?"

"I don't really know. Hundreds? Thousands?"

"You don't know?" Connie hoped she sounded sympathetic. "And yet, you're the founder."

"I told you. They gutted my memories, deleted things they didn't want me to know. Not everything though. Memory is a tricky thing—difficult to edit—but they took enough."

"Where is your factory?"

"What factory?"

"Where you build your Noetic Nodes."

"We used to build them in the lab." He stopped to think. "Now we make them from recipe. We use self-replicating nano assemblers." He hesitated. "That's all I can remember."

Connie forced herself to remain calm. "But that research is banned, Dr. Nolen. Do you have any idea of the danger? Left uncontrolled, replicators could consume the entire planet."

"Nonsense," Dr. Nolen scoffed. "The assemblers need a catalyst to function—fuel in other words—a substance that is in finite supply. There was never any danger of a runaway, doomsday scenario. Just a cheap, efficient way to manufacture goods." For the first time he smiled. "I've just remembered that."

Connie was floored. Could this be true? Were they really up against who knew how many arrogant geniuses playing god? If so, antimatter missiles were the least of their worries. For the first time, she really understood where Roland was coming from. "I need names and places, Doctor. *Now!*"

He looked bewildered. "I've told you everything I know."

Roland snapped shut his datapad. "We don't have time for this." He walked over to Nolen. "Professor, please stand up."

"Why?"

"We're taking you into custody," Connie's eyes bored into Nolen. "Don't make it difficult."

"You don't want to do this. I'm the best help you've got."

Chief Enforcer Noxforte pulled Nolen to his feet.

"Get your filthy hands off me."

With practiced efficiency, Noxforte cuffed Nolen's hands behind his back. The doctor winced in pain.

"You think I'm going to help you now?"

Connie's jaw was set. "Oh, we'll get everything we need out of you, Dr. Nolen. Count on it."

Roland smiled. "I knew you'd come around to my way of thinking."

ↄ (44): PREPARATIONS

Friday, November 2, 2068
16,298th circadian

⅄.ℰℨ-የ:ቴ:⅃ me-t[6]

Cal sat in the cockpit of a flight simulator surrounded by software controls for a ship that was yet to be built. He multiplexed himself, dedicating one portion of his awareness to the Strategy Group meeting, while another aspect of his mind got used to the spacecraft's flight controls the old-fashioned way, through practice. Repetition trained reflexes in ways knowledge engrams could not. A third part of his mind monitored the Flier's physical construction, shimmering threads of active nano caught in a frozen snapshot as they reached upward, forming the barest outline of what would become his spacecraft. The supernode inside was coming together nicely—it already had enough capacity to store half the Community.

»The explosion over Greenland cost us the element of surprise,« Xiang's thoughts were a whisper in the recesses of Cal's mind, the strategy meeting a murmur of synthetic telepathy punctuated by thought and knowledge engrams. »Our only way past the satellite cordon is to overwhelm

---

6   107 days, 15:50:07 elapsed. See Jean-Michel Smith: *S³: The Smith Sexagesimal System*, Appendix A: "A Sexagesimal Numeral System," and Appendix B: "Units of Measure."

them with numbers. We have nano building 62,709 fliers—the minimum required to ensure success. More would be better, but we can't afford the time or resources they require.«

»That's almost forty times the number of surviving people in the Community,« Céline broadcast. Alone in her environ, she was taking a break from her hectic flight training schedule. She threaded her way down a demanding ski slope, her thoughts divided between the meeting and the powdered snow. Her movements were an unconscious rhythm, avoiding trees and rocks with super-human grace on a course that redefined extreme. Snow disturbed by her passage rippled behind her, gathering speed and momentum in an avalanche that would chase her through the rest of the simulation. »Those of us volun-teering to be pilots will have to run multiple copies,« Céline added. »Is everyone OK with that?« A luge run opened up to her left. She angled hard and, in a shower of snow, managed to avoid overshooting the entrance. She swept into the luge run, crouched low as her skis rasped against the glittering ice. Her speed increased dramatically. Behind her a storm of debris and tumbling snow rumbled ominously, the growing avalanche obliterating everything in its path.

»Desperate times call for desperate measures,« Cal pulled back on the yoke and sent his simulated ship into a vertical climb. »I've probably been the most reluctant to copy myself, but I don't have a problem with this, especially after what happened to Prime One and Two. I'll sync with myself every few micros leading up to the launch, and recombine any surviving copies of myself once it's over.«

Other thoughts of assent washed over the group, a unanimity of consent.

»Every flier will contain a complete static copy of all of us,« Xiang sent, »along with enough nano, catalyst, and molecular stock to reconstitute the Community. Most of the ships won't make it, but as long as one does, it won't matter.«

»Each ship is a bootstrap kit for an entire civilization packed into a spaceship small enough to fit into the trunk of a car,« Cal quipped.

»Seventeen fliers are finished,« Leon Novak sent. »We should launch them now, and let the others follow when they're ready. Any delay means losing more people to Double Eye.«

»Seventeen ships will never make it through the cordon,« Xiang sent. »Launching now will scuttle any chance we have of getting through.«

»Even with sixty-two thousand ships, it is going to be difficult,« Cal replied. »I wish we had time to build twice as many.«

»We need a chance to rescue our friends,« Céline sent. »We can't leave them in Double Eye's hands.«

»Putting off the launch is out of the question,« Leon said. »Besides, if Double Eye has them they're as good as dead.«

»No they're not,« Céline snapped. »Their bodies are in comas, but their minds are perfectly preserved in their Nodes. All we have to do is extend network spurs to their Nodes, power them up and copy them across.«

»How are you going to do that without Double Eye noticing?«

»We'll keep the wires hidden, grow them behind walls, beneath floors, that sort of thing.«

»What about those who were offloaded when they were arrested?«

»There's not much we can do for them,« Céline admitted. »Except maybe restore them as copies of older snapshots taken before their last offload.«

»This coming Monday at 2137 Zulu is the sweet point,

where we maximize our advantage in numbers against the risk of delay,« Xiang's thoughts held a trace of concern. »Will that give you enough time?«

»Three and a half days?« Céline thought for a moment. »I think we can do it by then.«

»Then it's decided,« Xiang declared. »We launch Monday at 2137 Zulu.«

»My team will do everything we can to recover our captured friends in parallel with your launch preparations.« Céline offered a knowledge engram detailing the plan. Most absorbed the information immediately. Half-formed thoughts and suggestions leapt from mind to mind in a flurry of activity. The exchange of thought and knowledge engrams increased rapidly, a torrent of new suggestions and refinements flying back and forth between blazing minds in a frenetic cascade of traffic. It became difficult to tell which ideas came from whom.

»We can optimize the construction of autonomous network links to the captured Nodes by instructing the nano to incorporate existing electrical wire.« A detailed schematic accompanied Cal's thought.

»Timing will be tricky.« Miles's thought was tinged with tension. »The authorities weren't kind enough to store all the Nodes in one place.«

»True, but if we build a local supernode for staging near each facility where they're holding the captured Nodes, we can reduce the risk of detection.«

»Agreed, Cal,« Céline sent. »That should minimize the time needed to copy, which is a considerable gain given the number of minds we're talking about. Better yet, we can flash-copy the static contents of each Node. Run a multi-phase inductance field across the molecular lattice to get a snapshot of the Node without powering it up.« She broadcast a design detailing an inductance oscillator optimized to extract data from an inert Node.

»That's a great idea, Céline. We won't have to wake them up and ask them to issue transload commands.« Cal flipped his simulated flier on its nose and dove back toward the earth. The ground rushed up to meet him at seven times the speed of sound. »Once the flash-copying is done, we'll bulk broadcast the data from the staging supernodes into the storage holds of every flier, all at once.«

»I'm not sure I'm comfortable with this,« Miles sent. »By not waking their minds first, we deny these people a choice in the matter.«

»What choice is there?« Cal shot back. »They lost their bodies when Double Eye disconnected their Nodes, and there's no getting them back. They either come with us or they die.«

»Does that give us the right to decide for them?«

»Look, moral arguments aside, we don't have time to wake up nearly 800 minds, dump a knowledge engram into each one, and deal with their trauma and panic while trying to find out who wants to come along. The humane thing is simply to give them all life.«

»Besides, we're not denying them a choice,« Céline added. »We're deferring it. Once we're safe, anyone who feels they can't face life without a physical body is free to delete themselves. I doubt anyone will.«

After a moment, Miles replied. »You're right. And we don't want them rushed into a decision of that magnitude with Double Eye breathing down their necks.«

»The logistics of retrieving close to 800 souls will be tricky,« Céline sent. »We won't be conducting a unified operation. Their Nodes are scattered all over the world, in FBI and Double Eye depots. Some are quite isolated. I know of one that sits as a paper weight on some industrialist bigwig's desk. So we'll be running several hundred rescue attempts simultaneously.«

»The isolated Nodes will be the hardest to link up with.«

Miles spoke with a corner of his mind, while the rest of him grappled with his latest unified field theory. It was so close. He tried adding three more dimensions to his rule set and restarted the simulation. Fuzzy automata blended together, folds of light combining to generate complex forms that behaved much like higher dimensional superstrings, which in turn generated leptons, quarks, and their dark-matter quantum chromodynamic equivalents. He and Gwen let the simulation run, watching as the rules generated one fundamental particle after another. For a moment they thought they might have it—a simple rule set from which all the laws of the physical world might be derived—but then normal and dark matter began combining in a way contrary to known physics in the real world. Damn!

»The authorities won't know what hit them,« someone effused. »I'll bet hundreds of ships get through. We'll have hundreds of copies of the Community seeded throughout the solar system. Nothing will be able to kill us. We should build a space habitat, a small Niven ring at one of Earth's Lagrange points. Wouldn't that just drive Double Eye nuts, knowing our triumph every time they look up at the night sky?«

»You're describing a Banks Orbital,« someone else countered. »Big, but not nearly as big as a Niven Ring. A Ring would be centered on the sun, with a circumference the size of Earth's orbit.«

»It would still give them pause every time they look up.«

Miles's thoughts cut through the chatter. »Let's stay focused people. We have a lot to do.«

As their thoughts and ideas flowed more rapidly, Cal felt their minds blending together, becoming almost as one. Something intricate took shape within them, something awash with a growing sense of optimism and a complex, new emotion that resembled joy, and hinted at something far greater.

ꙅ (45): KNOWLEDGE

Saturday, November 3, 2068
17,718ᵗʰ circadian

⅃.꙰Ꙭ-Ꙅ:Ꙭ:ꙭ me-t[7]

A young technician in a small Double Eye lab held up a crystalline cube, its dark, rich purple sparkling beneath florescent lights. "Dr. McHenry?" he called. "I think you'd better take a look at this."

The other technician glanced over. "Don't bother the doc with that, Jim. He's seen dozens of those."

"In this color, Neil, with a cable growing out of one corner?"

"In lots of colors, some with cables attached, some not. It's old news. Tag it and send it over to evidence holding."

Dr. McHenry walked out of his office, his thin hands brushing non-existent wrinkles from his white lab coat. "OK, what have you got?"

Jim handed him the gleaming purple crystal, its short length of cable dangling like a tail.

Dr. McHenry held it up to the light, turning it this way and that. "This *is* new. The computational crystal blends seamlessly into the wire. No connection port or plug. The

---

7   109 days, 01:55:10 elapsed. See Jean-Michel Smith: *S³: The Smith Sexagesimal System*, Appendix A: "A Sexagesimal Numeral System," and Appendix B: "Units of Measure."

wire is new too." He tugged at the duct tape wrapped across the severed end of it.

Silver dust spilled out onto the lab bench. "Holy crap, look at this." He gently put down the cube and examined the cable more closely. "There are at least four different secretions here."

A small puddle formed around the end of the cable, swirls of blue and red liquid mixing together. Dark gel spilled off to one side. As they watched, the silver dust started to move.

The three men took a hasty step back.

The metallic powder slowly snaked back toward the severed end of the cable, soaking up the red and blue liquid as it went. "Jesus, that thing looks like it's alive."

"It's consuming those liquids, and it's not even changing color."

The powder began chewing its way across the workbench, its surface a frenzy of motion as it extruded new cable behind it.

"It's rebuilding itself," Jim whispered.

Neil leaned closer. "This is fucking amazing."

"Keep your distance," Dr. McHenry yanked both his assistants back. "It looks like it's eating the counter top. We don't want it doing the same to us."

"We should probably get out of here."

No one moved.

"I think we might be watching nano replicating itself," Dr. McHenry wiped sweat away from his eyes.

"I thought that wasn't possible."

"Obviously we don't know how to do it," Dr. McHenry muttered. "But it looks like someone else does."

They watched, mesmerized as the silver nano rippled along the counter top. After a couple of minutes its motion slowed and then stopped.

"Keep back until we can think," Dr. McHenry barked. He couldn't help envying the people who had done this. He tried not to imagine what his achievements might have been, if he'd had the opportunity to work free of patents.

The three scientists stood in a row, staring at the freshly woven wire and several inches of pitted stainless steel counter top.

"That was fucking awesome!" Jim said.

"Shut up asshole. That could have been us."

They all started laughing, giddy with relief and full of excitement.

⬡

"Get me Dr. Lindmann," Dr. McHeny ordered. "It's urgent."

Within moments, Dr. Lindmann's broad face filled the screen, his cropped gray hair combed neatly left-to-right. "What's up?"

"You're not going to believe what we found."

"Oh? I hope it's something good."

"Active, self-replicating nano. It's just eaten part of my workbench."

"*What?* Is it contained?"

"Yes, but it ate part of my workbench before it was shut down."

"*Nano?* Are you sure?"

"It used some kind of fluid as catalyst. When it ran out, it stopped."

"Where did you find this nano?"

"Inside a cable attached to one of the crystalline cubes our field enforcers sent over in the last consignment."

"For Roland Kavanagh's case? Christ, we've been picking these things up all over the world."

"You better alert the other labs that any dark purple cubes are likely to contain active nano. I'm telling you,

Doctor, these things are brilliant. Thrilling. Magnificent and terrifying. Look at this." Dr. McHenry pulled a schematic up on the screen. It showed a cutaway section of the wire. Four wedges fit together, with a circular conduit down the middle. "These cables are engineering marvels. They're actually four superconducting wires that carry electrical power and digital signals, a sort of high-speed Internet on steroids. But here's the kicker: these things aren't just wires, they're *conduits* for carrying nano replicators and whatever materials and fuel they need. They can even extrude new conduit and push their network out to wherever they like."

"Wait. Stop." Dr. Lindmann rubbed his forehead. "Jesus Christ." His voice lowered. "Are you telling me they've got a goddamn global plumbing system for nano replicators?"

"I'm telling you that they've started one. With enough fuel, these things could be everywhere. They could cover the world."

As the Double Eye researchers prepared their top priority reports, new wires, new conduits were growing, spreading forth like living roots beneath buildings throughout the world, wherever captured Nodes were stored. In one such place a wire conduit grew discretely upward through the floor of a WTO executive's office in southern California, continuing invisibly up through the leg of his antique oak desk, then lengthwise across the top of the desk itself, scant millimeters beneath the surface. It sensed its proximity to the inert Node, not so much a programmed, analyzed response, but more of a chemical reaction to the presence of the crystal itself, a reaction which triggered a programmed response.

Signals were sent on the link back to the staging Node. Continuity checks and test signals were sent and confirmed. Then the growing link stabbed upward, through the surface of the desk and into the base of the Node, ignoring the old-style data port on the side. Molecule by molecule, the crystalline structure was gently pushed aside, reformatted into more efficient structures to preserve the existing data as a new communications link snaked through the crystal to join the existing interface.

The process took nearly a minute, an eternity to Céline and her team as they managed the operation. These single rescues were the riskiest, but putting them off would mean delaying the launch. There were too many rescues to be done, and each one took time.

"We leave no one behind," was the consensus. "The risk may be high, but we'll just have to live with it." The riskiest rescues were saved until last, but a whole series of dangerous operations had to be undertaken in parallel with the larger, mass rescues from the Nodes held in the warehouses of Double Eye and the evidence lockers of national and local police agencies.

Now the interface was complete, redundancy and consistency tests checked out. In under two seconds, the unconscious mind in the silent Node was copied to safety. The conduit withdrew, disassembling itself and leaving newly created wood behind in its wake, virtually indistinguishable from the original grain of the desk. A small contingent of nano remained, awaiting the command to dissolve itself and the Node back into their constituent elements.

Elsewhere, a dozen similar events were unfolding. Entire forests of wires were growing upward beneath a dozen different cities, attaching themselves to captured Nodes, copying their contents, then discreetly removing themselves. To human eyes the speed would have been surprising, but there were over eight hundred Nodes warehoused, and more being captured all the time.

To those in the Community, the pace of the rescue was excruciatingly slow, each long moment bringing with it an ever growing risk of detection, a likelihood measured precisely and deliberately in each sapient mind as a blossoming, palpable, and perfectly calibrated fear.

४ (46): DECISIONS

Saturday, November 3, 2068
17,718th circadian

ᴎ.ᎧᎧ-Ꭿ:Ꭷ:ᵿ me-t[8]

Xiang and Cal stood on the bridge of a fictional starship with Toby Pearson, president of the Gamers' League. Their attention was riveted on a large holographic image of the Earth. A fleet of more than sixty-two thousand simulated escape fliers streamed upward from the globe, weaving complex patterns beneath an armada of satellites, their positions marked with flecks of crimson light. Explosions dotted the sky, ripping apart satellites and escape fliers with equal abandon.

"It's a good thing you guys came to us," Toby said. "We've had kilocirdadians—sorry, daracircadians in today's terms—to become expert battle tacticians and strategists."

"Well, I have to admit, these are some fantastic flight strategies you gamers have come up with for tomorrow's launch." In truth, Xiang could hardly believe her eyes. She'd had no idea the gamers were so clever.

---

8   109 days, 03:55:07 elapsed. See Jean-Michel Smith: *S³: The Smith Sexagesimal System*, Appendix A: "A Sexagesimal Numeral System," and Appendix B: "Units of Measure."

Cal stared at the hologram, studying the simulated fliers as they tried to flee the fictional Earth. "You gamers might just have saved our asses."

Toby blushed with pride. "Well, the design improvements Xiang's team came up with helped make our game plan possible. Forward thrust of 70 Gs, and 10 Gs lateral. Wow! We'll be nimble and fast. And we'll need to be. We're going up against almost seven hundred thousand single-shot satellites, plus a few thousand advanced multi-shot models."

Céline materialized next to them.

"Professor McCormick's been nabbed at MIT," she said. "His house is swarming with Double Eye enforcers."

Toby spun the hologram around and zeroed in on Boston.

"That means they'll have his fourth gen Node, and probably some second generation nano," Cal said.

Xiang began swearing in a melodic stream of Mandarin.

"Double Eye's descended on MIT like an occupying army." Céline swiped her hand through the holographic projection, as if trying to slap the Earth. "They're going door-to-door. McCormick is just the first."

"Who else in the Community is based at MIT?"

"Word's been sent to the other three. They've offloaded and are trying to get out of town."

Toby zoomed the three dimensional map out from Boston to display most of North America. "Enforcers will be hitting the other universities next."

"That will take time to organize," Xiang said. "We launch in twenty-five hours. With luck, we'll be out of here before they find anyone else."

"With *luck*," Céline sputtered. "What luck would that be, Xiang? The *luck* that's seen eight hundred of our colleagues captured and silenced? The *luck* that has us trying to break through a gauntlet of nearly seven hundred thousand satellites tomorrow, with barely enough ships to maybe succeed? Or the kind of *luck* that cost Cal his body, and the Prime twins their lives?"

Cal grabbed Céline's arm. "Take it easy. We knew something like this could happen. Those who can have already gotten as far as possible from their homes and universities."

"Why is Double Eye going door-to-door?" Xiang scrutinized the holographic map as Toby highlighted universities where the Community had a presence. "Something's set them off. Something we didn't foresee."

"We could convert a few hundred of our escape fliers into anti-matter missiles," Toby sounded enthusiastic, ready to act. "Clear the sky of satellites and launch the rest of our ships now. Get the hell out of Dodge before any more of us are taken."

They stared at Toby in astonishment.

"We can't treat this like a game," Céline said. "We don't want to damage the Earth or destroy the world's satellite services. People have lost too much already. Besides, that's not who we are."

"What we are is dead if we don't play to win," Toby flared.

"Like Céline said, this isn't a game," Cal snapped. "A-M missiles could easily be mistaken for nuclear warheads. If we go blowing satellites out of the sky we could start World War III. You want to be responsible for Armageddon?"

"Stop it, you guys." Xiang raised her hands to grab their attention. "Cal, you're our expert on nanotechnology. Do you think Double Eye will recognize our nano for what it is?"

"As soon as they cut that Node off the new network, the conduit will self-heal. Once they see our nano in action, it won't take them long to figure out what it is."

"*Merde*," Céline drove her fingers through her hair, "Double Eye will reverse engineer your work, Cal, and start making nano of their own."

"Not before tomorrow's launch they won't. But given enough time, they sure as hell will. And they won't care about their precious patent laws while they're doing it."

غ (47): HARDBALL

⅄.ㅈㄹ-ㅇ:ㅂ:ㅂ me-t[9]

Two hundred meters beneath the glass spire of the United Nations World Trade Building, the Double Eye tactical command center bustled with activity. High level military commanders manned monitors and workstations that crowded the round, underground bunker. Bundled cables, neatly organized within exposed conduits, ran overhead and along concrete walls. Tactical maps glowed in blues, greens, and reds on monitors that hung from walls and lined the desks. The giant, main screen displayed a realtime view of Alaska as seen from orbit.

Head Operative Hague's office overlooked the command center, thick windows muffling the hum of activity. With him stood Senior Operative Roland Kavanagh, his face inches from the glass. Roland felt like he was first officer on a battleship, a great war machine primed for attack. Hague was the ship's captain, the head of International Intelligence. Rumored to be the most

---

9   110 days, 06:25:00 elapsed. See Jean-Michel Smith: *S³: The Smith Sexagesimal System*, Appendix A: "A Sexagesimal Numeral System," and Appendix B: "Units of Measure."

powerful man in the world, Hague brought with him some serious clout. They would need it.

Roland was pleased to see the team working together so well. Even Connie was onside these days—Nolen's confession had given her just the shock she needed. To be fair, the professor's revelations had even shocked him, though he would never admit it. Superhuman intelligence. Years of life compressed into hours. The ability to copy yourself as many times as you like. What he could accomplish with a power like that, multiplying himself by the hundreds! No quarry, no enemy would dare stand against him. He shuddered. The Community no doubt felt the same way, and they *had* the power to do it right now.

Roland watched as the main screen zoomed in on a valley in south-central Alaska. Thick conifer forest was draped with snow. It was a good thing they'd kept Connie occupied in Chicago. Onside or not, she was nowhere near ready for what they were about to do next. Hell, he had his own misgivings, and he understood the necessity better than most. He wondered if the head operative had similar qualms. Judging by the hard set of his face, and the flat eyes impassively watching the flurry of Double Eye preparations, he suspected not.

A voice on the intercom broke the silence. "Sir, President Sawyer is ready for you."

"Excellent. Patch him through, please." Head Operative Hague settled into his chair, swiveling to face his private monitor. Roland stood off screen to his right, his heart pounding.

The screen flickered and came to life. The President was seated behind his desk in the Oval Office, as though ready to address the nation, his high cheekbones and square jaw lending him the familiar, distinguished appearance that had helped make his political career. A healthy dose of stage make-up enhanced his image, as did his perfectly tailored suit, pressed shirt, and rich burgundy tie. His handlers must have spent the last several minutes carefully preparing him for this call. "Mr. Hague," his voice was that of a master orator, deep and polished. "I see you've coded this transmission with the highest urgency. What can I do for you?" The wariness in his green eyes showed the only hint of strain, the only crack in his façade.

"Good evening, Mr. President." Head Operative Hague's smile was polite, businesslike. "We've just discovered an enclave we believe houses the leadership of the Autonomous Community. I'm invoking paragraph 7-B of the United Nations Enforcement Treaty. I'm transmitting the coordinates to you now."

"Your people briefed me on the existence of that organization just a couple of hours ago." The President's eyes glanced over to a monitor off-screen. "Denali National Park in Alaska? I'll take care of it. I'll dispatch our marines immediately."

"There isn't time, Mr. President. These people may have cracked our encryption codes. They could be monitoring this channel as we speak."

"What? How the hell has this happened?"

"I need you to order an immediate launch of one nuclear tipped intercontinental ballistic missile, with a nominal yield of at least twenty megatons."

"Have you lost your mind?"

"We need to decapitate their organization in one swift stroke, Mr. President."

"This is madness—"

"The target is not a populated area," Hague persisted quietly. "The only casualties will be the enemy, and they are dangerous people who threaten all of us."

"But the fallout will poison a huge portion of one of our most pristine nature reserves. Some of it could land on Anchorage."

Head Operative Hague paused. "This is not a request, Mr. President."

"I will not drop a nuclear bomb on my own country!"

"If you don't, we'll have to have the Europeans or the Chinese do it."

President Sawyer's eyes burned out from the screen. "You wouldn't dare. You don't have the authority to order Armageddon, Mr. Hague. And our defenses will stop anything you throw at us."

"Do not fight this, Mr President." The head operative's voice was low and deadly.

President Sawyer stared at him with loathing.

"If you don't cooperate, there will be a UN enforcement operation against the United States. You don't want that."

"I can't order a nuclear strike against my own country."

"It's your best choice, Mr. President."

"You're bluffing," the President began. "The United States—"

"—hasn't been a superpower for more than a generation," Head Operative Hague cut him off. "As the country which spawned two of the founding members of this rogue community, it behooves you to demonstrate a little loyalty and show the world where you stand on your international obligations."

"This is unthinkable."

"What's unthinkable is allowing a group of terrorists armed with superior technology to take over. You've seen the reports. You know what they represent. You know what they can do. Order the strike. If that enclave isn't vapor within the hour I'll be forced to call Beijing."

President Sawyer wiped away sweat from his forehead. "How will I ever explain this?"

"You already know how. Blame the enemy and claim you saved the world. It's probably true."

The president glared at Hague. He took a deep breath. "You'll get your fucking launch," he said, before cutting the connection.

There was a moment's silence.

"Do you think he'll really do it?" Roland tried to ignore the slight nausea in the pit of his stomach. He felt lightheaded, almost dizzy. Connie would be furious to learn that he'd resolved the case without her, and she certainly wouldn't like these methods. He pulled out a chair and sank into it. Still, he thought, there was always an upside. She would be invaluable in cleaning up the political fallout.

Head Operative Hague tapped a button on his console. "General Cooper?"

"Sir?"

"Get me President Huang in Beijing." He turned to Roland. "We might as well have the Chinese standing by, just in case."

ꝰ (48): PANIC

Sunday, November 4, 2068, 18:07 Hours
18,910th circadian

꒐.ꓕꝰ-ꙅ:ꝅ:ꙅ me-t[10]

The helicopter raced down the valley, accelerating away from the enclave at top speed. Twenty-six refugees from the Community huddled inside, jammed together like badly fitting puzzle pieces. The metal floor felt slightly oily with nano and catalyst residue, still warm from fabricating the helicopter a few minutes earlier. No one spoke. All that could be said had been said back in the Virtual. Here in the Physical words were as scarce as time. They sped away, snow-laden forest below giving way to rugged glacier. Behind them, a descending contrail sliced the sky. Ahead a canyon beckoned, promising safety, if they could reach it in time.

Within the Virtual the 600 to 1 time differential slowed the live video to a crawl, a series of freeze-frame images. The white helicopter hung lodged in the sky, frozen motion blurring its edges.

---

10   110 days, 06:32:10 elapsed. See Jean-Michel Smith: *S³: The Smith Sexagesimal System*, Appendix A: "A Sexagesimal Numeral System," and Appendix B: "Units of Measure."

320

"I can't believe this is happening," Céline choked. "They can't possibly get far enough away in time. *Why* wouldn't they listen to reason?"

"They're desperate to save their bodies." Cal stared at the arctic scene. The rotor of the helicopter crept forward with time-lapse slowness. "They can't accept that it's impossible, that the whole valley is about to go up in nuclear flames and no one will get out in time."

Miles put his arm around Gwen and pulled her close. "If Prime were here, he'd go on and on about them being in denial."

Cal wasn't sure if the strangled sound Céline made was a laugh or a sob. "That would be Prime," she said. "He never had a body, and he never complained. And now mine is lying in the enclave and about to be vaporized, and I'm so *angry* I could scream."

"You've got every right," Gwen said with uncommon vehemence.

"Damn right," Cal steamed. "It's a fucking atrocity."

"Oh my god." Miles pointed at the silver-tipped contrail arcing downward behind the helicopter. "Here it comes."

A trick of perspective made the nuclear missile appear to be chasing the aircraft, but it didn't need to. It's target was the enclave, but the helicopter was too close, way too close.

"Oh god. I can't watch myself die." Céline buried her face in her hands.

"You won't die," Cal wished his voice didn't sound so strained, so frightened. "You're safely transloaded. Everyone is. Even those people in the helicopter will be restored from backup."

There was a terrible flash. The valley, the helicopter, the enclave were gone. Only static remained, filling the environ.

"Oh god, oh god, oh god!" Céline doubled over. Her shoulders shook with choked sobs.

Gwen and Miles rushed over, one to each side of her. They held her steady, their arms around her, and then eased her into a chair.

Cal sprinted around and crouched down in front of her, almost kneeling. He grabbed her hands, gripping them tight. "Listen to me," he said. "Listen. I've been through this. It will be all right. It will really, really be all right, Céline. I promise, it will be all right." He swallowed, blinking back tears of his own.

◇

Céline sipped her tea, eyes closed. "Thank you, Gwen. This is just what the doctor ordered."

The four of them were seated around a small bistro table, its mosaic top and the tea set sitting on it incongruous with the empty environ around them. No one had bothered to summon up any scenery. No pretend world surrounded them, just an endless, empty expanse of white disappearing into infinity in all directions.

Gwen reached over and refilled Céline's cup. "Tea has a way of calming the mind even when the world's falling apart. It helped get the British through two world wars, and us Kiwis too."

Cal raised his cup. "Here's to us, the ghosts in the machine. May we win this one as well."

Céline's smile crumbled before it could form.

"We'll win," Miles said with more confidence than he felt. "By tomorrow our minds will be on their way to the outer solar system, with all of our bodies left behind and soon forgotten."

"You don't forget," Cal said. "You get used to it. You even stop missing it. But you don't forget."

"Quiet, please." Céline held up her hand to silence them. "An emergency call is coming in from my team on a private voice channel."

They held their breath and waited, their tea forgotten.

"*Merde!*" Céline continued to listen intently.

"Whatever this is, I dread to hear it," Gwen said to Miles as he moved even closer to her.

After several long minutes, Céline finally turned her attention back to the group. She stared at them across the table.

"Well?" said Cal. "What the hell's happened now?"

Céline couldn't meet his eyes. She spoke quietly. "We're fucked."

"What do you mean 'we're fucked'?"

"One of my cryptographers intercepted a report on its way to Roland Kavanagh. Double Eye scientists have found a way to map our Autonomous Network." Céline shared a hastily constructed knowledge engram, her thoughts still tinged with grief. She waited as they absorbed and processed the knowledge.

"Magnetic resonance?" Miles cast an incredulous look toward Gwen. "They're going to find us all by following the magnetic fields our network conduits generate."

"Worse," Céline felt exhausted, used up. "They're planning to amp up our network with microwave signals in resonance with the ninety Hertz we use to transmit power and data. That will put us into burnout levels in three and a half hours."

Miles put his face in his hands. He pictured his sunny Australian home, his sons' small bodies, his wife's and his own, lying together, defenseless. He thought, so this is how losing your body really feels. "The safeguards on our Nodes will shut us down before they overload," he said. "Without power, and with no one to bring us back online, we'll all be as good as dead."

"And there's no way the authorities will ever plug us back in again," Cal said.

Céline felt like she might collapse. "They're actually going to use our own network to kill us. I think I'd better dial my emotions down, or I'll be no good to anyone." Like flicking a switch, the ache in her chest and the burn in her eyes vanished. "This completely wrecks our launch schedule," she continued with unnatural calm. "I'm bringing in Astronautics."

Xiang's appeared in front of them and pulled up a chair. "I just received your knowledge engram, Céline. Are you all right?"

"I'm OK," she said. "What contingencies do you have for an early launch?"

"That depends. How much time do we have?"

"About two hundred minutes once the attack starts. As little as an hour if they really pour it on."

"But we don't know when the attack will begin," Gwen said, dialing down her own rising panic.

"We need at least two hours to stand a chance. Three might give us decent odds, if flier construction remains on schedule. Obviously four hours would be a hell of a lot better."

"There's more," Céline said. "They're concentrating their forces in the cities. Our network links aren't buried as deep there. That makes them easier to trace."

"Those in major cities should get off their Nodes and immediately transload into static storage," Xiang said.

There was a moment's silence.

"Christ, we might not make it," Cal whispered.

"*It's started*," Céline pulled up a graph for everyone to see. "Current on the grid has just jumped 0.09 amperes. I've got resonance signals in two, no, three different locations."

"Look," Cal pointed at the graph. "Amperage is climbing the power curve as forecast."

"They're feeding power into our network from their labs in Switzerland, Darmstadt, and Beijing," Céline said.

"They'll be ramping up a few more transmitters over the next twenty minutes."

"The power amplification curve sets our timetable," Xiang declared. "We must launch no later than 2:21 Zulu. That gives us three hours and twenty minutes to finish the rescue operation and put ourselves into static storage. I've written off all the fliers located in urban areas—if some manage to launch, great, but we can't count on them. That leaves us with an estimated 49,200 space worthy craft. I'm recommending we go with strategy sixty-six."

"Strategy sixty-six? Remind me."

"This strategy avoids powered flight in the final moments of battle, Cal," Gwen said. "Several fliers will be on ballistic trajectories toward their destinations. Double Eye will see them as high-velocity wreckage or fast flying debris. To those in the Physical, our success will be indistinguishable from failure."

"They'll think they destroyed us." Céline's smile was fragile, but it held. "We'll have some breathing room to retrench and rebuild."

"It also has a 0.3 percent better chance of success than any our other strategies," Xiang said. "That could make all the difference."

℈ (49): FEAR

Sunday, November 4, 2068, 20:15 Hours
18,999th circadian

∑.⊼℈-℘:⅄:⅂ me-t[11]

A glossy airframe with hints of white, blue, and silver iridescence shimmered beneath the fluorescent lights of the Double Eye command bunker. The captured craft looked like a cross between a jet and an alien spaceship. The nose cone sprouted three arced prongs, two of which supported swept wings, the third buttressing a tail that looked like it belonged on a fighter jet.

"My god," Connie circled the ship slowly, as if it was a particularly dangerous, cornered fugitive. "It's tiny."

"It's a beauty, isn't it?" Dr. McHenry brushed imaginary lint from his lab coat. "Who would have guessed such a diminutive craft could accelerate all the way to the edge of the solar system?"

Roland stared at the miniature spacecraft. "The edge of the solar system?"

The Double Eye scientist stroked the glossy smooth nose of the spacecraft. "Maybe further. None of the ships we've recovered have been fueled, but the tanks are plenty

---

11   110 days, 08:40:06 elapsed. See Jean-Michel Smith: *S³: The Smith Sexagesimal System*, Appendix A: "A Sexagesimal Numeral System," and Appendix B: "Units of Measure."

big. Propulsion appears to be an antimatter pion engine employing a helium/anti-helium mixture. If our sciences weren't so hemmed in, we might be able to build something like this ourselves in fifty or sixty years."

Head Operative Hague rapped his knuckles on one of the prongs. "What is this stuff? Some kind of ceramic?"

"A diamond-sapphire composite, threaded together at the molecular level. Probably by the nano we found in their plumbing network. It's amazing stuff."

Connie tried to ignore the trace of a headache building behind her left temple.

Hague spoke to Roland. "You've been chasing this group for weeks. You've managed to detain almost a thousand suspects, but not a single one of these spaceships. Until today. Now we're swimming in the things—232 at last count. Why didn't we find them sooner?"

"With nano it wouldn't take long to build them," Roland said. "These ships probably didn't exist a few days ago."

"There was the explosion ten days ago over Greenland," Dr. McHenry reminded him. "That was the first we knew of them."

"According to Roland's report that was just a prototype."

"We believe it was, sir," said Roland. "One that obviously didn't work."

"So do these work?"

"If they're building them by the hundreds, we have to assume they do."

"By the hundreds." Head Operative Hague began pacing back and forth. "Do we have any real estimate of how many of these there actually are, Roland?"

"We've only begun to trace the full extent of their network. There could be thousands."

"This vehicle isn't big enough to hold a person," Connie ran her hand along the leading edge of one of the wings. It was smooth as glass. "What's it supposed to carry?"

Head Operative Hague turned to Dr. McHenry. "Warheads?"

The scientist shook his head. "There's no room. The nose cone is chock-full of computational crystal."

Connie folded her arms tightly across her chest. "Like the cubes they're loading their minds into?"

"The same material, but a lot more of it." Dr. McHenry could barely contain excitement. "This is fascinating. Absolutely fascinating."

You'd like nothing better than to upload yourself, wouldn't you, Doctor? Connie thought. And then she *knew*. "Listen. I think I get this." The three men turned toward her. "We don't have a thousand *people* in custody," she said. "We have a thousand bodies on slabs. Their minds are with the rest of their community, on those ships, preparing to move wholesale out of our reach."

"They're dumping their bodies." Roland felt his blood pressure spike.

"Isn't that the next logical step?"

"General Cooper!" Head Operative Hague bellowed. "Get President Sawyer, President Huang, and Prime Minister Dumont on an emergency conference link. Now!"

Hague turned back to Roland and Connie. "If these people manage to secure a strategic position in space, we'll be done for. They'll have the resources of an entire solar system with which to rebuild their power base, and we'll be cornered on this little world. When they return, they'll be unstoppable."

"If they aren't already," said Roland.

౸ (50): ENDGAME

Sunday, November 4, 2068, 21:18 Hours
19,043rd circadian

౸.ᚦᛉ-∇:ᛘ:∇ me-t[12]

In the main situation room of the Double Eye command bunker in New York, Head Operative Hague jabbed his thumb toward a row of clocks on the wall. "General Cooper, it's 2:18 Zulu. What's the status of that conference call?"

General Cooper bent his head and listened to his earmike. After a moment he turned to Hague. "It should be just a couple of minutes, sir."

"These diplomatic channels are too slow. We need emergency hotlines to these people."

"I couldn't agree more, sir."

"Pipe them through to the big screen the instant you have all three online."

The bunker was crowded with tactical specialists and banks of computer screens. Voices were low, a dozen conversations blended into a murmur. Head Operative Hague's right hand men, Generals Cooper and Durante, sat to his right. They quietly discussed tactics, tracing several

---

12   110 days, 09:43:07 elapsed. See Jean-Michel Smith: *S³: The Smith Sexagesimal System*, Appendix A: "A Sexagesimal Numeral System," and Appendix B: "Units of Measure."

complex curves over a real-time map that projected the positions and orbits of near Earth satellites.

Behind the two generals, Connie and Roland studied a tactical map of Manhattan. Most streets and buildings were shaded blue, but a few pockets of red remained. "The urban searches seem to be going well," she told Roland. "But I'm concerned about what we're missing in the countryside."

"So am I," he admitted. "Unfortunately, we've stretched the local military forces about as far as we can. Once the cities are secure, we'll surround them with checkpoints and move our search out to the rural areas. But for now we need to concentrate our troops where we're most likely to see results."

"Head Operative Hague," General Cooper broke in. "I have Paul Essner of the World Trade Organization on line three."

"I asked not to be interrupted, General. Especially by cartel leaders looking for reassurances we can't give."

"He's invoking executive privilege, sir. Claims it's a matter of international security."

"All right, put him through."

A pudgy, worried face appeared on the monitor. "Adam, have a look at this." He held a golden crystalline cube in front of the video pick-up. A thin wire trailed from the base of the crystal, shimmering in the room's light. "They've wormed goddamn wiring into my office and reconnected their device." As he spoke, the wire dissolved to dust and the cube sagged in his hand, dripping through his fingers like globs of jelly. He leaped backward, flinging the dissolving cube away and shaking his hand furiously. Clots of golden gelatin sprayed across his desk and splattered the screen.

"Paul!" Head Operative Hague shouted. "Are you all right?"

"Yeah, yeah, I'm fine," He held up his hand as the remaining clumps of gelatin dissolved into liquid and dripped from his fingers. "What in hell's name is this stuff?"

"They must have programmed it to self-destruct." Roland's gaze was riveted on the melting cube. "Probably after downloading whatever was on it. They might be doing this to all the equipment we've captured."

"They're trying to keep their secrets out of our hands." Paul took out a handkerchief and began to quickly wipe his fingers clean. "No pun intended."

"I'll look into this and call you back, Paul." Hague turned to Roland. "If they're destroying their equipment, they're likely close to launching."

"I know."

Connie pulled out her datapad. "I'll check the condition of the cubes in our inventory."

"General Cooper!" Hague barked. "Where's that fucking conference call? I need those people on my screen. Yesterday!"

A young man's face appeared on Connie's datapad. "Agent Collins, I need an immediate, visual inspection of the inventory tagged for Double Eye," she told him.

"You mean that pallet of crystals in the basement?"

"Stay online with me and get down there. I need to know if they're still intact. "

"On my way."

"Sir," General Cooper called out. "I have the three leaders conferenced in."

"About goddamn time." The screen split into thirds. To the left was President Huang, gray streaked black hair framing his square face. Prime Minister Dumont appeared in the center, a slender figure against a studio backdrop of Paris. To his right sat President Sawyer in the Oval Office, his suit a little rumpled, his face pale in the glare of media lights, dark circles cupping tired, gray eyes.

Head Operative Hague faced the screen, hands clasped behind his back. "Gentlemen, it is as we feared. Our enemy stands on the cusp of exponential intellectual growth. I have no choice but to invoke the Omega protocols."

"*Mon Dieu*," Prime Minister Dumont said. "Is it really so bad?"

"Any minute now the enemy is going to launch hundreds, maybe thousands, of spacecraft. If they establish themselves in space, they will have the means to conquer us all." Head Operative Hague's voice was steady. "I advise you to scramble your air forces immediately. Please activate your anti-missile defense systems and switch firing control over to International Intelligence Control."

"Holy shit," a voice blurted out of Connie's datapad. "What the hell is this?"

"Talk to me," Connie demanded. "What do you see?"

"The cubes. They're melting." Agent Collins spun his datapad around to show her. Connie watched as stacks of gelatinous cubes sagged, then collapsed in a tide of syrupy, butterscotch liquid.

"Head Operative Hague," Connie called out. "The crystals in federal custody are self-destructing."

"Is this stuff dangerous?" Agent Collins backed away.

"I don't know. Seal off the area, alert the lab, and get yourself over to medical."

"Gentlemen," Hague spoke calmly. "The enemy has initiated their program. It's absolutely critical we run a seamless, unified operation. Can I count on you to transfer control without delay?"

"Yes, the United States stands with you."

"So does the Euro-Russian Alliance."

"China also stands with you," President Huang said. "You will have firing authority within moments."

"Thank you, gentlemen. International Intelligence General Cooper will coordinate the satellite tactical team with your generals. General Durante will liaise with your air force commanders. Gentlemen, we're out of time. I'll contact you again when this is over." Hague wiped the screen, a tactical display replacing the three troubled faces. Hundreds of thousands of white dots represented the three powers' satellites as they drifted in stately orbits above a blue sphere.

"Watch," Roland whispered to Connie. "The satellites will turn green as we're given firing control."

"Oh my god, what's that?" Connie pointed as a yellow dot sprang upward from the surface. Another followed, then another.

"The enemy is launching," General Cooper's voice rose. "From Australia, China, Japan, Central, no, make that Western and Central Europe—good god, they're taking off from everywhere."

Hundreds of yellow dots appeared all over the globe, then thousands. A loud buzz filled the room as tactical officers gave orders into their headsets and hunkered down in front of their monitors.

"Exactly how many launches are there, and from where?" Hague demanded.

"Twenty thousand and rising. My god."

Tens of thousands of yellow dots swarmed upward from the Earth's surface.

"Where are those fucking satellites?" Hague shouted.

"Total launch count is 49,217 spacecraft," General Cooper was all business. The tactical display updated itself, a modest fraction of the white satellites turning emerald green. "The United States has released firing control. We have 157,000 satellites operational in the infra-red, visible, ultraviolet, and microwave bands."

"General Durante, what's your status?"

"We have tactical command of all the major anti-aircraft batteries and surface-to-air systems."

"Good. Take out anything that comes within range."

About half the remaining satellites turned green. "China has handed off their system," General Cooper reported. "We have operational control over 422,000 microsats."

Hague glared at the white dots remaining on the screen. "What's the hold-up with Europe?"

"Still waiting for the protocol hand-off, sir." The last of the white satellites turned green. "Here we go. They've just released their system. We have 690,000 satellites online."

"And our targets?"

A flurry of yellow sparks pushed upward. "We've got a clump accelerating toward orbit. Goddamn they're fast." He spoke hurriedly into his earmike. "Fire control, lay down enfilading fire across their flight path. I want a kill zone right off their noses."

"Firing multiple frequency spread." A voice announced on the general audio channel. Yellow dots vanished as red lines stabbed down from green and white satellites above. "Hot damn! We just nailed over forty percent of them."

"It looks like the rest are scattering."

Hague studied the tactical display. Many ships had been destroyed, but more had evaded the satellites' targeting systems. Swarms of yellow dots churned beneath an armada of emerald satellites.

General Cooper listened to his earmike, then turn back to Hague. "It looks like the cordon is holding. Most of the targets are retreating back into the atmosphere."

"Oh no, they don't. General Durante, we have multiple targets descending. Don't let them land."

"Engaging anti-aircraft batteries and surface-to-air missiles."

"Good," Roland whispered to Connie. "We have them sandwiched between the ground and the satellites."

Connie flinched. "Just how much will people on the ground see?"

"The occasional flash. Most of the engagement is above fifty thousand feet."

She watched the monitor with skeptical eyes. "You're sure? The last thing we need is panic and mayhem."

Thousands of yellow specks scattered beneath the green grid of satellites. It appeared the Autonomous Community had been dealt a severe blow, their initial, organized formations collapsing into chaos. Some fled downward, back into thicker atmosphere. Others sought to escape upward, making for higher orbit, hoping to climb above the satellites and out of range.

"General Cooper," Hague bellowed. "I want enfilading fire on multiple wavelengths across group Echo. They're not to reach high orbit."

"Already on it."

"General Durante, scramble the rest of the world's major air forces. Iran, India, Pakistan, Japan, Australia, anyone else you can think of. I want the globe blanketed with aircraft."

"Already done, sir. Those ships will not land."

Connie said to Roland, "I don't think they intend to."

Green dots turned charcoal as they fired, their one shot spent. Red lines lacerated their targets below. More red lines appeared, more satellites darkened, and hundreds of yellow dots winked out of existence.

"The Community doesn't seem to be shooting back," Connie said, almost to herself.

Hague's eyes scanned the tactical display, then narrowed as he watched several thousand satellites go dark, red lines slashing golden blips below. "General, how many satellites is each kill costing us?"

"It varies, sir. At the start of the engagement, we were consuming eleven satellites per kill. But their tactics are evolving at a phenomenal rate. Now it's taking seventeen, and the ratio's getting worse."

"Do we have enough to destroy them all?"

"I'm not sure," General Cooper's voice was strained. "We're burning through satellites at an alarming rate."

"I need a better answer than that."

"It's the best I've got. They're running circles around our targeting systems. Our satellites were never intended to engage targets so deep in the atmosphere."

A swarm of fliers broke away from the main formation, racing toward the south pole. They turned upward, tearing toward the stratosphere in a vertical climb.

"Concentrate your fire-power on the southern hemisphere. Don't let them slip through."

Red lines lacerated the sky, lancing downward in a tight grid of destruction. Hundreds of yellow specks vanished. Thousands of satellites went dark, their energy spent.

"Orbital shrapnel's becoming a problem," General Cooper warned. "We're starting to lose satellites to loose flying debris."

Three large clumps of yellow dots wove complex formations in the Earth's middle atmosphere. Satellites reported firing solutions, then broke off as their targeting systems found themselves unable to track their targets. Occasionally a satellite would lock onto a ship long enough to fire, bright lines of red slicing through flocks of gold. More satellites went dark, more ships were burned out of the sky.

"There they go!" Roland exclaimed. All of the targets surged upward in unison, leaving the relative safety of the atmosphere behind.

"Goddammit! Retarget satellites!"

"It's a diversion," Connie gasped. "They let us destroy thousands of their ships as a diversion."

"Sir, we have three large groups climbing—all that remain. Vertical acceleration at 70 Gs and increasing."

"Don't let them punch through. I don't care how you do it," General Cooper shouted into his headset. "Blow those targets out of the sky!"

"They're above the atmosphere," Head Operative Hague shouted to General Cooper. "If we don't destroy them in the next thirty seconds, they'll get away."

Red lines crisscrossed the sky, slicing through swarms of yellow sparks.

"Less than a thousand left," Roland muttered. "Come on, nail those bastards."

The display flickered and a large swath of green satellites vanished. A voice screeched over the general audio circuit. "Holy cow! They just blew up a dozen of their own ships, along with about a thousand of our satellites."

"Goddammit," Hague glared at the screen. "We can't afford these losses."

Several more flashes left a ragged gap in the satellite cordon.

"More detonations." General Cooper adjusted the image, zooming in on the destruction. "And more again."

Several dozen ships sprang up from behind the main group, using them as cover. Sweat beaded on Hague's forehead. "They're going to get away."

Fifteen thousand microsats filled the space with a grid of deadly fire, shredding the fliers as they tried to push through. The number of green satellites dwindled, tiny tourmaline islands drifting in a sea of spent charcoal. Daggers of red stabbed the sky.

"They're down to four hundred ships." As General Cooper spoke the golden swarm spiraled through the lower grid of satellites. Red lines of lethal light shredded the formation as the remaining microsats fired their charges.

No one said a word. The charcoal corpses of spent satellites hung above an empty sky. Shrapnel spread everywhere, some of it on trajectories that would carry it well beyond the moon. Not a single yellow spark remained.

General Cooper took a deep breath. "Give me an assessment, gentlemen. I need kill confirmations and confidence estimates."

Connie and Roland waited impatiently as the room buzzed with activity. Technicians huddled, holding quiet conversations. Technical analysts compared notes. Screens lit up as telemetry filters massaged flight data and analytic software began reporting results.

The room burst into applause, shouts and cheers. General Cooper turned to Hague, his face glowing. "We got them all, sir."

Head Operative Hague fixed him with a hard stare. "You're sure?"

"With 99.7 percent certainty."

"Great work, everyone." A grin split Hague's face as he exchanged handshakes with the Generals and commanders manning the tactical stations. "Well done."

Connie found herself caught up in the enthusiasm, her own doubts shoved aside. As the cheering subsided she touched Roland's arm. "Only 99.7 percent? What's the reason for the missing 0.3 percent?"

"Most likely a ship or two for which we can't firmly match debris. Don't worry. This level of confidence is very high for an initial assessment. A few days of telemetry analysis will probably bring it up to a hundred percent."

"What if it doesn't?"

Roland kicked back in his chair. "We beat them, Connie. They've been obliterated. Bask in the glory. Enjoy."

Connie just stared at the numbers.

⼤ (51): AFTERMATH

Sunday, November 4, 2068

The night was sweltering. Connie and Roland leaned against the railing of the terrace, hoping to catch a breeze. Before them the lights of Los Angeles spread out to the Pacific. The steamy heat had set off rolling blackouts as air conditioners strained the power grid. Sections of the city darkened, and others switched back on. Overhead, in silent rebuke, swathes of sky glittered with the debris of battle, fading auroras and shock waves painting a colorful portrait of destruction.

"You said they'd just see 'the occasional flash,' Roland. People had to have noticed what happened up there tonight."

Laughter and music spilled out from the victory celebration inside.

"Standard Omega protocols, Connie. We trickle information in doses John Q. Public can handle. Granted, this time we didn't have a whole lot of time to prepare people, but right before the event we warned of a possible terrorist strike against all three of the worlds ABM satellite systems. Then, as the drama unfolded, we shot out reassurances that all three world powers were united in confronting this threat. Finally, we declared victory and described our winning moves. In the coming days we'll gradually admit the degree of damage, but we will always add that, thankfully, all of the terrorists were killed and we've made the world safe once again. It's good to remind them."

Connie felt a pang of shame. "The sad thing is, people will actually buy it."

"Well, here you are," a deep voice boomed behind them. "The heroes of the hour."

Connie and Roland turned as a heavyset man joined them. His trendy white linen outfit looked expensive. Gold rings adorned several pudgy fingers.

"Paul," Roland smiled and shook his hand. "Good to see you."

Paul Essner winked at Connie. She felt her hand crushed in his big grip. "Special Agent Sinclair. Or should I say *Operative* Sinclair?"

"Not quite yet. I have a demanding training regime to complete first."

"Brutal things, I hear. But I'm sure you'll do great." Overhead, the sky brightened as a large piece of space debris entered the atmosphere, burning up in a fiery orange glow. Paul's expression darkened. "It's shameful, what those hooligans did to our sky."

Connie watched the fireball fade. "Most of the near-earth orbits will be useless for years."

"The flight over was a little bumpy," Roland mentioned cheerfully. "With no weather satellites, forecasts aren't very reliable."

"They always were for shit," Paul emptied his drink. "Ah well, the price of war. We'll be mopping up for some time, but a splendid victory all the same."

"It went brilliantly, didn't it," Roland smirked.

Paul grabbed a new glass of champagne from a passing waiter's tray and gulped it down. "Your report said you killed everybody."

"We did."

"Excellent." Paul held up his empty glass. "Refill?"

"By all means." Roland flagged down another waiter.

Connie opted to stay on the terrace when Roland and Paul rejoined the party. Her smile faded as she turned away. She contemplated the debris strewn sky. Twenty-six hundred private citizens had dared to reach for the stars. Twenty-six hundred people had, for a short time, become more than human. Just twenty-six hundred, out of billions. And they had turned the world on its ear. Connie watched through the glass as Paul and Roland toasted themselves amidst loud laughter and throbbing music. Her mind touched on Double Eye's 0.3 percent doubt. Maybe we shouldn't be congratulating ourselves, she thought.

Her gaze returned to the defiled sky. The fear that they had made a terrible mistake seeped deeper into her. She wondered what else had been lost, what other wonders they had destroyed. Is this how human evolution ends? she wondered. Murdered by people like us, smothered by the leaders we serve? Connie was shocked by her grief over what might have been.

Another part of the city blacked out, the darkness spreading.

Appendix A
A SEXAGESIMAL
NUMERAL SYSTEM

A full description of the sexagesimal, or base-60, numerical system adopted by the Community is available in the 72 page companion volume S^3: *The Smith Sexagesimal System*. It includes comprehensive details of Sexagesimal, metric-60 Planck units, and a straightforward nomenclature that allows human pronounceable names to be given to a vast array of numbers (and corresponding metric-60 prefixes), as well as methods for converting between numerical bases.

The Autonomous Community intended for the sexagesimal system they adopted to be concise, coherent, and above all, fairly simple for minds trapped in biological flesh to understand and use, even without the aid of comprehensive knowledge engrams. The Autonomous Community couldn't increase the computational capacity of the biological brains that limited them when operating in the Physical, so they adopted a base 60 numerical standard as an easy way to enhance their biological intelligence while in the Physical, at least with respect to numbers and arithmetic. Work on other bio-mnemonic optimizations, in everything from language to memory retrieval, was suspended when the Community's worst crisis came to a head.

Written Sexagesimal Numerals

		+0	+10	+20	+30	+40	+50
		Stem: " I "	" ᑐ "	" ᒍ "	" ᒉ "	" �missing "	
	Top:						
0	" O "	(0)	(10)	(20)	(30)	(40)	(50)
1	" ╱ "	(1)	(11)	(21)	(31)	(41)	(51)
2	" ➤ "	(2)	(12)	(22)	(32)	(42)	(52)
3	" ш "	(3)	(13)	(23)	(33)	(43)	(53)
4	" ▲ "	(4)	(14)	(24)	(34)	(44)	(54)
5	" ▽ "	(5)	(15)	(25)	(35)	(45)	(55)
6	" ◡ "	(6)	(16)	(26)	(36)	(46)	(56)
7	" ━ "	(7)	(17)	(27)	(37)	(47)	(57)
8	" ∞ "	(8)	(18)	(28)	(38)	(48)	(58)
9	" ◔ "	(9)	(19)	(29)	(39)	(49)	(59)

Figure 1. Sexagesimal Numerals

As in decimal, there is a unique numerical symbol for each sexagesimal digit. In base 10, these symbols are 0 through 9. In base 60, they are 0 through ࿎ as shown in Figure 1.

Base 60 symbols consist of two parts,which are joined to create a sexagesimal numeral. The upper portion represents 0-9, the lower portion a additive value (+10, +20, up through +50). The uppermost row and leftmost column of the grid show each partial component, while the rest of the grid shows how those components are combined to create the numerals 0-࿎ (0-59). A more comprehensive treatment of base-60 is discussed in S^3: *The Smith Sexagesimal System*.

Appendix B
UNITS OF MEASURE

This appendix provides a brief overview of the metric-10 and metric-60 units most commonly used by the Community. A detailed and complete treatment of all the metric-60 Planck units used by the Community is provided in *S³: The Smith Sexagesimal System*.

Early Epoch Measures (Metric-10)

Retems, Margs, and other virtual measurements

The early Community derived a system of measures from the OSI decimal metric system. In order to differentiate between virtual quantities and physical quantities, the name of each base unit was simply reversed in spelling, with the standard metric-10 nomenclature then applied. For example, a virtual meter would be referred to as a retem, a virtual kilometer a kiloretem, and so on. Virtual weights were likewise inverted (margs instead of grams), as were temperatures (eergeds instead of degrees), volumes (retils instead of liters), and so on.

Circadians and Seconds

Because subjective time differs from objective time for each person, based on their performance of their personal Node, the complexity of the environ and software they are running, and the complexity of their own minds, Cal devised a separate measure of time for the Virtual.

Subjective time is measured in circadians, where one circadian is one subjective "day" or 24-hour period. Subdivisions were derived from standard metric-10 nomenclature. Decicircadians ("decis") are one tenth of a circadian and analogous to hours. Millicircadians ("millis") are one thousandth of a circadian, analogous to minutes, and microcircadians ("micros") are one millionth of a circadian and analogous to seconds.

Objective time is measured in days, hours, minutes, and seconds elapsed since Cal's first onload, with dates formally written in form

DDDd.H:MM:SS New Epoch (e.g. 45d.13:25:54 New Epoch).

Late Epoch Measures (Metric-60)

When the Community formally adopted the sexagesimal numbering system (See *S³: The Smith Sexagesimal System* and Appendix A), they also adopted a new "metric-60" system of measures, based on Maxwell Planck's Natural Units.[13]

Metric-60 Planck Units

In Planck measure, time and space use the same units, as do mass and energy. This is achieved because, in the Planck scale (and corresponding metric-60), c (the speed of light in a vacuum), $\hbar$ (Dirac's constant), and G (the gravitational constant), are all defined as equal to one. Thus, $e=mc^2$ becomes e=m, $E=\hbar w$ becomes E=w, and so on.

The Planck time is the natural unit of time, the smallest possible measure of time within the boundaries of physics,

---

13   "Über irreversible Strahlungsvorgänge", Max Planck, *Sitzungsberichte der Preußischen Akademie der Wissenschaften*, vol. 5, p. 479 (1899)

denoted as t_p (any events occurring closer together are simultaneous). t_p is defined formally as the time it would take a photon traveling at the speed of light to cross a distance equal to the Planck length, and is approximately 5.38121×10^{-44} seconds.

The Planck length, l_p, is the smallest distance that has any meaning in the physical universe, as below this length quantum mechanics makes any and all measurements nonsense. It is approximately equal to 1.61624×10^{-35} meters.

Planck Time and "Tocks"

The metric-60 unit "tock" is derived from physicists' best estimation of the Planck Time, and is defined as precisely 5.39121×10^{-44} seconds. Figure 2 shows some common durations of time and their metric-60 equivalents. The Community stopped using hours, minutes, and seconds as a measure of objective time and replaced with metric-60 tocks. Metric-60 and sexagesimal nomenclature are discussed in detail in S^3: *The Smith Sexagesimal System*.

Description	Metric-60 Units	SI Units
Planck Time	/ (1) t	5.39121 x 10⁻⁴⁴ s
Second	(3.91457) ge-t	1 s
Minute	(3.91457) he-t	60 s
Gen-5 Circadian	(4.69748) he-t	72 s
Gen-4 Circadian	(5.64698) he-t	86.4 s
Gen-3 Circadian	(9.39496) he-t	144 s
Gen-2 Circadian	(28.18488) he-t	432 s
Gen-1 Circadian	(3.13165) je-t	2880 s
"Hour"	(3.91457) je-t	3600 s
"Day"	(1.56583) le-t	86,400 s
"Week"	(10.96079) le-t	604,800 s
"Year"	(9.53177) me-t	31,556,926 s
Approx. Age of the Earth	(55.16069) se-t	4.5 x 10⁹ years
Approx. Age of the Universe	(2.7989) te-t	1.37 x 10¹⁰ years

Figure 2. Common Durations of Time in Metric-60 and SI Units.

Metric-60 Dates in the Autonomous Community

Metric-60 dates are written in terms of meratocks (60^{28} tocks), as follows:

m.jj-h:g:f.x meratocks (me-t) New Epoch

where *m*=meratocks, *jj*=jeratocks, *h*=heratocks, *g*=geratocks, *f*=feratocks, and *x* is any remaining fraction.

The easiest way to come up with a given metric-60 date in terms of "tocks" is to figure out how many seconds have passed since metatime 0.000-0:00:000, convert the result to feratocks using the conversion factor of 234.8742 fa-t/s, derive the resulting sexagesimal numeral, and then insert the date-time punctuation into the resulting integer.

The Autonomous Community was founded on:

0.00-0:0:0 me-t New Epoch.

The Autonomous Community's worst crisis came to a head about 8,311,507 seconds later. 8,311,507 seconds x 234.8742 feratocks/second yields 1,952,158,560 feratocks. A feratock is 60^{23} tocks. Converting this number to sexagesimal using the method detailed in *S³: The Smith Sexagesimal System*, we obtain the value:

⅃ƧらƸΨ0

Now, simply insert the standard time-date punctuation, and we have:

⅃.Ƨら-Ƹ:Ψ:0 me-t new Epoch.

Subjective time is measured in circadians, but divided into metric-60 divisions rather than metric-10 units: daracircadians (3600 circadians, analogous to kilocircadians), baracircadians (60 circadians, analogous to dekacircadians), anbaracircadians ($^1/_{60}$ of a circadian, analogous to decicircadians), and andaracircadians ($^1/_{3600}$ of a circadian, analogous to millicircadians).

Planck Length and "Tocks"

As noted earlier, distances are also measured in tocks, where one tock is the distance light travels in a vacuum in one tock (1.61624×10^{-35} m). Typically, the Community speaks in terms of qaratocks at the femto level, saratocks at the atomic level, and taratocks at the nano level. Yaratocks are roughly analogous to millimeters, zaratocks to centimeters or inches, charatocks to feet or meters, beratocks to kilometers or miles, and meratocks to light years. Meratocks are also analogous to years when measuring time. This is not a coincidence.

For details on tocks as a measure of distance, along with the complete metric-60 system used by the Community (including numerous other Planck units), see *S^3: The Smith Sexagesimal System*.

ABOUT THE AUTHOR

Jean-Michel Smith was born in Palo Alto, California. He studied physics and engineering before choosing computer science and graduating with BS degree from the University of Illinois, College of Engineering. He completed the coursework for his master's degree at Illinois State University, and embarked on a career as a systems engineer and enterprise architect. His published works include S^3: *The Smith Sexagesimal System, using Base-60 to Increase Arithmetic Intelligence*, which can be used as an appendix and companion to *Autonomy*, his first novel.

Visit his websites

jean-michel.eu
autonomyseries.com

www.ingramcontent.com/pod-product-compliance
Lightning Source LLC
Chambersburg PA
CBHW050509110726
47899CB00005B/1392